Depth Rapture

Depth Rapture

Carol Bruneau

The publisher gratefully acknowledges the support of The Canada Council for the Arts and the Ontario Arts Council for its publishing program. The publisher also acknowledges the financial support of the Government of Canada through the Book Publishing Industry Development Program for its publishing activities.

The following stories from the collection have been published previously: "The Tarot Reader" in *The Toronto Star;* "Family History" in *The Nashwaak Review;* "Refraction" in *Pottersfield Portfolio;* "The Park Street Bridge" in *New Maritimes;* and an earlier version of "Keepsakes" in *The Antigonish Review.*

This is a work of fiction; names and characters are products of the author's imagination, and any resemblance to persons living or dead is coincidental.

Cover design by Bill Douglas @ The Bang

Printed and bound in Canada.

CORMORANT BOOKS INC.
RR 1
DUNVEGAN, ONTARIO
CANADA K0C 1J0

Canadian Cataloguing in Publication Data

Bruneau, Carol, 1956-
Depth rapture
ISBN 1-896951-07-4
1. Title.
PS8553.R854D46 1998   C813'.54   C98-900010-9
PR9199.3.B7394D46 1998

for Bruce

ACKNOWLEDGEMENTS

I wish to thank my publisher, Jan Geddes, and Scott Milsom, editor of *New Maritimes,* for their wonderful encouragement; Pamela Donoghue for her insight and humour; Dr. Robert Scheibling and Mary-Jane O'Halloran of Dalhousie University for their expertise in marine biology; the late Nancy Lopes for her candour; my editor, Gena K. Gorrell, for her sensitivity. For their ongoing support I thank my family, extended and immediate, especially Elizabeth and Sara Erskine, Lawrence Smith, my father, John Bruneau, my aunt Elizabeth Williams, my 'partner', Bruce Erskine, our children, Andrew, Seamus and Angus, for putting things in perspective, and last, but not least, Clyde, my familiar.

CONTENTS

I hovered, contemplating the brink ahead. I stretched my arms and legs in space and greedily inhaled a lungful of thick, tasty air. Between the sibilants of my air regulator I heard rhythmic grating sounds and cycles of bubbles rustling overhead. Other human beings were alive nearby. Their commonplace respirations took on a cosmic significance. I was being seized by depth rapture. I knew it and I welcomed it as a challenge to whatever controls I had left.
Captain Jacques-Yves Cousteau, *The Living Sea*

KEEPSAKES

I 'm hiding under the hawthorns, between the peel
ing green fence and some branches with berries like
rabbits' eyes. I've got Aunt Laura's silver purse in my
pocket. A surprise, it was, something I'm guarding now
from the kids next door.

The Tattries, four or five of them, dressed in torn
shorts and overalls. Their faces are thin and pinched-
looking, streaked with dirt — "coal dust," Aunt Laura says.
Even their name reminds me of raggedy, ripped clothes.
"The Tatters," I heard Mum call them, helping Aunt Laura
fix lunch. Aunt Ardith was upstairs putting on her face.

Through the thorny branches I watch their shins scis-
sor past, bare feet flattening the grass. "Are we warm yet,
Barbie? Can ya tell us if we're gettin' hot?"

I clap my hand over my mouth and count, *one, two,
three....*

"Putting on her face" — that's what Aunt Ardith was doing when I peeked at her in the bathroom the day she
arrived.

"What a surprise!" Mum said, kissing her cheek,

though Aunt Ardith is the reason we're here. Aunt Laura called long distance when she heard Mum's sister was coming.

"I don't know how long she plans to stay" was how Aunt Laura greeted us.

"That's all right." Mum shrugged. "We were coming anyway."

"Ready or not you shall be caught!" the Tattries yell. "We're gettin' warmer, warmmmmer, warmmmmmmer! Ya may's well come out now — we're gonna gitcha sooner or later!"

Come *oat,* they say, like something you'd feed a horse.

I'd like to make a run for it, Aunt Laura's purse in my hands. Back into the house, her cool, quiet house. But no. The Tattries are here to play. Aunt Laura hardly said boo this time when she looked out and there they were, whistling through the fence for me.

"This'll be like any other visit." Mum rolled up on her tiptoes to kiss Dad goodbye, rubbing her big, round stomach and sighing. I felt like sighing too — these trips to Aunt Laura's aren't much of a vacation. Here, time slurs by like the skatebugs on the flat, winding river behind her house. Aunt Laura says the Indians used to set fire to the river, its banks were so gassy with coal. Rub two sticks together and *whoosh!* watch the whole thing go up. Now there's something I'd like to see, but no dice.

We've been here four days, Aunt Ardith — my real aunt — three. At least with her around it's been different. From the moment I saw her bumping up the road with her suitcase, I knew it would be.

I love her bright red lipstick, the black stuff she twirls on her lashes with a little wand. Everything about her makes Mum and Aunt Laura seem quiet and plain. Her laugh sounds like glasses clinking together — Aunt Laura's fancy glasses, the ones she fills with tomato juice. "Vedgetable cocktail," she calls it, pronouncing each letter.

Those glasses make me nervous. I nearly broke one at lunch, pinging it to get that tinkly sound like Aunt Ardith's laugh. It was then Mum suggested some fresh air.

"But the Tatters...."

Oh, she knew they were outside. All through the salmon sandwiches we could hear them: screams and wails coming through the window, the *plonk* of a ball, "booger this," "booger that." It must be their favourite word, something to do with the things up a person's nose? Something rude, anyhow, by the face Aunt Laura made, dabbing her mouth with her serviette.

"Barrrrbieeee! Come on out! Barbie? Come on, we know you're in there somewheres! We're gonna start countin', then you better tell us if we're cold or hot!"

There are lots of things I like about my Aunt Ardith. Though if she weren't here, I wouldn't be hiding this way; I'd be inside sipping tea with the grown-ups. Well, milk with a spoonful of tea, in one of Aunt Laura's teacups — but just a spoonful, so as not to stunt my growth. And I'd moon over the cookie tin till Aunt Laura offered me one, then another. And maybe she'd forget she and Mum still had things to catch up on — who else died or got sick since our visit last summer.

If my dad were here, I'd sit on his knee (though I'm a bit big for that) and pretend not to listen. Without Aunt Ardith, Mum and Aunt Laura would be talked out by now. But with her around, they have more than ever catching up. Fifteen years, that's how long she's been away. A lot of people dying, a lot of sicknesses to cover.

"Barrrbie! Barrrbie! Ya little booger," the kids yell.

"Come on out now, can ya hear us? We give up, ya have to come out."

Their eyes are wild; their skin looks freckled with sunlight. I don't know their first names or ages, only that they're bigger and rougher than me.

"You run along now, sweetie." Mum gave me a poke getting up from the table. I helped her fold the serviettes, the ones that didn't look used, and put the clean knives back in the case.

In the kitchen Aunt Laura started washing dishes. Mum leaned against the counter with her hand on her stomach.

"Run along now, those kids won't bite." This she whispered as Aunt Ardith reached for a tea towel, nudging her out of the way.

"I don't want to," I said.

If Dad were here....

I knew Mum meant business. The glint in her eye told me how itchy she was for more titbits from Aunt Laura's store of news. Their visits are like eating in a Chinese restaurant: they start off peckish, but helping one another to tiny, finicky bites from each of the mysterious plates. Finding something familiar, a shred of celery or onion, they chew it over, each little mouthful; then, seeing how good it tastes, dive in for more. But politely, always politely. Ladylike.

"You mustn't be piggish," Mum tells me all the time.

But since Aunt Ardith arrived it seems they've gotten greedy, shooing me away at the most boring subjects, things they talk about all the time. Not just sick-beds and funerals, but babies too, and men, grown-up men like Dad, and my Aunt Ardith's husband, Uncle Jarvis. You can feel it coming — "run along now" — by the way Mum leans close, nodding when her sister opens her mouth to

talk. Sometimes Aunt Laura puts a finger to her lips —
"shhhh" — but that doesn't make Aunt Ardith stop or
lower her voice. This may be what I like most about her.

I'd still rather Dad were here instead. Then Mum and
Aunt Laura would turn a blind eye and keep talking, but
low, low as if neither of us could hear, or would want to
anyway. But he couldn't leave the office on such short
notice — how he put it when Aunt Laura phoned.

Mum decided on the spot that we'd make the trip
from the city while Aunt Ardith was *down home*. Which
is what she calls Pictou County, though on the map it
looks up from everyplace else. Especially Florida, where
Aunt Ardith lives. She showed me a pink thumb of land
on Aunt Laura's globe.

It's not as though we come here often. Once a year,
that's all, though it only takes a few hours on the train.
Or so Mum says to Aunt Laura, as if explaining to herself
why we don't visit more. Aunt Ardith has a better excuse;
she lives too far away, which is why this visit is special,
special and unlikely as spotting blue butterflies in May.

"Come on out, Barrrbie! We know you're in there! You
git out here now, ya little booger! You come on *oat* or
else."

One of them has spotted me — a stray shoelace,
maybe, a fleck of red through the sun-specked bushes. A
boy with bright, hungry eyes pokes in a stick, a long,
green stake from Aunt Laura's dahlias. Branches crackle.
Bare knees dance and jiggle inches from my face. Aunt
Laura won't appreciate them trampling the lawn, pulling
leaves off the hedge. Neither would Mum if it were our
yard. Though she's happy I have playmates; a few broken
stems for a little peace.

I hold my breath.

One of the boys starts bowling, using Aunt Laura's

purple phlox for pins. The ball is red and blue with a white stripe like the equator, the chewed-looking rubber showing through.

If this were home, I'd yell "private property" and tell him to quit it.

I might do that here, if Laura were my real aunt, like Aunt Ardith. Maybe then we would come oftener. Mum says she and Aunt Laura are cousins, which makes us cousins too. Impossible: I'm only eight; Aunt Laura looks ancient, though Mum insists she's not. Her hair is grey and she wears tidy, good dresses and nylons the hottest days of summer. "The holidays," she calls them. *Our* holidays, she smiles, because school is out for both of us. Aunt Laura has an important job at the consolidated school, according to Mum. Consolidated — the word reminds me of when it hurts to do your business, as Mum says.

"She's a teacher? Aunt Laura's a teacher?"

I was thinking of Miss Wilson this year in grade three — pretty and young, with bouncy black hair.

"No," Mum explained. "But she has a very important job. The principal's secretary."

I picture Aunt Laura in her straight blue dress, the cameo brooch on her big, smooth bosom. Bustling around the principal's desk, watering geraniums, making sure the strap's there, ready.

The Tattries dart back and forth, prancing over the grass. The biggest girl reaches in. Her grubby fingers yank at my hem.

"What're ya hidin' for? Come out and play wit' us. Finders, seekers, losers, weep— Come on, my turn now. *You* gotta be it."

Through the leaves I see her mouth, the white triangle of her underpants. I close my hand around Aunt

Laura's purse, tighter and tighter. One of the boys squirms in on his belly, peering at me with lazy eyes.

The quick brown fox jumps over the lazy dog, I think. (Miss Wilson made us memorize this because it has every letter, including *zed*.)

"Hey, skeeerdy-cat! Whatcha got there anyways, skeeerdy-cat? Come on out an' let us see!"

"Yeah, we gotcha now, Barbie. Ya may's well give up and come on *oat*."

Zee, Aunt Ardith says. Mum gave me a tap when I tried correcting her the first evening, after she'd come from the train.

Aunt Laura's neat white house is just up the hill from the siding, a wooden platform with a sign for "Ferrona/Eureka." It's a short walk past the post office and a store with dusty fishing tackle in the window, a broken Fanta sign. Next to that is a tall house with a wide veranda, the lattice missing. That's where my mother and Aunt Ardith grew up. Mum gets quiet whenever we go past, slowing down to steal a peek through the ripped screen door. Though she never says, I know she wishes it were still their house so we could stay there instead of Aunt Laura's.

"I don't like to impose," she says, which sounds a bit crazy to me since it's always Aunt Laura inviting *us*.

I wish we didn't have to come at all. But Mum says she needs to keep in touch; with her sister so far away, her cousin is all she's got.

"You come on out now. We knows you got somethink in your pocket. Come out and show us what you got, Barbie!"

If not for Aunt Laura, why would I be here, cornered like a cat with a bird in its teeth?

Mum doesn't know the people in the old house, the place

where her mother and father used to live, my grandparents who died before I was born. Aunt Laura never mentions the new owners, except to say the children are at school and often make trouble.

"Like the Tattries, you mean?"

I'd like to ask her what kind of trouble — what they do that's so bad. Pull the fire alarm, maybe, throw rocks, play hookey — as bad as that? Or worse? Those are as bad as it gets, at my school anyway.

"What do they look like, those kids?" I did ask, one afternoon in the parlour. Imagining the Tattries, of course: big, runny-nosed boys being hauled from their seats into the hall. The principal's low, stern voice; the loud, stinging smack of the strap, hardly muffled by the coats and schoolbags hung there.

But Aunt Laura clucked her tongue and smiled faintly, setting her teacup in the saucer. Then Mum came in and flopped down on the sofa.

"Whew, it's hot," she said, looking from me to Aunt Laura. I don't know where Aunt Ardith was — upstairs, maybe. I yawned; there's nothing to do at Aunt Laura's but sit, or eat. I would have liked to go to the river and put my feet in, or to MacKenzie's for a treat, as we did our first day. Mum was woozy from the train and Aunt Laura told her to lie down.

Oh, it was dusty in that store! The air smelled of dead flies and the Windex the man sprayed on the countertop, so smudged the candy underneath looked faded. I asked for a Popsicle, a Crispy Crunch too, which Aunt Laura bought without any coaxing. I ate it first, while Aunt Laura held the Popsicle dripping from the wrapper.

The bar tasted salty-sweet, the ripples in the chocolate melted smooth. Passing the old house — that's what they call the place with the ripped screen — I popped a big hunk in my mouth. Aunt Laura didn't blink. She was too busy tsk-tsking about the weeds out front.

"It's just a house," I almost said, but my mouth was full.

She shook her head, the same as when she tells Mum something she's just remembered in her quiet, no-nonsense voice. The same voice you can imagine her using, doling out late slips to pupils. I expected her to frown and bite her lip, as she does waiting for Mum to say, "What about that puzzle in the kitchen, Barbara?" or "Weren't you going to go draw something?"

But instead she started talking. "See that window? There, above the porch? That's right, that one. That was your Aunt Ardith's room, before she got married. And that window, that one at the side. That was your—"

"Aunt Ardith's?" I repeated, my mouth sticky brown.

"She'll be over the moon with you," she said, pulling a Kleenex from her sleeve. "The only time she saw you, you were eight months old."

"Her husband," I said, pushing the tissue around my lips the way Mum puts on lipstick, "is he coming too? Uncle Jarvis?" I felt grown up saying his name; its sound reminded me of pickle jars for catching grasshoppers, with rusty lids that *scritched* twisting on.

Aunt Laura sniffed and shook Popsicle juice from her hand.

"Oh no, dear. Not now."

"Why not? Why isn't he coming? Too short notice?" I liked how reasonable this sounded but felt a pang for Dad, wishing *he'd* heard me say it.

"Jarvis?" Aunt Laura seemed distracted, glancing up and down the road as if watching for cars. Cars once or twice a day, maybe. Grabbing my hand, she said, "Come, Barbara. Your mother will think we got lost. And I have a little something waiting for you."

"A present?" I blurted out, curiosity louder than the

*shhhh*es in my head. Aunt Laura doesn't often give me things, you see; she's not that kind of cousin. She doesn't send birthday gifts, though every Christmas there's a silver dollar taped inside her card.

"It's a surprise," she said.

"For grading, Aunt Laura? More crayons? What *is* it?"

See, the one thing she does give on these visits is crayons, something to keep me amused. All year she saves the cards from nylons for me to draw on. This time she'd handed me a new box of crayons as soon as we unpacked. "How thoughtful," Mum said, patting Aunt Laura's arm, her other hand on top of her tummy. It's gotten like a shelf; when she sat down for tea, I half expected her to rest her saucer on it. Maybe she would've, too, at home. But not here; it would've been disrespectful — of Aunt Laura and of the baby, the one that's inside Mum.

I spread the colours across the table, with the puzzle Mum brought along, a picture of a farm with a red barn and Old MacDonald in straw hat and overalls. I tried drawing a horse, but it was so muggy the wax came off on my fingers, warm and greasy through the little paper tubes, the colours refusing to stick to the shiny white card.

The crayons had been my surprise. What else could she possibly have for me?

"Let's see, Barbie! Let's see what you got in your pocket! Give it here, eh? Don't be skeeered, I'll give it back to ya. I will."

I don't budge, just keep my fingers wrapped round the purse.

Mum was upstairs lying down when we came in from the store.

"Leave her be," Aunt Laura said, and went to plug in the kettle. "Your mama needs her rest, dear. We'll sit and have a cup of tea now, all right?" She flitted around setting the table as if she'd never mentioned a surprise. I waited and waited while she filled the sugar bowl, the matching creamer — slowly, carefully, not at all the way Mum does things in the kitchen, but as if she was thinking about every little detail, the sugar, the milk, and enjoying it, too. Setting out cups on the clean white cloth, she also seemed to forget my age. Mum never lets me have tea at home, not even milk with an inch of tea. A spot, as Aunt Laura calls it. "A spot, what's the harm in a tiny spot?" I opened my mouth to remind her, then thought better.

She made the tea and sat with me at the table.

"Your mama's tired, dear, from your trip."

I hoped she'd start talking about the baby, the mysterious baby. I tried picturing it inside Mum but couldn't, not at all.

It's okay, I know already — soon I'll be a sister, I wanted to say, to loosen her up. But Aunt Laura just sat rubbing her knuckles, so I thought better of that too. What I really wanted was to ask her questions: Where did it come from, this baby? And how did it get inside my mother?

I could see Aunt Laura wasn't the person to ask. After a minute or two she reached over and patted my hand.

"She'll need a good rest before all the commotion tomorrow," she said. "The commotion" being Aunt Ardith's arrival.

She sniffed and poured a cup for me, a tiny splash of tea, then half the pitcher of milk. Using a small silver spoon she measured two hills of sugar, and then she stirred them in slowly, with a regular kitchen spoon.

"Mustn't tell your mama." She gave me a funny smile, watching me drink. "She might think I was interfering. But when I was your age I had a cup of tea every night with my parents. A little won't hurt."

I looked at her across the table. Of course I believed her. Aunt Laura was not an awful lot shorter than my mother, not really.

I'd practically forgotten her promise of a surprise, another surprise, when she pushed her cup aside and got up, straightening her skirt. The knees of her nylons wrinkled like elephant skin, loose and grey. Taupe, I thought, the shade stamped on the cards for drawing; but what kind of colour is that?

"Come here a minute, Barbara. There's a little something I've had set aside for you for a while, but I was waiting. I was afraid, see, your mama might think it's too old for you, not quite right for a little girl. But I'd like you to have it anyway, dear. I want to give it to you before I forget."

It wasn't like the tea; she never said, "Don't tell." But something about her voice — like another child all of a sudden, shy almost, but half sneaky, half regretful — made me figure this would be best kept secret.

"Shhhh," she said, "we don't want to wake your mama. We'll let her sleep for a little bit, then take her up a cup."

I followed Aunt Laura to the sewing machine in the dining-room. It had been her mother's, she'd told me once, running her hand over the scratched wooden lid. It was hard to imagine Aunt Laura young enough to have a mother.

I breathed in as she slid open the narrow drawer where she keeps her thimbles. Oh, I'd taken a peek in there now and then, looking for something to do while the grown-ups were busy. Goody, I thought, biting the callus on my finger as she rummaged. Her soft, freckled hand sifted through squat spools of thread, skinny gold bobbins. There was a new, never-opened case of white-headed pins that looked like the lightning rods on the roof. It still had the price tag from Woolworth's. I leaned closer, peering into the drawer — hoping for a thimble, the little one she said was hers when *she* was eight.

But instead she pulled out a tarnished silver purse — an evening bag, she called it — and dropped it in my palm. Knit of tiny silver loops, it made me think of the sleeves in knights' armour, a fine metal fringe dangling along the bottom. It had a fancy, thin clasp; "filigreed" was the word she used — which made me think of Mum upstairs, her favourite warning: Don't be *greedy.* "It was my mother's," Aunt Laura whispered, closing my fingers around it.

Small enough to fit in my hand, the purse was heavy as stone. But when I clicked it open it was empty. Not even a penny — Aunt Laura calls them coppers — for good luck.

An "heirloom," she called it. To me it just felt cold and slinky, made me long for the pink patent one Mum kept saying she'd buy at the Metropolitan back home. I'd have it by now, if not for this trip.

Right there I wanted to hand the purse back. But I couldn't, not with Aunt Laura being Aunt Laura. "Mind your manners," in my head my mother's voice woke up. "And always eat everything on your plate. Don't forget, dear, you're a guest."

"Spoilt-sport! Spoilt-sport! Barbie is a spoilt-sport! Some fun you are, won't even come out and show us what you got! Some fun, you skeeerdy-cat! Skeeered of your own shadow, I bet!"

If my dad were here, he'd stand by the door with his newspaper and, after a minute or two, step outside to ask what was going on.

I roll myself into a ball, thorns scraping my arms. The purse is tucked in one hand under my thigh, the clasp digging into me. The big girl and her brother get up and pace over the lawn. I'm still not budging.

Sprinkled over the grass are petals from Aunt Laura's nasturtiums. The sight makes me queasy, the same feeling you get when the teacher yells at someone though it's you talking. I wonder — if I give up and come out, will the Tattries get bored and run away?

But even as I'm untangling myself, they start to wander off, kicking up dust by the road. When their shouts fade, I wriggle out, my hair in my eyes. A few pulled threads, that's all. I go and sit on the shiny grey steps, tickling the purse's fringe up and down my arm, jiggling the mesh just so to catch the sun. I try to picture Aunt Laura using it, wearing her blue dress with the cameo — at a Christmas concert, a home-and-school meeting. A church supper, maybe, or a funeral. It would have to be a school or church outing, since Aunt Laura would never set foot in the Legion, the only place besides bingo where grown-ups go around here. I can't imagine Aunt Laura dancing, the purse tucked under her arm, or laying it down on a long shaky table with some cards and little plastic chips. And I certainly can't see her shaking dimes from it at MacKenzie's, either.

Playing hot potato, I flip it from palm to palm till the tarnish rubs off. It's so clumsy and old-fashioned, heavy but too small to hold much of anything — my treasures at home: the rabbit's foot Dad won at the fair, the piece of fool's gold I found once by the road.

I think up ways to get rid of it. No one would ever find it buried under the hawthorns, or the porch. I could just put it back in the drawer with the dusty thread and frayed scraps of ribbon. But Aunt Laura would see it and think me rude, rude and spoiled like the girl with her nose stuck up in Snakes and Ladders. Or see it and chastise herself for again forgetting to give it to me. Chas-*tise*

— which is what Aunt Laura says instead of *strap*, on the rare occasions she brings up school.

I sit there wondering what to do until a shape comes up behind the pebbled window. I shove the purse in my pocket just as Mum sticks her head out the door.

"How come it's so quiet? Where'd all the kids go?"

She rubs her cheek, tic-tac-toed as a waffle from the blanket on our bed. At home she never lies down afternoons, but here Aunt Laura keeps telling her, "Rest while you have the chance." Even with Aunt Ardith visiting, and nobody sure how long she'll stay.

"Well, as long as you're okay," Mum says. Without noticing the lump in my dress, she steps back into the porch, a shadow again behind the silly glass. What's the point of a window you can't see through, I'd like to know. But, this once, I find it has its benefits — a word I learned from Dad on the phone getting people to buy policies. Both words sound to me like names from the Bible.

Next door the Tattries' yard is quiet, empty but for a bucket and a headless doll lying in the dirt. A tire swings from the rope on their veranda. Slowly — as if they're only hiding, ready to ambush — I get up to slip around back. Pushing past the dahlias, their smell like tinned mud, I stick to the side of the house farthest from the neighbours', the side with the kitchen window. Taking giant sliding steps along the foundation, passing below the window I hear their voices, Mum and Aunt Laura's, secret, hushed. I don't hear Aunt Ardith; who knows where she can be, but it's plain she's not there. Through the wide-open window their voices swoosh like a bus down a quiet street, making up for lost time.

"Well, for pity's sake, Laura. You know that Jarvis never was any good."

I stop, hold my breath.

"Oh, but he looked so handsome in a suit, don't you

remember?"

"But what do you expect? From a Tattrie...."

This makes me listen harder. I think of the photo Mum has in her top drawer, of Aunt Ardith and her husband. In the picture my uncle is tall with curly hair and a big, wide smile, and he has his arm around my aunt's waist. She has her eyes closed, her head tilted up and her mouth open, laughing. It was taken, Mum told me once, at their wedding. I thought that couldn't be right since Aunt Ardith is wearing a suit, a short, dark jacket with a skirt that looks hard to walk in.

"If not for the drinking...."

"But you think she'd've known."

"I guess he surprised her."

"I don't know *what* she saw in him. Ardith's no lame-brain, you know. Heaven knows why she'd get mixed up with a fellow like.... If you remember, Laura, she could've had her pick of any number of...."

"Perhaps it was just meant to be. One of those things, you know...."

"No. She *had* to know, Laura. It's not like she's blind...."

There's a long silence, and a picture fills my head of Aunt Ardith at a party, being spun around with a wide black scarf over her eyes. Pinning a tail on the donkey's nose.

"I wonder where he is now, Jarvis—"

Next door the clothesline squeaks, a loud, shrill squawk like the noise blue jays make in the trees out back. Then comes some shouting, crying and threats.

"Good riddance anyway" is what I think Mum answers, though with all the racket I can't be sure.

She comes and scrapes the window higher; I know it's Mum because she puffs a little, leaning over.

"I don't know why she doesn't stay for good. She's

got nothing down there to go home to."

After a minute or two, I slink around back, where Aunt Ardith is sunning herself in a lawn chair. Her face turned towards the sun, she looks like she's asleep, her turquoise blouse rolled up for a pillow. She has on matching shorts, her long smooth legs stretched out, and on top a red halter that cuts into her armpits. Little ribs of sweat spread under her bosoms, two soft-looking mounds nested together like sleeping kittens. I tiptoe past, making for the screen door, when she opens her eyes and smiles.

"Hi, doll. Whatcha been up to, huh?"

She speaks in such a warm, cosy voice it's as if we've known each other for ever.

Before I can answer, Aunt Laura comes out and feels the sheets on the line.

"Children all gone home?" she asks, a clothespin in her mouth. Reeling the laundry in, she tucks the corners under her chin to fold them. As the weight comes off, the line snaps upwards; the forked pole propping the middle flips to the ground. I run and grab it, jabbing the slack towards the sky.

"Easy there, sweetie!" Aunt Ardith yells, jumping up to hold the door for Aunt Laura and her sheets and pillowslips. Stacked like newspapers, they'll smell like the wind when the bed's first made up. But after a while they'll get a peppery scent, like everything else in the house. Lavender, Mum says.

"It's all right. She's not hurting anything, are you, dear?" Aunt Laura shouts back, heaving the clothes basket inside.

I miss our pillows at home. The tiny feathers work their way out of Aunt Laura's; the ends poke like straight pins through the blue-flowered ticking.

I follow Aunt Laura into the porch, past the wringer

washer under its yellow oilcloth, the pile of *Atlantic Advocates* beside it; the neat tower of ice-cream containers. The air is hot and dry with the hum of flies, the smell of warm plastic.

"Where's Kaye disappeared to, anyway?" says Aunt Ardith behind us. "Must be nice to sleep the afternoon away." She's put on her blouse over the halter, is busy tying the shirt-tails.

Mum isn't in the kitchen. Aunt Ardith moves the laundry from the chair where Aunt Laura has set it. The knotted blouse cuts into her waist, the roundness at the top of her shorts. She looks soft as a pillow with a string around the middle.

"Did you have to do all this wash today, Laura?" she sighs. Then, to me: "So, the kids didn't stay long, did they? I thought you might have them in for a cookie." She glances at Aunt Laura peeling potatoes.

"Such a lovely day," Aunt Laura says, staring out the window. She shakes her head at Aunt Ardith leaning against the counter, rubbing a finger along the chrome edge.

Reaching into the cupboard, Aunt Laura brings out a wooden box of dried cod. I watch her pry it open and set the fish to soak in a speckled bowl.

"Your auntie works too hard," Aunt Ardith says, touching the part in her wavy red-brown hair. (I have her sister's colouring, Mum tells people, with her Oh-well-we-can't-always-have-what-we-want look — pleased or jealous, it's hard to tell which.)

Swinging my legs beneath the lace tablecloth, I see my puzzle's been put back in the box, set aside with the crayons. On the wall, the pendulum sways back and forth in the dark wooden clock. Its chiming makes me think of castles, of the Friendly Giant.

"How old is a grandfather clock?" I ask, not expecting

an answer, not the kind of answer I want. When I was small, I used to think Mum's father lived inside this clock.

"That's way too small for a grandfather clock, Barbara." Aunt Ardith laughs with her mouth open, her teeth small and yellow between her deep red lips. "A grandfather clock would never fit there — the ceiling's too low."

I quit swinging my legs and slide off the chair to watch Aunt Laura. Sometimes she saves the cod boxes for me to take home. But this one Aunt Ardith picks up and drops in the garbage under the sink.

"Fishcakes." She says it the way Mum says "You shouldn't've." "Really, Laura. Don't fuss on my account. I'm not that hungry."

"The more for us, then," Aunt Laura jokes, though she's not smiling.

I close my eyes, imagine the buttery taste of fish and potato. Aunt Ardith goes out to the porch and comes back with a magazine. Flipping the shiny pages, she blinks at the pictures of dories and fall leaves.

"Do you get much fish in Florida?" Aunt Laura says, more politely than usual. She clangs the masher against the pot. "You used to love a nice white fillet, if I recall."

A quiet spreads between them as though I'm not there. I might as well be under the table, watching their legs through the lacy cloth. I feel for the purse against my thigh.

At last Aunt Ardith speaks, slowly, as if picking chicken from a bone.

"Jarvis and I—" She gazes at the fridge, her voice breezy, wisping off. Aunt Laura sets the masher in the sink, waiting, but Aunt Ardith has clammed up again. Their silence is like a staring contest, each wondering who'll blink first.

Finally Aunt Laura shrugs. "Never mind," she says. "I'll make plenty in case you change your mind." And in a tone light and airy as the see-through scarves she ties over her newly set hair: "Ardith, can I get you to do the ved-getables?"

It seems to me that she's won.

Whittling carrots, Aunt Ardith flicks peelings into the sink. She glances over and tries to smile.

"So. You never did tell me what you did with the Tattries."

Then Mum comes in, leaning over Aunt Ardith. "What can I do?" she asks, her face the same shade as the mashed potatoes.

Aunt Laura ignores them both, shaping fishcakes — a speeded-up game of pat-a-cake so the potato won't burn her palms.

"It's like he never existed," Aunt Ardith suddenly bursts out. Shaking peel off her fingers, she flies from the room, leaving Mum standing with a potful of water. I have to stop to think who she's talking about.

"Ardith's still upset about your uncle," Mum whispers, holding a finger up to *shhhhh* me. I start to roll my eyes.

"Perhaps she *is* lucky to be rid of him, then," Aunt Laura says, loud enough for the neighbours to hear. Dragging the frying-pan over the burner, she hacks off some butter and taps it in.

"I'll say," Mum mutters.

"That crowd next door, too."

"I know."

Mum's eyes have the same shininess as when she laughs with Dad about things I don't find funny.

I wonder what kind of monster my uncle must be, picturing his tiny black and white smile. Mum and Aunt Laura sound so sure; he must be guilty of something godawful, whatever it is.

Now's the chance to ask what I've always wanted to

know: "Why doesn't Aunt Ardith have any kids?" Out it jumps before I can stop myself.

Mum and Aunt Laura turn and gawk as if I've done something terribly rude, turned up my nose at supper or wet the bed.

"Not everyone is so lucky," Mum says after a while. Aunt Laura squints through the hiss of the pan.

"Go into the parlour, Barbara, and draw me some pictures till supper's ready." Mum shakes her head and I giant-step away, one side of my dress drooping from the purse. She still hasn't noticed.

"The things kids come up with," I hear her trying to joke.

And Aunt Laura: "They say when the Lord closes the door he always opens a window."

I wake next morning to screeching, doors slamming, a ball thudding the dirt below our window. Mum rolls onto her side and says she's not feeling well. I bounce off the soft, lumpy bed, jingling the springs. Ours is the guest room across from Aunt Laura's; Aunt Ardith has the little room next to hers.

The ceiling slopes over the fancy bedstead, white with rust spots showing through the paint. Sunlight seeps through the turnip-coloured blind; the air itself feels yellow.

"Ask Laura to get you some cornflakes," Mum moans into the pillow.

I put on my pink housecoat, check the pocket. The purse is there, where I slipped it last night after Mum turned off the light.

Between the houses rise shouts, the dull slap of rubber on a wall. *Queenie, queenie, who got the ball?*

The purse settles like cold pudding in my pocket. A plastic one would stand out square like the cigarette deck in Dad's shirt. If he were here, he'd be up by now, shaving, calling out riddles through the bathroom door.

Downstairs Aunt Laura is doing the crossword from the paper. As I come in, she looks up and smiles, laying it down to go find the dictionary. Aunt Ardith pours herself some tea, starts cutting toast in little triangles.

"Hi, doll," she says. Her lips are painted, her hair rolled on top of her head. She's still in her housecoat, though, her white slip showing underneath. "What would you like?"

"Nothing." I'd rather wait for Mum to get up and fix my cereal like on the box, with banana. As I pull up to the table, the purse clunks the chair. Aunt Ardith glances down.

"What've you got in there? The Royal Bank? Or the First National?" Ever since she arrived, she and Mum have joked about their days as tellers up in New Glasgow and Stellarton. ("Best job a girl could get, just out of high school, before you got married.")

I shift in my seat and she eyes me more closely. "Or could it be somethin' from your pals next door? I s'pose they woke you up, did they?"

The hands on the clock stutter forward.

Aunt Laura never told me *not* to show it to anyone.

Aunt Ardith bends so close I can see the little screw on the back of her earring.

"What is it?" she says, her lashes curling as I draw out the purse. "Where'd you get that?" Under the beige makeup her cheeks go pale but for two rosy circles, like a clown's.

"Aunt Laura," I whisper, shoving it back in my pocket. "She said I could have—"

"It's — it's just I haven't seen it in years." Aunt Ardith slaps at her cheeks like she's swatting flies. "Well—" One side of her mouth pulls in. "If Laura said you could have it...." She sniffs, then goes and dumps her tea in the sink. "It just doesn't seem like something a *little* girl would want."

I reach down, spilling the fringe through my fingers. I don't appreciate being called little. I'm practically an older sister, I want to remind her.

"Ardith?"

It's Aunt Laura, the soft, heavy book in her hands. My aunt, my real aunt, gives her a look and brushes past, trudging upstairs.

Aunt Laura pours cornflakes in a bowl and passes me the sugar. The milk tastes wrong, but I pinch my nose and try not to notice. While I eat and she does dishes, we listen to Aunt Ardith up there opening drawers, snapping her suitcase.

"Maybe she has been away too long, like your mother says." Aunt Laura's sleeves touch the soapsuds, but she pays no attention. "Or maybe *they're* just too close for comfort." She starts to laugh then, a dry, puzzled laugh. "Like your mother, I never could understand why anyone would get hooked up with that bunch."

I'm not even sure she's talking to me. She says "bunch" the way Mum says "shoot" when she's baking a cake and forgets the Magic powder.

"Why?"

Like the baby questions, it seems only right to ask. But all Aunt Laura does is stare.

"You know who I mean, dear. I'm afraid your uncle was no better."

I think of the boy poking the dahlia stake in the bushes.

The worst, what's the *worst* a person can do? I need to know.

"Did he *die*, Aunt Laura? Is that it? Is Uncle Jarvis *dead?*"

Her look is a mix of shock and fun, as if I've just re-peated a joke, one of Dad's from work.

"Oh no, dear," she says, slow and gentle. "But they say it's in the genes."

In his picture he's wearing a light grey suit.

"Your aunt and uncle, dear, they're getting divorced."

"Divorced — what is *that*?" I want to ask.

But there's no chance; Aunt Ardith comes clumping downstairs, the red suitcase in her hand. She's put on a polka-dot shirtdress; I like how it pulls in at the waist, the skirt twirling out like a lampshade. Mum's always talking about her sister's "fashion sense".

"Time sure flies, Laura." Aunt Ardith sniffs.

"But I thought you'd be staying. You mustn't let those people upset— Look, we've lived side by side like this all these years and they've never caused trouble, not really. Just because we're not friendly. I thought when you and Jar—"

"Never mind, Laura. You knew I wouldn't be — wouldn't want to wear out my welcome."

"But where will you go? You only just got here." Aunt Laura shrugs like a bird fluffing its feathers. "Besides, who do you have down there in Florida?" She pronounces it as carefully as the name of a flower.

Aunt Ardith whistles through her teeth.

"Friends, I have plenty of friends. An' I plan to get a job."

"I hear they're looking for someone up at the ban—"

"A real job, Laura. A secretary maybe, like you."

The look on Aunt Laura's face makes me want to slide through the cracks in the floor.

"All because of that crowd next door—" It sounds as though she's pleading.

But Aunt Ardith is already leaning outside, pulling a pair of wet nylons off the line. She opens her suitcase and stuffs them in.

"Give Kaye a hug for me, will you?" she says, without looking up. "You too, kiddo."

"Where will you go?" Aunt Laura says. She grabs a dish towel and sits down heavily at the table, twisting the cloth in her hands. She stares at the crossword as if she's speaking to it (*three down, four across*), and Aunt Ardith is already out the door, halfway across town.

Without another word my aunt lifts her suitcase and bumps through the door, turning long enough to blow a kiss through the dark screen.

"Is she going back to Florida?" I ask, to shake Aunt Laura's silence. When she finally looks up she has no answer, just drops the dish towel, then taps her pencil on the folded page.

I wonder what the purse has to do with what's happened, but of course don't dare ask. Aunt Laura's too busy anyway, listening for a whistle echoing along the river.

Lord knows how long she'll have to wait there on the platform by the tracks. But in Aunt Laura's eyes I can already see Aunt Ardith handing her bag to a man on the train, her high heels on the steep, grilled steps to the coach car. Her smooth, pretty hand on the railing.

"How will she get back?" I'm too nosy to feel sad. What I want is to get the globe and have Aunt Laura point out the stops, each starred city and town. But you know what she says?

"Barbara, take some milk up to your mother, would you please? And when you're done that you might go out and play. It's too nice to be inside, dear. Then perhaps the others will come out too, and keep you company."

She speaks with her back turned, has forgotten I'm not even dressed.

I take out the purse and tickle my palm with it.

"But I'd rather stay inside with you," I tell her, though this isn't altogether true.

She shakes out the dish towel and hangs it to dry on the oven door. "I know," she says softly. "But what you need is someone your own age, isn't it?"

She tucks the purse back in my pocket, her face so close I see the yellow spots in her eyes. "An hour or two in the fresh air won't hurt. You might even take a jaunt down to the river."

My disappointment's like a Mr. Freeze that melts too fast on your tongue. I feel let down, not so much by my real aunt — no one ever expected she'd stay — but by this one. Let down, yet comforted too, in a way strange but ordinary as a spider spinning a web.

It could always be worse — I'm not being sent next door. I know, at least I hope, Aunt Laura would never do that.

After Mum's sister leaves, it's quieter than ever — in spite of the ruckus next door. The Tattries never do come back to play, and after that one afternoon they even quit spying through the fence. Mum gives up her naps to be with me and after a day or two tells Aunt Laura that Dad has likely run out of clean socks and casseroles, and that we mustn't wear her out.

Mum says we make too much work, though as far as I can see Aunt Laura would have us stay for ever. She's started slipping me gum and round white mints when Mum's not looking. To me there's something sneaky and mean about Mum packing our bags, then announcing we'll leave in the morning, just like that.

"Suit yourself" is all Aunt Laura says, though you can see she's surprised. "Don't stay or leave on my account."

"You'll be getting tired of all the company, Laura."

"Whatever you think, Kaye," says Aunt Laura, though

she knows she won't see us again till next year. Since Aunt Ardith's visit, she's been politer than ever — the kind of woman you can see copying tests, purple ink from the machine and the gluey smell of paper on her hands. She seems too tired to argue.

Mum blames the carry-on next door. As we're leaving she makes sure our blind is drawn — to keep the sun from fading the bedspread, she says. But I know it's to shut out the view.

The whole train-ride home, I keep the purse in my pocket. Mum says the rocking upsets her stomach, and sits most of the way with a hand on her forehead. She pays no attention to me, except to smile weakly when I take my eyes off the trees and fields zipping by, to make sure she's awake.

Dad meets us at the station, his round, tanned face nodding in the crowd behind the big brass doors. He tries to swoop me up in his arms.

"Feels like Laura's been slipping you treats," he teases, eyeing my hem. "Whatcha got in there? The Crown Jewels?"

I giggle, pull the purse out to show him.

"Barbara!" Mum frowns. "Did Laura give you that?" She forgets to say "aunt".

The purse feels greasy and warm. Walking to the car, I'd like to let go of it, watch it slip through the sewer grate by the curb, disappear.

"Oh God," Mum suddenly groans. "I hope Ardith didn't see."

"It's just an old change purse, Kaye. Your cousin unloading more old stuff." Dad gives my hand a squeeze.

"Aunt Ardith didn't mind," I say.

"Laura wanted Ardith to have that for her wedding. Goodness knows why. But I'll tell you, she was miffed all right when it came back in the mail. Exactly as she'd sent it."

"Some wedding gift." Dad laughs. Mum clicks her tongue.

"Laura's father gave it to her mum when they got married — if Laura's told me once, she's told me a dozen times. He bought it in Boston, genuine sterling. Her mother never used it, of course. Too fancy, I guess. She worried it might attract thieves."

"Or the Tatters?" I pipe.

Mum looks down at me, lets Dad go ahead with the luggage.

"Aunt Laura shouldn't have given it to you, Barbara."

From the way she watches me, I know she can see it at the bottom of my toy-box, jumbled up with the crayon bits, the little, cupless tea-set saucers she thinks should be thrown out.

"Maybe we could send it back," I say, though of course I already know what her answer will be.

WHERE ADDERS LIE

Mum had her reasons, I guess, for inviting the deaf girl. One spring's worth of Sundays, that's how many times Corinne came to play. She was the daughter of a friend, someone named Shirley who Mum grew up with in Ferrona. Not someone she saw much; they just came from the same small place.

Corinne — the name made me think of a slim, dark-haired girl in pink leotards, a soft angora sweater. But no, from my first glimpse I figured she should've had her mother's name. Shirley, she looked like a Shirley, with pale, plain-looking skin and straight-across bangs.

A sense of duty — maybe that's what made Mum invite her, that and all the other things she started doing after she lost the baby. "Lost" — that's how Dad put it, explaining to someone on the phone. All I could think of was another child, Hansel or Gretel maybe, roaming around the forest. Or the time I wandered off in Simpson's, my heart pounding like crazy the instant I lost sight of Mum. No — people lost *things*: mittens, pencils, dimes in the gum machines at Sobeys. Losing a baby made it sound like a purse left somewhere by accident.

But maybe that's how it was for Mum. It was soon after that she got so busy, as if on the lookout for a missing dollar bill, figuring ways to find it again. Waking one morning with an IOU and no way of paying it back. I think Corinne was part of this, I do. Part of Mum's trying to find something gone.

Of the baby there's nothing to tell. I just remember being woken up and thrown in the back of the Volkswagen, still in my pyjamas. The dark, empty streets, dead quiet; yellow lights flashing. There were no other cars, no honking. Just the steamy sound of tires through the open window, Mum's queer, sharp breaths.

"Where're we going?" I kept asking, cold and queasy from being roused like that.

"Hoss-pital," Mum gasped, as if blowing up a balloon. Dad kept real silent, his face close to the windshield as we screeched round a corner.

I waited, curled up on the seat, while he helped her inside. It seemed like hours before he came out again, alone, not saying a word the whole drive home. He must've thought I was asleep; I let him carry me up to my bed and tuck me in, as if nothing had happened.

Next morning I figured it was just a dream, till I went into their bedroom. There was Dad alone in the bed, staring at the ceiling. He told me the baby didn't make it. Didn't make what? It sounded like someone not getting on the school dodge-ball team.

"Where's Mum?" I wanted to know, thinking of the cat. The time she had kittens, how one never opened its eyes.

When Mum finally came home, she was still fat. She never mentioned the baby, not once, and I wondered if perhaps it had been a hoax, as they say in Nancy Drew. Then September came and school started — business as usual, Dad said. Except that's when Mum stopped being home the way I was used to; started smoking, too. The busier she was, the faster she'd lose the weight, I heard her tell Dad.

Meetings, that's where she went night after night, through the fall and then the winter. She'd explain that it was volunteer work, while making supper, stirring peas and carrots and checking the meatloaf. We'd eat when Dad came home and, later, while I did homework, she'd get dressed in her matched sweater and skirt, sometimes a string of pearls. Once Dad, drying dishes, said, "I thought it was in a church basement."

She gave him a funny look, putting on her coat to go see these women she'd met someplace — at church, the hospital, I'm not sure where. They were collecting for people in Korea, that's all she said. The name reminded me of sickness, a bad stomach flu. At least — thank goodness — Korea was far enough away that you didn't have to worry about catching it.

Sometimes Mum brought stuff home from the meetings, boxes of clothes that needed mending. It was her job to get them ready for sending in the big wooden tea crates she had the stevedores save down at the waterfront.

The mornings after her meetings — always schooldays — if I got dressed without a fuss, she let me dig through the boxes in the dining-room. She'd sit drinking coffee in her housecoat, watching me, humming "Spanish Eyes" with the radio.

"What *can* they be thinking?" she'd say, shaking her head at some of the donations — a word that reminded me of doughnuts, sugary, sweet.

Among the stretchy pants and pilled, shrunken shells were laddery nylons, blouses with no buttons. But it wasn't these that got Mum so much as the *nice* things — a dress, one time, or maybe it was a slip, the same colour gold as inside a sardine tin; a stiff, shiny gown another time, cut like a sleeve. It was a deep rose, all lathered over with purple lace — a dress you could see your Barbie doll in, but not your mother, not a real person. Not even my Aunt Ardith with all the flashy clothes.

"Can you *imagine?*" Mum said, blowing smoke rings in one long, disgusted breath. As if nowhere in Korea was there anyone so shameless as to wear something like that, and the donor must be crazy — or just plain insulting.

I thought it was beautiful — I'll bet plenty of people would've died for such a dress. I almost told her so, but changed my mind. Maybe, if I just kept quiet, she'd let me....

In the same box was a skating costume, too — red velvet with a short, twirly skirt lined with satin, trimmed with white fur like Santa's jacket. It was just as lovely.

"How impractical!" Mum uncrossed her legs, pulled her housecoat tight across her bosoms and reached down, tossing the costume over a chair. "As if anybody skates there."

I kept my eyes on the red velvet, but then she pulled out the purple-rose one and threw it over the chair too. A picture filled my head of myself grown up, on a date. Wearing that dress, my hair piled on top of my head.

Lifting her eyebrows, Mum stubbed out her cigarette, dainty and slow as the school librarian stamping books. You could tell she was considering it.

"Pleease? Pretty pleease? We could use them for dress-up." I could see her start to give in.

"Wellll...."

"The next time Corinne comes over—"

I knew that would do it. Mum's mouth loosened at the corners.

"Oh, all right," she said, "Just this once. But don't tell anyone, now. These things are supposed to be for charity."

"Where are we going?" I had to know, the first time we went to pick up Corinne. "Where is it, again?" I yelled from the back seat, though I'd already had it explained. The tall grey school by the harbour where pupils stayed year round, the School for the Deaf.

"Why does she live there?"

"Because she's deaf, silly. She can't hear a thing."

I thought this over, swinging my legs through the gap between the bucket seats.

"Sure," I said, after a minute or two, not quite convinced. It sounded kind of fishy to me, Mum talking through her hat again, the same way she spoke of starving kids when I wouldn't finish dinner.

Everyone hears *something*, I decided, even if it was just the windy space between their ears.

The school was in the north end, on a hill overlooking the shipyards. Outside were some dead-looking elms and a scrubby yard, the places next door either falling or being torn down — old flat-roofed houses folding like accordions, whole sides sheared off. The rooms inside looked cut open, naked as the ones in a doll's house; some still had wallpaper.

"You wait here," Mum said, putting on her gloves, yanking up the brake.

Bracing both hands on the tops of the seats, I hoisted myself up, kicking back and forth between them. Waiting, half scared, half gleeful, to get a look at this deaf girl.

Nobody had prepared me for the fact Corinne didn't speak either.

After a long time Mum came outside, smiling, leading the girl gently by the sleeve of her thick tweed coat. Corinne wasn't smiling; she had no expression. As Mum helped her into the car, Corinne's face reminded me of butter sculptures at the Atlantic Winter Fair, bland and smooth, the noses and mouths so easily smeared.

Sliding back on the hard, cold seat, I stared at the side of her head, the red tam on her dull brown hair.

"This is Barbara," Mum said in a slow, loud voice, patting Corinne's arm with her glove. "I bet you two will have some fun!"

Corinne just stared at the harbour, the peaked green bridge over it. Mum caught my eye in the mirror and didn't quite wink, stealing a look at Corinne as she started the car.

At home the idea was we'd eat dinner, then Corinne and I would spend the afternoon playing Barbies. Mum hinted for me to show her the ballgown we'd bought, let her dress Midge in it. I had some doubts about this, since Corinne was a couple of years older than me.

Dinner was mashed potatoes and roast beef, with lemon pie for dessert. Corinne picked at her food, avoiding their eyes as first my mother, then my father tried talking to her.

"So how's school?" Dad shouted and cleared his throat, reaching for more potatoes. Mum shot him a look that said: You don't have to yell; it won't help. Glancing at Corinne's plate and smiling, she said in a loud, *loud* voice, mouthing each word, "So. How. Do. You. Like. The. Big. City?"

Corinne put down her fork and held the sides of her face, looking baffled.

"I promised your mother so long as you're here I'd keep an eye on you. Besides" — she watched me roll a pea across the tablecloth, blinked hard and swallowed — "Barbara loves having someone around to play with, another girl. Don't you, dear?"

I stopped long enough to gaze at Corinne, expecting *something*. But no, not a flash or flicker of anything, just that blank softness, her too-short bangs like the lid on an empty jar.

So much for pink angora, the gentle bossiness of someone older. All I saw was Corinne's brown corduroy jumper, her beige leotards bagged at the ankles.

"Why don't you take Corinne up to your room now, honey, and show her your Barbies? I bet she'll get a kick out of them," Mum said, the meringue off my pie barely swallowed. Her voice was still loud enough to cut plaster.

You don't need to holler, Mum; she can't hear you anyway — and how clever, I thought, running up the stairs. I turned to watch Corinne following, quiet as Hiawatha on *Merry Melodies*.

You're just fooling, aren't you. Of *course* you can hear. Everybody hears. Don't they? I felt like hissing it in her ear as she leaned behind me, a soft brown presence breathing starch and hard yellow soap.

In my room the dolls lay naked on the white poster bed: Ken with his smooth, straight body; Barbie and Midge, pixie-nosed, their hard, pointy bosoms like the shells my dad's brother Vincent made into lamps. Beside them were the clothes: tiny sweater-dresses, blouses and skirts that snapped up the back; the satin ballgown with matching gloves and sparkly slippers Mum helped pick out. It was the colour of the ocean on a hot, sunny day, the same shiny green-blue, with netting over the wide, puffy skirt.

Kneeling, I started poking Barbie into the dress, biting my tongue as her hand snagged the fabric. Corinne came and sat on the edge of the bed, hands in her lap. I handed her Ken and his one-piece tuxedo, black and white with a glued-on bow tie. She fumbled with the snaps till finally I took him and did them myself. Sighing, I handed her Midge, the red sweater set Mum knit.

"Here," I said. "Try this."

But Corinne didn't seem too interested. She stuck the stiff arms through the sleeves, then dropped the doll and went to stare out the window. Who knows what she was looking at — our yard or the neighbours', our identical pea-yellow lawns, or maybe the grey woods at the end of the street. It wasn't quite Easter, see, not warm enough yet for things to be green.

Spying something, she made a grunting sound, a croak like a window sticking shut, or someone breaking wind. I let on I didn't hear and she stayed by the window, hugging herself. It looked so funny, those thick arms of hers in the greyish blouse, both hands sticking out the sides as if sewn to her jumper.

I said, "Are you cold or something?"

When there was no answer I went and changed Ken into some jeans — just like the ones Dad wore cutting the grass, blue with yellow stitching, and a real fly.

I changed the others to match, then stood them up along the footboard.

"They're going on a *date*, see? You can be Midge — I'll let you be Midge — and I'll be Ken if you want. Midge can go with Ken. Okay?"

No answer.

It was spooky being in the same room with someone yet feeling alone, all alone but for the dolls lined up in their outfits. I felt lonelier than I ever did playing by myself, even when Mum would come and stand in the hall, listening. Making like a mouse or a spider on the wall. I hated it when she did that, especially if the dolls were busy talking. It made me cold and shivery, as though I'd grown too big for my skin and she'd come to unzip it.

But this time I felt grateful when Mum tiptoed upstairs and tapped on the door, saying we had to take Corinne back to the school. And would I like to come for the ride?

"No," I said, not even trying to sound sorry.

The next Sunday and the Sunday after that, things went about the same, though Mum made no mention of bringing me along when she got Corinne. Lord knows what she talked about on the drive home. I imagine she smiled a lot and patted Corinne much the way she would've had I been there, desperate to fill the air with something — her work for Korea, maybe: socks darned, buttons replaced. Or maybe she quit bothering altogether. It got kind of tiring, I heard her tell Dad once, holding conversations with yourself.

At dinner nobody said much, except to remind me to finish my vegetables. No such reminders were given Corinne, who looked at her food the way she did at my dolls. From the start, I think Mum could see we weren't exactly hitting it off like trees on fire. The second visit she had us bring the Barbies downstairs and play with the TV on, so she could listen to *Hymn Sing* and keep an eye on things. Maybe she was scared I'd forget to share. When it was time to take Corinne home, I told everyone I had a stomach-ache.

Not long after, Mum let me keep those clothes.

"As long as you put them away afterwards. And remember, you mustn't tell *anyone* where they came from. Heaven knows those poor souls could prob'ly use them — more than we ever will — even though they're not too practical. All the same, these things *were* given for a purpose."

Souls. Refugees. These were the names she used, talking on the phone. By now she was in charge of shipping the clothes too; I could tell when she was arranging things at the cargo pier by the way her voice would speed up, get high and shrill and out of breath. I don't know why, but the strain to make whoever it was understand made me think of Corinne.

The next time she came over, I didn't wait till after dinner to show Corinne the dresses, piled in a box in my
closet. I made her turn around while I took off my sweater
and slipped on the skating costume. It was a bit big, the
waist hanging down to the top of my thighs. For one
split second Corinne's eyes lit as I spun around, sock-feet
slipping on the hardwood floor.

I grabbed the other dress, the lacy, purplish one; held
it out. It looked so grown-up, I was sure she'd want to try
it on.

"Go ahead," I mouthed, tugging at her cuff. "I don't
mind. Come on, there's time before dinner."

I was dying to get a look at her, what she was like
under the jumper, the same one every week. I made a
face, pulling at the neck of my skating dress.

"Like this," I mouthed, reaching behind my head for
the zipper, undoing it till the collar flopped. "Go on. Take
off your jumper, like this, and try it on."

After some coaxing she finally pulled the dress over
her clothes, blouse, jumper and all, a sad, sour look on
her face as if she'd had enough already, trying to please
me.

"It's s'posed to be *fun*," I said, in the same fast whisper Mum uses, scolding, when she doesn't want Dad to
hear.

Corinne stood there scowling, the dress bunched up
on her hips, her arms stuck out like broomsticks.

"Fine, then."

I turned away, spinning faster and faster, till my skirt
stuck out like the bench round the tree in the grade-two
reader, the story about Jane and Dick, their pets Bunny
and Flip.

Corinne shook off the dress like my cat wiggling out
of her flea collar.

"Barbara?" At last Mum hollered upstairs. "It's ready!

Come and eat."

Though it was raining, after dinner my parents decided to take a drive. "Just a jaunt," Dad said, the four of us crammed in our small blue car. I was horrified at the thought of having to sit there in the back seat with Corinne in her damp wool coat, her see-through rainboots; of having to look at her and smile each time someone opened their mouth to talk. Praying the car would put her to sleep, I kept my eyes on the mirror, hungry for Dad's smiles.

Once Corinne caught me glancing over, her pale green eyes so wide and open you could see the grey flecks in them. Eyes that could skim a layer off your skin, it seemed to me. How, I wondered, could she not know everything going on?

After the dress-up clothes I'd quit bothering to speak to her, my parents the same. Even Mum, sitting stiff and straight in the passenger seat, cooing at the scenery.

When Corinne caught me looking, I tried climbing over the seat to the cubbyhole above the engine. I shut my eyes, sniffing the warm, gritty smell of exhaust and road salt.

"Get out of there, young lady! You're much too big to be in there," Dad hollered, and the car wobbled and hit the shoulder, just for a second. Mum gasped and threw up her hands. I rolled back onto the seat.

"You wouldn't catch Corinne doing something like that," Mum muttered, wiping circles on the windshield with her fingers. It was so fogged up you could barely see the passing houses, the grey blur of ocean ahead.

"How much farther?" I kept asking, till Dad said, "That's enough."

When at last we turned back to the city, it was time to take Corinne downtown. All of us — no chance for

Dad and me to stop at home and let Mum go by herself.

At the school, Dad asked me to move and let Corinne out. Standing by the curb, Mum gripped my hand and said, well now I was here why didn't I come and see where Corinne lived.

Inside was a hallway with a big, wide staircase. It smelled of stew, the warm, soupy odour of radiators, and something else, the smell of visitors maybe, stale perfume on wet fur. At the foot of the stairs Mum helped Corinne out of her coat, then bent to kiss her, a quick, waxy peck on the cheek. A shade of something — embarrassment, shame? — passed over Corinne's mouth as she stood there, arms by her sides.

I'd hoped for a peek at the dorm where she slept with the other girls, but that didn't come. Waving, half shy, like a baby to a stranger, Corinne looked at us, then disappeared, taking the shabby, carpeted steps two at a time.

Not long after, the school was closed and moved to Amherst — a newer, bigger building, Mum said, though even farther from Corinne's home, her real home. This ended that string of Sundays.

I heard Mum talking about it, see, the night she had the charity ladies over. Dad and I stayed upstairs, not that it was much quieter. Oh, even with the doors closed you could still hear them down there laughing and carrying on. They were supposed to be sewing, fixing a big batch of clothes to go by boat that same week. I'd heard Mum on the phone inviting the women, saying in that soft but jittery voice, "Many hands make light work."

Dad fell asleep reading papers from his office. During a lull in the laughter, I slipped downstairs in my nightie; stood for a minute by the living-room, listening. Mum sat in the wing-chair, a big pair of pants on her lap; on the couch were three ladies older than Mum. One waved some scissors as she talked, the others nodding along. Mum stared at the pants, her needle weaving in and out. The woman with the scissors was going on about somebody having a baby with water on its brain. I pictured an ice cube melting on someone's head, the little pool it would leave.

The woman kept talking, the others looking up from their mending long enough to shake their heads or click their tongues. All except Mum, her eyes on those pants till you figured they'd burn a hole through. Without looking up she cut in.

"I know someone that happened to," she said in a quiet, cool voice that made my shoulders prickle. I thought at first that she must be talking about the baby, the one that got lost — after so long, I'd almost forgotten it. But then she glanced up, catching me there in the doorway. The look on her face wary, watchful but indifferent too.

"You know who I mean, dear, don't you?"

Corinne, of course. Or Shirley, Corinne's mother. One or the other, I realized it had to be them. Who else?

The other ladies hushed up, waiting for more. But Mum didn't go into it; she reached for the scissors, snipped some thread.

That was the most I ever heard about Corinne's problem.

We did have one more visit, though, a couple of months later, one Saturday in June before school, my school, ended. Corinne came to see us, this time with her mother.

Mum peeled off her apron when she saw them at the door, two surprise guests. You could tell by the look on her face that she wasn't all that pleased. She was in the midst of washing something in the kitchen sink, trying to get the stains off a blouse she'd fixed. Her hair was stuck back with bobby pins.

"How nice to see you," she said without much cheer, straightening the doormat with her toe.

As they came in, it struck me how Corinne and her mother didn't match — like Cinderella and one of the step-sisters. Corinne had on a pink dress, a bit too short, her purplish knees showing below the lumpy hem. Her mother, though, wore a shiny suit the colour of cantaloupe, with cream-coloured gloves and high-heeled shoes the same shade. Mum stood with her back to the sink, running her hands over the hips of her old blue skirt, the one she wore doing housework.

"Stay for a cup of tea?" she took her time asking.

"Love to," said the mother, giving Corinne a nudge. "You two run along now, give us old birds a chance to catch up!"

Outside, I tied my blue-striped skipping rope to the telephone pole at the end of the driveway, and started right in turning pepper. Balancing on the curb, Corinne watched but didn't jump in. I slowed to salt, the rope sagging and slapping the ground. But by this time she'd turned and begun walking away, quickly, down the street.

"Hey!" I yelled. Letting the white handle skip over the pavement, I ran after her.

"Where do you think you're going?" — "young lady," I almost shouted.

I followed her past the neighbours' driveway, past the black-speckled boulders at the end of the street.

"Mum says it's not right, we're not s'posed to go in the woods by ourselves," I said, making a grab for her arm. She gave me a funny look, like the cat watching a flea, holding her arms up to push through some alders. My eyes shut to the snapping branches, I waded after her, snatching at the back of her dress. But it was no good; whatever she had in mind, there was no keeping her from it.

"There's nothing down here." My voice was like Mum's, nattering, talking to myself as she stepped over roots and rocks, some crumpled Kleenexes.

"I'm gonna get it if Mum— I'll be in for it now, Corinne, don't you know—"

Then I heard. A choked-back giggle, next a wheezy, mewing sound like someone having the wind pumped from them.

It was Corinne who stuck out her elbow and gave me a knock hard enough to stop my breath. She put her finger to her lips.

"What now—?" I groaned. But then I saw it too. Something, somebody, squirming behind the bushes, a bare bum round and white as a beach stone among the bright green huckleberry leaves. Underneath, someone with long yellow hair in her eyes, her mouth half open.

"What the—?" The boy lifted up on his knees, turning just as we backed away. "Dirty little bitch—"

He was like a dog, reared back, snarling.

A giggle popped from Corinne's lips, a bright, hiccuppy sound, as I pulled at her, yanking her back through the tangled branches. Her cheeks looked hot, a funny glitter in her eyes, then her mouth split open in a big, wide, gasping laugh.

"Run!"

I kept dragging at her, sure the boy *must* be coming after us. We were done for, I knew, after whatever we'd seen him doing. My blood pounded at the thought of what might happen if he caught up.

"Come on, come *on*!"

I wouldn't let go of her arm, even once we reached the pavement. She was snickering into her hand, a noise like somebody blowing their nose. I kept pulling her along the curb, my heart still hammering.

"Stupid!" I hissed. Though by the time we got to our

driveway I'd begun laughing too, sort of, wiping sweat off my forehead, trying to catch my breath and calm myself.

Corinne shook me off and marched up the steps.

"Not yet!" I tried stopping her, but it was too late. Her mother was just coming out, Mum in the doorway looking glad.

"Where did you disappear to?" my mother wanted to know, as Corinne's picked a twig from her hair. Corinne flinched, fixing me with a smug, secret grin, a grin that sent little chills down the back of my pop-top. I chewed my lip, trying not to smile.

"Kids," said Mum, breathing in deep and sighing, letting the door spring shut as the guests moved down the walk. As if remembering something, she tapped on the glass and waved, mouthing, "Bye-bye, Corinne." But neither of them turned or looked back, getting into their brown car.

"So." Mum rolled up her sleeves, plunging her hands back into the sink.

"Where'd you go?" she asked again, glancing at me, this time shaking her head. "I don't know how often I've told you, Barbara Anne Mossman—"

The smell of bleach made my eyes sting. It was awful when she said my whole name like that, as if counting the hairs on my head, going over each one with a fine-tooth comb.

Mum sniffed and held up the dripping blouse; dipped it back in.

"You mustn't go into those woods by yourself. Do you hear me? You just don't know who could be down there. I mean, what if something happened to you? Or Corinne?"

She looked at me and sighed, her eyes watery from the Javex.

"Some people," she muttered, rubbing away at the greyish cloth, holding it up to the window. The stain was a long, yellow-pink splotch the colour spaghetti would leave.

"Some people."

Dipping it once more, she started wringing the water out.

"Well, I hope *you* two had a nice time, at least."

Mum rolled up the blouse and set it down while she rinsed her hands under the cold. She let it run and run till the pump came on in the basement, and Dad had to yell up the stairs.

DAYS AS IN THE TIME OF NOAH

S even days and nights it rained, one entire week with out let-up. It was as if some giant sluice had opened, spilling every drop ever drawn into the sky. Creeks choked with overflow, and above town the Salmon River backed up like a faulty sewer; instead of emptying into Cobequid Bay, it spewed without mercy across the marsh.

Laced with salt and cow-dung, the river carried with it the stink of tar and ruined wood, chunks of buildings, barns and pavement — anything unsecured by dike. Across the flat and yielding land it spread till houses bobbed like islands, and by the hour more homes, farms and businesses were under threat. And not a thing could be done but watch and wait and hope the rain would stop, the Salmon subside below banks swollen as the edges of a deep, ugly wound.

1. Contract

On the sixth day Arthur Mossman disregarded RCMP warnings to avoid the hardest-hit areas. He had Kaye dig out an old pair of gumboots from the basement, which thus far had escaped with only a tiny leak around a window. Their house, purchased with caution and much fortitude, stood on a hill on the outskirts of town.

It was a Sunday, around noon. They'd slept in, wakened by their daughter, Barbara, going off to her friend's. Kaye was edgy and irritable, as she often got during stretches of bad weather. Arthur tried to ignore her fussing over the coffee, the scrambled eggs. If not for her grumpiness, he'd have preferred to stay home with her, as he had the day before, puttering around his desk in the basement with the radio on, the new country station that played some of their favourite songs.

But he had work to do. Still grateful he hadn't been called out the night before — which the radio labelled the height of the storm — Arthur figured it was time he got a handle on the extent of the flooding.

Kaye was still in her quilted bathrobe, sorting through some old raingear in the basement closet. She gave him a sulky look, watching him gather things from his desk — a clipboard, some pens, a sheaf of claims forms.

"But Arthur, you haven't even had a claim come in yet, have you? I really don't see why—"

The sullenness of her voice — was it any wonder he preferred the quiet of the car, the solitary pleasure of being out on a job, driving?

"Well?" Kaye stood there with a small red all-weather coat over her arm, something Barbara had outgrown. Her hair was flat at the crown, grey showing through the auburn rinse. The corners of her pale mouth sagged a little; her eyes, bright and suspicious, were like his daughter's. Perhaps that was where Barbara got her disposition, he thought — the dismissive pouts, disgusted sighs; the childish spurts of anger that often left him baffled. Yet at other times she seemed practically grown up; "out of his hair", he'd joke with the fellows in the office. Imagining it was the same for most fathers with teenaged girls.

"Don't try to understand me, just love me," he'd seen once on a T-shirt at the mall. At the time Arthur had considered picking up three, one for each of them, small, medium, large. Not that it seemed a bad thing, putting oneself in another's skin — something, he told himself, Kaye might have attempted now and then. But no, like Barbara, he could scarcely expect his wife to put herself in his; to appreciate, for instance, how it felt to do his line of work.

Arthur went in to use the bathroom. Spread beside the sink were some tubes of cosmetics, an eyelash curler that looked more like a cooking gadget or mousetrap. The thought of someone using it made him cringe.

When he came out, Kaye was in the front hallway, holding his trenchcoat.

"I suppose an umbrella would be silly." She tried to sound cheerful, watching him load his camera.

"A rubber raft might be more useful, hon." He dropped the camera in his briefcase, snapped it shut.

"You're not going all the way out past the marsh, I hope. I mean, couldn't you just take a look, say, out Bible Hill way?" There was a long pause. "Really, Arthur, I don't see why you won't wait till the office calls — wouldn't it be easier to check the damage once the flooding stops?"

She eyed him with that wary, fretful look of hers, checking him over like a newly scrubbed floor, searching for a spot she'd missed, some reason why he shouldn't go. Fifteen years of marriage, he thought despairingly, and she still wasn't used to the incidents that were his business — disasters big and small: kitchen fires, car crashes, flooded basements. If anything, she'd gotten worse since he'd started adjusting. As if he had any choice but to go and do his job: assess damage, assign liability.

The radio was on in the kitchen. Arthur hummed along with a Porter Wagoner song, suiting up for his drive across town. He was shoving his feet into the gumboots, still dusty with cobwebs and cat hair from the basement, when a voice cut in to announce the mall was being closed, Zellers' parking lot under two feet of water. Firemen were on the scene assisting evacuation.

Without stopping to kiss his wife, Arthur rushed out to the car. As he jiggled the key in the lock the rain fell in sheets, a curtain of grey needles. Like being under a waterfall, he couldn't help thinking. It reminded him of his honeymoon with Kaye — a lifetime ago, it now seemed — when they drove all the way to Ontario and took the tour at Niagara, donning black rubber slickers to walk the tunnels beneath Horseshoe Falls. They had stood back from a gaping hole in the rock and watched the water cascade above them, thick and white as the spume from a snow-blower. Kaye had clung to his arm while he snapped a picture, ducking her shoulders in the long, stiff raincoat as if she feared being crushed by the roar, the thunderous weight of so much rock and water. When they emerged ten minutes later, Arthur was still trembling from the noise, the pressure on his eardrums.

The Chev didn't want to start at first; some water had trickled in through the vents, leaving a small, shiny puddle on the floormat. No sweat, he thought; bought slightly used, the car never liked dampness, rarely started first crack in wet weather. Waiting for the engine to turn over, torrents lashing the windshield, Arthur thought once more of the falls. That endless volume of water, where on earth did it all go?

As fast as it hit the driveway, the rain seeped into the lawn. From the road it swirled in the ditch and disappeared through a culvert. Turning onto the pavement, Arthur switched on the country station, barely audible with static; caught the end of a newsflash. "Sandbagging...a rising tide of water...."

He twiddled the volume for the forecast: "...four more inches by nightfall, showers tapering to drizzle...." At high tide, around three that afternoon, the cheery car-sales-man voice predicted, the floodwaters would peak, when the bay, at its highest, pushed back the river.

Slowing to avoid a slippery patch, Arthur sighed and clicked off the radio. So often reporters exaggerated; wasn't it their job, after all, to go out and find the worst possible situations?

From what he could see, the fields and yards along the road acted like sponges, soaking everything up with no problem. The furniture store was open at the end of the road, where it met the two-lane highway into town; there were cars parked outside. Near the intersection some children played in a puddle, their bright yellow raincoats flattened against their bodies. Arthur thought for a second of the mother indoors, smoking a cigarette, talking on the phone perhaps, or having a shower. Kids, he thought. When Barbara was small she had loved playing in the rain; Kaye would have to call and call, then bribe her with TV and cookies to come in.

He was reminded briefly of his own childhood, too, growing up in a town in the Annapolis Valley. How when it rained he and his older brother, Vincent, would put on their boots and play near the pond by the sock factory, collecting slugs and corralling them in the runoff till they drowned. Vincent would pick them up with his bare fin-gers and shove them down inside Arthur's jacket, his thin white face up close and taunting if he cried.

"They can't hurtcha, what're ya cryin' for, ya big friggin' baby? They're already dead, don'tcha know? What the frig are ya cryin' for anyways, huh?"

Vincent would chase after him and rough him up by the shoulders when Arthur ran home to tell. Their mother, Rowena, would be at the wobbly kitchen table, nursing a

cold cup of tea; their father Lorenzo — when he was home
— sleeping it off in the cellar, on the broken-down iron-
ing board she made him use if he'd had too much to
drink. Arthur could still picture it next to the washtub,
propped between two old chairs.

The sky opened up, the sound of rain spilling and
beating the roof — this was what it brought back, when
he allowed himself to think of it. His childhood, his father asleep in the cellar, as well as the day with Kaye in
Niagara Falls: the two of them newlywed-shy, asking strangers to snap shots of them in their hooded black coats.

2. Premium

As Arthur turned towards town, nothing looked out of
the ordinary: vehicles ahead splashing jets of water from
the potholes, the asphalt slick and shiny as the glaze Kaye
baked on chicken. Nothing to get too excited about. If
damage existed, from the car it was invisible.

Past the tavern and the Chinese restaurant, traffic
moved as usual. Arthur slowed enough to glance from
time to time at the roadside, the muddy front yards and
storefronts. There was nothing amiss or alarming — no
downed power lines, no cars abandoned by the sidewalk,
no one waving helplessly from front porches; not so much
as a fallen branch. "What's a little rain?" he said aloud,
waving to someone in a passing car. This is nothing, he
thought. Twenty-four years in this business; I should
know.

It was only his second year, however, as an adjuster.
After twenty-two years in sales he had decided one day
he'd had enough; studied and wrote all thirteen exams
for his licence, then transferred up here from Halifax as a
career move. No easy thing, moving a wife and daughter
from the city to a town this size. Having come from a
village in the middle of nowhere, Kaye hadn't minded

too much; she'd never enjoyed being in a bigger place, having no connections there. Hubville, their new home, was halfway in between, a clean break for both of them. And for Arthur it offered clear-cut opportunities, not the least of which was the freedom of working as an adjuster. After all those years selling — life insurance with Foresight Limited, then basic, across-the-board coverage with General Accident — it was the independence of his new job Arthur found most appealing.

The position involved travel, of course, sporadic travel to the scenes of wreckage. Yet there was something solid and dependable about adjusting, a kind of assurance he'd found lacking in sales. It was much easier, Arthur knew from experience, to go in and assess a calamity after the fact than to try to convince people of one that hadn't yet happened. Boom, just like that, out of the clear, blue sky: that was how disasters usually occurred. House fires, fender-benders, farm mishaps — in a good mood Kaye would joke that he should've driven an ambulance, he spent so much time pursuing accidents. Accidents and acts of God, equally capricious. Except for flooding. At least once each spring one could depend upon the Salmon overflowing, and this lent a grain of comfort and predictability to Arthur's work.

Stopped at some lights near the foot of a hill, just before the road dipped below a concrete railway bridge, Arthur glimpsed the marsh through a gap between two buildings. From this vantage-point it spread like a rippling grey sheet between town and the hills opposite, the broad, brick-coloured river like a gash through the centre. The sight was so startling he missed the light change until the car behind honked. As he pulled away, the sudden, unforeseen view of so much water tightened his chest with glee. Though this was something he would never have admitted — not even to Kaye — for fear of sounding callous.

Just do your job, he told himself, gathering speed. The town's grid ingrained in his mind like a waffle, he rolled over figures: trying to imagine the acreage, the sheer area under water, estimating ongoing salt damage. Every angle, all the variables of destruction and devastation. Just do your job, he thought, and it will be easy. So long as there was no personal injury to contend with and his own house remained on high ground. Twenty-four years in the industry, he reassured himself as he stepped on the gas, trying to think of the best point from which to gauge the worst of the flooding. *Fires, floods, explosions, crashes.... Till it washes up in your own back yard, you just go ahead and do your job....*

When Arthur first sold insurance — back when he began with Foresight, before he met Kaye — he used to prickle at the idea of reaping profit through others' misfortune, others' fear of misfortune. Hell, he would assuage his guilt, the price of soothing their fear is my commission. Never, never bite the hand that feeds you. What folly that would've been. And really, when he thought about it, nobody lost. Premiums paid for assurance, no more and no less.

Now he worked on his own time — as much as the uncertainty of accidents allowed — and on straight salary. There was no more worry over racking up commissions, and the stress of competition was largely removed. Switching from sales meant, of course, no more company car. Which wasn't so bad really, Arthur told himself now; a small price for being pretty much one's own boss.

Approaching the business section of town, Arthur braked for another light. The rain was coming down in sheets, coursing along the curb and buckling over storm drains. From the spreading pools the car sprayed waves over the sidewalk — had there been pedestrians, they'd have been drenched. He listened to the long, deep swoosh from the wheels, the ticking of dirt and grit up inside the fenders. Yes, it would've been better, he thought quickly, to have the use of a company car.

But there had been more to Arthur's decision to change jobs than comforts or money. There was a certain excitement, witnessing the aftermath of events — so much more interesting to be out surveying and taking pictures and estimating the effects of calamity both natural and human; trying to assign dollar values. So much more satisfying than shuffling papers and going over the no-fault policies of the parties involved. Adjusting, at least when dealing with property, was so much cleaner, he felt, so much more objective. Things like house fires, flooded basements — you went in and looked over the damage, the injuries, then reported back to the company. There was no dealing with weeping victims or their families, people crying into the phone about their losses. In Arthur's experience as a salesman, people never took out enough coverage, never half enough. Mention it and they would look at him, wary and defiant, as if he was trying to pull the wool over their eyes, gyp them.

"Oh no, that will never happen to *me*."

But it might, Arthur would always say to himself, shaking his head politely, putting the papers back in his briefcase. It might and could and usually did, and then who was the one crying? Left standing outside their burned-down house with nothing but the pyjamas they'd been wearing when roused by smoke. Oh, it was sad, of course; and these were the lucky ones.

It was a different thing altogether dealing with the bad fires, the ones where there was loss of life. The awful details, the things Arthur didn't or couldn't put down in his report: the charred remains of a teddy bear, a melted bicycle seat. Things that put you in mind of your own loved ones. Once Arthur found a scorched makeup case near a foundation, all that was left of the neat split-level house — everything burned black as toast, even the patchy snow stinking of smoke. The case was one of those small, boxy affairs with a mirror inside, ringed with tiny, battery-operated lightbulbs. When Arthur saw that, he had to stop his inspection and find a coffee shop with a payphone to call home.

"Kaye, Kaye honey? Everything all right? ...Why, I was just having a doughnut and I felt like.... No, no it's fine, everything's fine. And how was Barb this morning, getting off to school? Good, oh that's good. No, I'm fine. Really. I'll see you tonight."

The fires were bad, very bad. But it was the car crashes that affected Arthur most, though this was something he'd reckoned on before making the move, the number of traffic accidents he would have to cover, Hubville being the juncture of two major highways. One spring night Arthur had to go out in the fog, assess what was left of a carload of people hit head on by a tractor-trailer. It was the worst thing he'd ever seen, though by the time he arrived the bodies had been removed, the wreckage towed off the pavement. The sedan was barely recognizable as a car; in the dark and the slow revolving light of a police cruiser, Arthur shone his flashlight in upon the crushed and bloodied interior, bits of skin, hair and glass laced and spattered over the seats. He had to turn aside quickly to reach the ditch in time to bring up the tea and pie he'd been enjoying with Kaye when the call came.

For a month or two after, he had wanted to quit adjusting; had wanted to pack up everything, move back to Halifax and try for his old job selling policies. But Kaye convinced him otherwise, saying it would interrupt Barbara's schooling, so late in the year. Wait till next fall when she starts high school, she said, and Arthur kept working. And after a while he found he had grown numb to the incidence of smashed metal and remnants of life. Had stopped seeing bits of his own body spilled on the road, and of his wife's and his daughter's. The accidents were a staple of his work, and after a time he simply got used to them.

For some of the other fellows in the office, it was the death and injury of children that lingered when they shut their eyes at night. With Arthur this wasn't quite the case; no, it was more the thought of men losing wives that kept him awake nights after somebody died. His own child seemed inviolable somehow, removed. Safe. But only, perhaps, because he could look at her now and wonder, quite honestly, how it was she'd come to be so tall; where she'd gotten the two flat little breasts under her top, more than just a wrinkle in the fabric. The first time he noticed them, it made his breath snag, the thought striking him all at once that he barely recognized her. As if he'd been out of town working fourteen years, then come home to find a stranger. That had been part, a big part, of his choice to leave sales, so he could cut out some of the regular travel, spend more time at home. Not, apparently, that it had made any difference.

3. Risk

Past the bank and the courthouse the water deepened. At the next light the car sputtered a little; Arthur braked and pumped the gas, pumped it hard to rev the engine. He pictured the floodwater splashing up and wetting the spark plugs, cursed under his breath.

He was just pulling into an intersection when a car swerved in front, the rear end fishtailing and splattering mud on his windshield.

"Hey, watchit, you! What the hell you think you're doing?" he yelled, the window rolled up tight. Ahead the driver crept along as if watching for something, a certain shop or restaurant. Arthur slowed down, listening to the water swish around the tires. The noise beneath the fenders no more a ticking but a long, steady rush, loud as the wind in the trees behind their house the day the rains started. Both hands on the wheel, he glanced at the crack below the passenger door, half expecting a trickle there. He was still looking down when the driver ahead slammed on the brakes, his rear end wallowing into the curb. Arthur, lucky enough to stop in time, rode the gas to keep from stalling.

He cranked down the window and shouted as the fellow turned into a parking lot. "Where'd you get your licence? The goddamn drugstore? I hope you've got insurance!" But the man didn't so much as glance back, the water splitting from his wheels in a long, smooth V.

The rain seemed to lighten slightly, the drumming on the roof growing softer. Arthur turned down the wipers; the windshield blurred grey as the surface of a lake. It was only another couple of blocks to the mall, the area nearest the river. By the bowling alley a town policeman stood in water up to his shins, diverting traffic. Arthur pulled over and got out, flashing his adjuster's licence. Water tugged and sloshed over the tops of his galoshes, mixing with the grit inside them. The officer nodded and Arthur jumped back in the car, his feet soaked now, the icy wetness swilling between his toes.

Along Prince Street, floodwater spread over the sidewalk. He heard it swish along the running boards.

"Should be driving a boat, for Chrissake," he said to himself as the engine sputtered again. Riding the brake, he gave the gas an extra couple of pumps. It was getting hard to see — the window kept fogging up, but it was still pouring too hard to roll it down even a crack.

Passing a corner he peered at two teenaged boys

clinging to a telephone pole, like something you'd see on television — news reports from Florida, whenever hurricanes hit. He thought at first they were fooling around; there was something comic about it, exaggerated, the way kids behaved in extraordinary situations. One held his hand out to the other, pulling him in as people did on TV clinging to buoys or rubber dinghies. The current tugged at their knees like a frothy soup. Arthur honked the horn and kept going. Hanging onto each other the boys stared, one of them shouting as his friend stumbled, the water sucking at their jeans like a vacuum. With a chill Arthur realized they weren't just carrying on. But what could he have done? He might've thrown them a rope, he supposed, had there been such a thing in the car. But there wasn't, and besides, had he stopped to check the trunk, no telling whether the engine might've died altogether.

The bright green Zellers sign soon came in sight. Outside the mall, sandbagging had begun; the entire fire brigade appeared to be present in all their gear, hand-over-handing drenched-looking sacks. Arthur thought of pulling in where a row of cars sat submerged to their bumpers. A brown tide swept and spread to the doors of the mall — he could see women in Red Grille uniforms stranded inside, waving for assistance. He almost stopped then and got out to help, when the engine choked again and started to stall.

"For the love of Jesus!"

Keeping to the road, Arthur could feel himself sweating under the clammy trenchcoat. He felt like hell driving past those people; knew he should've stopped and given a hand. But if he had, he was sure he'd have gotten stranded too; might as well wait for a miracle as get the car started again once it quit.

The water was rising, no question. He imagined it

coming in and slowly filling the car, an inch or two at first, then up past the pedals. In front of a garage, its gas pumps like islands, some firemen worked a pumper engine sucking up water — like drinking the sea through a straw, it struck Arthur. One of the men waved him over.

"Where you headed?" he shouted, eyeing Arthur as if he were crazy. Arthur cranked down the window to explain but the fireman spoke first.

"RCMP got this whole end of town closed off." The fellow shook his head, rain dripping off his face. "My advice would be to turn around and go back wherever it was you came from. Or ditch 'er right here and come up in the truck with us."

Arthur shrugged. "How bad, up ahead?"

"Well, this here's where she's crested. I s'pose it's no worse once you hit higher ground."

"Up past the highway? I've got business up there. Want to see how the farms are doing. You know, damage to fields, that sort of thing."

The man leaned inside the window. "I guess if ya got a job to do — I know if it was me I'd be home right now sucking back a beer and watchin' the tube. Best place to be, I can tell you, day like this. That is, if you're lucky enough to have a place that's dry. But you're this far now, buddy, I guess what the heck—"

Arthur gave him a nod and pulled away, winding up the window. Ahead he could see the ramps to the highway; just beyond, the hills slanting up from the marsh, the fields and pastures he hoped to inspect.

Farm insurance — it was big business in these parts; like the promise of flooding, another factor which had drawn Arthur to this market. He'd had in mind an image of green rolling hills, red barns and wire fences; a ready supply of cases, but nothing, surely, too grisly or demanding. It was the prospect of being in farm country again that had convinced Kaye to move. He remembered the day she agreed almost as clearly as the day he met her, going into the bank in New Glasgow to cash a cheque. Back in the days he was still travelling for Foresight.

The night before he'd been just outside Halifax, visiting his brother Vincent and his family. Pearl, the wife, had invited Arthur to supper; reluctantly he'd accepted. He'd ended up drinking too much and leaving with a headache, glad to be away from their small crowded house, the sound of their little boy's humming. Jeremy, that was his name; an odd child. Not retarded, no, not exactly; but different. An accident at birth, a lack of oxygen perhaps — all through the meal of fried sausage and peas Arthur couldn't help wondering what might have happened. Beside him at the table, the boy fidgeted and fussed, then crawled underneath to chew his food. Arthur put on his best selling face and tried not to notice the boy at his feet humming, a sound soft and thick as a mouthful of potato. Who knew but this was normal for a kid his age, three or four, maybe — Arthur was a bachelor, with no other nephews or nieces to compare.

But it wasn't Jeremy, or Pearl smiling nervously, knocking over the salt when she poured more beer, that made him uncomfortable. More, it was his brother's sullen gaze, as if begging Arthur's assurance while denying, flatly denying, there was anything amiss. No, it wasn't the wife who acted cold and awkward — she had a quiet if cheap warmth about her — but Vincent himself, who, despite being his brother, seemed more a stranger. With Vincent's taste for Oland's and the dull tattoos on his thick, greyish arms, Arthur wondered how they could be related.

The next morning he woke with a hangover, recalling the appointment he had that afternoon a hundred miles away in New Glasgow. There wasn't time to go to the bank near his room in the city, which was how at a quarter to twelve he ended up at Kaye Rushton's wicket. His tie was askew, his suit creased from the car — his hand shook a little signing the cheque — but she didn't seem to notice, snapping the crisp new bills and sliding them over the counter. It shocked him when he heard himself asking her to lunch, just like that, the question popping out before he could stifle it. Never, never in his life had he been so bold; he mightn't have spoken at all, if not for the hangover and his feeling so shaky and desperate. It lent an urgency, which Kaye must've felt standing there patting the pearls at her throat, taken aback.

"Pardon me?" she said, the red creeping up her neck and into her cheeks.

"I have to see a client at two; maybe we could grab a bite and you'd be kind enough to direct me...."

She laughed and shook her head, looking around at the other tellers as if a customer had entered and politely asked her to empty the till. A polite kind of stick-up, some crazy prank. But fifteen minutes later, there she was at the corner with her purse and her swingy red coat undone, as if she couldn't get out fast enough to meet him. They ate tomato soup and crackers together in a dingy café with dark, narrow booths, and Arthur arranged to meet her again, when the bank closed at three.

After that day Arthur swore off drinking, said he'd never touch another beer so long as he lived. It wasn't worth it, he later explained to Kaye, the way you felt afterwards, dizzy and out of sorts as though trying to function underwater.

4. Loss

Proceeding at a snail's pace — his stomach clenched as if that would prevent the water seeping in — at last Arthur reached the turnoff to the highway. The car jerked slightly as if running low on gas. Glancing down, he saw there was a good half-tank, and he had only a few more yards to the on-ramp.

Water sluiced along the incline, pooling at the bottom and sliding off into fields awash on both sides of the road. In the distance he spotted the river, the green railway bridge across it — still in place, but surrounded and skewed as if afloat. The engine sputtered, for a brief second the oil light flashed, but Arthur had no trouble getting onto the highway.

As he climbed the overpass above the marsh, the road cleared and he picked up speed, his breath keeping time with the wipers' rhythm. The car zipped along now like a sewing machine, puddles stretched thin as cellophane across the pavement. He felt himself relax, the clamminess beneath his coat evaporate.

At the next exit he should've turned right and followed the hills beyond the marsh back home. But lulled by the rain, the steady beat of the wipers, he kept on following the bay's outline past the bloated mouth of the river. How bad can the flooding get, he asked himself, his eyes peeled for sagging barns and silos. Convinced he'd come through the worst of it.

The car began acting up again near the top of a steep hill. Gunning the gas twice to make the crest, Arthur barely had time to brake for what lay over it. Ahead was a gully, at the foot of the slope a creek churning with debris — the jagged remains of a white, two-lane bridge.

Speeding downhill he was lucky to spot it soon enough, the ugly brown gap where the bridge had been, its struts and pavement washed away. He slammed the brake pedal so hard the engine quit; there was an eerie silence the split second before the brakes grabbed, tires screaming, the car skidding off into the ditch.

"Oh my Jesus!" Arthur just had time to breathe, his eyes squeezed shut till the car came to rest. Upright, in a patch of drowned alders a few feet from the creek.

"Oh my Jesus."

Afraid to move, afraid the slightest movement might somehow dislodge the Chev and send it drifting over the brink, Arthur sat hugging the wheel. The trembling in his fingers was like the end of a raw, exposed circuit, nerves jumping like sparks.

When at last he was able, he pushed the door open and slid out, sinking to his knees in the watery mire. Thick as a milkshake, it eddied around the wheels, just touching the bumper. There was hardly a scratch, though — lucky, damned lucky. The fact of his luck sent a shiver through his guts.

Dragged down by his boots, he sensed the ground beneath him spongy as quicksand. Leaning against the car, he felt it settle, the water level with the doors. All around him the rain fell like a soft grey blanket. Squinting, he watched the top of the hill for cars, the opposite stretch of asphalt where the bridge was sheared away. But there wasn't a vehicle in sight, and it was a good five-mile hike to the last house he'd noticed. Nothing to do but wait.

He was soaked to the skin now, his body's warmth a feeble flame inside his sodden clothes. His head ached, a sliver of pain lodged in his brow; the muscles in his neck stretched taut. It was getting late; the wind had stopped, the sky growing dimmer and dimmer, the stubborn clouds thick now as a window-blind. And still the rain kept coming, a thin, pissing rain so steady and pervasive it scarcely pocked the surface around the car.

Arthur got in and tried the engine — if he could get it running at least he'd have heat. It turned over once, then died, a slow, growling sound measured by the patter on the windshield. He turned the key again, just enough to try the radio. It crackled and sputtered and then went dead too, the voices swept from the sky.

From the sky — wasn't that something Barbara had said once in the car, when she was small? The people on the radio — where do they live, she'd wanted to know, and he had looked back at her and burst out laughing. They were coming back from a day at the beach, he and Kaye and their little girl; she would've been around three.

There was a place Arthur liked taking them near Peggy's Cove, not far from the city. He'd found it one day before he was married, out walking on the rocks. The first time they went, the three of them as a family, Kaye was skeptical. They parked near the lighthouse, then started to walk, Arthur in the lead, Kaye sighing as they picked their way around peat bogs and boulders; great shelves of granite, the tidal pools barnacled black mirrors.

"For goodness sakes', Art. It's not much farther, I hope." Kaye, straggling behind with Barbara. Little Barbara, in a terry-towel beach coat printed with sea-horses, her small, bare legs underneath.

"Just over one more big rock, I promise."

He stopped to swoop the child up on his hip, her small, wiry warmth in his arms. The sun was hot; he had to look away from the sea's glare, holding her close as they continued. The clean, soft child's smell of her hair in his nostrils, that and the salt-scented wind, the sharp perfume of wild bay and juniper.

Reaching a rocky crest, Arthur slowed down to wait for Kaye. She had the plaid picnic blanket over her arm, Barbara's red pail and shovel. He wanted to see the look on her face when she spotted the narrow, secret inlet below.

The tide was out; a long, straight arm between the

rocks, the channel empty but for a shallow stream in the middle. On either side glinted pink and white sand. Wedged between two massive boulders sat an old ship's boiler, as old as the rock it seemed, the metal feathered and lacy in spots, rusty-red against the sun-bleached granite.

Kaye looked away from it, blinking, and spread the blanket on a rock above the strand of coarse, crushed shells.

"I was hoping we'd swim," she said, not looking at him. Watching Barbara squatting with her pail and shovel, tugging at her sneakers. "Don't take them off, honey. You'll cut your feet!"

"All right, then, we'll try somewhere else," Arthur almost said, but instead took off his shoes, picking his way over the shards of limpet and periwinkle and broken angel wings. At the water's edge he rolled up his trousers and waded in, the salty coolness licking his shins. Beyond the ship's boiler he could see the tide start to turn; another couple of hours and it would be deep enough for swimming, water warmed by the sun and sand.

Settling on the blanket beside his wife, he pulled off his shirt, ignoring the disappointment on her face, their daughter's happy chatter at their feet. Kaye had on a pink sundress over her bathing suit; leaning close to kiss her bare shoulder, the spot where the straps left white stripes, the long, freckled curve at the top of her spine, he thought in that instant he'd never seen her so lovely.

And slowly, surely, she came out of her snit, peeling off the dress to stretch beside him, watching Barbara play. Soon they were scraping up the walls of a castle with their feet; then kneeling to cup and mound the sand with their hands. Barbara cried when it wouldn't stick together, the sharp, clumsy grains falling away, but Arthur hugged her till she stopped. By then the tide had come in enough to fill the centre of the channel, rockweed lifting and waving from the sides like hair. While he swam back and forth, up and down its length, Kaye waded in with Barbara, holding both her hands. *Hen, rooster,* their voices rang bright and shrill above the sparkling green ripples. *Chicken, DUCK!* they squealed, squatting.

5. Settlement

It was almost dark, the sky a soggy canopy over the black-green spruce. From the car he watched parts of the creek's banks succumb: chunks of frost-splintered earth, rock and the webbed roots of trees sucked into the current, then spinning and bobbing away. He caught a glimpse of something else flying by, stiff and black with patches like snow. Realizing it was a cow, he shut his eyes, tried not to imagine it washed ashore later: bones propping up the hollow hide, eyes ringed with maggots.

He felt the water drag at the wheels, a steady trickle beading the bottom of the doors. The rushing sound filled his head now. Something started to tug on the back bumper, gently at first, like a huge, smooth hand pulling with a force so subtle it seemed almost funny. Funny, had he been above looking down. Watching, absurdly, like the gulls and crows that circled and screeched overhead as if waiting for prey.

Disbelieving, Arthur gripped the wheel, all his weight pinned to the brake. There was a sucking sound and he felt the tires loosen, the back end of the car slide almost gracefully sideways, then catch on something, like a chip bag or pop tin snagged on a twig.

The obstacle gave way, the car swinging gently as a partner in a slow-moving waltz, then wider, wider, the screech of rock on metal slurred and hushed by a thick, muddy *swooosh*. And Arthur, snapping alert, finally let go the wheel and jumped, as the front end lost its grip and gave in to the current.

If not for the bushes, he might have been swept away. Clinging to the slimy, weak branches, water dragging at his groin, he managed to pull himself free and climb beyond some rocks to safety.

He didn't stop to watch the car slide and tilt closer to the brink; knew the sight of it going over would make him want to tear his skin. The sound, too — enough to grind the fillings in one's teeth. He did look back once, though, from the top of the hill; felt a foolish burst of hope when he saw it was still there, poised near the edge of the roiling white torrent.

He couldn't have said how long he walked, braced against the wind. For in the pitch-blackness Arthur lost track of time, slowed by the cramps in his muscles and by clothes so wet it took him a while to notice the rain had stopped, the air cold yet drier against his face.

After he'd walked four or five miles — or farther, perhaps; with no houses or lights, there was no way of measuring — the road flattened out and a light came in view, a light at the end of a lane. It was an imitation coachlamp on a pole, the kind more at home in a subdivision than out in the country. A marvel, his mind lit on the idea, that it hadn't been uprooted and washed away. A good thing, too, since without it he'd have missed the house hidden behind trees below the road.

From the doorstep he could hear a TV; when he knocked a dog barked. Through the door came a man's voice and a low growling. After a long time a face appeared in the window, an older woman with her hair in curlers. The man shouting above the TV, asking who was there. ("Tell him we don't want any!")

She wouldn't let Arthur in at first. Who could blame her, he thought, summoning his most businesslike expression. The one reserved for claimants, those lucky enough to survive the accidents that took parents or children. As if everything that happened were a daily fact of life, be it an act of God or a simple twist of fate.

"Please! I just want to use your phone for a minute, please, if I could," he yelled through the glass. "I've had an...accident." The word seemed so crazy coming from his mouth. Shivering, weary, he felt a foolish, desperate smile spread over his face.

"Please!" He banged on the door, the metal frame around the glass. "I only want to call my wife."

"Oh, for the love of God, Mabel, let the poor bastard in!"

Pushing her aside, the man appeared and unlocked the door, scarcely looking at Arthur. A heavy fellow in green pyjamas, he shrugged and pointed at the phone hanging on the wall in the kitchen.

"Don't mind her," he said, "she's just the nervous type, is all. Got her reasons, though; you can never be too careful. Well help yourself, then. It ain't long distance, is it? Well that's good, take yer time."

Dialling the number, he heard the man tell his wife to put on the kettle. ("Buddy looks like he could use a cup a coffee.")

The phone rang only once, but to Arthur she seemed to take for ever to pick it up, her breath catching before she said, "Hullo?"

Her voice cracked with fear.

"Kaye?" he cried out, suddenly sobered, almost awed by her familiarity, the depth of his relief — as if there could've been anyone else at the end of the line. Who knew him so well, he thought, she could probably almost see him standing in this strange kitchen somewhere, the muddy tracks from his boots all over someone else's floor.

"Arthur? Honey? Where are you?" Tiny at first, her

voice wavered like a seismograph, rising steadily in pitch. "My God, I've been climbing the walls, just lit'rally climbing the WALLS! I've called everywhere, all over hell's acre, Arthur! The office, half the numbers in your files. I called and called, and no luck. Nobody'd seen hide nor hair — like you'd left the planet or something. Oh, honey—"

He braced himself, awaiting a hectoring tone. Instead, Kaye's voice strained like a net, dipping.

"—the only reason I gave up was Barbie saying, 'Muuuuummm, what if Daddy's trying to get through?'"

Beside him, leaning against the cluttered counter, he could feel the strange couple watching, listening. The light from the overhead fixture was making him dizzy. He blushed, smiling weakly, apologetically, his face washed with relief. Avoiding his eyes, the woman scrabbled through the cupboards, grabbing a jar of Nescafé, a box of arrowroot cookies.

"Arthur?" Kaye appealed, slightly calmer. "Are you okay? Look, I've been scared sick, Barbie too. The two of us, dear, all evening, sitting by the phone!"

An edge of admonishment had crept in, but Arthur ignored it.

"I'm fine, sweetie. Look, I've had a...mishap. But I'm okay, everything's okay, really."

The husband grabbed a biscuit and crunched it, scratching under his waistband. Never leaving Arthur's face, the fellow's stare was curious, downright nosy, almost amused.

"Just one thing — Kaye? Like I say, everything's all right, nothing to worry about. Except the car, the car's not in great shape." He imagined the Chev gliding into the creek, the clatter of chrome and glass, then pushed it out of his mind.

"Kaye? You listening, sweetie? You think you could have somebody come and get me? One of the guys from the office, maybe, I don't care who."

As Arthur spoke, he heard someone pick up an extension, the one on his desk in the basement. For a moment there was breathing, hovering tears, next a satisfied sigh.

"Barbie?" Kaye's voice lifted, and the line clicked. "Arthur?"

"Hang on a minute, honey."

Capping the mouthpiece with his palm, Arthur gazed back at the man munching cookies, unable now to stifle a foolish, cock-eyed grin.

"If you don't mind, mister, could you tell me something? I need directions. I know it sounds crazy — but where the heck are we?"

THE PARK STREET BRIDGE

T he road was deserted. I mean, Marilyn and I must've stood with our thumbs out for an hour, and nothing. Not a car in sight, not even a grubby half-ton, some old farmer going to town for liquor. A Saturday afternoon, too, deader than an all-girls sock hop!

Marilyn kept gazing at the store across from us.

"Look, let's go use the payphone. Just this once. We could get a lift. If my mum's not home we could phone yours."

"No way." I had two-fifty in my pocket, left from babysitting, and I was saving every cent for Frenchy's — best place in the world to shop. Don't be a drip, I felt like saying but didn't. Marilyn can be such a browner at times, but she *is* my best friend.

Besides, Mum would've hit the roof if she'd known where I was going, second time this week. Bad enough she didn't approve — if only she could've kept it to herself. But no.

"You're *not* going there again, you girls!"

Mum after breakfast the other day, having a cigarette

before she finished cleaning up. She was drinking from this mug someone gave Dad, with a naked woman on it; the heat from the coffee melts off her clothes. Mum sniffed and set the thing down with a clunk, not batting an eye at the sugary-pink nipples. I had a couple of minutes before running to catch the bus with Marilyn.

"Don't expect me home right after school" I said lightly, as if planning a trip to the washroom. But that didn't throw her off.

"What does Mrs. Guthro think of Marilyn buying clothes there?" Mum started turning the mug in her hands, gawking now like Marilyn and me pointing at safes on the neighbours' lawn the time their sewer backed up. She gave the same half-amused, half-disgusted laugh as she had then, drawing the drapes so we wouldn't have to look.

"I mean, the queer old stuff, Barbara. You don't know where it's been. You don't know who's been wearing it, who it's *touched!*"

She got up and started scouring the counter with Javex, her free hand waving the cigarette. Her lips looked dry and faded, the cracks stained pink. Still in her robe, she had a scarf tied over her rollers, one of those see-through jobs she wears while Dad's at work.

I glanced at her feet, the shiny green mules she wears around the house — for all I know she stays in the same get-up till we come home and she has to start supper. Though weekends when Dad's around she does house-work with her hair perfectly set, her nails painted. All dolled up and nowhere to go — that's my mum.

Except this particular Saturday — she and Dad were supposed to be going to a dance that night. So you'd have figured she'd be in a good mood. But nope, that afternoon she had to come sit on my bed while I was getting ready to meet Marilyn. She flicked through Sears' catalogue while I dabbed on perfume, orange-blossom stuff from this aunt of mine in Florida.

"I think it's a waste, spending all your money on someone else's junk. Old throw-away stuff they don't want. Have a look through this, why don't you? Mark down what you like and I'll order you something. New."

I breathed in deep and sighed. "No thanks."

How do you make someone whose favourite colour is beige understand that people in catalogue clothes look like dorks? Or that Frenchy's has some real finds, genuine treasures beyond being great deals — if you stick with it and go often enough.

This month Marilyn and I are into short, big-shouldered peplums from the fifties. ("Suit jackets missing the skirts," Mum says. They remind her of outfits her sister Ardith used to wear — that's my aunt, the divorced one in Florida.) Well, Frenchy's is a gold mine for clothes like this, and other things too. We're always on the lookout for fat-waled hiphugger cords, fringed purses and crocheted ponchos. We find they go perfectly with our long, middle-parted hair and yellow Kodiak workboots.

"Barbara? I don't like it. Your father'd have a fit if he knew. I mean, dear, what if one of his clients saw you there? Do you have any idea how that would make him feel? Our daughter, buying second-hand clothes."

"Who said we're going shopping? First I'm meeting Marilyn, then we're — we're going for a walk. I'll be back by six, okay?"

"How'll you get home?"

"Marilyn's mum," I shot back, quick, before she could ask anything else.

"What's *wrong* with people?" I was starting to get antsy, marooned on the highway — well, so it was a road, okay?

Two lanes through some fields and our subdivision at the foot of the hill — the Mountain, we call it.

It was still only March, the sun trying to come out, the wind damp and raw with the smell of mud and cowpats, rotting hay. I had on a short-sleeved shell under my latest jacket, its chilly, ripped lining sending shivers up my arms. Marilyn was dressed the same, hopping from foot to foot like she had to pee.

"Jeez, if we don't get a ride soon the place'll be closed!" I danced around her, tucking my hands up into my sleeves.

"At this rate all the good stuff'll be gone." She kept staring across the marshy fields, at the embankment where the train tracks snaked past. The wind picked up the smell of tar with a salty tinge from the river beyond. All at once I got this bright idea:

"Okay, let's try the shortcut."

Marilyn knew what I had in mind. Under her big, wide shoulder-pads she seemed to shrink, her small blue eyes daring me.

"You wouldn't — would you?"

"Oh, let's give it a try anyway — this money's gonna burn a hole in my pocket!" For fun I clapped her on the back. "C'mon, there's no train for another hour. At least."

Jumping the ditch, we waded across the spongy field, then climbed the steep gravel bank to the tracks. Way in the distance, you could just make out the end of town spilled like little grey blocks against the river's reddish glint, and the exit off the Trans-Canada, lined with burger joints and bodyshops. Frenchy's was under the off-ramp.

At first it was easy going. We walked fast, skipping from tie to tie, the wind whipping hair in our mouths. Any fear of the train coming as flighty and ridiculous as the seagulls swooping over the wide, muddy river ahead. For a while we hopped along, hardly looking over our shoulders.

"No sweat." Marilyn shrugged. "We see it coming, we just jump down into the grass."

"Yeah, that's right. No problem."

We started in about some boys who liked us, Ricky and Chris: what nerds they were, but how we'd gone for a drive with them anyway, one night after the high school dance. Flicking hair out of her eyes, Marilyn went over all the details — about us parking by the river and watching them drink and smoke up. How there was dog hair on the seats in Ricky's dad's car, a first-aid kit in the glovebox. And what a joke it was, we shrieked with laughter, when that stunned Chris pulled out a Band-Aid and asked if we'd play doctor.

"His hair—!"

Marilyn only had to mention that and we broke up.

"The way it shows his ears! Like a frigging Mormon —" I threw in.

"Yeah, and his pants—"

"Oooooh."

"Yuck!"

"If there's one thing I *hate* it's those skinny grey cords—"

"Pressed!"

"Yeah. Ooooh."

"And that Ricky—"

"Don't remind me!"

"Remember how he panicked 'cause it was late and he had to get the car home?"

"Yeah, and how when we were getting out he yawned and threw his arm over the back of your seat. 'See ya later,' he goes."

"Yeah. Fat chance."

"'Thanks for coming,' he goes, all moony-eyed."

"Yeah, right. 'Don't thank me,' I should've said, 'thank

God we were stunned enough to give you guys the time of day!'"

Roaring so loud I had to clutch my stomach, I gave her a poke and we started jogging. But not before she dug me back: "You were the one ended up drinking their beer!" She pulled a face, our sleeves rubbing.

It was true — I stayed over at Marilyn's that night, so I didn't think twice about guzzling down one of their Alpines. The dope you didn't worry about — like vodka, Chris said, it doesn't stay on your breath. Afterwards we made them drop us at the end of Marilyn's street, the two of us doubled over on someone's lawn giggling, me sucking Clorets so her mother wouldn't suspect anything. Like my mum, she always waits up.

That night Mrs. Guthro was sipping cold tea at their dining-room suite. "Brand-new, French provincial," Marilyn snickered as we stumbled in. "That's why she uses a saucer, even at this hour." Who knows how long her mum had been sitting there waiting. She reminded me of Mum in her quilted housecoat, those slippers with the toes out — except her toenails were painted pink, her hair in a neat yellow beehive. "What were you up to tonight?" she yawned, patting the needlepoint seats beside her, as if expecting us to tell.

"What a hoot!" I was shaking so hard now I could barely spit it out. Marilyn looked over her shoulder and tugged at me. I stopped long enough to glance back — still no sign at all of a train. I sighed, and we launched into "Little Green Bag", this stupid song about losing something on some tracks. Marilyn did the chorus in her deepest Tom Jones voice, which cracked me up so badly I thought I'd die laughing.

After that we got serious, going over what we hoped to buy — if we managed, that is, to make it before

Frenchy's closed. Fair Isle sweaters for twenty-five cents, button-up painter pants for seventy-five. Boys' tweed blazers for a buck — never mind if the sleeves were a tad short.

"Heck," I said. "Think if we had our own apartment — you could decorate it for ten bucks! Curtains, dish towels, sheets...." Marilyn made a clucking sound, her face going dreamy.

See, these trips to Frenchy's mean more to us than just getting clothes. We like to linger there and browse. Check everything out, from strings of beads and plastic hoop earrings to men's ties and boxer shorts. If you go often enough — or luck out and get there when the clerks unstrap a bale of clothes jammed tight as cars in a scrap-metal heap — no telling what gems you'll find. And it's all good stuff, shipped up from Boston.

Designer labels, as Marilyn always points out. Rich people's things. Not like it's used stuff from Canada. Yes, you can get anything there — bras, even underpants, the skimpy kind with lacy hearts and the days of the week sewn on. Of course Marilyn and I draw the line there: no underwear. Or kids' clothes — no *way!*

"Imagine someone being that cheap—" I said once.

"Yeah, how disgusting!" she agreed.

The two of us swear that no matter what happens in our lives, if we ever have kids we'll *never* buy their clothes there. It just isn't right. Still, we take a sick kind of delight sometimes watching people root through the kids' bin, seeing the sorts of things they dredge up.

We were starting to lose steam, getting hot and sweaty under our jackets. Marilyn dawdled behind.

"C'mon! It's just over the bridge now, then down Park Street! Someone'll pick us up there, no problem. We'll make it, I know we will. C'mon! Last one across is a rotten—!"

"This time of day it'll be all picked over. There'll be nothing left to buy," she moaned. But I could tell what was really bugging her.

"Oh come on. If we hurry—"

Across the marsh you could almost see Frenchy's, one of a string of squat buildings, the small, shiny hoods of cars speeding past on the highway practically on top of them. But just ahead of us lay the bridge, and our feet started to drag.

"I dunno, Barb. I dunno—"

"C'mon," I coaxed. "It'll be fine — the train's not due for another half-hour, at least. C'mon. Just don't look down."

I ventured out first, edging along one of the rails — it's a low trestle bridge, just the tracks laid over steel supports. The river below was one swirling brown mess of whirlpools and mud.

"Barb?" she said again in this weak little voice. "I don't think—"

"Oh, don't be a chicken," I hissed, stepping sideways from tie to tie, holding in my stomach. Like walking a tightrope, trying not to look down. Through the gaps you could see chunks of ice flying by, an old rubber boot. And all around us the churning stink of wet tar and rusty metal.

"What if— Barb?"

"Shhhh."

"What if—?"

"*Marilyn!*"

"But what — if the train comes?"

"Don't be such a worry-wart!"

I made it seem like a lark, balancing with both hands stuck out, waving like Mum's when she smoked.

"I...don't...like...it." Her voice like a magnet behind me, till I tuned it out.

"Well. Too late now. Come on, we're almost there."

I turned once and gave her a big smile, even tried to laugh, though my stomach felt like a fist. For one godawful second I did think: what if the train comes? What then? But I shook it off.

"Maybe that coat you liked will still be there, Marilyn—"

"What? Oh. Yeah. Maybe."

"I hope nobody found that shirt — you know, the one I hid under the Crimplene dress on the ladies' rack? Hope it's still there. I *love* the colour. Burgundy. It'll go with—"

My tongue loosened the closer we got to the other side. Just a few more churning brown gaps to jump over....

"A chocolate shake," I said, when at last we made it. "That's what the water looks like — a big chocolate milkshake!"

"I guess." Marilyn let out a big breath.

"Whew." I undid my jacket, let the wind flap through it. We gave each other a look, then started jogging again. It wasn't far now — just past the siding where the tracks cross Park Street, the signals that make you wait for ever if you're unlucky enough to get there when the train does.

Both Marilyn and I have wasted *days*, if you add it up, stuck waiting on the schoolbus or in the car with our mothers. The Park Street "shortcut" — Mum always rolls her eyes and sighs, blowing smoke in the rearview, humming along with Charley Pride on the radio, her fingers tapping the wheel. I mean, no wonder they call this place The Hub of the Maritimes, with a bloody train passing through everywhere you turn.

"It's gotta be four o'clock. It's only open for another hour!"

"One quick ride and we'll be there in a sec."

We raced to the end of Park Street, then stopped by

some dirty patches of snow and stuck out our thumbs. Leaning towards the traffic, giving each driver this *how-dare-you* stare as one after another passed by. After a minute or two a man in a dusty green car stopped and we jumped in beside him. The interior smelled of Thrills and damp plush, the pine-tree deodorizer dangling from the mirror, and the man's belly spilled over the top of his brown polyester pants. Marilyn and I kept our eyes on the road straight ahead, the two of us squeezed close to keep my arm from touching his. Pretending he wasn't there, we chit-chatted about the deals we hoped to find.

After a bit the man cleared his throat and broke in: "I'm just goin' to Wilson's for gas. Okay if I let yuz off there?"

"Great." I tried to sound bored.

"Thanksalot," we yelled at once, jumping out and giving the door a slam.

Frenchy's was just ahead, past the Ford dealership and a couple of bodyshops. You could see it: a small, concrete-block and tarpaper building wedged between the Esso and a green metal warehouse. We ran past the car place and the garage, past some eighteen-wheelers fuelling up, slowing a bit once the sign came into view. F-R-E-N-C-H-YS, it says, in crooked, kid-like letters, red, yellow and blue. Inside, the lights were on; outside, a couple of cars were parked. One was a black Chev like Mum's. Stragglers, I guess, scrounging for the last of the day's pickings. Though with Frenchy's you never know — like I say, no telling what you might find.

I felt for the rolled-up bill in my pocket, the two warm quarters. Marilyn's face glowed as we opened the springless metal door, let it flap behind us.

"We close in twenty minutes," the clerk yawned from behind the counter. She was cutting the buttons off something, tossing them into a big glass jar, the kind pickled eggs float in at the corner store.

Overhead the bare bulbs flickered — dim and tired-looking as the clerk anxious to lock up. We had to hurry, we knew, but all the same we stood there for a minute, taking in the rows of grey wooden bins filling the narrow, dingy room. High up the walls a couple of dresses danced — that's how they looked, anyway, bright flouncy things with the skirts spread and thumbtacked in place. Someone's sad attempt at making it like a *real* store, Dalmys or Fairweather's.

A couple of women stood around bins picking and sorting, every now and then holding something up, a blouse or sweater, checking under the arms for rips or stains. Marilyn sucked in her lips, glancing around, deciding where to hit first.

The trick, see, is being open-minded. You have to be patient; it's not like you can just go to a bin and *poof!* there's a perfectly good, practically new turtleneck, or some never-worn Levi's, 28-30s — you know, something so nice even Mum would be impressed.

We slipped over to the underwear, out of habit I guess. It's something we do for a laugh before getting down to serious picking. Marilyn started tugging at a clump of bras and black nylon panties, the elastic cracked and yellow, showing through like skin. The smell of mouldy latex and damp concrete made me sneeze. Bent beside her, I yanked a girdle from the tangle and held it up like something poison, jiggling the rubber garters.

Marilyn let out a squeal and doubled over, her legs crossed to keep from wetting herself. Next she dug in and pulled out a bra, a huge D-cupped thing. The row of hooks at the back was wide as a thigh, the straps held on with gold safety pins.

"Va-vooom, va-voooooooom!" she tittered, collapsing against the bin. Me too. The two of us howling and slobbering into our hands till our ribs hurt.

We hardly noticed the woman who'd been looking at sweaters slip over.

"Ahem."

I ignored her at first, till she said it again, louder this time. Then she coughed, a loud, dry bark, her bifocals sliding down her nose. When she pushed them up — her eyes round and staring — you could see the flashy big diamond on her finger, a set of silver bangles jingling up her sleeve. She looked about Mum's age, I guess, maybe a bit older. She was wearing an expensive-looking blazer and pressed wool slacks — the way Mum dresses when she goes for groceries.

We went on waving pieces of underwear, buckling under with giggles.

"Fifteen minutes," the clerk yelled.

Marilyn picked up a black push-up, the kind advertised in the back of her mother's *True Confessions* magazines.

"Whoooo!" she snorted, and that did it. I collapsed, helpless, my face buried in scratchy damp lace.

"Girls."

I couldn't move, bent there gasping and snorting; Marilyn the same.

"Excuse me.

"EXCUSE ME."

We both stopped, gawking up at her. The woman was glaring, her face fuzzy through the tears I had to blink back. There was an awful look in her eyes, mean and spiteful, as if it was all she could do not to reach out and slap us.

"Listen here," she said in a quaky voice, snooty and indignant, "I'll have you know" — she stopped and sniffed — "I'll have you know the Kennedys, the *Kennedys*, donate their clothes to Frenchy's. You have no, *no*— If you want to be insulting, maybe you should go someplace else."

"Ten minutes," the clerk croaked. "Everyone outta the change rooms." (The change rooms — two dusty cubicles with stiff, lopsided drapes dragged across.)

Marilyn and I dropped our hands, stood gazing at each other with our mouths open, as the woman stomped to the cash and paid. At the sound of her car starting we unfroze and started giggling again, sort of, though for some reason nothing seemed quite as funny.

"The Kennedys!" I dug Marilyn with my elbow. "What a bag!"

She rolled her eyes and shrugged, going for the sweater bin.

"Five more minutes, girls, that's it. Then we lock up."

Going like a maniac, I rooted through the jumbled piles. The blouse I'd had my eye on was gone, but I managed to find a pink Orlon cardigan with rhinestones on it, a short maroon blouse with a bow at the neck, and a couple of boys' white shirts with only a button or two missing. A buck twenty-five total. I stuffed the change back in my pocket.

I never did see what Marilyn bought. By now the clerk was tapping her foot, her finger on the light-switch. When we got outside the sun was low, sinking over the highway.

"I hope something comes soon. I'm s'posed to be home by six. And I hate hitching in the dark," Marilyn started in.

"Take a Valium," I tried to joke, then started humming one of Mum's songs, "The Most Beautiful Girl in the World", nudging Marilyn to join in. But she didn't, just clutched her Sobeys bag full of clothes, her shoulders hunched for warmth. It was cold enough now for a thick winter coat. I stood shivering in my skimpy gabardine.

"We *could* put on some of our Frenchy stuff," Marilyn said after a truck passed, then a string of cars.

"Yeah. *Right.*"

Like buying the underwear or kids' clothes, you wouldn't dream of wearing any of this stuff till it's gone through the wash a dozen times.

"I'm already itchy," I teased, my plastic bag at my feet, both hands jammed into my tight little pockets. I rubbed my fingers together; thought better of sniffing or blowing on them.

"Come *on*," I moaned as yet another car went by.

The sun was directly over the off-ramp now, each car exiting in a bright orange flash.

"I said I'd be home for supper." Marilyn stamped her feet to keep warm. "Shit." She shook her head as a car slowed, then sped past.

I twisted the bag's handle round my fingers till they went numb. For a second, one quick second, I thought of going into the Esso and phoning Mum to come get us. Then, just as quickly, let the idea pass.

"Someone'll give us a lift," I shrugged, as a beat-up half-ton turned off the highway and came our way. There were two guys in it. Sure enough, it slowed down and veered to the shoulder, the engine racing.

"Told you so!" I pinched her as the fellow on the passenger side jumped out to let us slide in. I scrunched beside the driver, pressing my thigh away from his so we didn't touch too much. He glanced sideways at me, leaning over the wheel as he tugged the thing into gear and pulled onto the pavement. When he turned to check the side mirror I stole a quick look at him. An older guy; university age, maybe? He had longish auburn hair that curled over the greyish fur collar of his bomber. Not one of those thin-looking vinyl things from Sears, but a real one — thick black leather with sheepskin inside, the kind bikers wear. Except he didn't look like a biker, not with those freckles, those deep brown eyes.

Not bad, Marilyn shot me a look — the secret look we give each other when someone cute walks past our lockers.

The friend wasn't too hard on the eyes either. So tall he had to hunch a little, he had dark hair to the shoulders of his jeans jacket. He had a moustache, and looked like he hadn't shaved in a while. Under his jacket he wore a dark blue work shirt with a purple T underneath. They both had on faded jeans frayed at the knees. I thought of Ricky and Chris, and pressed Marilyn's arm.

"Where you girls off to, anyways?" the driver said.

When he flicked his hair I noticed the earring — a little silver cross dangling from a shepherd's hook. He eyed the Sobeys bag between my feet.

"Out spendin' your money, were yuz? I seen the Newfie luggage, that's why I stopped." He gave a little laugh and looked across at his friend, who smirked and gazed out the window.

Marilyn kicked my foot and we giggled.

"Yeah. Newfie luggage. Huh. Frenchy's, we were...."

I felt her shrug. The friend grabbed a pack of smokes off the dash and lit one. Sucking in his jaw to inhale, he held the cigarette clamped between his thumb and pointer the way you'd hold a roach — as we'd seen Ricky do that night by the river. Except this guy was cool; you knew with him it was second nature.

The driver's leg brushed mine as he stepped on the gas. I didn't move — couldn't've, anyway, with all of us squeezed so close together. The cigarette balanced on his lip as if stuck there, the friend draped his arm over the back of the seat and leaned forward. Marilyn shot me a glance, wrinkling her nose, but otherwise didn't let on she noticed the hand dangling over her boob.

"So where'dja say you girls were off to?" The driver glanced at something in the rearview, then slouched back, half watching the road, the bodyshops and warehouses sliding by.

"Park Street." I coughed and cleared my throat. "You can let us off down the other end of Park Street."

He ignored me and smirked at his buddy, who smirked back but said nothing.

"Goin' for some bodywork, were yuz? Whadja say your names were?"

"Darlene," I lied. "And she's Wanda." This is what we tell anyone who asks, usually just the geeks. I waited for Marilyn to nudge me and start giggling, but for once she didn't.

"Oh yeah. Where'dja say yuz were goin' again?" He started braking for a light, reaching for a cigarette. I had this weird urge to grab the wheel as I'd done when Ricky was driving us home to Marilyn's and kept weaving on the curves. But I stopped myself, of course. It wasn't like these were boys, the type who play hockey and borrow parents' cars for dates. Dates: I thought of Ricky and our cold, clumsy necking in the front seat.

"You girls wanna come for a ride?" The driver exhaled the words in a blue cloud, his voice flat and familiar. Chummy. "C'mon, whadidja say your names were?"

The light changed. He stepped on it, then looked me in the eye.

"Barb," I said. It came out weak and feeble, like the way I felt when Ricky went and slipped his tongue in my mouth. I wished I could've said "Linda" or "Sheryl" or "Darlene" again. Anything would've sounded better.

"So what's your girlfriend's name, Barb?"

We were creeping past the mall now; the parking lot was emptying.

"For fucksake," the friend muttered as the next light

went red.

"Wanna go to a party?" the driver said. His voice coarser, prickly as the wiry white hairs on Ricky's car seats.

"Whereabouts?" Marilyn said in a little girl's voice, digging me with her elbow. The light changed, the truck lurched forward and the friend's hand reached down.

"I don't think so," she whispered, digging me harder.

"Um...we've got plans," I said, picturing Mum with her hair in rollers, taking fishsticks from the oven.

"Don'tcha like to party?"

"Where d'ya live anyways?" The friend hawked into his hand and sighed.

"Out past Park Street, out past the railroad tracks, the other end of...." A little high-pitched quiver, you could barely hear Marilyn's voice over the truck's rattling.

I kicked her hard, my plastic bag falling over. You didn't want to get too specific, hitch-hiking. What if they drove you right to the door? I mean, I could just see Mum peeking through the sheers at the strange truck in the yard, wanting to know who they were, why I didn't ask them in for a pop. Her way of keeping tabs.

"Park Street," the driver said in the same wiry tone. "I dunno if we're goin' that far, eh Russy? This party's up the other part of town, up by the Legion...."

"You wanna get stoned?" The friend sneered; I felt Marilyn shrink away from his hand.

"Or is your mama home waitin'?" The driver stared past us, gawking at some girls waiting by a bus stop.

Marilyn sniffed, nudging me. Daring me, I could tell, to say: "Yes. Yes that's right, my mum's there at this very moment waiting for me."

Marilyn squeezed her hands together, her face a pale shadow. It was getting dark now, the tail-lights in front of us bright red, the streetlights aglow with faint specks of snow wisping down. Just ahead was the Park Street intersection.

"You can let us off here," I started to say, as we spun round the corner, barely slowing. The four of us bunched together as we made the turn. On Park Street the marsh rolled up black on both sides, the streetlights a string of pale yellow dots funnelling with the tracks towards the river. In the darkness I could see the outline of the trestle bridge, the signals where the road cut over the railway.

"Why don'tcha wanna party? What's wrong with you girls?" The driver reached out and laid his hand on my knee. It felt hard and cold as an ice cube through my jeans.

"C'mon, you don't wanna go home do yuz? Sa'rday night, for Chrissake. Nothin' wrong with havin' a little fun is there?"

The friend started to grope under Marilyn's jacket — I felt his wrist bump my shoulder.

"I don't think the girls really wanna go home, do you, Russy? I think they wanna party, don't you?"

We were speeding now, the cab bouncing up and down over the potholes. The driver leaned on me, that hand sliding up my leg, the other barely holding the wheel. Beside me Marilyn had gone stiff. I felt something inside me slide, then coil up tight, like a Slinky at the foot of some stairs.

The friend shifted in the seat; Marilyn pressed against me like a board as he reached inside his jacket and pulled something out. It was really dark now, just the watery glow from the odd streetlight shining in on our knees, our hands, his hand against my dark blue leg. There was a click, like a lighter being flicked, and Marilyn gasped, bracing herself against the seat. I caught the greenish flash of a blade. Marilyn's hand slid between us and grabbed mine, clutching it like a vice.

The truck wove a little; the driver slowed, let out a

laugh like a boot crunching through snow.

"I guess ya got 'em talked into it, Russy. Eh Barb? That's yer name isn't it?" His hand slid up my thigh, the flesh dead as wood under the stiff denim.

I took a deep breath and held onto it, counting, as if that would make his hand go away.

The friend put up the knife and checked it over. It was long and skinny, the handle dark as blood. Not like the kind Ricky'd used to open the beer, a Boy Scout one with little attachments — corkscrew, nailfile, things that come in handy.

Then the fellow flicked it before Marilyn's face, laughing with this awful, gleeful, choking sound, like he couldn't believe how easy some things were.

"Let us out." I barely heard myself speak, my voice no bigger than the engine's growl. Then louder: "Stop, I said. We want to get out here."

The driver made like he didn't hear, stepping harder on the gas till the truck careened — you could feel it fishtailing. Marilyn's nails dug into my skin, her fingers squeezing harder and harder like they were losing their grip. Squeezing back till I thought my knuckles would break, I clenched my legs, my jaws, my fist — every last muscle tight, tight and rigid as steel, as though that would slow us down.

Way ahead tail-lights bobbed like the ends of cigarettes, us peeling after them as if in some crazy race to catch up and get there first — "there" being a secret place these fellows knew but weren't telling. The only sign of life or hope those car lights speeding off. My eyeballs stung, my throat was dry as ice. The faster we chased those lights, the farther they seemed to get.

Somebody. Stop. *Please* stop. I could hear my own breathing, tight and raspy, or maybe it was Marilyn's. *Somebody. Please.*

I felt the driver's eyes on me, on my leg. He had an ugly smile on his face, his hand between my thighs now, clawing at me through the creased denim, the elastic underneath creeping up. *Injun underwear*, Marilyn and I would've laughed. In any other situation.

Please don't go any higher. I may have said it aloud; now I honestly don't remember. But that's what was playing over and over in my head when suddenly I heard the train. Can't be, I thought first, glancing at Marilyn. Her lip was quaking, her face green as a Martian's in that queer, awful light. I knew I wasn't just dreaming when her hand went limp and I could tell she'd heard it too. Like dull, distant thunder at first, a low, fast rumbling over the marsh. And then the whistle sounded, a shrill, bleating wail that set my teeth on edge. The far-off, grinding squeal of the wheels growing louder and louder, till the noise seemed to come through the tires and the cold, rusted floor, right up into my toes.

Just ahead the signals started flashing, the semaphore like a white-armed bandit bowing over the road. Traffic stopped, strung like a red-beaded necklace.

From somewhere out there in the dark I could almost feel the rush of the cars, the charge of cold air in my face. Getting closer, closer.

"Fuckin' shit," the driver swore and stomped on the brake, as if he hadn't seen any of this coming. Tires squealing on the slick black pavement, the truck skidded sideways and bit gravel for a second. We stopped just short of the car ahead as the train clanged and swayed past, lights flashing, everything washed red.

The friend rolled down the window and spat. "Fuckin' six-oh-five."

The Ocean Limited — a long, long train, the longest train in the world, coming through from Montreal. The lights near blinding us, it barely had time to register.

The driver grabbed the crotch of my jeans and twisted, twisted hard, jeans and nylon, flesh, hair. *Hard.* And he said: "Get the fuck outta here. Go on, get the fuck out."

And next we were scrambling, Marilyn and me, clawing at each other to move it. Sliding, shoving, climbing over the friend. The door squeaked wide and we fell, tumbling past him onto the wet gravel. His feet — all I saw were his feet, the chains on his square-toed snoot boots — as we rolled and slid into the ditch, the frozen black mud.

"Run, ya fuckin' teases! Run, an' go fuck yourselves."

Half running, half crawling through the dead, spiky grass, we could hear his voice, ugly and full of hate. Even with the roar of the train breaking up in the wind, we heard it.

Us. Not *us.*

Not Marilyn and me.

Our hands were full of splinters, mud squishing up through our boots like some queer frozen dessert. (Whip 'n' Chill — Mum makes it from a box sometimes.) We ran and ran — blind we might've been, racing across that field. The pulse in my throat kept time with the clickety-clack till it grew fainter and fainter, the road behind us no wider than a skinny black choker, a sparse row of pearls sewn over it.

"Man!" Marilyn let her breath out in a rush, stumbling beside me.

The clanging had stopped. Traffic started moving, like slow red fireflies flitting over the marsh, so tiny and low to the ground you could hardly make one car out from another.

"Man, for a minute I really thought they'd come after us," she said, her voice like the air, thin and whispery.

Back there the road lay empty and still, nothing but the windy blackness stretched around us, the cold glimmer of town in the distance.

"What?" I said, and for one split second, I have no idea why, I could've slapped her. Slapped her hard, on the side of the face, like they do on TV. I had my hand up, I did, almost as though I couldn't help myself. But then she started laughing, this low, squeaky giggle like something unwinding inside her. The way she'd laughed when I told her, after a day or two, about Ricky and his tongue, how hard and slippery it felt in my mouth.

And I laughed too, leaning against her, our damp stringy hair in each other's teeth, ears aching with the wind.

"Thank God, eh Barb? Thank *God*."

We both let out one whooping howl, staggering away from each other. Straightening up, I brushed off my jacket, patting my pockets.

"Shit!"

"What's wrong?"

"Our stuff. Our *stuff!*" I yelped — as if this was the worst that could've happened. I blew out a sigh, tried mimicking Mum. "One person's junk...," I began, then broke off. "Which way you figure there's a payphone?"

But Marilyn didn't seem to be listening.

"Barb," she said, "what do you s'pose they'll do with those clothes?"

"Finders keepers," I sniggered, and we collapsed against each other. In hi-sterics, as Mum would say, at the idea of those two awful guys finding our stuff in their truck.

"Losers weep—" Marilyn burst out, bending over; her legs twisted together like a pretzel, trying to hold it. Too late, though. I could tell by the way she stood up that she'd gone and done it anyway.

NOTES FROM UNDERGROUND

"Better wear a hat, unless you want bat droppings in your hair," the teacher warned them.

At this the class broke out laughing — all but one student near the front. Chris Kynock already knew about spelunking; to him it was serious business. Since childhood he'd dreamed of caves, a glorious underworld of pink stalactites and stalagmites, and bottomless, mist-covered pools: a fabulous mix of Jules Verne and Disney.

Yet, counting the hours to tomorrow's field trip, he was barely listening to the teacher. Of greater urgency was a chunk of amethyst circulating round the room. When at last it reached Marilyn — the girl ahead of him, who'd brought it in — Chris craned behind her, studying its cut-glass angles.

"Best example of a gypsum cave in the province," Mr. Hincks went on as if from another room. "Just don't expect Hayes Pit to be like something outta *Peter Pan*.... Think of it, errr, as a spelunker's bread and butter."

Chris breathed in deeply as Marilyn turned and handed him the amethyst. For a moment he forgot Hincks's voice, the upcoming trip. The rock was a geode, the sort of specimen Chris had only seen before in books: stone cracked like an egg, crystals spiky as teeth inside.

"But don't get me wrong. Like most caves of this type, Hayes is one spaghetti junction of tunnels behind the main cavern. Just because it doesn't look exotic...."

Cradling the amethyst in his palm, Chris glanced up just as the bell went and Mr. Hincks rubbed his diagram of the cave off the board.

"...accessible through sinkholes in the surface, big enough for small animals to squeeze through. Maybe."

Gathering up his books, Chris tried replaying what he'd half heard, aware of Marilyn with her hand out, chewing gum poised on the tip of her tongue. She didn't smile or speak when, reluctantly, he handed over the rock.

"Don't forget your flashlights!" Mr. Hincks shouted. Behind him Chris heard someone razz Marilyn about where she'd got the diamond. Remarks like that made him cringe.

Geology was Chris's best subject, the field in which he planned to specialize at university and later find work. His *life* was rocks; he longed for the time when he could say that and not have people frown in sympathy. Not that everyone was that way. Not Marilyn, perhaps — you had to admire a girl with specimens, even if she did crack her gum.

Marilyn *had* to be different, Chris figured, not that he knew her much outside geology class. He'd sat with her in the back seat of his friend's father's car once, the night after the dance — the one and only time he'd decided to go. Of course, it was his friend Ricky's idea, not his, to get Marilyn and a girlfriend of hers to go for a drive with them. But it wasn't as though anything had happened.

There was also the time he'd seen her at a party at Ricky's, sitting on the couch in the Deacons' basement.

Marilyn had pale blonde hair that stood out against the rec-room panelling; she'd looked up and smiled the second he peeked in before retreating back upstairs.

In the kitchen Ricky and some other boys hunched over the stove doing hot-knives. Bright as a fishtank, the window was wide open, as if to let the entire street know what Ricky got up to when his parents went out. Watching them, Chris sat at the breakfast nook and tried sipping a warm beer. From the living-room came giggling, the keening part of "Stairway to Heaven".

"Hey Kynock!" Ricky glanced up and started coughing. "Have a toke."

"Naaa."

"Take off yer coat an' stay awhile." Ricky looked at the others and burst out laughing.

Slowly, Chris got up and followed the music to the living-room. All the lights were off, the needle bumping around the record. Sliding into a La-Z-Boy, the beer between his knees, he leaned back and shut his eyes, trying to ignore the rustling from the sofa, the sound like someone sucking Life Savers. Till Ricky came in and pulled him out by the sleeve, hissing: "You some kinda perve or *what*?"

Back in the kitchen he watched Ricky top up his father's rye with water and slump to the floor, snoring beside the dishwasher. Dumping his beer in the sink, Chris stubbed out a cigarette left burning on the counter, then crept downstairs to the rec room.

Marilyn was cross-legged on the couch, deep in conversation with a boy in a jeans jacket. She blinked when she saw Chris, shrugging as the boy stopped mid-sentence.

"Sorry," she muttered. Chris had no idea why or to whom she was apologizing. Gritting his teeth, he tiptoed past, stumbling on the shag carpet.

"No, no — *I'm* sorry," he said, letting himself outside.

The damp, late-winter wind stung his eyes, lifting the smell of dogshit from moonlit patches of snow. But he breathed in deeply — such a relief, to be alone under the cold white stars.

In the hallway, as if she'd just remembered something, Marilyn caught up with Chris.

"You goin' to Ricky's this Saturday?" Tucking her notebook under her chin, she unzipped her purse and threw in the amethyst. "His parents are going away for the whole weekend," she said. Looking away, she pulled crumbs of mascara off her lashes.

"I don't think so."

"See ya tomorrow, then."

"Yeah," he said, his eyes drifting to her cheap-look- ing purse. For all his excitement about the trip, he could still feel the stone's weight in his hand, its cool planes and soft graininess. He'd have liked it on his dresser, with the rest of his collection. To study at leisure under his magnifying glass.

For his sixteenth birthday Chris's mother — his parents were divorced — had given him the magnifier, a folding glass on a nylon cord. She'd sent away to Minnesota for it; Chris kept the supplier's catalogue under his bed. His mother worked as a loans officer and didn't have time to shop (she said), though there was just Chris to buy for. He was genuinely surprised when he opened the gift. Horrified, too, at the thought of her riffling through his room for the catalogue. Not that she'd have found any- thing amiss — it was the thought of her touching his rocks and field guides that troubled him. Enough to keep him in his room with the door shut, pondering his next acquisition.

Chris had hopes — not unreasonable — of amassing a decent collection of rocks and minerals by the time he entered college. This was something he kept to himself, of course; the only one who might have been interested was Mr. Hincks. Examining his samples — slivers of obsidian black as the ice on a frozen pond; slabs of bloodstone marbled like steak — Chris often longed for someone who shared his interest. But from others his age, especially Ricky, whom he'd known since fourth grade, he got nothing but glib looks and quiet, mocking stares. As for his mother, she was glad he had a hobby, though the breadth of his knowledge of rocks often left her stumped. Especially at dinner, when he'd tell her what he'd learned in class and proceed to explain. She'd listen patiently at first, then excuse herself to serve him more casserole.

He'd always been what some would call obsessive. "Touched" was what they said at school, where his keenness for rocks had set him apart as an oddball, even in junior high. On summer afternoons while Ricky and the others lolled around listening to records, Chris would take an old magnifying glass, a hammer and chisel, and wander through the woods at the end of his street.

He'd study the granite outcroppings spread like bald patches among huckleberry and wild pear, brushing away lichens and broken glass to inspect their glittering properties. Even the most ordinary granite fascinated him: its texture like sugar, colours from salt-and-pepper to canned-salmon pink, dark specks of mica like the flecks of skin mixed up in the fish.

Rocks reminded him of food, the earth itself a huge oven: everything mixed up and baked, ready for sampling. When he looked at granite he felt a certain purity, as if the world itself were laid bare, details of peat and topsoil scraped off by glaciers. Thinking of Ricky smoking up in his parents' basement, he wished life could be that straightforward. His friend, however, had no inkling of Chris's perspective. Less and less often did Ricky invite him to parties.

"Dork," other students snickered, sometimes within earshot. The school staff reserved judgement, though by eleventh grade even Mr. Hincks began to wonder about Chris. His interest was so intense for a kid his age, no one knew whether to encourage it or treat it like a phase. And teachers had worse to contend with: pupils dealing dope and feeling each other up in the stairwells. In a way Chris's oddness made him easier; it kept him insulated.

His mother was no buffer. Things could be worse, she told herself, especially on nights Chris stayed up all hours reading. She'd wake at three sometimes and his light would be on. *At least it keeps him out of trouble.* All the same, it cheered her the evening she phoned to say she'd be working late and Chris told her he was going out. He couldn't help but note her hopefulness when she asked, "Should I leave a light on?" Meaning: should I wait up? You don't have to be home by any special time, you know.

Chris took his time walking home that night from Ricky's. He had no idea what the hour was, but prayed his mother would be asleep when he got in. He couldn't have borne her questions, or to sit with her at the dining-room table. His mother in pink robe and slippers, nursing a cup of tea. Her cheery need to know: "Any *girls* there tonight?" He wondered what she'd do if he told her the truth, about the dope-smoking, the wet, mucky sounds coming from darkened rooms.

Thankfully, his mother was in bed when he came in, the light on in the kitchen and a bottle of Coke on the counter. *Hope you had fun,* said the note scribbled on a grocery receipt. *Just thought you might be thirsty.*

The morning of the cave trip Chris was first on the bus; he chose a window seat near the front as the others filed past. The bus was full by the time Marilyn got on, out of breath, flopping down beside him.

"So," she said, twisting a shank of hair round her finger, inspecting the split ends. "Thought any more about Ricky's tomorrow night?" She looked like she'd just gotten up; there was toothpaste on her lip.

"Excuse me?"

"Ricky's — it'll be a blast!"

Chris thought of his mother, the nudge she'd given him before leaving for work. You should go out more, she said, though as far as he could tell the only place she ever went was the bank. Why not bring somebody here, then, she kept on, after he insisted he was fine, he saw all he wanted of people at school.

He felt his face burn. The least of his interests was the party at Ricky's; besides, he'd been up half the night anticipating this trip.

"I'll have to think about it," he said.

Marilyn folded her arms and shut her eyes, resting up for the outing ahead. Seated opposite with the vice-principal, Mr. Hincks eyed Chris and winked.

"Y'all remember your flashlights?"

The cave was an hour away, a spot on the map where two dirt roads converged, remote enough that only locals and dedicated spelunkers knew of it. Spelunkers and the Mi'kmaq, who considered it the entrance to the underworld — or so Mr. Hincks said. Legend had it you could enter the cave and emerge at the far end of the province.

This set off waves of stupid jokes about a brave and his dog reputed to have come out the other side without clothes or fur. Chris did his best to ignore this, trying to picture instead what it would be like in the cave. The teacher had told them to expect water. A pond — or did he say a lake?

"Everybody got hats? Boots?"

As they left the bus, the giggling and scoffing gave way to a reluctant, jittery quiet. The cave lay in a hill beyond a river churning with runoff. When the others balked at shimmying over on a fallen log, Chris pushed ahead and side-stepped across, swinging his knapsack and trying not to look down at the roiling brown water. Once across, he ran on, pausing only to dig out his flashlight, having forgotten to pack his ballcap.

The entrance was easily missed — a rocky cleft small as a basement window, a chip bag on the ground beside it. Chris squeezed through head-first, feeling his way with his hands. Inside, it was cool and perfectly still, no sound but water dripping, the faint rustling of bats. Three or four footsteps and absolute darkness, a darkness Chris could never have imagined. Soothing, it was, in a curious way. Like being swallowed by some vast, unseen beast and finding yourself intact, held and rocked inside its dark belly. It didn't occur to him to feel frightened but, like Jonah praying inside the whale, he felt his muscles slacken, his spirit wrapped in an endless blood-warmth. An envelope of faith, no trace of doubt.

The flashlight cast a thread of light that went nowhere, its frailness quickly swallowed up. Behind him Chris heard a girl — Marilyn, perhaps — tittering about who'd go next. He tried tuning out the sound, moving forward until the entrance was a pinprick of light. Near his feet he sensed water still and unruffled as the air; aiming his light, he could just detect the gleam beside his boot.

"Hey Kynock?" As if miles away, Mr. Hincks's voice bounced off rock, rippling through darkness. It set off peeping, a shrill whistling like wind blowing through a crevice; more rustling of wings. Someone gasped — yes, it *was* Marilyn — and muffled a scream.

"Over here," Chris replied hesitantly, his voice a whisper. The sound made him wince; the darkness was so complete, he hated to stir it.

"Stay with the group," Hincks's voice echoed, unravelling.

"Yes," Chris hissed, barely opening his mouth.

Sticking to the water's outline, he picked his way over boulders and debris, using his palms as fish use sonar. The gasping and squealing never far behind — never far enough; the dance of flashlights just inches away as he stumbled along. The light at the entrance had vanished altogether now.

After a while — Chris didn't know how long — he bumped against something, a rockface taller and slimier than what he'd been clambering over, half crouching, half crawling, using his fingertips to see. On one side of the rock seemed to be another opening. He could feel the sides and ceiling narrow, the furry brush of bats — though it was harder to tell where air ended and rock began, the mind rushing in to fill the spaces. The same way he lost track of the voices behind him, didn't notice them fading until they were gone. He was so content to be away from the screams and Dracula jokes.

The clay-cool air was like salve on a sunburn at first. It didn't bother Chris at all being alone like this, until he realized he'd lost direction. *A labyrinth of passages behind the main chamber, typical of this type of cave.* He thought of Mr. Hincks's chart on the board. *Accessible through sinkholes big enough for a squirrel or rabbit....*

Chris went over and over the number of times he'd stopped and turned, which way his feet had pointed. To pluck himself up he thought of the naked Mi'kmaq emerging by the ocean, dense green water roaring through the mouth of the cave. The air felt clammy as sweat now, warmed slightly by his rapid breath.

"Stay put," he spoke out loud, no longer caring what he disturbed. "They'll come and find me. Won't they?"

He must've crouched there three hours, his back to wet stone till his jacket was soaked through. His absence wasn't noticed until the rest boarded the bus. Mr. Hincks paid the driver not to let anyone off while he and the vice-principal went back to look. Cracking gum and bragging about how scared they'd been, it took the others a while to realize something was wrong. Right away, though, Marilyn knew it had to do with Chris. She pointed out his empty seat, setting off laughter and cruel speculation.

"Prob'ly back there somewheres jerkin' off," someone yelled. But as the wait dragged on, jokes turned to curses.

Mr. Hincks discovered Chris near the end of a passage, mumbling to himself about metamorphic rock. Wiping sweat from his face, the vice-principal said it was a good thing they heard him talking, otherwise he mightn't have been found. All the way out, he kept one hand on Chris's shoulder, while Hincks stumbled ahead trying to make light of things.

"Whole new meaning to the term 'get lost', eh Kynock? God, I had no idea you took those turkeys so serious!"

When the driver let them on, Chris was greeted with spitballs and hoots, taunts that stuck like the bat guano on his clothes and hair. He slid into the seat beside Marilyn, who pressed her face to the window.

"Three frigging hours!" someone moaned, neither Hincks nor the vice-principal offering any explanation.

All the way home, Marilyn gazed at the asphalt flying

past, as if to punish him. Even after the insults died down, she refused to speak or look at him. He thought of the amethyst, longed to ask her about it as a kind of reparation. But he couldn't find the words.

Back at school, Chris expected them to phone his mother, but if they did she never mentioned it. The only real consequence of his misadventure was Mr. Hincks putting an end to such excursions; after that, field trips were kept to the woods behind the school.

The last thing Chris felt like the next day was going to another party. He stayed in bed till noon, when his mother tapped on the door and announced she was going shopping and out for supper with people from work. She wondered if he'd like to come.

He waited till he heard her pull out of the driveway, then got up and made some toast. The rest of the afternoon he lay on his bed and tried reading an article on volcanoes. After that, he fixed himself a hamburger, drank the rest of the Coke in the fridge. By six o'clock he decided he would go to Ricky's, combed his hair and put on some clean jeans.

Above the stove was a bottle of Bristol Cream his mother kept for "special occasions". She rarely drank, except the odd glass after work, particularly if she'd had a long day. Chris rinsed out his tumbler and filled it with sherry, took a deep breath and thought of other things as he downed it. Then he went to the bathroom and brushed his teeth.

It was just getting dark when he started for Ricky's, three streets away. All the way up the block, TVs flickered in picture windows, the same dim blue as the sky. It felt cold enough to snow; the wind pushed him along in his thin jacket, his hands shoved in the pockets. Outside Ricky's house, two kids got off their bicycles and stared as he approached. On the frozen lawn a group of teenagers milled, as if waiting for something to happen.

Music blared from the split-level house, bass notes rumbling like a tremor through the stiff grass. The kids wheeled their bikes closer, yelling something. Not hearing, the teenagers moved to the porch. Chris watched them go inside before slouching up the steps. He hesitated before pressing the bell.

After a while he let himself in, his head spinning in the splintered light from the hall chandelier. "Deep Purple" was blasting from the stereo, voices pealing above the noise. In the living-room he spied Ricky, his hands cupped around something burning. On the sofa sat Marilyn, drinking beer and laughing with her mouth open. Between her breasts dangled a pendant, a gaudy, purple, heart-shaped stone. The boy in the denim jacket tugged on the chain and bent to kiss her lips. The rest of her obscured, Chris saw her knees jerk up as she leaned back, her hair falling across one eye.

Lingering in the hallway, he thought perhaps he'd try the kitchen, maybe stay for a beer. But from the living-room he heard Marilyn laugh again and knew before long the lights would go off.

Outside the stars had come out one by one, the sky a stolid mauve. The street was emptied of kids, their bicycles abandoned in driveways. Chris stepped quickly to the curb, the wind in his face now. Above the party's rumble he heard dogs barking, a sound quaint and cold as stone. First one, then another: a chain of backyard replies. It grew louder the farther he got from Ricky's, bouncing and rolling and filling the sky as it followed him home.

IF WALLS WERE GLASS

F irst thing I did was paint the whole place white:
walls, ceiling, trim; both rooms, kitchen, bedsitting.
Not that it needed it. The suite, as it was listed in
the classifieds, was spotless, not a bad shade of beige. But
the fresh coat covered the smell of previous tenants —
mothballs, mostly — and the Comet I used scrubbing everything down. It made it seem more mine, homier, if you
can say that about someplace a continent from home.

The landlady supplied the paint in crusted, dribbled
tins. She told me to keep my damage deposit — just glad,
I guess, to have someone willing to keep the place up.
Not that it was run down, mind you. It wasn't. The house
was a neat, three-storey stucco like all the rest on the quiet
eastside street.

The man down the hall kept the bathroom spick and
span. I know, because we shared it. I hated to think of his
strange bum on the seat, though any signs of another
body's functions were carefully Pine-Soled away. He kept
to himself; oh, I'd hear the odd cough sometimes, footsteps on the stairs, the toilet flushing, but that was all. It
was easy enough to forget we used the same facilities —

the only drawback, really. A small inconvenience in exchange for cheap rent. My job at the aquarium was just for the summer and didn't pay a lot.

"The suite has a *great* view of the mountains!" I wrote Mum the day I found it, leaving out the part about the bathroom. Had I mentioned that, a cheque would've come in the mail.

At the airport, Dad pressed five crisp hundreds into my hand. There was no room to argue since Rick, my boyfriend, had come along too and was making a bit of a scene. Well, not making a scene so much as stirring things up, making it sound as though I were leaving the planet, going to Mars or someplace, never to be seen or heard from again. All the way there in the car — Dad driving, Rick in front, Mum and me in the back — nobody talked. It was like going to a funeral. Mum kept picking a thread on her new white purse, arranging her feet in her matching sandals. Sprawled beside my father, Rick looked like a gorilla. He made Dad seem so small.

"I love you, Barbara," he had to say, right there in front of my parents, as if it were just us in the steamed-up car.

"I know," I muttered, hoping that would shut him up. Praying Mum would keep quiet.

Surely you can find something down here — why the heck so far away? Look at Marilyn; she didn't go away for work! I'd expected Mum to be happy for me when I landed the aquarium job, but instead she'd looked dismayed. The choice after graduation was waitress or move back to Hubville and work for Dad. A secretary or filing clerk? Yeah, right. Just like Marilyn, my old friend and my roommate until she quit university to get married.

But the issue here wasn't jobs.

"When did you say Marilyn's baby's due?" Mum asked coyly, watching Rick's neck as we pulled up to the terminal.

"September, maybe?" I couldn't wait to get on that plane.

"Lucky Darrell," Rick joked, but when he lifted my bags the nerves around his mouth were twitching.

Airborne, I loosened my seatbelt and counted Dad's bills. Only then did I feel a tug about leaving — a drag, actually, like the weight of a suitcase full of pennies. What else can you say about twenty-five years in the same gold-fish-bowl of a province? The sum of my life.

The tour-guide job at the aquarium was a dream come true, at least when I applied and actually got hired. Plenty of room for advancement, they said, a distinct chance of being kept on after the season. The ideal entry-level position for a biology major.

They must've liked my résumé — of course I jazzed it up. Stressed the marine biology paper I wrote once which got an A+; played down the fact I'd been waiting tables since. What they didn't know wouldn't hurt them; applying from a distance, I figured my lack of experience didn't matter anyway.

When they phoned to offer the job, Rick and I had one of our blow-out fights. He'd been at me to move in. I told him I was going.

"What about me?" he wanted to know, leaning over the bar where I was working. It was one of those new family restaurants dark and plush enough to attract adults too.

Typical, I thought, his first concern always himself. He'd just finished his commerce degree, had a couple of lines on sales positions but no bites.

I knew the best thing for both of us was a summer apart.

"I love you," he said once more by the security gate. The

Mountie didn't bat an eye going over me with his wand; my arms stuck out like brooms, Dad's money in one hand. Mum gave Rick this querulous, last-ditch look.

I mean, it's not as if it was easy leaving. I'd never been farther west than Edmundston. God knows what awaited me out west, a place I'd only seen in tourist brochures — pretty sunsets, snow-capped mountains. Still, as the plane climbed I felt the weight of everything slide and streak away like blobs of rain on the window.

"You like white, no?" The landlady stood in my tiny kitchen watching me pry open the paint. She was oriental, middle-aged, her English rather wobbly. One by one she'd carried the tins upstairs, feeling every now and then for her earrings, large dangling stars.

"This for you," she said, handing me a paper bag from her purse. She stood twisting an earring as I opened it.

"For me? Oh, Mrs. Lee—"

"Please, my name June."

It was a pink satin pincushion ringed with tiny pigtailed men.

"How nice—"

"You good girl, Ba-bhlah. That your first name, eh?" She blinked approvingly. "You met Earl yet, huh?"

"Earl?"

"Man in next apartment, Earl. He lovely housekeeper too, eh. You see?" She waved towards the bathroom in the hall, then sat watching me spread newspaper over the dinette. Not that paint would've ruined it. The suite was furnished — with stuff from better days.

"You do nice job, eh. That a good girl."

As I dipped my brush, she came over and kissed my cheek.

"You need anything, my place just two streets over. You got my number."

That was a Saturday, after my first week at the aquarium. I'd stayed at the Y while apartment-hunting. The suite was almost too good to be true; I found it on Thursday, moved in Friday after work. That was how things seemed to happen for me. Call it serendipity or plain good luck, I took it as a sign of choosing right: taking the breather from Rick, doing something on my own for once.

Even if the job turned out to be a bit of a bust. At first all I did was clean — scrape white scum off the rocks inside the tanks, Windex away fingerprints and mouthmarks left by kids. Allison, a guide from the summer before, showed me how to squeegee without leaving streaks and scoop out "morts" without letting visitors see.

"I didn't expect it to be...custodial," I finally told her when, after a couple of weeks, my duties hadn't changed. "I thought I'd be helping with the animals, giving information."

Allison was tanned and lean, with kinky blonde hair, her legs brown and unshaven under her uniform's dark-blue shorts. She reminded me of the people in the brochures skiing in bathing suits. She was studying political science, halfway through her degree.

She looked at me and laughed, spraying cleanser and talking to the fish as she rubbed and wiped.

"Well, if you don't like it, look for something else. I mean, it's just a job. But I hear you — all this crap we use on the tanks? Ten years from now they'll find it causes cancer."

Allison was always talking about toxic substances; had picked up right away on the paint under my nails, the tiny white specks in my hair.

"It's not that easy," I said, "just getting your foot in the door."

"I guess. But there's more important stuff out there than jobs. I mean, doesn't it just bug your ass to see all these things in *cages*?"

I shrugged, looking around at the invertebrates. From what I could see, anemones and jellyfish were as happy in tanks as in the ocean — and safer. You could say the same for the salmon and wolf eels, their open, toothy snouts bumping the glass, their cold, unblinking eyes. Far as I was concerned, there wasn't much debate over quality of life.

"But doesn't it *get* to you?" she kept on, eyeing me as if I had two heads.

I shrugged again. "Beats me." As I picked up my squeegee she tapped my shoulder.

"What're you doing here, Barbara? I mean, really, you come all this way—? For *this*? I mean, if you were really into it.... But seriously, what are you doing on the west coast?"

"Getting away?" I looked at her and forced a laugh. I hadn't meant it to come out a question.

"What does he look like?" She gave me a sly look, her eyes wet and inquisitive as a seal's.

"I forget."

A week or two later, on the spur of the moment, I invited Allison for supper. We'd been swamped all day with bus tour after bus tour. At lunch break we sat near the killer whales, Allison taking deep sips of bottled water. It struck me how, after all my work making the suite cosy, I still hadn't shown anyone. Mum had written, of course, wondering what I'd done for curtains and to say she'd seen Marilyn in Sobeys buying chips for a shower at her mother's. "Anyone to chum around with yet?" she also wanted to know.

Once the paint smell disappeared, I'd gone to Woolworth's and bought a set of dishes — white — feeling a weird joy rinsing and putting them away, one by one, in the tiny cupboard. They were a bit of an extravagance; I still can't imagine needing plates for four! Another thing I had to buy was sheets — yellow flowered ones that didn't clash too badly with the orange carpet, the brown pull-out bed. Though a little dated, at least the furnishings were clean. On the dresser was a lamp that looked like molten lava, ugly enough to laugh off as a conversation piece.

After work Allison rode the trolley with me along East Hastings, scarcely blinking at the grungy hotels, the derelicts hanging off the sidewalk. It started to drizzle, neon melting onto the pavement. A man in a grey cap got on and jostled past us, loaded. He took a seat near the back, slurring threats at the other passengers. We sat rigid, staring straight ahead until a couple of blocks from my stop the driver pulled over and put the man off near a tavern. The sign had palm trees, advertised rooms by the hour.

At home, I rushed around fluffing pillows, pulling up blinds. The mountains were blocked out by fog.

"On a nice day you can see the Lions," I said, but Allison was too busy looking around to hear. Hands clasped behind her back, she stood by the bed, gazing at the carpet as if it were quicksand. When I switched on the lamp, her hand came up to cover a burst of laughter.

"Nice, eh? Came with the place, what can you do?" I tried joking, handing her a cider sweet and fizzy as pop. Lucky I had two in the fridge.

"Cheers," I said as she took it to the dinette and sat sipping, still gazing around.

"Where's the can?" she asked after a while.

She wasn't gone long before she came back looking indignant — or embarrassed, perhaps, as if she'd forgotten to flush. She kept tossing her corkscrew hair, crossing her legs and pursing her lips, sipping from the bottle.

"You want a glass or anything?"

"No." She wiped her mouth on the back of her hand, shaking her head. "You actually share the bathroom? Wow."

I couldn't help prickling at that — she shared a place somewhere in Kitsilano with seven or eight other people. When I said I lived in the east end, I had to give her directions.

"Poor you," she said now, polishing off her drink.

For supper I made salad and macaroni and cheese — Marilyn's favourite when we roomed together. Sure, we'd joke about it, but studying we'd make double potfuls and take our time eating it, savouring each spoonful like some exotic gourmet treat.

Allison made a face as I dished hers out; took a few polite bites and pushed away the plate. With a cringe, I noticed the smudge from the price sticker.

"Like something else?" I sniffled, praying she wouldn't notice the mark.

"It's okay. I'm not very hungry, that's all." Her elbows on the woodgrain tabletop, she watched me eat. "We should go out sometime — you like sushi?"

I got up and scraped my supper into the garbage.

"Like the things at work, isn't it? Practically still moving."

"Marinated," she sighed, rolling her eyes upwards along the edge of the ceiling.

Below, a door opened and there was a thud; heavy, shuffling footsteps on the stairs.

We stopped talking as they came closer, pausing for a second by my door.

"Neighbours?" Allison said in a flat voice, as the shuffling continued down the hall.

She stood up, her eyes on the stove.

"Oh God, is that the time? Look, I've gotta take off now. Thanks, I mean for the cider and everything. On me next time, okay? See you tomorrow at work. Wonder who we'll get to check out the piranhas?" It was a joke for obnoxious tourists.

I listened to the slap of her sandals on the stairs, the sound echoing down the wet sidewalk.

Cleaning up the dishes, I felt myself sweating, the air steamy and close. I'd been skimping a bit on baths — like a child almost, comfortable with the feel of dirt. But with the heat I knew one couldn't be put off much longer. Besides, the cool water would feel good.

Gathering towel, soap and the loofah sponge Mum had sent, I tiptoed out — almost going back to lock up, then leaving the door ajar, the radio on. In the bathroom, I switched on the light and bolted the door. The walls glistened blue under the bare, frosted bulb. Below the sink were a new tin of cleanser, a blue toilet brush. As I ran the bath I tried not to notice the frayed towel hanging by the deep, old-fashioned tub, the sparkling rim of the bowl with the seat flipped up. Everything gleamed as usual, and a new roll of tissue was set out to replace the one getting low.

I kept my clothes on while the tub filled, listening for the TV in the next apartment, the squeak of kitchen drawers, any sound drowned out by gushing water. Undressing quickly, I lowered myself in. It was too hot, but I made myself crouch, my thighs reddening, and dip backwards to wet my hair. Easing down, I let the water fill my ears, a heavy, soothing burble. As it cooled I soaped myself, was lathering under my arms when the lock next door clicked and I heard the man step into the hall.

Dropping the soap, I lay still, arms folded over my breasts. He rattled the knob and I heard him sigh, muttering something under his breath. There was a pause, and I pulled my knees to my chest, splashing loudly with both hands.

After a second or two — it seemed like for ever — he grunted and moved away. I waited till his door clicked shut, then resumed washing. I took my sweet time rinsing off, running plenty of water. When my fingers started to pucker, I stepped out and towelled off. Getting into my robe, I took a good look at my face in the mirror, pausing to inspect a pimple. I was so concerned about that zit I think I might've forgotten and left the soggy bathmat on the floor. But when I went back later to brush my teeth, there it was, hung as usual over the tub.

Sometime before dawn that night the phone rang. It was Rick; he'd forgotten the time difference. At first I thought I was dreaming, my mouth sticky with sleep.

"Hello stranger — thought you said you'd call. I miss you, Barb. I just needed to hear your voice."

I had nothing, absolutely nothing to say, grunting, "Me too," before hanging up. I never did get back to sleep, thinking about him at the airport.

"Phone me!" Rick was shouting as I climbed the escalator. At first I wouldn't turn around, knowing how geeky he looked waving and carrying on. But near the top I couldn't help myself. When I glanced back he had his arm around Mum's shoulder; she was leaning into his shirt like a starlet in a movie. Dad was off to the side, jiggling his keys.

As July wore on, tourists swarmed the aquarium. After a while I was allowed to feed the fish three times a week, blending concoctions of shrimp and squid the look and colour of barf — "Calamari," Allison joked. I took my time dumping cupfuls of pink goop into the tanks, holding out tweezerfuls of fish to the crabs. They'd have eaten my fingers too, if I'd let them. You had to wonder why, cooped together like that, they didn't go for each other.

Between tours I'd lose myself sometimes watching

them, oooohs and aaaahs from the killer whale show drifting right over my head. When there was no one around, I'd feel like Alice down the rabbit hole: invisible. Which I was as far as Brent was concerned — the attendant who ran the show, flinging fish to the whales from a platform. He was blond and muscular, with such rippling biceps you wondered sometimes who the cheers were for. Allison called him an asshole.

As the weeks dragged by, the heat spread like glue over the city. Some days the breeze off the harbour was barely strong enough to budge the tops of the giant firs, the sun burning down on the pavilions till the windows acted like a magnifying glass. Beyond their glare, above the tourists' squeals you could hear ravens gliding through the thick air overhead.

One especially muggy day, Allison strode over after work and asked if I felt like going out to eat. The restaurant had black lacquered dishes of sushi in the window — plastic or real, it was hard to tell. A chart showed the different pieces you could get, like the map in a box of chocolates. Allison pointed to something pink and white as a set of dentures.

We left our sneakers at the door and crouched at a table, our knees cramped under us. Strange music tinkled in the background. The other diners spoke in whispers. The waitress bowed when she took our order, Allison rhyming off the odd names like ice-cream flavours.

"Sashimi, for both of us," she leaned close to whisper.

The food was pretty to look at. The waitress brought chopsticks, impossibly tiny cups and bowls. Following Allison, I tweezed up my dinner one piece at a time, thinking of the creatures at work. Everything tasted of the sea; the fish was the texture of butter.

"Wasabi?"

It made me think of *The Lone Ranger*. Allison passed a thimble of green paste; hesitating, I dipped in a chopstick and spread some on my next bite.

Like a trail of blazing gas it flared up my throat into my nose till my head throbbed and tears sprang.

"Whoa—!"

Allison covered her mouth and tried not to laugh, flinging her hair back.

"Careful," she said, too late.

"I won't ask what *this* is," I said, gulping pale green tea and grabbing the next thing on my plate, a wad of rice topped with something spongy and orange, artificial-looking as a Buried Treasure, the kind with a plastic toy inside. For a second — who knows why? — I pictured Marilyn, her belly bulging in a floppy pink top.

It tasted like Halifax harbour at low tide, but at least it cooled my mouth.

"Urchin," Allison said, watching me eat. "A delicacy in Japan."

"You're kidding." I felt the bile rise, carefully spitting the mouthful into my black linen napkin.

"I can't believe you never had it before. I mean, coming from the east coast and all." The way she said it a mix of wonder and contempt.

We finished eating in silence.

Outside Allison said she had to meet some friends. On the way home I stopped at a bookshop, the kind with comic books and funky postcards. There was one with a mushroom cloud spread over the city: "Getting bombed in Vancouver," it said. Made me think of Marilyn, our old flat; her boyfriend Darrell drinking rum and Coke, watching *Six Million Dollar Man* reruns on TV. At the time it had gotten on my nerves, but now it struck me as funny, quaint. Cosy. She and I cooking supper in the tiny kitchen, the figurines she saved from tea lined up above the sink.

"Bring me another, wouldja Maaar?" the boyfriend would yell from the couch, enough to make you gag. God, and she married him. All the same, I picked up the card and took it to the cash.

When I got home, the landlady was at my kitchen sink, wrench in hand, fixing the faucet.

"Excuse me—" I tapped lightly on the door.

"There!" She turned around, a trickle of sweat down the side of her nose. "See, no drip now." There was a tight pause. "So, you meet Earl yet?" She gave me an odd, quizzical look, almost impatient.

"No." I folded my arms, waiting for her to leave.

"Oh well. Earl a nice tenant, no trouble. He keep things nice. Now anything else you need fix, you tell me, eh? I bring my husband for the big jobs."

"Drip?" I felt like saying, having barely noticed one. "I'd...I'd appreciate it if you called first—" I began, as she bustled past with her toolkit, smiling.

After she left I went to the bathroom — spotless as ever, except the tub faucets were disconnected, a gaping black hole where the plumbing had been. Just as I flushed, footsteps started upstairs, shambling, uneven, like something rolling wall to wall. They stopped outside the door. As I stepped towards the keyhole there was a movement. Covering the hole with my hand, I waited for the sound of his key turning farther down the hall, the TV springing to life. I made a dash for my apartment.

"Having a wonderful time," I scribbled on the postcard. "Any baby yet?"

The next day at the aquarium was unusually slow. A steady rain beat down all afternoon, bringing giant slugs onto the pathways around the pavilions. Fog backed up the length of the harbour, blotting out all but a few dark wisps of mountain. I hung around the ticket kiosk in my rainjacket, moving only for the odd straggle of visitors — foreign-speaking mostly, which made things easier. Without saying much, just smiling, I led them around the exhibits; waited patiently while a man photographed me with the piranhas.

After work Allison invited me along for a cappuccino with some friends. We took a bus to a dingy coffee shop across the street from the postcard place.

Around a red Arborite table huddled some people my age, maybe slightly older, dressed in black leather jackets, bright batik scarves wound round their necks like bandages. I thought they must be students, though there was an intensity about them — the kind of worry you'd see on someone plotting things: revolutions, coups, bank robberies. Their tall, napkin-wrapped glasses of coffee, pale and striped as strata of sand, sat untouched, milky foam melting on top. They scarcely blinked as Allison and I pulled up chairs.

"Make the rich pay," one fiery-looking guy was saying, intent on his cigarette. "Leftist insurgency . . . Salvadorean peasants. . . ."

It was hard to make sense of what he said — he seemed to speak in code. The others nodded. Allison grabbed a Player's from the pack on the table; threw her head back exhaling. The fellow launched into an analysis of Marxist theory. He looked as though he hadn't shaved in some time, a smudge of foam stuck to his moustache.

"This is Barb," Allison said impassively during a pause while his ideas sank in. The others ignored her, slouched back in their chairs, waiting for more.

"So how are things at the aqua-prison?" The man who'd been talking suddenly switched gears, as if for a breather.

Allison waved her cigarette, flinging ash.

"It's a job, okay?"

"For the co-opted, maybe." I expected him to laugh but he rubbed his jaw, scratched the back of his rat's-nest hair.

"So what's up?" Allison flicked her ringlets and butted out her smoke.

"Big demo this weekend, Robson Square. Refugee speaker. U.S. ambassador's in town...."

The words "struggle" and "united" kept cropping up.

"If you're not for us, you're against us," concluded rat's nest, and for the first time the others turned and looked at me.

"Look, I've got an errand — nice meeting you, though—" I got up awkwardly, squeaking my chair on the dirty tiles.

Their faces seemed hostile yet blank too, as if they hadn't seen or noticed me at all, my getting up to leave as predictable as rain.

"Ciao," Allison called out, a hint of sarcasm in her voice. Glancing back, I saw her leaning over, deep in conversation.

When I let myself in, there was a bathtub in the middle of the kitchen — modern, rectangular, robin's-egg blue. The landlady's voice came from the next room, speaking rapidly in Chinese.

"I tried to call!" She waved at me, cupping one hand over the phone. "But you not in."

Hanging up, she stepped towards me, smiling.

"You like? Nice new tub for you and Earl. It match, eh. Old one go better somewhere else, downstairs maybe."

"But why my place?" Irritated, I caught myself enunciating each word. She eyed me as if I were nuts.

"Somebody might steal, out in hall. It get in Earl's way. My husband, he come tomohlow and install."

I put on water for tea and after a minute or two she nodded and left. I listened to her stump downstairs in her flat black pumps, then sat at the dinette and began a letter to Mum. I didn't get much past "Dear," however, seized by this weird sudden urge to write Rick instead. Rick of all people. It was just that he'd have enjoyed hearing about Allison and the coffee shop. With him, I could've joked about it.

I ended up writing to nobody; spent the rest of the evening listening to the CBC, something about conflict in Nicaragua. I made myself concentrate; at least it drowned out the car radios and shouts of people outside enjoying the night. My mind kept drifting to Rick — for some reason I kept thinking about the time we met up after high school. We'd both left Hubville to go to the same university. Marilyn and I were downtown having a beer when he came up to us. I hardly recognized him; he'd grown a foot and his hair was styled — not at all like the Ricky Deacon we knew before, that skinny teenager with bad skin, always sucking on a joint.

"Barb! Marilyn! How *are* you? What're you girls drinking? Shit, what a treat! Fucking small world, can you believe it!? Wow, you look *great* — no, really, I mean it, Barb. Lemme buy you one — or ten! No, truly, I can't tell you how good this feels—" His voice had gotten deeper, too, and it turned out he was living on the same street off campus. Something just clicked between us, you know? Not much later we started going out.

At bedtime I was about to go brush my teeth when I heard Earl from next door come home and go into the bathroom. So I used the kitchen sink instead, wiping the spit off with a Kleenex.

That night I had a hard time getting to sleep — the sounds outside, too much tea. When at last I fell asleep, I dreamed I was back east at a party with Marilyn and Rick. We were dancing in a basement with panelled walls, swinging and flailing to the Beach Boys while people stood around drinking beer, watching.

It was the frat house where Rick lived in first year — weird, since in real life we always stayed at my place. (More privacy, he said.) In the dream Marilyn took off and I ended up alone with Rick in his room. There was a beer-can collection above the bed. Rick staggered over and pulled me to the mattress. "Ricky!" I said, my head spinning from too much drink. He pinned me down with his leg, working at my buttons. There were people by the door, gawking at us. Cheering. His jaw unrolled like in a circus mirror when I pushed him off and jumped up. Should've seen the look on his face, the others skulking away.

The rest of the night I dreamed I was cleaning fish-tanks — squeegeeing off the fog from the tourists' breath. But the more I wiped, the harder it was to see, until the things inside were just vague, dark shapes. I woke with a headache. All day at work the feel of that leg kept coming back, its weight making me sluggish and low. Or maybe it was the heat.

Allison cooled towards me after the coffee bar. At break she started making herself scarce; I'd see her over by the belugas, chatting up Brent the attendant.

As August slouched by, the heat made you think of a jungle. At night it would rain, a soft, drenching down-pour; steam rising from the sidewalks by the time I went to work, dead slugs frying like dog turds on the concrete. Some days I'd get off the bus a few blocks early and walk. Allison would be at the entrance gates when I arrived in a sweat. She'd nod and say hello, but that's all.

The tourists flooded in: pudgy kids in fluorescent

shorts, their parents in tank-tops and sun-visors, cracking gum and drinking cans of pop. Their faces, the slant
of light from the tanks on their jaws, chewing; their eyes
on the cold, fishy ones behind the glass — when I was
bored I'd try to picture them inside, on exhibit. Sometimes you'd wonder, seriously, who was on display.

By the end of the day "B.C. Hall of Fishes" would
come out "Feces Hall of Wishes". Not that anybody noticed. Heck, after a while I stopped feeling contempt for
the job, the visitors, and started feeling sorry — not just
for the animals, but for all of us there watching them,
part of the same exhibit. Meanwhile the aquarium asked
if I'd stay on after the season; Allison, I heard, was going
back to school.

Mum's voice would come to me at the oddest times,
once when I saw a pimply boy with his face to the glass,
watching salmon spawn: his eyes wide open, one hand
moving in his pocket. "Easy to be critical, Barbara," her
voice would say, and then, "Written to Marilyn yet?
When's that baby due, again?"

By the time I got home in the evening, it was all I
could do to wolf some yogurt from the carton, maybe a
peach, washed down with a couple of ciders. I'd peel off
my navy shorts and polo, and sit by the window in my
underwear, listening to the radio, the sash thrown wide
to get some air. The CBC got monotonous: non-stop
shows about Central America, a different, troubled country every night.

A bath, a long, cool bath — that would've been the
ticket, as Mum would say. The landlady had installed the
new tub, a poor replacement for the old curved one. On
the hottest nights it would've been perfect for stretching
out and relaxing. But as the heat held, it wouldn't've
mattered: Earl, my neighbour, seemed to be spending
more and more evenings home, and I didn't feel right

hogging the bathroom. Perhaps, had things developed differently with Allison, I'd have gone out more.

The heat seemed fixed like a lid over the city, oppressive and scary — a climate for fights. You could see it in the black eyes and bloodied faces of drunks on East Hastings. After the long bus-ride home, I figured it was better to stay in, alone — safer — even if the time got long, the air in the apartment stifling.

Once, desperate, I stripped and lay naked on the cool tile floor; I could hear Earl through the walls, feel the vibrations of his feet. When I realized he was going out, I got up and threw on a T-shirt, grabbing my towel. From the window I listened to him leaving, waited long enough to glimpse him below on the sidewalk. I'd never actually laid eyes on him, you see — all along I preferred to think of him more as figment than real; a poltergeist watching TV.

His head was bent down, face shaded by his peaked grey cap. From up above he looked tall and stiff in his windbreaker, his neat, pressed pants. Dodging something on the sidewalk, he staggered a little. It took a moment to click — then like a cold shower it hit me. I'd seen him before, all right, that day on the bus with Allison.

I ran to the bathroom, stuffed a sock in the keyhole; took a shallow bath. The water was too cold to enjoy. I scrubbed like someone with lice, then, wrapped in the towel, sprinted back to the apartment.

There was a small blue card from Marilyn waiting next evening. "Seven pounds, nine ounces," she wrote proudly, under the baby's name: Jason Todd Jeffrey (Guthro) White. At the bottom was a hastily scratched note: "Thirteen stitches — couldn't sit down for a week. P.S. Loved your postcard — Darrell says they should do one for Peggy's Cove."

I found some paper to start a reply. It was hard to know what to say. "Seven pounds, nine ounces" reminded me of Mum pricing rump roast. Not to mention the approval — from someone I didn't even like.

"Dear Marilyn...Dear Marilyn & Darrell...Dear Marilyn, Darrell & Jason Todd...," I doodled over and over. I was thinking what to write next when the door slammed below, a noise erupted like a barrel being thrown upstairs. "Congrats on the baby—" I began, as the racket got louder.

It stopped outside my apartment. From the dinette I could hear breathing, smell a strong whiff of liquor. The hairs on my arms pricked up — everything around me suddenly, instantly quiet, the radio awaiting the time beep. Frozen to the wobbly chrome chair, I watched the knob twist and rattle, the flimsy door shaking as fists came up and pounded. The pounding went on till I thought it would splinter, the lock wiggling like a tooth.

Afraid to breathe, I rose, my back to the stove. *Better play dead, better play dead*, went a voice inside, *better play dead than let him know you're in here.* A flash of eyes came to me, the image of them staring through glass: the eyes of fish.

The whole room was shaking, floor to ceiling. A string of garbled curses rushed like wind around the door. "Dirty fuckin' bitch don't fuckin' clean up after yer fuckin' self! Lemme in an' I'll fuckin' teach ya...!" Spit clicked and rattled around the words.

I shut my eyes, my heart thumping fit to explode. Thinking crazily of when I was small and the cat brought home a robin, stone dead with no sign of injury. Dead of fright, Mum said.

Crazy, crazy, the things that come to you.

Fuck this, fuck that, the cursing kept on.

I put my hand over my mouth and started counting, imagining each fish in the aquarium circling endlessly around its tank.

I was making my way through the pavilions, counting, when the pounding stopped and there was silence. I swear I stopped breathing, my heart in my mouth. Then — as likely as a dead bird opening its eyes — I heard his jagged footsteps lurch away, his door slam shut. Springs groaning, a burst of TV laughter.

I tiptoed to the next room and phoned 911, sweating with each whirr of the dial. Sweating blood, it felt like.

The dispatcher's voice was calm and ordinary as my parents' rec room: "We'll see what we can do, ma'am." I stood by the window waiting. When the cops finally arrived at my door, they tipped their caps, jovial as brushcut jocks at a barbecue. One was burly and tall as Rick. I wanted to fall into his arms.

I held a glass to the wall, listening while they roused him. I heard them explain they were taking him somewhere to sober up, heard his low, growling slur. They kept calling him "pal".

As they led him outside I turned off the light and watched them load him in the paddy wagon. He was crawling drunk, but they'd given him time to put on his cap. Even in the dark, from that high up, his clothes looked pressed. One of the cops, the big one, gave him a little push, patting his back before slamming the door.

When my pulse slowed, I went and ran a bath — a long, deep one with bubbles, just the right temperature. Working Mum's sponge over my skin, I tried not to think past its brusque, slippery feel. But that flood of cursing kept echoing back.

Sponge baths in the kitchen — maybe. But how the hell would I manage the toilet? "Life in the big city" I could see myself sloughing it off on a postcard to somebody. Rick?

I didn't think so.

The landlady was abrupt on the phone.

"Why you call this ungodly hour? You got problem, I get to it tomorrow. My husband might be able to fix—"

"But, see, June — you don't understand — there's nothing broken—"

"Then why you call, huh?"

"It's the man next door—"

"You mean Earl? Whassa matter with Earl, huh? He a good, good tenant, he never no trouble—"

I stared at the page on the table addressed to Marilyn.

"Not like you, Barbara. He so quiet, so clean, and you so messy. Always got that radio on, never clean up bathtub. Nice blue tub. He say, "You know that girl, she drive me clhazy—"

"I see—"

"I thought you be good girl. I give you presents. I give you discount—"

"I'm sorry—"

"It no good, you bother other people—"

"I—"

"You have till end of month, okay? I be easy. That's it."

Her words seemed to come through a funnel; there was a sharp click as she hung up. As I laid down the phone my ears burned.

Numb, I slumped at the table, picked up the pen.

"Dear Marilyn," I started to print in small, shaky letters. "I'm happy for you and your baby.... Having a wonderful time...." My fingers felt weak and fuzzy gripping the pen, my wrist limp. "Life...." I dotted the i, then crumpled the paper in my fist.

Taking a deep breath, I got up and rummaged for a fresh sheet, tuning the radio — to an AM station. It was music I wanted, any kind of music. I found one playing a Loverboy special, not great but catchy, upbeat; better than a documentary.

Starting fresh, I closed my eyes and thought of what to say, the sharp, tinny drumbeat urging me on, bringing strength back to my fingers.

"Dear Dad," I wrote, in my neatest possible hand, "I've decided...maybe's Mum's right. Vancouver's nice, but — the rain, the rain really drives you nuts after a while. And the job, well.... So I've decided — could you...would you mind lending me the money for my ticket? I could be there by next week!! Thanks, I know you will. I love you. Oh, but one thing, okay? Please, *please* don't let Rick know."

DEPTH RAPTURE

The lab's a cocoon, like being inside a seed, a cell. No windows, no distractions; just the sound of running water, the squeak of my labmates' shoes on the scuffed floor. Stacked atop some metal shelves are buckets and nets, the prof's kayak; the sinks and counters crammed with things in bottles — chaos. But a week into the term I feel a weird bliss here, the same quiet peace you find lying on a beach. The same comfort, maybe, some people seek listening to windchimes or nature tapes, records of frogs and whales singing.

We don't talk while we work, Michael, Jennifer and I. Talking wrecks your concentration. One sharp, sudden laugh and I could foul up what I'm doing, tweezing tiny, wriggling larvae into a petri dish. I'm studying sea urchins, you see; part of my thesis is watching them reproduce.

"It stinks in here," Michael mumbles. Strange he'd notice — this is a guy who'd bring his dog to class if the prof hadn't told him to keep her outside. Michael's from Orillia, qualifying for med school. ("Some bedside manner *he'll* have," Jennifer jokes, behind his back.) For someone who wants to be a doctor, he seems kind of squeamish.

"I like the smell." I keep squinting at the squirmy specks in my dish. It's something you get used to, the scent of dead, fishy things, of algae left standing too long. After only a week, it's in my hair, my clothes. Even my socks smell. Yet I find it soothing, like the gurgle of water through the tanks, irksome at first as a toilet running, then lulling you to work.

"Coffee?" Michael mumbles, his silver Thermos beside him, surrounded by scummed-over cups and plastic bags. He brings fresh-ground from home — won't touch the stuff Jennifer and I buy from the basement vending machines. A couple of times I've seen Beulah, his golden retriever, tied next to them. "You never know what they put in that shit," he's always telling us.

I glance up and shake my head, wiping my hands on my jeans. He looks at me with disdain and wonder — same as when Perling, the professor, first threw us together, hoping, maybe, my interests would rub off.

Michael couldn't give a flying fuck about invertebrates, it's clear. Transparent as a specimen slide, he has a face that changes like clouds. He's tall and lanky, but it's not his body you notice so much as his face: long, strong-jawed, with very even white teeth. Then again it's not his features either, but the rosiness of his olive skin, his colouring that strikes you, that makes you think of the sky. He's not so much handsome as — God, I hate to say it — lovely. So lovely I felt sick when the prof put us in the same lab: jittery, unsure. Until the urchins put me at ease, stuck to their tanks like spiky green islands. And Perling too, a leprechaun in lumberjack clothes, stroking one like a pet, speaking in his soft, New England drawl:

"Barb Mossman, Mike Easton, Jennifer Boyd — I want you three in the urchin lab, the rest doing molluscs."

The Greek root of "plankton" means "wanderer", which is how sea urchins begin, as tiny, swimming larvae. For my honours thesis, I'm studying the adults — something bigger, more substantial. Studying cells is okay, but what drew me to biology in the first place wasn't the protozoan. Oh, I have immense respect for those who spend days gazing into microscopes — solving tiny pieces of the puzzle, as they say. Call me impatient, but I prefer a wider view.

My parents, though, weren't impressed when I phoned to tell them my topic — the ecology of urchins. "Good luck then, dear," Mum sighed, meaning: "My land, don't tell me you're becoming a professional student." Dad teased, "All that work, Barbie — on seagull food? Well, I s'pose it beats getting an MRS!" He'd happily forked over the money for tuition and rent for my bachelor apartment, glad just to have me back east again. "Well, I'm glad you've found your niche," Mum finally allowed before hanging up, still baffled.

Once I decided to return to school, it didn't take long to get back into the routine. Within a few weeks of leaving Vancouver, I was ready to hit the books. It was after I chose sea urchins the dreams started — only natural, perhaps.

Finning through a huge kelp forest, I slither and weave like a fish through ribboned fronds of weed. Horsetail kelp and devil's apron sway like trees in the soft, fluid breeze. Leather-tough, gelatinous as eyeballs, plants brush my skin. I'm wearing an orange bathing suit, one-piece, with a blue mask and snorkel. On my feet are matching flippers.

It's daylight, the forest full of shadow. Sunbeams flicker on the green rippled sand; plankton dance like confetti. Slippery as seaweed, I knife between thick, roped stems, supple as a moray eel.

I'm the only creature down here, or so it seems. Besides dazzling flecks of krill, no fish dart. Not so much as a sea-star or lobster creeps across the sand; no sculpins scud in and out, nothing so homely. No urchins either — which explains the kelp's proliferation.

If menace exists, it lurks farther out, where sand and light slope away. Where my frail human lungs will not take me, the water so deep and dark you need special equipment to touch bottom.

Perhaps the other creatures have simply been frightened off. It's not as if they're extinct, or non-existent here in the forest. I sense their presence somehow, hiding. The presence of life other than mine, palpable as the sun's filtered warmth. Yet it's their absence I notice — though underwater the eye falters, looking forward only, missing the periphery. Absorbing only part of the picture.

What I do know is that in the dream there are no predators; no creatures get hungry. I'm safe, perfectly safe, swimming down here alone. There's nothing to fear; my only feeling regret, vague but intrusive as a pulse, that I'm not wholly of this element, or the sea wholly mine.

Through the corner of one eye I detect movement. A diver appears, a black shape scooting above me. He has an undersea camera; peering down, he snaps a photo. "Don't stay down too long," he mouths before stroking away. Ascending, he resembles an oversized fly, the tanks on his back thick, folded wings.

Eventually I swim up for air. On the smooth blue surface there's no sign of him. Nothing. The water's warm as soup, the sun a lazy, slanting brilliance. I roll onto my back, warmth soaking into my belly, threads of rockweed and eelgrass wisping past like shredded clouds. The sea is thick and slow as the Sargasso, a pale blue bowl; the horizon encircling me a faint pencil-line meeting sky, and I a tiny floating petal.

The dream is so real — the swish of kelp, the water's *glug* against my eardrums — I wake needing to tell someone. Jennifer? Behind her wire-rimmed glasses are such steady, earnest eyes. Not that we're close, but she's the type who appreciates details. You can imagine her stopping to ask the colour of a certain weed or species of algae. But when I get to the lab there's only Michael.

It's not that I dislike him — I've seen him around campus with his friends, guys with the same careful messiness, like people always practising for something. Hard to tell what, except there's an ease about them, an air of everything being fun. You can imagine them in T-shirts saying *I never let school interfere with my education,* except that would be tacky. The last thing Michael is, is tacky.

He's bent over his microscope when I come in. Glimpsing his profile, I envision his face — its openness, the way expressions bloom and fade — and think maybe I'm being unfair. After all, there's something enviable about Michael's manner, so unlike what I grew up with: my mother's caution, for instance, as if the sky's waiting to fall. She's like the coyote on *The Road Runner,* Michael Easton, I can't help thinking, the lucky, smart-ass bird.

At my desk, I unload my backpack quietly as possible so as not to disturb him. Not that I'm too concerned about that — I'm just afraid if we start talking I'll let the dream slip, give myself away somehow. Like pulling a rock from a dam and having water gush out, I figure it could be dangerous. Michael's the last person you'd open up to.

He's wearing an expensive-looking button-down shirt, wrinkled, with faded jeans. Something about their colour reminds me of the sea in my dream, bleached and calm. I open my parasites text and start reading, glancing from time to time at his back, the neat, small vertebrae.

Remembering the cool, slippery feel of kelp, I bite my tongue, try focusing harder on the page. After a while Michael smiles over, pushing his hand through his hair.

"You have an early class?" He never says hello first; if Jennifer were here, she'd smirk. Far as she's concerned, Michael treats us equally — with the same polite (Jennifer says smarmy) dismissal he gives our experiments.

I close the book on my finger and cough. I can feel the salt, balmy wet on my back....

"Have you ever—" I start to say, without looking at him. Afraid, perhaps, to see his smile harden to mockery.

But he appears not to hear. When I finally glance over, he's looking down again, the back of his neck smooth and brown behind his collar. From my desk I can see a grimy smudge inside, which surprises me a little. For all his ease, he's the type who never wears something two days in a row — though we've all been putting in extra hours, writing our thesis proposals.

Michael seems too composed to sweat.

I pretend to keep reading, then clear my throat.

"You working on that invertebrates assignment?" It comes out timidly, half whispered.

"What?"

"Your invertebrates paper — how's it going?"

"Oh, that."

An awkward — sullen? — pause.

"I wasn't sure you were talking to me, that's all."

He leans against Jennifer's desk watching me, his sleeves rolled up. I can't help studying the fine black hairs on his forearms.

His cool hazel eyes drift to the urchin shells above my desk — green and purple, in various sizes, prickly to smooth. The animals themselves are missing, pecked out by gulls.

"Nice shells." For a second he looks embarrassed, at a

loss.

"Tests," I correct him, thinking of my research: how little you can tell about urchins by their exteriors. The sex, for instance, indeterminate from the outside.

"Goddamn things don't even have a cardiovascular." He shrugs and I have the weirdest sense of being challenged.

("Cell pathology," I heard him one day kibitzing with Jennifer. "Or parasitology — now *that's* useful. But this invertebrates stuff, talk about a bird course!")

I open my book and reach for one of my specimens. A pale mauve-green one, the delicate sun-washed shades of a watercolour; feather-light, perfect. Clearly visible are its five double rows of pinprick pores, symmetrical as a cut-paper lampshade's; the minuscule joints where the flexible spines were attached, prickly once as spruce needles.

"Useless little critters," he keeps on, and I see then he's teasing. He comes over and picks up my favourite thing, the miniature set of urchin teeth I found on a beach once, bleached white jaws shaped like a lantern. I cringe, the tiny, calciferous treasure in his slender fingers.

"Barely have the parts to reproduce," he sighs, setting it down again — with care, I notice, a feckless care.

Like a draft through my clothes, the dream returns: the absence of predators and prey, below in the kelp bed. There's mating, of course, but invisible: the silent, microscopic mingling of drifting cells.

"Have you ever—"

As I open my mouth, Michael reaches for another test, this one dark green and spiny, salvaged from the lab.

"Charming" — he doesn't know when to stop — "I can see how you'd get attached."

This is driving me nuts.

"The spines allow the animal to move and feed," I burst out, my ears hot. The amusement on his face melts into surprise.

"They pass specks of food to the mouth — like relief workers passing bags of rice." My voice sounds rough and offended. I feel instantly stupid.

"Whatever," he says, turning back to his microscope.

My face burns as I watch him prepare a slide, his long, deft fingers holding the tweezers, nudging something I can't see into a drop of water. His hands, I can't help noticing them — surgeon hands? Swallowing my distaste, I hear him sigh. A long, pissed-off sigh, as though such care, such precision, is just being wasted.

Later, the two of us are sent out collecting. God knows why Perling keeps pairing us off — he takes a queer delight in it, perhaps. Michael digs for his keys; I've seen him a few times off campus, driving a beat-up Volkswagen van.

"No, no, guys. I meant on foot." Perling holds up his hands in front of the class. "See what you can find within a couple blocks."

"I don't have time for this," Michael grouses, following me down the hallway. The science building is concrete, grey and labyrinthine as a beehive. Outside, the sun is brilliant, blinding after the dingy corridors.

"You got something in mind, Barbara?" The way he says my name sounds mannered, rehearsed. He strides beside me towards the street below the university.

Heading down the steep hill to the harbour's arm, I pretend not to notice the large, well-groomed houses and lawns — as if it's familiar territory and I, at least, have that much over him. He lags behind, taking things in. I sense his easy, unspoken approval and realize it's the sort of neighbourhood he feels comfortable in.

The pavement ends at the shore, rusty-looking rocks strewn with garbage. Tampon tubes litter the mud, condoms lapping like jellyfish at the water's edge. Amid the debris are shells, some slime-covered periwinkles and broken mussels.

Shoving his hands in his pockets, Michael stares at the spruces on the opposite side.

"You'd never see stuff like this where I come from," he finally says, nudging a bread bag with his foot. His sneakers are the flat black canvas kind with white rubber toes; they remind me of little boys.

I squat to turn over a rock, poking the mud with a stick. He stands over me, his eyes on my back. I can't help wondering if the bra lines show through my shirt.

"Perling says there's a pipe somewhere, pumping seawater up to the labs," I say, to make conversation. He smirks, gazing at the mud as if he's dropped something. A penny, maybe, or a gum wrapper, something of no consequence anyway, amid all the flotsam.

Straightening, I hold a tiny black periwinkle up to the sun. The animal inside blinks like an eye.

"Molluscs," I mutter, feeling myself blush. My fingers close around the shell. "It's echinoderms we want."

Michael gives me a strange look.

"You really like this stuff, don't you?"

Then I spy what I'm looking for, a fresh green urchin still wet, a yellow thread of guts inside, enough to put on a slide. I toss the periwinkle back, watch it skip once and sink.

The wind comes up, ruffling some gulls bobbing farther off, bright white specks on the brisk, sparkling blue. Michael shields his eyes, watching them.

"They like the sewage," I try once more, shrugging. He shakes his head, as if to ask: What galaxy did you say you're from?

"Bloody waste of time," he laughs, and goes back to class empty-handed.

That night I dream of fish, of diving in a tropical lagoon. The beach is a scorching white crescent fringed with palm.

First I must wade through waves of turquoise glass, cresting, breaking — heavy enough to knock me down. Salt tingles my hot, tanned skin. I'm wearing the same orange suit, the colour now faded from the sun baking down.

I'm not equipped to dive, have left the snorkel and flippers home, knowing they'd be useless in the surf. I've decided to take my chances, lured by hopes of an under-sea kaleidoscope.

The trick is getting under, timing my dive between rollers once I manage to get past my waist. Then it's sim-ply a matter of pinching my nose, kicking with one sharp thrust of my legs, my body slicing through the weight of curling froth; of pushing out, giving up on air.

Once I get going it's not difficult at all. Instantly the sand gives way to coral, bubbled pink ridges at first, razor sharp; then coned and crested, dotted with purple sponge, orange-fronded anemone. Sea-fans and stinging coral reach out like hands. I swim well above, to keep my belly from touching.

The turquoise deepens to blue, a deep Aqua Velva blue, alive with schools of fish above and below me, bright and shimmering as metal. A merry-go-round of angel-fish, yellow-striped goatfish, parrotfish electric blue, vio-let and gold, lurid as a black velvet painting. Purple pipe sponges, feathery mauve tubeworms petalled like daisies wave from mats of yellow coral. They tickle my arms, my legs. It's like watching a treasure chest spill open in space: a glittering, silent ballet, choruses of sea feathers waving from the wings, singing silence.

No need any more for air — for sound, any sound beyond the deliquescence of glass, this silent symphony. I take a seat on a mound of brain coral, clapping. My hands pulse together, slow-motion, palms barely touching. The current is gelid, soft as wind.

But just as I lose myself in the performance, something spooks the fish flashing past. They scoot for cover in folds of rock and mouths of coral. There's a greying, like cloud covering the sun, and looking up I see a school of hammerheads, shadows like torn laundry bent in a gale, the sky layered with their shapes. The absurdity of their jaws: hard, blunt tools that shatter the scene. Everything scurrying for shelter, the kaleidoscope split in a million blurred pieces.

In panic I shut my eyes, imagine their cool, scaleless skin touching mine; the dense, cold weight of their boneless bodies as they circle, blind. Their crude, unfocused eyes are like lights on the wingtips of a plane.

Lucky thing I haven't scraped or cut myself. No blood to draw them, or scent, here, out of my element. Or so I believe, a small reassurance.

I wait, then an odd thing happens. As if scared by thunder — its feel rather than sound, a rumbling through the deep — the sharks dissipate, finning off into thin air. Leaving only an empty, murky green.

Gazing up through the fuzzy strains of light, shielding my eyes for a better look, I see something descend, slowly, jerkily: a gleaming white saucer lowered notch by notch from a thick steel cable.

The sight fills me with awe. Behind the thick, wavy glass sits a man in an orange toque. It takes a minute to recognize his sharp, inquisitive face — the Gallic nose, the toque. He doesn't see me at first. I can tell he's busy concentrating, his hands on the controls but his mind outside, in the depths. From my hill of coral I wave —

cautiously, in case the movement brings back the sharks.

After a moment Captain Cousteau squints in my direction through a veil of fish, the slowly resumed carousel. Looking baffled, even slightly piqued, he raises a glass of wine, his lips pinched. Mouthing *"Salut!"* he throws a switch and the diving saucer quickly ascends, to a fading white mushroom-shape high overhead.

On the weekend Dr. Perling organizes a field trip outside the city. It's only mid-September; Jennifer and I look forward to a day in the sun, beachcombing. Michael gives us a ride in his van, the dog panting in the back. Leaving the city it's hot and sunny, but near the coast clouds thicken. Michael doesn't talk much as we bump along the patchy, winding road. Through the fog bright shapes loom, wisps of turquoise, red and yellow — sides of houses, mobile homes with tires on their roofs, rusted cars sitting in bare, rocky yards.

From time to time, checking the dog in the rearview, Michael catches my eye. Both of us look away, as Jennifer in the seat beside him harps on about urchin gonads.

The road to the shore is so riddled with potholes, the whole van rattles and shakes. I imagine bits of it strewn in the bushes with the parts of other dead cars. We park and start for the beach, a chain of white crescents strung like a necklace between outcrops of boulders.

The sand is banked with seaweed cast up from storms at sea — the ocean gearing for winter. There's an icy chill to the fog for which we're unprepared, wearing nothing but shorts and sweatshirts.

A raw wind whips the beach, numbing our hands and faces. Out of the greyness Perling's blue Volvo pulls up and Jennifer waves, her hair already in wet strings. Michael stands with his back to the heavy grey-green surf, his shoulders hunched for warmth. I wait for him to start complaining. Instead he whistles for Beulah, smiling as she bounds over heaps of kelp — so much of it I picture the sea floor scoured like linoleum. As the prof approaches, carrying large white buckets and cone-shaped green nets, my teeth start to chatter.

He glances around at the seaweed and shrugs.

"Doesn't look too promising, guys — with this kind of forestation I doubt we'll see much evidence of urchins. No urchins, no lobsters — few of their predators, in fact, though with growth this thick you'd have to figure out there's an ideal feeding ground...."

The theory is that urchins graze whole forests of kelp till not a shred remains, laying barren huge areas of ocean. Only when the urchins die off — killed by predators or parasites — will the kelp come back. An endless cycle, the classic chicken and egg.

Michael starts whistling again, not for the dog but perhaps to fill the silence. Heads down, we follow Perling to some granite ledges at the end of the beach, scaling rocky slabs towards a point where waves break and spray. It starts to drizzle, a fine cold mist that soaks our clothes and running shoes.

For a while the four of us comb the rocks, the wind cutting our faces. There isn't so much as a shard of urchin shell scrubbed white by wind and sea.

"It happens." Perling shrugs again, looking bemused. "We're dealing with nature here — another piece of the puzzle. So much *depends*. You have to realize coming back empty-handed sometimes is part of science."

The sky looks bruised, the wind driving rain down the beach. I glance at Michael, can just imagine what's going through his mind. The cold seems to sharpen his features; the hair plastered to his forehead makes his nose look bigger, his face set, somehow, in a way I haven't noticed before.

"Well, Barbara" — he looks over and grins, as if in some odd way he's caught me out. "You had enough of this yet, or what? If you want I can run you back to town."

Jennifer and Perling stay behind to sort through the weed. In the van Michael rubs his hands together, glancing over his shoulder at the dog. Bouncing back along the road, the noisy heater blasting, he whistles "Martha My Dear", as if it were just he and Beulah together. I breathe in, gazing at the goldenrod in the ditch, self-conscious but cosy somehow, comfortable in the warmth of the rickety old vehicle, fogged-up windows blocking out the cold.

Outside my apartment building, Michael keeps the motor running, his foot on the brake. But as I'm getting out he puts his hand on the back of my seat and looks at me, leaning close — close enough that I see the shiny dark bristles of beard, the amber flecks around his pupils. Something inside me snags, and for an instant I have the cool, quiet urge to lay my palm against his face — that's all — to see how it feels.

He smiles, his eyes still on mine as he tugs the van into gear and I hop out. Wondering, yes wondering, what on earth I've just allowed to happen.

Inside the apartment, when I go to dry my hair, I'm smiling — grinning like the Sphinx, actually. There's a funny tightness inside me, my breathing so shallow I tap my chest as I catch my eyes in the mirror.

Michael Easton, I tell my reflection. Of all people.

In the dream I'm wearing a wetsuit the colour and texture of tangerine skin. It's a brilliant tropical day, the sun burning directly overhead. I'm on the deck of the *Calypso*, standing over the diving bay. Tanks are strapped to my back, a mask being pulled over my head and fitted into place, the breathing apparatus hooked up.

Captain Cousteau has on an identical suit and mask, his keen eyes shining approval through the glass. He dangles his legs over the side, thin, strong frog's legs sprouting black rubber flippers. Holding up one hand, he gives a nod, then rolls in, descending quickly into the opaque green water.

We have decided to explore the vent of an ancient volcano, its cone submerged in a coral lagoon. The water's dark as a bottle of food colouring, so dense it looks black. The top of Cousteau's head resembles a dirty orange basketball. A few slow bubbles stir and pop the sea's surface.

The look of the water gives me the creeps but I swallow fear and, closing my eyes, leap in. Reaching out both arms, I spread my fingers wide, feeling my way through the thick, fluid night. In their black neoprene gloves my hands seem webbed.

Breathe, breathe, don't forget to breathe — Cousteau's instructions, his lively accent, replay themselves. My eyes search for his orange shape but find no sign of him. Yet I know he's down there somewhere, and try to keep calm.

Dark shapes float past — no fish, only feathery scraps of weed at first, then clots of algae. Even through the regulator I can smell the strong fishy stench of rotting plants. They drift and waver through the darkness like veins of ink trapped in dark green Jell-O. They cling to my wetsuit, a pale, murky yellow in the turbid, airless water.

The algae is so thick the sun can't penetrate. It gets thicker the deeper I go — like falling slow-motion down a dark, endless well. My hands reach for bearings but there's nothing to grasp, only the slippery black decay bursting in slow, soggy clouds at my touch.

Cousteau is nowhere to be seen. Panic builds inside me like trapped air. Bubbles rise in a lazy chain: languid, eerie. As if dressed with nowhere to go, they stall, disappear into nothing.

The water feels viscid. A stinging starts under the edges of my mask and where the gloves meet my sleeves. My eyes burn; I have a terrible urge to rub them.

Then something beyond me jerks — a strong, quick motion in the fetid gloom. Cousteau's suit bobs into view as he scissors up from the depths.

His eyes closed, he grimaces in pain. He doesn't see me — his eyes are squeezed shut — but senses me. One hand clutching his air hose, he waves frantically, a wild, exaggerated gesture as if flagging a plane. Though my eyes are stinging — raw as peeled bladders of weed — I glimpse his face long enough to catch the message: "*Vite! Vite!*" Without further thought I obey, muscles spurting to action, my legs propelling me upwards. Knowing now there's nothing down there, nothing but the acids of death.

Slowly, slowly, we climb to safety, millimetre by millimetre, millisecond by millisecond, a painstaking ascent towards light. Looming above: a sieved luminescence; water the colour of leaves, the sun-scalded surface. We burst forth, air and skin blazing with gilded heat; blind.

Aboard the *Calypso*, the crew peel off our wetsuits, bring Evian water to flush our eyes. Sight returns, though hours later they still smart. That night at dinner we squint as we eat and sip wine, the cabin bathed in candlelight.

Slumped slightly, his gestures small, diminutive, Cousteau describes what we've seen to the others. *The Dead Zone*, he calls it. But they're only half listening, lulled by full stomachs, the ship's gentle rocking.

The next week Michael and I are sent out in the field again. It's a fine fall day, the sky high and cloudless. Perling suggests sites where we might have better luck, anxious,

perhaps, to make up for last time. Because of the weather
— a burnished warmth, leaves just starting to turn —
Michael chooses the farthest place from the city, a rocky
bay an hour or two beyond the first. We need all day,
which means skipping classes. Nothing we can't make
up later, Michael says. For some reason he leaves Beulah
home; "She gets jealous," he jokes, loading gear into the
van.

This time I've come prepared with a jacket and duck
boots, a pair of jeans should the weather change. As I
climb in beside him, he glances at my knees, sturdy and
brown below my hiking shorts. I clap my hands over
them, but his eyes linger, sliding — approvingly, it seems
— to my ankles, the work socks rolled over the tops of
my hiking boots. Our eyes meet. *Yes?* I think, looking
straight at him.

"Think we could just tell Perling we went, and bug-
ger off someplace instead? Tell him we looked but couldn't
find anything?" Seeing my dismay, he makes a face. "Just
a joke, Barbara — you've got to learn to lighten up."

For most of the drive we don't talk, but it's not an
awkward silence, no. More the easy quiet of two people
with the same thing in mind. A couple of times we
take wrong turns and end up in people's yards, mangy-
looking dogs racing out, teeth bared, charging at the
wheels.

"Man, Beulah'd have a field day, wouldn't she?"

Stupid dog, I can't help thinking, feeling mean for
doing so.

Finally our bay comes into sight, a broad blue inlet
surrounded by rocky cliffs. The road winds past a white
church named Stella Maris, a graveyard with rough
wooden crosses; small, peeling houses with lawn orna-
ments out front, plywood Snow Whites and the Seven
Dwarfs. Michael drives past without seeing — or perhaps

he's just being polite, not commenting.

We follow Perling's directions to the end of a road, a short stretch of sand bordered by white granite. A blackened rope of seaweed shows the high-tide mark, studded with crab claws and bits of shell, a dried purple sea-star. I follow Michael to the water. It's crystal-clear, cold as melted iceberg. Flecks of mica sparkle in the gentle wash of waves.

The bay is sheltered from the ocean, perfectly flat, a serene, pale blue. A soft wind rustles the bushes on the hill above. Without looking back, Michael makes for the rocky shelves ahead in search of tidal pools. There's a purpose to his walk, a determination this time, perhaps, not to return empty-handed.

I follow, my boots leaving faint impressions in the fine, wet sand. Michael swings a pail, a big one from the lab. In it he's packed other things — zip-lock bags, a couple of nets better for scooping fish than the creatures we seek. On the rocks lie scattered bits of urchin shell, some still with spines, others chalky as unglazed porcelain. I feel suddenly foolish, ill equipped. If urchins habitate here, they likely lie in deep beds offshore.

The sun is strong for September, yet the water too frigid to consider swimming. Michael marches ahead, the muscles of his calves knotting as he leaps from rock to rock. A chill ripples through me — care? He's not thinking about jumping in, surely.

When I catch up, he has set down the bucket and found a sheltered gap in the rocks, a crevice where the sun funnels down amid the granite. He's unbuttoned his shirt, is spreading it out on the rock.

"What are you doing?" I sound like Jennifer: wary, suspicious. Impatient, too, dazed as I am by the sun, the effort of clambering over boulders.

"We've got all day," he says, smoothing a place

beside him. I think of his shirt, its soft weave against the grainy rock. He reaches into his packsack and pulls out a green apple, a Swiss Army knife. Carefully, quickly, he divides it, handing me half. His fingers are tanned, his nails very clean, with perfect, pale half-moons. He leans back against the rock, munching.

"This isn't like you — you're usually in such a hurry," I say between bites, as he tosses away his core. We watch it roll and disappear down a crack.

He looks piqued somehow, almost offended. I open my mouth to explain — and he reaches for me, pressing my back to the rock. I swear in that moment I stop breathing, the only certainty the rough warmth through my T-shirt. Every nerve roused, alert, as he puts his hands to my face and pulls me close. His lips are warm and dry, his breath cidery, vaguely bitter too, like strong black coffee.

"There," he says, in a soft, soft voice, warm as the sun in my ear; coaxing. He doesn't need to — I'm ready, have been for some time, I realize, the knowledge stiffening in me like the breeze shirring the ocean.

"What's wrong?" he asks.

"Nothing. Nothing." I shut my eyes and imagine his hands are the sun, a yellow strength spreading everywhere.

He is quick and agile, adept at getting us out of our clothes, arranging them on the rock like a lumpy quilt. I melt to his touch as he enters me, his back smooth and warm under my nails.

I would like to see the expression in his eyes — whatever it is taking shape, passing over — but he keeps them closed, lashes like spiders on the hollows beneath. Without his eyes I haven't a clue.

"Barbara," he says a couple of times, moving against me. "Oooh, Barbara."

Afterwards I notice the freckles on his shoulders. He

throws on his clothes, almost shyly. Starts singing that silly Beach Boys song "Barbara Ann" under his breath, not quite to himself.

"Don't make fun," I mutter, zipping my shorts. Aware now how easily someone could stumble upon us, this place in the rock so open and exposed. I feel grumpy, shamed; afraid, of all stupid things, to look at him, to see his easy smile.

Michael quits rolling up a sleeve, giving me a puzzled, horrified look. The cuff flops as he reaches out to squeeze my shoulder.

"Fun? For *shit*sake, Barbara — whatever would make you think I was making fun?"

He holds out his hand to help me up the rockface, the two of us staggering a little under the dazzle. We start searching for tide pools but there aren't any, the bay too sheltered for waves to reach that high. But we do find urchins — the remains of them — still wet from the sea, a couple of large tests almost intact. The sated gulls nowhere in sight.

We don't talk much, wrapped now in a wordless comfort. Michael holds the bags open as I drop in the specimens, gently as though the animals were still inside. We lose ourselves, combing the shore for shards and remnants till the sun shifts and the bay darkens, a deepening chill rising from the water.

I have this crazy longing that the day never end, that we might keep wandering along this coastline and beyond, to the next small cove, and the next...just keep going.

Then Michael asks, "You figure that's enough now? Think this'll keep Perling off our backs for a while?"

"Live ones would've been better."

Michael shakes his head, mimicking Perling's laugh.

"So much just *depends*," he shrugs, turning back

towards the van.

Back in the lab I lose track of time. Hours flow past like water. Hours and hours of poking at tiny grey larvae, watching for growth. Out of the dishful of larvae I cultivated, only a few still squirm. I hold it up to the light to make double sure, the thick glass bottom scummed with what looks like something from the bottom of a fridge. After a while the eye trips into seeing movement where there's none. A window would help, some natural light.

"God, if we had some air in here...," I complain to Jennifer. "No wonder the things keep croaking like flies."

"You could try growing some more," she sighs, distant, remote, as if threatened by my restlessness. Both of us know how useless her suggestion: even in the lab urchins go into a reproductive hibernation, hold off producing eggs and sperm now till spring, the end of the school year.

This is ridiculous, but I'm close to tears. I feel as though I live here, in this airless, windowless room. Today is Tuesday; I only know because we had a parasites quiz. But I couldn't tell you what it's like outside, rainy or dry, day or evening.

I can't recall the last time I showered or had a full night's sleep — or the last time I dreamed. It's as though every brain cell, every ounce of concentration, is tuned now to work. No thought left for dreaming, as if that part of my mind has absconded. Or maybe I'm just too tired to dream.

I wait for Jennifer to share some of her larvae — God knows she has enough to spare. She watches them like a mother her babies, feeding droppersful of microscopic food, her tongue between her teeth, concentrating. But she doesn't so much as offer, groaning when Michael comes in and drops his books on the counter. I half expect her to start cooing at the squiggly things in her petri dish, turning a blind eye when he spills the coffee pouring out a couple of cups. He ignores her, handing over my mug, the extra one he's brought from home.

"You work too hard," he says, kneading my shoulders. His fingers smell vaguely of formaldehyde. "What you need, Barbara, is some fresh air."

The sound of running water is like the urge to pee, the lab itself a brook that neither swells nor slows. Michael's right — the steadiness, the *closeness*, is enough to make you stir-crazy.

On the way out I glance at my adult urchins sturdy and round as stones. Not one has moved or changed since I last checked, sometime before the quiz. In captivity some have grown long, furry spines — sharp as pins to the touch but too weak to fend off enemies.

Carrying my coffee, I follow Michael down the hall to the fire exit. He holds the door long enough for me to slip outside blinking, stunned to see daylight. To hear birds, the soft rumble of traffic. The laughter of students walking to class.

Before my pupils adjust, I reach for him. But already he's clinking his mug with his nails, saying he's got an anatomy class. I gulp down the gritty dregs and we saunter back to the lab.

When we come in Jennifer doesn't turn around. Michael stops long enough to grab some books, giving my waist a squeeze on his way out. I take a deep breath, determined to forget the mess in the petri dish. I go over to a tank, dip my hand in to check the temperature: a perfect, steady chill. It must be all right — the urchins haven't moved a hundredth of a millimetre.

Perhaps it's the sound of the water that makes them sleep.

ASPIRATIONS

B oys are murder on the furniture, not to mention the Gyproc. I've got four, you see, ages two to eight, so I should know. And after the morning I've had! Box spring caved in from kids jumping on it, toilet overflowed because someone flushed a toy cannon — lucky I got the mess mopped up before it went through the kitchen ceiling. And snow, snow for the seventh bleeding day in a row. When I looked out and saw that, I thought, "If I don't get outta the house I'll—" That's when I decided we'd go bowling. Kids'll get a kick out of it, I figure. It'll get me out, plus give them something to do.

So here we are killing time till the Bowlarama opens, another half-hour to go. Me a human coat-rack in the middle of the mall, trailing snowsuits and scarves. Kids squalling over who rides next in the Space Shuttle Discovery — a small white replica, of course. The security guard keeps walking past; I don't like the way he's eyeing us. I'm just waiting for him to waltz over and ask us to move on. But so far he hasn't said boo, not yet anyway. Probably he feels sorry for me.

I've already spent a bagful of quarters, see, watching

each child take a turn in the tiny cockpit, getting jerked up and down. Jason — my oldest — has already snapped off a piece of the wing. Darrell Jr.'s dumping slush from his boots onto the seat.

"Jason. Jason, put that down, please. Honey? Honey, no. Don't. I said, *don't.*"

Oh *sugar* — here comes that security guy again, mouthing things to his walkie-talkie. Maybe we should've stayed home; the kids could've trashed the place. No.

Don't get me wrong, now — it's not like our house is *Better Homes and Gardens.* If I'd stuck out my degree maybe it could be, but I've been too busy raising kids to worry about a real job, one that pays. Though Darrell — that's my husband — says if I applied myself, the typing I learned first year would come back, enough to make me a receptionist. But for now it's scrimp and save, scrimp and save, so I can stay home with the boys.

Which is why the kitchen's the same harvest gold as when we bought the place, and the rec room panelling still needs redoing. I'm ashamed to say that hole's been there since last summer when Darrell Jr. — the second-youngest — drove his Tiny Tots forklift through it and his older brother Joshua tried fixing it with his dad's hammer. That happened in a thunderstorm. Kids were so cooped up, I tried not to blow my top. I mean, you could hardly blame them. But Darrell went wild. "Kids'll be kids," I kept saying to calm him down. That's what he always throws at me when I'm fit to tear my hair out.

"Relax, they're just havin' fun," he says, even when he knows my period's due and I could rip their heads off but I go scrub the toilet instead. I chant it to myself — a mother's mantra: *just having fun, just having fun* — working the grunge off the seat with an old toothbrush. The boys often miss, see. I grew up in a houseful of girls, so I'm sure my mother didn't have this problem. I'm just scared Joey, the youngest, will find the brush under the sink some day and try it on his teeth.

"No honey, don't lick slush off the floor," I tell him now, shifting from foot to foot. The things in my arms smell like an old, wet dog.

The security man hovers nearby, behind some plants. Voices crackle over his two-way radio. Shit, I think, as his eye catches mine through the palm fronds, and Jason stuffs the chunk of wing in my pocket.

"Jason! NO!"

"Mom? MOM? I thought we were goin' bowling, Mom. MOM?"

"How much longer, Mom? MOM?"

"Yeah, Mom. I wanna go bowling! Now, Mom. I wanna go bowling NOW!"

Beady and narrow, the man's eyes stay on me as he holds the radio to his ear, listening. With his free hand he strokes his moustache, wide and stiff-looking as a whisk, then the top of his head, a shiny pink dome under his sparse, broom-straw hair.

There's something familiar about him, I can't help but think — I mean, beyond all the times he's walked by. Something that'll bug me till I put a finger on it. But I can't, and I don't like to stare. Someone I went to high school with, maybe? Though usually they recognize me and speak first: "*Marilyn? Marilyn Guthro?*"

Joey starts crying because Joshua won't share his gum. I grab a piece and shove it between his little white teeth. Behind the palms the crackling stops. When I look up the fellow's gone, marching off towards Zellers.

"No honey, don't swallow it," I say five or six times, squinting so I can read the sign in Suzy Shier. Stirrup pants and tank-tops, $14.99 and up. I'd have to drop twenty pounds first, I think. Guilt shoots behind my ears like a wasp sting.

Exercise class — I skipped it again today so I could take the kids out, something special for a change. I didn't want to park them in front of the TV at Darlene's again. Really, I didn't feel like forking over the ten bucks for her to sit there and eat the kids' Chee-tos. That pudgy daughter of hers, too — Brandy — the child lives on junk. Besides, I couldn't face my perky instructor, the one with the permanent smile. Not that it's the smile I mind so much — though frankly I don't get it. What's to smile about, watching a bunch of overweight sleep-walkers do leg-raises and sit-ups when you know they'd rather be home eating Mars bars? She's probably gloating, that's what it is: Get a load of *this*, girls. Twenty-inch waist, belly like pavement. No lard-arse here.

She'd be right, too. Not a dimple of cellulite on those thighs, I can't help but marvel when she does jumping-jacks with her back turned. But you know what? It's not her trim little body that bugs me. Not even her perfect perm or perfect red nails. No, it's more the look of her teeth when she curls back her lips to yell, "Wup, wup." That's to make us jump higher.

I couldn't've stomached those teeth today, not after the toilet and everything else. So that's why I'm willing to wait as long as it takes the Bowlarama to open. Twenty more minutes. Heck, maybe we'll stay there for lunch and all afternoon, too. All-you-can-eat pizza and free shoes for each string bowled. Five bucks a kid. If they behave. If the security guy doesn't throw us out first.

Darrell would say we can't afford it. But what's a little treat now and then? Besides, I'm desperate, I *need* to be out of the house. I'm having what Oprah would call a bad-hair day, normal now my perm's grown out. I want to get it cut at Aspirations, see. Though the name makes me think of a cat ralphing a hairball. Or Darrell's brother, Russy, who almost choked to death once on his own vomit. Aspirate: I think that's the word the cops used when they called Glad — my mother-in-law — from the drunk tank.

Darrell says I should take the scissors to the bathroom and give myself a trim. He's even offered to watch the kids so I can take my time getting off all the ratty ends. But no, I think I'll wait till the baby bonus comes and treat myself. Till then I'll keep my hat on in public. It's not so bad — a ski toque Darrell's mom gave Jason for Christmas. He won't wear it, and I like hot pink.

"Mom, Mom. How much longer? How much longer, Mom, how much longer?" he whines, starting a chain reaction.

"Yeah, how much longer, how much longer?" They're all clamouring now, tipped off like a set of candlepins.

"Fifteen more minutes," I yell, snatching the wad of green gum from Joey's mouth before he swallows it.

The smell of cigarettes wafts from the food court and my eyes start to sting. You'd think I'd be immune — Darrell's up to two packs a day now. Stress, he says. Things aren't too rosy down at the terminal. He's already been laid off twice, once in Toronto and once down here.

He was in a union up there, see, big plant making mud-flaps on Eastern Avenue. Jason was just an infant. When Darrell was on days I'd bundle the baby up and push the stroller across the Queen Street bridge, watch the cars whiz up and down the Don Valley Parkway. We'd go into Bargain Harold's, spend hours looking at tinned goods, dish soap and baby socks.

Every afternoon we did this, till Jason started grabbing things off the shelves. But it got me out of the apartment. I had no friends and the Eaton Centre made me too lonesome. Lonesome and sick, actually, swarms of teenagers reminding me of my life, once, when my old friend Barb and I used to hang around. Before I got married, before she and I lost touch.

Last time I heard from her was when I had Jason. She sent him the funniest gift, this little satin ball with tiny men holding hands around it — cute, but more of an ornament than a toy. I was scared shitless he'd choke on the men. Can't remember now if I ever wrote back to thank her, it was such a weird thing to give a baby. Jason loved it, though; I hung it over his crib like a mobile, till he got big enough to pull himself up.

Anyway, those mall kids made me think of being a teenager. Pushing the stroller, I'd feel hot and itchy as if wearing someone else's clothes. Like I'd gone to bed one night and woken up in my mother's stretchies.

There were no teenagers in Bargain Harold's. And it was cosier than the Eaton Centre, though it meant passing the drunks outside the strip joint by the bridge. Me so scared of getting vomit on the wheels.

So I was just as glad, after a year or so, when Darrell got laid off — though of course I didn't tell *him* that. We moved back here and right away he got on at the container pier. His brother's best friend works there and helped him get hired.

Then I kept getting pregnant.

Well, there's a bit more to it than that. After Jason I wanted a girl: someone to dress up in little white shoes and pink jogging suits. Someone to trade recipes with when I got old. Darrell didn't care what the kids were, so long as I was the one changing the Pampers.

I nearly haemorrhaged to death with Joshua. And when I heard Darrell Jr. was a boy — right there on the delivery table, my feet still in the stirrups — I said I didn't want to see him. While they were stitching me (his head was so big, nearly tore me apart) I told them to wrap him up and send him to my sister-in-law — Darlene, Russy's wife. And Darrell, looking like a spaceman in those green hospital booties and mask, went over to the nurse and took the baby. The only one he ever held when it was first born. I nearly rolled off the table, half stitched, scared he'd snap the neck. But he seemed to know to hold the head, though it beats me where he learned.

So after a while I came around and had Joey. By then I didn't mind him being another boy. I figured raising him would be like Darrell's old job grabbing mud-flaps off a conveyor belt and drilling some holes, then flinging them down to the next guy for stamping. What else could I have done with all the sweatpants and grey-striped socks piling up in the basement, barely worn before they got outgrown?

But after Joey I got my tubes tied. I mean *right* after Joey, from the delivery room to surgery. Seemed like they just finished sewing me up when they took the knife to me. But I was glad. The extra pain didn't hurt a bit, neither did the stunned look on Darrell's face. I just hoped it'd be the last time I'd get poked there or have my parts on display, for a baby or anything else. Was I dumb.

"Joey! Joey, put that DOWN!" — he's found an old piece of bubblegum under the spaceship — "NOW!" I holler, as he starts to pop it in his mouth.

They've all got their boots off and Darrell Jr. has chucked his mitts down the escalator. Joshua's doing circuits around the plants, and Jason's trying to unwire the little red light on the ride.

"Mom. MOM! Can we go now? Puuhhllleeeease? It must be open. It HAS to be open!"

"Eight minutes. Just eight more minutes."

"MOM!!!"

"Seven."

The girl in Suzy Shier keeps shooting me dirty looks. A woman with shiny bobbed hair strolls past with a little girl in a pink snowsuit. She lifts her eyebrow and yanks the child in a wide loop around us. You don't know the half of it, I feel like hissing at her. You don't know the—

Nobody does, I tell myself when I'm home, drinking cold coffee at the kitchen table. Trying to tune out the Lego crashing to the floor, the Ninja Turtles sailing through the air, bashing the fridge.

"Come on, guys. Six more minutes."

Hiking Joey onto my hip, I herd them towards the escalator. Darrell Jr. whines to be high up too, so I hoist him on my other arm. The other two stumble behind, hanging off my coat.

"Now you have to promise, *promise,* you'll behave."

At the top of the escalator I set Darrell Jr. down and grab his hand. Then I notice something hanging from Joshua's sleeve — a bigger, sleeker piece of wing this time, like the dorsal fin of a shark. Wrenching it from him, I haul them back to the spaceship. While Joey scoops dirt from a planter I almost manage to reattach it.

But not before Security comes. I sense him at first, a blue-grey blur behind me; feel those slippery-looking eyes burn through my toque. The kids have gone dead still. Smoothing the ends of my hair, I slowly straighten to face him. Under his light blue shirt he wears a white T-shirt, which makes me think of a cleaner. The hem of one grey pantleg is dragging. When he opens his mouth, his breath smells like an ashtray.

"What's the problem, lady?" he says. His voice bored and put-upon as if it's the zillionth time he's had to come and rescue the spaceship. He looks right through me, past my kids as if they're not even there.

Problem!? I feel like blasting the guy.

Next he'll ask if they're all mine. I get that all the time in malls, see, total strangers coming up and asking. You don't know me from the next mall-crawler, I always want to answer back.

His eyes drift to my son trying to stick on the other piece of wing. I want to slap Joshua's mittened paw, but something stops me. Cold.

The eyes, it's the eyes, sludgy and brown as furnace oil. I should've known. Once I would've recognized them anywhere. The moustache too, though the hair's so thin now I wouldn't've thought.... The roll of flab above his belt — that's new, too. I have to remind myself it's been twelve years. At least.

"Boys! BOYS!" I yell, but it does no good. They've come unfrozen, gone back to crawling in and out of the Discovery, swinging off the nose. Their noise could be five blocks away; I scarcely hear it.

I'm back in university; my best friend, Barb, and I have just moved away from home and gotten an apartment together. A bit small, but reasonable. Clean, if you over-look the smell of cat pee in the foyer. After a month or two of school, she and I throw a party, invite the people who sit near us in class — nobody we know too well. Only a few turn up and all five of us sit in the dark listen-ing to my Cat Stevens records, Barb and me too mopey to dance because *he* never shows up, this guy we know from the cafeteria. Not a student, exactly, but older; the type who spends a lot of time drinking coffee — says he does something in the library. A heart-throb.

Afterwards, Barb and I tell each other he probably would've laughed at our music anyway, figuring he'd like Deep Purple, and decide maybe it's a good thing he didn't come. A cloud with a silver lining, as I try to point out. It's not long after that Darrell and I first get together.

"That's *enough*, guys! Settle down."

But there's more: Barb and me in the campus pub, with a tableful of draft. She gets up to go to the can, winking over her shoulder at me. He's at the next table, see. And while she's taking her time putting on more mascara, he slides over and helps himself to my beer....

He puts his arm around me and next thing I know we're in Point Pleasant park, sitting at a picnic table in the fog. I can't believe my luck! I don't think about Barb alone in the pub, as he pulls a couple of beers from the case at our feet. But before I can take a sip, he's all over me like a wet shirt. One hand down the neck of my peasant blouse, his tongue half-way down my throat.

I could unravel, I could, right here in the middle of the mall. The whole of me, come apart at the seams and unravel like a chunky-knit sweater, the kind made on fat needles, with holes so big it takes no time to undo. Unravel till the only thing left was a pile of kinky wool — plus the pom-pom, maybe, from Jason's hat.

Mr. Security looks me in the eye and for a second I know he recognizes me.

"Kids got cabin fever, eh?"

That's all he says as more garbled messages spark over the walkie-talkie on his hip. He shrugs and shoves his hands in his pockets, eyes like a lizard's watching Joshua give up on the scrap of wing and biff it into the plants.

"You wanta tell 'em to take 'er easy, okay? Tell 'em this isn't a playground?"

Voices keep jumping, sputtering, breaking up, till he reaches down and switches the thing off. Then without another word, no warnings or threats, he moves off, not exactly running or walking either, towards the supermarket.

"Come on, Mom! It's gotta be time now. The Bowl-arama's *gotta* be open by now." Jason grabs my hand and for once I'm glad he's so wilful.

After the park, buddy drives me back to the apartment. Barb's not home; I guess she's still at the pub. As soon as the door shuts, he's all over me again, pushing me down this time on the living-room davenport. It's a one-bedroom place, all we can afford.

I push him off and jump to my feet.

"I'm not sleeping with you — tonight," I announce, quavering a bit at the sound of my voice. The look on his face, as though I'd just sloshed beer in it!

He gets up and skulks to the door like a dog wanting out. Except there's this hot, smarmy look in his eyes. Stung. Disgusted. And as he twists the knob, I panic and blurt out the first thing that comes to mind: my phone number. Start reeling it off, like saying: "Screw you tomorrow for a hamburger today."

"Mom! It's open, Mom! The lights are on, I can see 'em! Come on, come *on!* Let's *go!"*

And all these years I've been so proud of telling that guy — you know, his name escapes me now — I was no one-night stand. At least that's how I liked to remember it, especially once I met Darrell. With him it was all or nothing, first date. One night out at a movie, then BINGO! Next we're doing it on the Hide-A-Bed, Barb in the bedroom with the door closed, listening to eight-tracks.

Somehow we make it down the escalator, kids hopping and doing armstands on the rubber handrail. They're just opening the doors to the Bowlarama, a hot whiff of cigarettes, Coke and shoe deodorizer hitting us as we pour in.

"Two lanes, please," I tell the man at the counter. "One with bumpers. And shoes, we need shoes; one adult, four kids." He makes me repeat the sizes, but that's okay, we have time to burn. We're the only ones here; we have our pick of lanes. We can stay for ever if we want, the man yells over as I dump boots and snowsuits on the curved plastic bench.

And we very nearly do, too. I give myself up, no problem; lose myself in the low, rolling thunder of balls, the echoing clatter. I forget everything, really, watching the kids take turns, sometimes lobbing the ball across the next lane. They love it, of course; pretend they're firing cannons at straight white armies. And there are no rules — I just let them keep throwing till each set's a strike.

THE TAROT READER

I t's like being married to a spider, I think, watching
Michael get into his jogging suit. Curled on my side
with the duvet pulled up, I watch him work the black
spandex over his knees, his hips, tucking his parts into
place. (He never wears underwear with it — that would
ruin the effect.) I watch him push his arms in, then his
shoulders, like a kid wriggling into a snowsuit, except
lithe, almost sinister, his arms and legs shiny black sticks.
The villain in a cartoon show. Except that my husband's
a good guy — a miracle-worker to his patients, a cardi-
ologist. A heart man.

"See you tonight, Barbara." He bends over my pillow,
gives my cheek a quick peck. His lips feel cold though
he's just out of the shower. He hovers beside me for a
second like a machine idling, silent. Same routine as always, every morning of our seven-year marriage: Michael
slipping out at dawn for a five-mile jog before heading to
school, now the hospital.

In the days before children he used to run with the
dog; I'd wake to the sound of her clicking down the hall,
tail thumping the floor to go out, then silence. After a

while I'd get up and eat breakfast, glance at the paper before going to work. I had a job in a lab at the university; it paid the rent while Michael studied. Slicing a grapefruit, I'd have to remind myself to save him the other half — that's how much we saw of each other. But in a way it kept things interesting, until the kids came along. Just hang in there, I'd tell myself then: one more year — year after year. Hang in till he's done his residency, and all the waiting will pay off. That's how we managed, though God knows now I wonder if my head was screwed on straight.

He missed our daughter's birth because of exams; the entire pregnancy with our son he was on call. "It'll get better," Michael would whisper, getting up for his jog, when Tyler was colicky and I would fall into bed after walking the baby all night and comforting Amy from nightmares. "It'll get better" — but if it has, it's only as far as the money.

The kids never see him. Till lately it hurt, competing with strangers for his attention. More and more, though, it's like a pain near a filling that just goes away. A habit that fades to relief.

"Barbara?" He nudges my shoulder and, as I open my eyes, drives his fingers into the gloves matching his suit. Fingers most at home gloved, I think.

"Yes *darling?*" It sounds like a slur, though that's not my intention. Michael sighs.

"Got a bypass at four so don't hold dinner. I'll grab something on the way home." It's meant as a concession.

"Oh. Yeah, okay."

Then he's off, a shadow slipping out the front door. I picture him sprinting down the sidewalk past driveways, the contours of his bum neat and taut as his thighs, not an extra ounce anywhere.

"Not bad," his friends say, "for a guy who's forty. When the rest of us, ha-ha, are into relaxed-fit jeans." And they're right. Except for the grey hairs you'd never guess Michael's age as he runs along the street, arms pumping like pistons. Legs scissoring like the pieces in Tyler's Meccano set.

No, I take that back — that implies something humble, endearing. I prefer to imagine Michael in white rubber gloves wielding instruments over an open chest, the roiling red mess of somebody's heart.

I burrow under the covers waiting for the kids to stir, a reason to get up. It's March break, so Amy's off school. I'd stay in bed all day if I could, if there were someone else to make breakfast for her and Tyler, someone to dress and play with them, ferry them around on errands. Of course Michael and I can afford help now. But then where would that leave me?

Marry a doctor, my mother always coached, back when I was at university. Even then her advice was embarrassing, but I fell for it just the same. Finding a guy like Michael, his future gleaming, was like winning the 6/49, gift-wrapped. Nobody said I'd end up like part of the packaging, a doctor's wife. My life, a glossy, perfect bow.

The kids start cooing and chirping from their beds and for a second I picture Michael again. Jogging in the park, his Nikes on the frozen pine needles. Nobody around but other joggers, professionals like him, and people walking dogs — big glossy purebreds, never beagles or mutts, not at this hour. Michael's breath fogs the air beneath the branches. He doesn't slow down. He just nods to these people he sees each morning, nods without smiling, like a Doberman in his spandex suit.

If he misses anyone, I bet it's Beulah, our ancient,

drooling Lab. Only time I've ever seen him cry, when we had to have her put down. He'd have gone right out and bought a pup, but Tyler was just born, and of course there was the expense. "Kids need a dog, and once you got it house-trained, Barb, it'd make great company — you could start taking it for runs!" His less than subtle suggestion I could shed a few pounds, my baby weight. I finally put my foot down: no pets, not until the children are grown. And no early-morning jogs — not for me.

You see, I'm no runner. Not once in our lives together have I gone running with Michael, not even before the kids were born. But I've seen him, sprinting past the shops on Spring Garden Road, giving people a terse little nod. Former patients, some of them. They beam and nudge their wives, and watch him disappear. *A young fella who practises what he preaches*, they say. *Some good shape, that Dr. Easton.*

I get the same from the other wives. *He's incredibly fit,* they cluck, checking to see if I'm wearing the latest from Mills' window; warming slightly if I'm not.

What's your excuse? their eyes say. *He's the one under stress.*

Yeah, stress. So much stress that he hasn't touched me in weeks. But like the long hours, the wrecked weekends, it matters less and less — I've known for a long time that I made a mistake. I suspected it soon after the wedding, when Michael got accepted to med school. And later, when he decided to go on and specialize.

How was I to know? This was a guy who brought his dog to class when we first met, when people still did that. It was fourth-year biology. Beulah was a big golden Lab who slept at Michael's feet. Instead of a collar, she had a red bandanna tied around her neck, cowboy-style. It was Beulah caught my eye first, though I've never been a dog person — I tolerated her lying on his futon and, later, slobbering on the kitchen floor.

The kids come in and start bouncing on the bed, their hair tangled and eyes full of sleep. I pull them under the covers, smell their warmth through flannelette, their icy feet on my shins. I hug them until they squirm and wiggle away, pulling off the duvet. I lie there among the twisted sheets a few minutes longer, concocting lists, lists of things to do, to give the day shape. Dry-cleaning to pick up and groceries, always groceries. Errands, a trip to the mall. Either that or stay home, building toy railroads and making Play-Doh pies.

I dress quickly and make the bed, fluff the shams, adjust the balloon shades. The list in my head grows: pick up Michael's tweed jacket, buy salad things and maybe something nice to eat later (tomorrow?) with Michael once the kids are asleep, a bottle of sparkling wine. At least he still has the occasional glass, though he tells everyone else to stop drinking.

Late that afternoon we stumble out of the supermarket into the mall. Tyler is asleep in the stroller, his round blond head lolling like a flower. Amy drags along, kicking at the wheels. I bend to straighten his head and when I look up there's a woman with yellow hair staring at me. She's sitting at a table with a cardboard sign propped on the dusty cloth. *TAROT. $10.* She smiles hopefully as Amy flops down by the table, whining that she's tired.

"This way," I coax, but Amy clings to the plastic chair.

"It's okay," says the woman, fluffing her bright hair.

Goldilocks, I think. A middle-aged Goldilocks in stretchy blue pants.

"Want yer cards read," she says, "while you're waitin'?"

The only thing unusual about her is her jewellery, heavy turquoise rings on every finger. Apart from that she looks like the women you see going into the Bi-Way, riffling through the lingerie.

"This way and we'll get a treat," I say a little louder as the woman lights a cigarette and props it on the foil ashtray. Amy sinks deeper into the chair.

"Treat yerself!" the woman says. "Can't hurt."

Clenching the cigarette between her lips, she brushes flecks of dandruff from her blue sweater as shoppers pass in droves. There are swarms of teenagers with babies, and women my age, with frizzy perms and wide behinds, men in ballcaps trailing after them. Not a soul I'd recognize.

"Not today, thanks." I smile, trying to pry Amy off the seat.

"Tough age," the woman says, her watery eyes grazing the crowd. "I know. I had five. It's okay — she can stay put till someone comes. A customer," she adds coolly.

Feeling guilty, I reach into my purse and slip her a ten. I can't believe I'm doing this: *Mrs. Easton getting her fortune told. In the Spryfield Mall, yet.* Something worse creeps in as I pull Amy, wide-eyed and grumpy, onto my lap: what if she tells Daddy about the woman with the funny rings? He'll have a bird, an absolute bird.

"Well." The woman smiles at Amy and starts unwinding the tasselled scarf from her deck of cards. Her fingers flutter through the deck, light as flies despite the jewellery. Glancing down, she arranges the cards in paths over the black tablecloth. I look at her frothy hair, the pink scalp showing through, her lips grey under the peach lipstick.

"It's late. We really have to be getting—" I shift Amy on my knee. "The kids are starving and I—"

"It don't take long." The woman frowns and shakes her head. "You mustn't let *them* dictate, dear." To Amy she says, "You're all right, aren'tcha honey? Let yer mum have a little break now."

Then, gazing at the card in her palm, she looks at me and snorts.

"You a secretary or somethin'? Good at rubbin' things out, I can see. Ya must be handy with the white-out." She turns over another card. "Keep erasin' an' there'll be nothin' left!"

I look at her, embarrassed. What the hell am I doing here? I have no idea what she's talking about. She gazes at me, her eyes slits now, lined like a tabby cat's.

"So dear, what is it you wanna know?" she sniffs.

"Five minutes and we'll get a treat," I whisper to Amy, my eyes on the cards in front of me.

"Nothing new in your love life, not for the next six months anyways." The woman sighs, sliding the cards over the cloth like bumper cars. She lays one face-down at the top of each path, her hands moving so fast I barely glimpse the pictures on them.

Tell me something I don't know, I almost say.

"Ahhhh. Your husband is a successful man. A lawyer, maybe," she says, squeezing her eyes shut as if to wring something out. "Excuse me, not a lawyer. A *dentist!* The kind that does braces!"

I shrug, jostle Amy on my knee.

"Oh yes," the woman coos and starts to cough, covering her mouth with the back of her hand. "Sometimes a person's gotta blot out a few things. You know, like whitin' out typos."

She waits for me to nod. When I don't, she draws another card and flashes it at me. It looks like Narcissus in a loincloth, leaning over a pool.

"The father figure," she says knowingly, taking a deep breath and fidgeting with her waistband. "Your husband is an excellent provider, isn't he?" She speaks in a voice that would melt rock.

"Yes, yes. The perfect husband," I agree hastily,

setting Amy on her feet. "Look, it's been *really* interest-ing—"

The woman seems startled.

"But we haven't got to the good stuff yet," she says, suddenly annoyed. "I promise I won't tell ya anything bad, if that's what you're scared of."

I'm standing now, smoothing the creases from my wool slacks. A catty smile creeps over her face.

"Ohhhh," she sighs. "He's tall and dark. A little on the heavy side. But not fat. No dear, not at all what ya'd call *fat*. Oh yes, yer husband's a handsome one, but you gotta watch what ya feed him now. You'll see." Her voice trails off. "The rest of yer life will be fine, just *lovely*." Abruptly she begins wrapping the cards back up in the scarf and digging through her purse for something. As I start to move away, Amy hanging off the stroller, she passes me a black card with a phone number and *Faye's Fortunes* in gold letters. "No appointment necessary," she calls. "Thanks now and have a nice day."

Out in the parking lot it's almost dark, bright beads of snow falling beneath the floodlights. Tyler wakes up as I slide him into his car seat. He starts to scream, Amy crying over and over that she's starving. I've kept them out much too late.

Trudging up the front steps, juggling Tyler and a bag of groceries, I hear the phone ringing inside.

"Maybe it's Daddy saying he'll be home early after all," I say, jiggling the key. The phone keeps ringing — most people know to let it ring more than ten times. Still, there's a queer aimlessness to it, the sound bouncing brightly through the cold, dark house. I get the door open and the kids flop down in the hallway crying, their noses running. If I had half a brain I'd hire help — someone to have dinner waiting, to straighten the boots in the entry, *to keep house.*

The phone is still ringing but I take my time getting it. Nobody calls this time of day — suicide hour, with small children — nobody but teleresearchers and people selling vacuum cleaners. I stop and hang up my jacket, taking care to brush the wet flecks off the lapels. Then I make my way to the kitchen, the comfort of gleaming tiles, and grab the receiver.

"Yes?" I'm too tired to say hello.

"Mrs. Easton?" It's a man, no one I recognize, but with a voice like Michael's, cool and businesslike.

"Can I help you?"

"Mrs. Easton, I don't mean to alarm you but...."

"*Yes? What is it? Who's calling—?*" I'm exhausted now, kids dragging at my knees, trying to pull me to the floor.

"It's Dr. Easton, I have to tell you he's collapsed...."

I wait, holding my breath.

"A colleague of his, coronary...happened in the OR.... We're running tests.... I think you should come as soon as poss—"

"*Michael? What's happened?*"

"Two hours ago, myocardial infarc— We've been try-ing to reach you...it would be best if...."

"The patient," I mumble stupidly. "What about his patient?" I'm crouching, the children clinging to me, the mess from Tyler's nose on my neck.

"What?" The voice impatient, incredulous. Then a pause. "It's not the patient we're concerned about. I think you'd better come right away."

Stunned, slow as stones underwater, I watch myself hang up, my hand trembling. Amy and Tyler rolling around at my feet, kicking their wet boots in the air. I squat down, hugging myself tight to keep from shaking. Inside there's a cold, bleached feeling, as though all the blood has drained out. I don't know what to tell the kids

— how to say we have to go out again, how to get them back in the car.

At the hospital a nurse offers to watch the kids in the reception area outside intensive care. She takes off their mitts and presses Gummi Bears into their fists. A man I've seen somewhere before emerges through the swinging doors, beckoning. His smile cool, impassive. Dr. Lismore, one of Michael's superiors. His fingers feel dry as leaves when he removes his glove to take my hand.

I don't know my husband at first. His eyes are closed, his face ashen, flat and grey as sand. The lines around his mouth gone. Oxygen whistles through a tube in his nose, fluids drip through others in his wrist, his groin. His chest is wired like a circuit board. His stillness deeper than sleep, but for the faint lift and fall, the slow, steady beep of a monitor, the fine green line snaking across the screen.

My stomach lurches, hollow. I'm shivering, it's so cold in here. Deathly silence enveloped in the noisy bustle — the drone of voices, phones ringing; the harsh buzz of fans, oxygen; equipment bleating. An image flashes of Michael's face, once: smooth, rosy, slick with rain.

"Shhhhh," I hear myself whisper, reaching for his hand. Laying my cheek against its vague warmth, against the icy sheet. "Shhhhh." My face is wet. His fingers move, ever so slightly, in mine.

Someone touches my shoulder, leads me outside. The doctor is waiting, his voice soft but firm. "First twenty-four hours, critical . . . blockage . . . but given Mike's shape . . . minimal damage."

Warning? Reassuring? Whatever his words, they pass right over me, scarcely sink in. As though something inside has taken flight, leaving only the cold white space under my heart.

REFRACTION

The fire engine looks clumsy and out of place pulled up beside the lake with all its lights flashing. A team of emergency workers in yellow suits clamber up and down the steep embankment, hauling lengths of cable with heavy, brutal-looking hooks. They're a cheery burst of colour in the soft dusk, the pale blue sky splintered in a million blue-black ripples on the water's surface.

Jesus, mutter a couple of men, swatting blackflies, while others lean from the dam dragging the hooks through the deep, still water. Fishing.

Trout rise, nipping the air for insects, pooling the surface into widening rings, the water tepid and brown as molasses. From the woods, unseen, spring peepers trill, *neee-deep, neee-deep*, their throaty music echoing louder and louder as darkness falls. An alien sound, hollow and unearthly, pulsing from swamps and spruce thickets around the lake.

There are few spectators. Reports of the incident are still too fresh, the dam too secluded.

Cables unfurl, descend like the long thick stems

anchoring lilypads. One of the hooks snags something, a dense liquid weight. The man at the other end freezes, glancing for a moment up at the sky.

The little girl's face is white, white as the flesh of pickerel lurking near the bottom. As her body is pulled up, a swath of dark blonde hair sways and wavers above the head in the brown shallows. Everything tinted, her pink T-shirt stained a pale flesh colour, oddly bright in the dimming twilight. Tea-stained as an old sepia photograph.

Her parents only just reported her missing, said she'd disappeared from a neighbour's swing-set sometime after supper. They went over to call her in for a bath but she was gone.

New-budded twigs shiver in the soft June breeze. The mother, a gaunt young woman in jeans, trembles ever so slightly, jaw clamped shut with one skinny, quaking hand stopping up a scream. And all around her the sound of lapping, lapping, and the long gentle *shhusshhh* of traffic sweeping along the road.

She finally lets go, starts to cry with her mouth open in one long tight gasp.

At the dam the father kneels, helping the yellow-suited firefighters haul the body up onto the rocks. He slides one thin, tattooed arm under the child's neck, fragile as a flower stalk, to keep the head from snapping back and cracking against granite.

Seven. She would've been seven next week.

And darkness soaks up the last slivers and smudges of light, the trees and lake melding into a solid blackness. The frogs' voices deepen. Last call, last long lizard tongue rolling out to snare a blackfly. Apart from this it's so quiet you can hear the fiddleheads unfurling, the beat of a loon's wings as it propels itself across the last bit of blueness. Dampness swells from the lake, the peepers serene now, fading. Their quiet's like a warning, a warning from some other planet.

At first nobody sees Jeremy Mossman wading through
the weeds along the road, between the ditch and the edge
of the woods. In the twilight he walks slowly, as if either
lost or tracking new ground, his thick dark hair blending
with the black of spruce. Only his face stands out, a waste
of pale skin in the glare of headlights, accentuated by the
dense backdrop of trees.

Sauntering along the roadside Jeremy hears the sirens, the measured radio voices bouncing over the treetops. The sounds carry over the lake. He knows that something unusual has happened, probably something bad.

He sticks close to the edge of the trees. There's a
sidewalk on the opposite side of the busy four-lane road
but he prefers the feel of moss and spruce needles, of soft-
packed earth underfoot. If it were lighter out he'd be
watching the ditch for beer bottles and pop tins, which
he collects sometimes and turns in for the change.

He's aware of cars slowing down to make the deep
bend in the road, more a highway than a street winding
through a suburb, this edge of the city bordering wilder-
ness. Miles and miles of swampy woods behind the strip
of muffler shops and Burger Kings; rocky lakes, brooks,
and freshets running through abandoned farms, recognizable only by bent apple trees hung with old man's
beard.

As the cars round the curve, headlights looming, the
people on the passenger side lean towards their windows.
In a flash they seem to gape at him, this middle-aged
man dressed in a natty dark suit jacket and ragged pants,
ambling along the ditch. Through rain and fog, sun and
muggy heat, oblivious of weather, Jeremy wears the jacket,
threadbare at the cuffs but still dressy, at least from a distance. He hopes the dark colour will make him invisible,

let him disappear into his surroundings.

You'd think by now he'd be used to strangers' brief gawking stares — this is how it is for him doing the most ordinary things, even buying groceries or housewares over at the mall. He had a job there once at the drugstore, stocking shelves. Not a bad job, he thinks now, for a fellow with only grade ten. Unloading crates of shampoo and toothpaste and cigarettes, the kind of work you could do pretty much on your own, not having to deal too much with other people, the other stock-handlers, the skinny, pimply salesgirls, except when they wanted to know what plans you had, when you were going out on a date. Jeremy kept his eyes on the clock, the big grimy ramp into the rear of the tractor-trailers, his hands on the red metal dolly, the clumsy cartons. He worked steadily, he did, till each truck was emptied, even while the others huddled round the door of the dingy freight elevator having a smoke, snickering and hooting at his dogged effort.

"How many a them guys ya figure it'd take ta change a lightbulb?" he heard them say one day, among some other things that stung his ears: crude, suggestive words with vague, spongy meanings, things he knew better than to repeat to Pearl, his mother. She was home then on her first bit of sick leave, recovering from a bad back.

When Jeremy lost his job at the drugstore it seemed only natural that he'd stay home and keep Pearl company. By then she was spending most of her days on the couch in their small, musty living-room, watching television. At first he found something distasteful about this. But soon he scarcely noticed his mother's addiction to *Another World* and *Days of Our Lives*, and before long Jeremy was calling them "the stories" too. Somehow the days flew by, the two of them living off Pearl's pension cheques. As her health declined, she relied more and more on Jeremy to do errands, to help her get around the cluttered, decaying house. She'd send him to the mall, to pick up their weekly supplies — tinned food for the cat, cheap cuts of meat and canned peas and milk, and the bags of marshmallow biscuits she enjoyed while watching her shows. On rainy afternoons Jeremy would sit with his mother tucked up on the couch under a worn plaid blanket, eating cookies and watching TV. By then he was struggling to do all the cooking, the housework too. The place was in disrepair, the roof leaking when it rained, the front steps rotting and sagging into the weeds. Inside smelled like catfood and the sweet, cloying odour of tinned milk left out too long.

Before long Pearl grew heavy, so heavy it was difficult for Jeremy to help her from her bedroom to the couch. It was then she started spending more time in bed, with only Jeremy to attend to her more intimate needs. This he did without complaint. When he helped her to the toilet, his mother would grip his thick arms and wonder how it was he'd grown from a skinny, freckled boy to a stocky, middle-aged man with sour-smelling breath, the flesh loose around his waist and flecks of grey in his black hair. As for his circumstances, she refused to let herself think about them.

This was precisely the way she'd managed after Vincent left, all those years before. Not that one could ever forget. It happened a month or so before Jeremy began kindergarten — and everybody said it was school where his problems started festering, like a splinter working its way to the surface. *Oddball, retard, fruit:* names that followed him home like a pack of yapping dogs. Only Pearl knew none of it was true.

When Jeremy was small Pearl would take him outside to play in the swamp behind their house. She'd stand nearby, her arms folded against the cold as he jammed sticks into the slimy water, poking and prodding, dredging up dead leaves in the hope of finding frogs or squirming tad-poles. In the woods he'd turn over moss-coated rocks, one by one, searching for wood bugs. Once he discovered the shed skin of a garter snake, brittle and almost transparent. Picking it up he'd gasped at how dry and rough it felt, his mother suddenly wide-eyed, grimacing over his shoulder. It used to bore her silly, standing around watching while he played; she'd think of the chores waiting for her in the house, the dirty clothes to be washed, the mud on the kitchen floor, the supper to be cooked. When Jeremy asked to bring the snakeskin home, Pearl shook it out of his hands. Then for a moment she almost relented, knowing that after a week or two she could have simply swept the thing into the garbage. But there were limits, she told herself, there had to be, even to Jeremy's uncanny love of nature.

For a while she tried dragging his toy trucks out to the scrubby back yard, a patch of mud and weeds, the grass beaten down by rain and snow. She'd show him how to throw spoonfuls of dirt into their little metal dumps, and for a few minutes he'd oblige her by playing along, then without fail abandon this and wander towards the trees. It nearly drove Pearl out of her mind, so hopeful was she for a minute to herself, to sit on the step perhaps and drink a cup of coffee, skim through one of her magazines. *Modern Confessions, True Crime.* These were the sorts of things Pearl loved to read, though her husband, Vincent, mocked her tastes, so much so that she kept her reading for the daytime while he was off at work. Up until the day he left, he had a steady job as a bus mechanic.

One hot afternoon, just after Jeremy's fifth birthday, Pearl allowed her son to venture past the swamp alone. She sat at the kitchen table, the screen door sprung wide, glancing up every few moments to catch the flash of his red T-shirt or his thin white legs moving through the scrub maples.

"Stay where I can see ya!" she yelled two or three times, before turning back to an article about teenaged call-girls. Jeremy was such an obedient child she never feared him straying too far. It never occurred to her that there could be other dangers, that he might get lost.

At three o'clock Vincent came home from work, startling Pearl from her reading. Leaping up from the table, she opened a cola and handed it to him. He stood there drinking it down, the back of his dark blue coveralls droopy with sweat, slamming down the empty bottle before looking around and asking, accusing, "So quiet it's like a goddamn morgue in here — where the hell's the kid?"

Where minutes before — one ear cocked for the faint happy hum of the boy's singing monologue, his thin sweet harmony with crickets and birdsong — Pearl had glimpsed Jeremy, a playful weaving of red through a leafy screen, now there was no sign of him. Rushing out into the yard, she pushed through the branches with her bare arms, calling, calling his name, a note of hysteria lifting at the end. Vincent shoved her aside, trampling bushes and saplings, shouting over and over, his voice held in by the damp, swaying umbrella of branches.

Weeping, Pearl found a seat on an outcrop of granite, put her head between her knees and waited, listening. No sound save the gentle swaying of limbs, the crush of leaves, crows calling. *One crow sorrow, two crows joy.* At last she heard their voices, the sharp cry of the child. Rising, she began wading through the snapping sea of huckleberry up to her armpits, twigs tearing at her clothes. The voices louder, pulling her, until straight ahead she glimpsed them in a clearing ringed by scrawny birches — the boy with his shorts round his ankles, sobbing, the father's grease-stained fingers gripping the child's small white arms. Even at that distance she could hear the boy's teeth knocking together, spy the bloody dents in his bottom lip. And Vincent, sensing her presence then, getting up off his knees and making some threat, loud enough for her to hear. "Don'tchu ever wander off like that again, ya hear me? Don'tchu ever ever wander off, or next time I'll—"

A week or two later, on a day so muggy the heat seemed to ripple from the road in waves, Vincent went off to work at the usual time of five in the morning and did not return. In the chaos and upset following her husband's desertion, Pearl never once mentioned that day in the woods, and Jeremy didn't ask, and eventually each assumed the other had forgotten all about it.

Jeremy is sure now something terrible has occurred — not just from the whine of sirens rending the still June evening, but afterwards, when the shrillness fades and the frogs and birds and earthworms take over. He knows something awful and earth-settling has happened, somewhere, to somebody.

For a while longer he continues along the shoulder, waiting for a string of cars to pass, the red flicker of taillights. Looking both ways, he steps cautiously over the curb and runs as quickly as possible to the other side, his stomach in his throat from the sudden exertion. Once safely across, it's only another five minutes to his house, up the potholed lane behind the Tim's and the Petro-Canada station.

When he lets himself inside, his mother is asleep, the jumpy blueness from the TV filling her doorway. He peeks in just in time to catch the final scenes of a local newsflash, a fevered reporter with the rear of an ambulance behind him. Its red light rotates across his face, the camera panning to the lake, the dam, where the last of a group of

grim-faced workers haul up straggling pieces of equipment.

It took her a while to tell him her name, when he first
stumbled across her sitting on the rocks. She was swinging her legs over the water, playing a game with the lake,
she said. To see if it could swallow the dinosaurs on her
shoes.

"Where's your mother?" he wanted to know. She
seemed so small to be there on her own.

She was shy at first, kept looking down at the dark
toes of her sneakers, dipping them a little deeper with
each swing. He didn't want to alarm her, couldn't help
feeling big and awkward standing there in the bushes,
watching her. Like one of those bears that shuffled from
time to time out of the woods, foraging weedy lawns and
dumpsters for food. If anything, he was afraid of children, but knew enough about them to hesitate over leaving her there.

"What didja say your name was?" he asked again,
squatting down among the alders, shielding his face. This
time she glanced back at him without fear, a brazen curiosity in her eyes.

"Amanda Dawn Boutilier," she said, unfazed by his
shyness. For a moment she even looked straight into his
small blue eyes, eyes that seldom looked straight ahead,
trained always on the periphery.

"Careful you don't fall in," he now remembers yelling, or something to that effect. "Watch yourself, Amanda
Dawn, those rocks are slippery!" He also recalls vaguely
the peculiar gleam of her dirty blonde hair, the sun slung
low in the sky picking up traces of gold in it.

He hadn't wanted to leave her, would have waited
there with her until someone came looking. Her mother
or father. He would have stayed there all night, keeping

his distance behind the granite boulder next to hers, watching out for her. The two of them listening to the frogs, waiting there till the moon rose and fell if necessary.

But something spooked him, the sound of teenagers coming closer, slouching along the road towards the lake. A string of them in baggy pants and ballcaps, oversized T-shirts. They spooked him all right, their mocking voices growing louder through the trees, curses hurled like sharp stones.

He reacted; forgot the little girl perched there over the water, knowing only the instinct, tried and true, of making himself disappear.

But when the officers came to the door — the cruiser's lights splashing everything orange — all Jeremy could say was that the lake had done it, the lake could swallow dinosaurs if you didn't watch out.

LOBSTER IS NOT AN APHRODISIAC

For a while now Rick had been finding sex with his wife more like a medical exam than anything else. "Talk to each other," said the articles in those magazines Maureen was always leaving on the kitchen counter. Talk to each other, reasonable enough advice — had either been thinking with their heads. But since catching "the baby bug", she'd become like a walking uterus, a whole other woman, one he hardly recognized. And Rick himself? He was almost afraid to speculate which of his parts had taken control.

What had begun five years back as the perfect marriage — happy if placid and at times even dull — had turned, or so it seemed, like a game of Monopoly: landing repeatedly on Free Parking, with never a measly buck in the middle. His wife, the winner who refuses to quit: "Just one more hotel, honey, then we'll stop." Except in this case it was a baby she was hellbent on having. But that was Maureen, determined, some might say dogged; this quality of doggedness, of knowing her own mind, what had attracted Rick in the first place. Unlike girlfriends he'd had who changed their minds the way most people changed jackets, Maureen refused to quibble.

She was the type of person who delighted in making plans and sticking to them, a quality he found comforting. The ideal spouse, Rick had always thought; the perfect complement to his own equanimity and ambition. Except there was one problem. People like Maureen hated having plans thwarted, for, when fate did not comply, who was left holding the bag? — a bag full of empty schemes and schedules, like a blue-box of unrecyclables. A thwarted Maureen, as Rick was quickly discovering, was not a happy camper.

And all this fuss, he thought, over starting a family, her delay in conceiving the only explanation Rick could find for his wife's recent moods. Just because it was taking a bit longer than expected.... But talk about it? The very thought of talking made Rick seize up inside. Knowing Maureen, what was there to say?

Besides, it had nothing to do with him, did it?

Rick sold real estate, though to look at him you might not guess. He was fond of black, had an idea that it set him off, apart from the other agents, that it made people overlook his thinning brown hair. He had a certain way of dressing — black trousers and turtlenecks, sunglasses, wool sportsjacket. Understated, cool. He felt it put people at ease, gave them the impression of someone on the ball, not *too* homey but not exactly a fast mover either.

He and Maureen lived in a new construction on a suburban cul-de-sac, in a subdivision where the streets were named "wynds" and "closes". The subdivision was Maureen's idea, part of their decision to start a family. At first Rick had felt a little uncomfortable — he was much more a downtown type of person; his ideal home would've been a Victorian townhouse, lovingly restored. But he'd known in his heart that Maureen was right, that the place they chose had a better resale value, and after a while he could tell clients with a little flourish, in a casual, upscale monotone, that he himself had bought a place on Brierwood Wynd.

Everything was fine, in fact, until Maureen quit her job as a mortgage officer — she said the stress was interfering with her ability to get pregnant. This had been some time ago (Rick had lost track of when exactly since the money hadn't been a factor) and Maureen still hadn't conceived. Not that she seemed to dwell on it — oh no, after dealing with snivelling customers, Maureen was just as glad to stay home keeping things clean and well appointed, seeing to it that dinner, most nights many-step gourmet, was on the table when Rick came in from work.

This past autumn, though, it seemed she'd been getting stuck a lot with the pastry falling on the *pâté de fois* while Rick tore around with clients, driving his black 4Runner too fast along suburban streets, working out details on the car-phone.

"I'm doing it for you," he'd say, when he crawled in beside her at midnight, sometimes later. "I'm doing it for *us*," he'd correct himself, rubbing a tired hand over her flat white belly. Maureen would lie there patiently, her eyes wide open, focused on the perfectly replicated moulding around the ceiling light fixture. "I know, baby," she'd sigh, visualizing how she'd do the bathroom.

If he wasn't too tired they'd make love, quickly and unemphatically, his wife's body like a map — Rick knew it so well it hardly seemed necessary to go to point A before point B. In fact, sex reminded him of those dot-to-dots he'd see kids doing in the back seat while the parents went through yet another back-split: why take the slow route when any idiot could already see the picture?

Lately Maureen had stopped telling him if she was ovulating or not, and afterwards, before they drifted off, she'd ask him things like what he thought about purple, aubergine actually, with cream and dusty rose woodwork. "It'd show well," he'd mumble his approval to her latest project. Even half asleep he knew that for a new home theirs had all the touches of an older, more elegant one — thanks to her.

Since summer she'd taken up stencilling: painstaking florals on the wall above the kitchen cabinets and over the dining-room buffet, Rick's mother's crystal under nothing more than a thin sheet of glass.

"I won't be able to do it when I'm pregnant," she said in a pinched voice, one October evening after Rick had had an especially hectic day. It seemed there was a boom in the metro area, though one that nobody expected would last, and Rick figured with a few more sales — one or two executive homes, a few bread-and-butter bungalows, four percent commission — he'd have a decent crack at being the year's top seller. He could just taste the bottle of Henkell head office threw in with the big prize — a trip for two to Jamaica, all expenses paid. Just a couple more months of really busting his ass, he decided, and by Christmas he'd have it nailed. Then the work would pay off, the evenings and weekends dragging half-hearted buyers through places hardly worth showing, laundry bulging from closets, plates stashed in the dishwasher, rings on the countertops.

"You need to make it *inviting*," he was always telling people. "It's not just a house we're selling here, it's a *home*." Forget the brochures suggesting clients have bread baking, kids playing board games in the rec room — lately it was enough just getting them to keep their carpets vacuumed, fingerprints off the walls.

It was like that with Maureen and what they did in bed, too. A means to an end, he kept telling himself. Though as months passed and she still hadn't conceived, he had to admit he was beginning to feel a little edgy about how much time — and money! — she was spending sitting around the house all day. When by late November his phone stopped ringing so much (as though the market was suddenly, mysteriously running dry), Rick began dropping hints about the classified ads next to the real-estate ones. ("I see there's a finance company needs somebody," he might say as she was slipping on her nightgown. But she'd just shrug and go off to brush her teeth.)

At first, still sure he'd meet his year's objectives, he put things down to Christmas. A simple sign of the season, that fallow period before the depths of winter drove people — especially well-heeled, empty-nested snowbirds — from their homes like sheep. Head office took such swings into account; there was still January to make up for the shortfall. And then July and August, waves of rich tourists searching out summer homes, to make up for the bust period every spring. But too late to compensate for the present dip in sales.

Rick tried not to let himself get too depressed.

At the height of his winning streak (mid-October, when he genuinely believed it would not end), Rick had gone out and splurged on Maureen's Christmas present. A diamond pendant, to match her engagement solitaire. There was also a matching diamond hair clip you could buy, which Rick had considered. Maureen was a sucker for those large velvet bows and barrettes women wore in their hair. She had started getting her short brown hair streaked with blonde, pulling it back in a stubby ponytail. Like the Duchess of Windsor, she'd joked when Rick mentioned it, then she'd looked embarrassed, hurt even. He'd thought long and hard about getting her that hair clip, but at the last minute decided against it. Good thing, he told himself when business slumped. Now he was counting his blessings.

With three weeks to Christmas things were getting tight. He could hardly believe it himself, much less break it to Maureen. Why spoil her fun, he thought, as she threw herself into trimming the house. Hand-cut spruce twined around the banisters, red velvet bows at perfect intervals; the same for the bay windows at the back and the front, inside and out. Ten dollars a bow, he happened to see the receipt. Ten dollars times three hundred, plus GST. *Don't spoil her fun*, he had to bite his tongue. Not that she appeared to notice — Maureen just seemed pleased he was spending more time at home.

A cheque bounced, then another. Rick had to charge the Christmas cards he was giving out to clients. Not that he had many — by mid-month they'd stopped calling altogether and he was considering turning in his cellular phone. Then Maureen started getting miserable. She'd snap at him in the morning when he poured himself a second cup of coffee, shoot impatient glances his way when she was vacuuming, bumping his feet while he was sitting on the sofa reading.

Two weeks before Christmas Rick found himself putting in time at the office. All his clients were on computer, some from as far back as ten years; no telling when they might decide to turn around some property or want to buy up. As he scrolled the list, something twigged: a gimmick. If it worked for cars, why not houses? His wife's voice came to him.

It was lobster season, Maureen had been reminding him. On the news, cargo planes were shown taking off for Europe, loaded to the hatches with Christmas lobster. People liked that kind of thing, tradition, just as much as they liked the taste. It was the idea that sold, anyone could see.

Free lobster with every referral — it couldn't have been simpler. On the way home for dinner he stopped at a printer's and ordered a rush on two hundred calendars, his name, Richard W. Deacon, and the slogan on each one. That night he ran his plan past Maureen. She seemed to think it was all right — he dismissed the fact that she was rather distracted at the time, thumbing through her magazines for holiday recipes, "country Christmases with 90 percent less fat."

After he picked up the calendars, he spent the rest of the morning rolling them up with red ribbon. For the next two days he drove around delivering them, stepping inside to see the new shade somebody'd painted their kitchen, the double-paned windows somebody else had installed, their new bathtub.

Maureen was making cheesecake when he finally came in, exhausted but optimistic, even cheerful. She slapped his fingers when he reached for a curl of chocolate off the top.

"It's for company," she snapped, as if saying so for the thousandth time. Then she clutched her stomach and made a face, and Rick remembered her period was due — not that it had much to do with him, only that he thought he recognized the expression she wore sometimes coming out of the bathroom. *We'll just have to keep trying,* she'd sigh, but now she looked at him with hate.

Two days before Christmas the calls started. First one, then another, then a string. He phoned a lobster pound and talked the manager into letting him buy on credit. The fellow finally agreed when Rick assured him he'd be buying in bulk, and then gave Rick a deal on a hundred pounds, so long as it didn't interfere with their European commitments.

"Some party," said the clerk behind the counter, fishing lobsters from the tank.

"Business," Rick said, watching as he threw them into bags, claws twitching through the plastic.

"That's *another* twenty pounds ya wanted?" The fellow shook his head and smirked.

"What the hell," said Rick, pulling out his wallet.

"That'll be $503.83, please." The clerk rocked back on his heels, tugging at the cap on his head — it reminded Rick of a shower cap, the type of thing doctors wore in the delivery room.

He only knew this because of some pictures Maureen's friend had brought over once showing the birth of her baby. Maureen had gone pale and excused herself to check the hors-d'oeuvres while the father flopped the infant over his shoulder. Then the phone had rung and Rick had had to leave, right in the middle of drinks. The couple hadn't been over since and Maureen had stopped mentioning them. Rick had trouble now remembering their names.

"Have a good one," the lobster fellow sneered, handing back Rick's credit card.

Rick felt a lump in his throat, a little thrill of excitement, as he carried the squirming bags out to the car. He filled the back seat with them, the plastic crinkling with the slow-motion movements of the about-to-be-cooked. A client had told him once you could anaesthetize lobsters by tickling their bellies. Driving home, Rick winced when he imagined the squeaks they'd make being plunged in the boiling water, made himself think instead of the *beep* of computer keys, the sound of money going into the bank. He began to whistle, switching on the radio. He turned it off, though, when he heard what was on — someone arguing the pros and cons of vaginal birth.

A hundred and twenty pounds. He glanced in the rearview at the back seat's cargo. It was enough to make Maureen flip.

His wife's car was in its usual spot in the double garage when Rick pulled in — he couldn't remember the last time he'd seen her take it out. She wasn't in the kitchen when he let himself in, which struck him as a little odd — so close to Christmas Maureen usually had the place upside-down getting things ready for when his mother came to dinner. The recipe magazines were in a pile on the table.

He browsed the answering machine, jotted down a message about square footage, another about insulation, then remembered the lobsters.

"*Moe?*" he shouted up the stairs, and when there was no answer he hoisted half the dripping bags, carried them up to the bathroom. Maureen was there wrapping a towel around her head, the front of her blouse wet. She gazed at the mirror when he slipped in and turned on the cold, started filling the tub with water.

"Oh my," she said as he began lowering in the bags. For a second he paused, wondering if he should remove the lobsters, let them crawl around like they'd done in the tank, then thought better of it and gave the twist-ties on the bags an extra yank. Maureen stood over him, the towel sliding off. "What the heck—?" she sighed, jerking backwards at the scrabbling of claws up the sides of the tub, the thud and scrape of shells against porcelain.

"There's more downstairs," he said, standing up.

"*Oh?* So where do you expect us to bathe? You're not keeping them for long, I hope." She looked at him aghast, a wet strand of hair falling across her eyes.

"Well...."

"I said, where will we *wash?*" Her eyes were like pieces of steel through the wet bangs, and Rick thought she might cry.

"Look, it's only for a day or two." He put his arm around her shoulder. "You've heard the phone."

"Oh *that,*" she sniffed. "That's been driving me nuts."

As if on cue, the phone downstairs started ringing,

an insistent, low-key warbling. Maureen rolled her eyes, blinking back tears.

"Honey, look," he said in dismay, his face getting flushed. "Look, how 'bout I boil up a couple. For us. Tonight. We could melt some butter, open a bottle of wine...." He reached up and rubbed the back of her neck, the way he had when they were first married, before this house, before she started keeping a basal thermometer by the bed.

"Oh Ricky." She rolled her eyes again as she plugged in the blow dryer. He thought he saw a glint there all the same, a pinkness to her cheeks that couldn't have been from the bathroom. The water in the tub was ice-cold.

"Which one of these suckers would you like?" he said, massaging her upper arm.

"Surprise me." She shut her eyes and leaned against him. "So long as it's not a female — those yucky eggs make me sick."

Rick waited till after the news to put on the water. While it boiled he set the dining-room table for two, put on Maureen's favourite Céline Dion tape. Before she came downstairs he wanted to have everything ready — candles lit, a brilliant red lobster on each plate, wedges of lemon, champagne flutes though the wine was a Chardonnay. He'd drunk a glass before pitching the lobsters in to cook — it always made him squeamish, how they'd keep squirming even in a rolling boil. Once the lid was on, he polished off another glassful, felt its warmth moving down through his belly. First they'd eat, then they'd....

He was still making the salad when Maureen came into the kitchen, wearing the same blouse she'd had on earlier except now it was dry. No makeup, her hair tied back in the ponytail.

"Oh! You've really fussed!" she yelled from the dining-room, a tinge of crankiness to her voice. He could hear her in there inspecting things, probably holding up the glasses to make sure they weren't spotted.

With a flourish he set her plate down, then went to the kitchen for his own. On his way back to the table he flicked on the answering machine.

"The evening's ours," he said, sitting down, shaking out his napkin. He shut out the cookbook voice in the back of his mind, *Best when boiled live, lobsters won't keep unless they've been cooked. Do not eat if already dead....*

"Butter," said Maureen, twisting off the tail. "You forgot the butter."

Rick ran to the kitchen, stuck half a pound in the microwave. While he waited for the *ding* he dashed upstairs and threw a boxful of salt in the tub.

By the time he set the butter down, an oily scum had formed on the surface. Maureen was on her second claw, the body with its clot of roe abandoned on her plate. Her chin glistened with lobster juice, there were bits of shell in her hair, and she held out her fingers as if she'd just done her nails and was waiting for them to dry.

"Sorry, hon. It was too good to wait." She leaned back in her chair, sipped the last of her wine. "Even though you must've got the male."

Then she rose and took her plate to the kitchen, switching off the answering machine as she went past. Right away the phone started ringing.

"You get it, Rick, it's probably for you," she yelled from the sink, and then her voice hardened. "The way I see it, you've got twenty-four hours to get rid of those things."

A SPORTING LIFE

Gloria. The name alone reminds me of those machines advertised on TV: "10 ways to the perfect body", "abs and buns of steel". Gloria, G-L-O-R-I-A. As teens we'd shout that song at the top of our lungs, driving around in our parents' cars, the radio blaring. Sticky summer nights at the cottage, a warm, soft breeze coming off the lake. When I was still a kid, sixteen or seventeen. Young.

Gloria.

"You're kidding," I said, when she told me her name.

"No." She held her smile, looking bemused. "Gloria Coombs. What's it to you?" And she rolled her head from side to side and bent flat-backed from the waist, stretching out her legs. Her "hams", as she explained, grinning and squatting into a deep knee bend. Fingers laced together, she pressed out her palms; even in the shadow of the trees you could see her forearms tensing. Such definition. She wore no ring, no jewellery of any sort besides the thin gold chain around her neck.

Some warmup, you had to marvel, watching her. If the park hadn't been empty, I'd have felt compelled to remove my training jacket and drape it over her. Look, I'm no prude, and as a doctor, believe me, there's nothing I haven't seen. But...it wasn't as if she were an old friend, or a patient. Not even much of an acquaintance, at that point.

"Your shades," I reminded her. She'd pushed them up on her head where they tilted precariously — these which I'd retrieved the day before from the path, and been kind enough to keep to return the following morning. By chance, of course — everything unfolded by chance, you realize. I had nothing to do with it. Meeting Gloria was something that simply happened. It wasn't that I — a happily married professional — had been out looking. Christ, no. It's just that she happened to be....

Oh, I'd seen the lady around town, even before the MI — the heart attack. She was an early morning person. Likely we'd crossed paths, doing our usual laps through the park. At dawn, always the same faces — those keen enough to be up and active — bobbing like lanterns through the dark trees. Though with little chance for more than a nod or a breathless "hello", there's a certain camaraderie — God, kindredness? — between those who begin the day while the rest of the world is rolling over, catching a few more winks.

I won't say I was already attracted to Gloria, definitely not before my MI. Until recently I scarcely noticed her, just another jogger. Let's be frank; until you really look, the truly fit wear their bodies like uniforms. It's those with excess rolls of flesh or saddled thighs who catch your eye. Here in the park, at this hour, lithe, supple bodies blend in with the trees; faulty, unhealthy ones stand out like burls.

But I should talk.

Gloria. Five foot eight, one hundred and fifteen

pounds. If she weighs more, it's pure muscle. Not that she's one of those body-building types — those women frighten me, built like fullbacks with their masculine bulges and ripples, triangular torsos and lack of breasts.

Not Gloria, thankfully, too mature for such extremism. Her emphasis is on endurance; she teaches aerobics full-time at the Y. She's no spring chick. But she's gorgeous — what can I say? — absolutely gorgeous. Strong as a team of oxen, but feminine, the sort of woman who looks lovely in pink, equally appreciated in a suit and a string of pearls, or damp with sweat, wearing a thong. "Butt floss", she calls those skimpy get-ups she wears instructing. My wife would be disgusted. But Gloria can say the crassest things and get away with it, uttering them with a bright, impish sparkle — an unquenchable *joie de vivre*.

The first time I saw — really saw — her was the day she dropped her sunglasses in the park, running. She flashed me this broad, toothy smile, scooting past in a crinkly nylon track suit, purple and green. It was around six-thirty, I was due at the hospital in an hour. The sun was just rising over the treetops, a bright, blinding orange. I had to slow my pace, in fact, rounding the curve towards the sailors' monument. The edges of the large stone cross were etched orange, brilliant as the flame from the refinery across the harbour. A Sea King helicopter roared overhead, on some sort of patrol.

I slowed to a power walk, stepping aside to let her pass. She was going the opposite direction, with a wide, determined stride, fists clenched. Not puffing, not even breathing hard, and barely perspiring, a pleasant wash of colour in her cheeks — from the morning's chill, most likely. She wore a pair of dark Ray-Bans like a hairband pushing back her thick gold bangs. Who knows how they stayed on; you had to wonder how she could run at that pace without the damn things falling off.

But that's just Gloria. She's not like most people. No, she certainly isn't.

As we passed, close enough to brush arms, I thought for a split second she'd stop. As I was saying, she gave me this broad smile as if we had known each other all our lives, and in that instant I realized, yes, maybe I *had* seen her before. Running, of course. In purple tights; usually alone, occasionally with a girlfriend, one of the nurses, perhaps. I say "girl", though these women aren't exactly teenagers. Me neither, though, believe it or not, since the bypass I sometimes forget my age, forget that I'm a middle-aged man with a wife and two kids, a two-car household in the south end, a mega-mortgage. To be honest, I never felt better.

Before I could speak, she made the top of the hill, a purple and green sprite vanishing, without hesitation, into the blackness of the woods. A sylph of a woman, alone but unfazed. A girl with a purpose. Too fast for even the most determined of perverts to assail; God, she was fast. I couldn't help thinking of Barbara, my wife, alone in the woods at this hour: jumping at the sound of her own footsteps. And as I watched this purple blur disappear up the path, I noticed her drop something, her shades. Without pause I turned back to pick them up — deep violet, wrap-around frames, the black lenses slightly scratched. I toyed briefly with the idea of catching her up, but by then it was too late. I could have left the sunglasses on a tree stump, the way people leave lost gloves on fences. But instead, without further thought, I stuck them in my pocket. Which is how I came to introduce myself, the following day in the park.

She's forty-three, divorced. No kids. God knows what she'd

be like to live with. She's a bit of a card; when they made her, they threw away the mould — I could see that from the word "go", our earliest conversations. But it didn't stop me from confiding in her, and vice versa.

After I got to know her, I asked once about her marriage. It was a foggy morning in the parking lot; she simply stopped and started stretching her neck till you could hear the tendons flexing. "Wore the son-of-a-bitch out," she laughed, then galloped ahead, slowing slightly when she remembered.

"Have you taken your heart pills, doctor? Don't forget, Michael; go at your own pace! Think of Jim Fixx — I don't want a corpse on my hands. A body, maybe, but not a corpse!"

Very funny. I jogged after her, laughing, but matching my stride to the slight pull in my chest.

"You can resume your normal activities, Mike. But you've got to remember to listen to your body. And don't overdo it, unless you want to wind up in cardiac again — on your back." My colleague's advice, after the bypass operation.

Barbara was a basket case, wouldn't allow me to lift so much as a milk carton for the first month. And our first try at sex, she was like a mother, guiding me, instructing. Sounded exactly as she did teaching our son to tie his shoes: circle this end like *this*, that's right, honey; then you stick this loop through *here*. I thought she'd never shut up. "You okay, Michael? You really okay? Now you tell me if it starts to hurt. You will, won't you?"

My wife. I love her. She's a good mom, she's smart and she's usually right. How smart and how right, I realized that horrible afternoon in cardiac, lying flat on my back, the pain like a bus driving over my sternum, my eyes on a water stain on the ceiling. The last place I ever imagined ending up.

"You're not," Barbara said, the first time I went running afterwards. I'd taken all the stress tests, passed with flying colours; Lismore had given me a clean bill of health. It seemed so easy — too easy, in fact. I had no bad habits to give up, no smoking or fatty foods. In place of coffee, I took to drinking hot water. A man can get used to anything after a while, which is what I tell my patients — with new authority — when they whine about cutting out cigarettes and doughnuts.

"Do it," I say, "or you'll be a statistic in six months." Dead, I mean, though I have a bit of trouble using the word now, not like before, when I could say it with smart-assed resolve. Impunity. Now I couch my warnings. "A statistic." When I see the fear, the pleading in their eyes, I can almost feel and taste it: the rankness of that rust-brown stain, the quickness of instruments laid out sterile and shiny, the iciness of the air in the surgical suite. I swear my body temperature drops, like the climate-control in the OR, conserving energy for the bypass pump.

"Well," Barbara sighed, and for a minute I thought she was going to cry, and thus prevent — or at least delay — my run. "If you must," she finally said, forcing the same weak smile she'd worn holding my hand when I came out of the anaesthetic. "Go easy on yourself. Okay? For me, Michael. Okay?"

But all this was two years ago. I scarcely think about it now, honestly, as though my illness happened to somebody else. Except when colleagues come up and ask, "So, Mike — any problems? No signs of angina?" Physicians — other physicians — can be heartless, a tendency I'm learning to curb. It's something I decided, between gazing at that spot on the ceiling and waking wired for sound, my wife beside me, weeping — that if one continues in this business, one must never forget how the patient feels. One has an obligation to remember, for their sake. How it feels. If I was to continue.

The other big "if" was whether to continue running. I went through a terrible time, the first couple of months, of being afraid to move. Of wanting to die — there, I've admitted it — of feeling guilty that I'd done myself a disservice by not dying only to face a life sentence waiting for death to come. To end up once more on a stretcher, helpless, wondering, finally, if this was the real thing. Almost craving the finality, just to be spared enduring it again.

How irresponsible, how ungrateful this must sound. Barbara would divorce me for having such thoughts — and she'd be justified. But during my recuperation, amid the flashes of despair, I did a lot of reading. Forced myself: *The Lancet, The New England Journal of Medicine* — every article I could get my hands on, the pros and cons of bypass surgery, the prognosis of a guy like myself. A go-getter with a drive to succeed. A patient. Weekly, I had Barbara check the med school library for the latest studies; with the kids in school, she was already spending a good deal of time around the university, considering doing some graduate courses. I even sent her to the public library and had her borrow everything Jim Fixx ever wrote about running.

"Oh Michael. *Please* don't do anything stupid." She was sitting on the bed in her nightgown, watching me pump up my runners. My first time back out.

"If I can walk, darling, I can run. Well, a couple of kilometres, anyhow. For starters," I said, tuning out her sighs.

Gloria wouldn't have been so apprehensive — surely not so openly fearful, so self-interested in my welfare as

Barbara was and is, and perhaps even has a right to be. Which brings me to our introduction, the hot midsummer morning I happened to return her sunglasses. I had them in the glovebox of my little black Celica, the car I take to the hospital — Barbara drives the Cherokee.

It was a Saturday, around eleven. Not my usual time for a jog; a time when those who enjoy the outdoors are already off sailing or golfing, or whatever people do on a fine weekend. Clean the garage, eat waffles with the spouse.

Barbara had the day mapped out for me: she wanted the lawn mowed, the flowerbed by the driveway weeded. She hadn't been able to get hold of the landscaper, I guess, and she was in a lather about the mess, the neighbours, the mess...on and on. "I'll do it after my run," I told her, having already lost the best part of the morning sleeping in with her, then drinking coffee (in my case a herbal substitute) — the two of us alone, out on the deck. Barbara can spend a whole day sitting on her ass. Really. Though she knows how restless that makes me.

I kept getting up and wandering around the yard with my cup, checking the new sod we'd had laid. That's when the dispute erupted, Barbara in a flap about how little time I actually spent around the house, with her; and when I was there, why the heck couldn't I just *sit down*.

After a while I went inside and shouted through the sliding doors, "I'll do it when I get back — the grass'll keep till then, surely. It isn't going anywhere."

I drove to the park — not my usual means, but that's how uptight I was feeling. How put upon, if you will; I wish Barbara would learn to pick her spots — when to argue, when to let sleeping dogs lie.

The lot was almost empty, the only sound the roar from the container pier, the only sign of life the huge cranes moving overhead. The harbour looked perfectly calm, a slight haze over the horizon. Almost like a day at the cottage on Georgian Bay, when my mother would pack sandwiches, iceberg lettuce and ham, and my brother and I would take the canoe and row to the island. It was just off shore, though it felt like the middle of the lake. On the way out we'd glance back and watch our parents, Dad practising his swing, his back to the dock; Mom kneeling, weeding the petunias. The silly, floppy canvas hat she wore gardening, but nowhere else, thank God. And we'd use our folks as a means of measuring distance, two diminishing dots on the shore, Dad's green golf cap eventually merging with the leaves. When it merged completely, you knew it wasn't much farther, though sometimes in the sun you'd lose track of time and forget. On the hottest days, the island would seem to quaver in the distance, hovering like a hummingbird above the turquoise surface. Tantalizing. We'd get a bit rowdy, careless from the heat, break rhythm paddling, while ribbing each other about girls we'd been with the night before in the old man's new Cutlass, the radio blasting....

This is what the morning reminded me of as I pulled in and parked near the canteen, a cedar shed with a plastic ice-cream cone on the side and a pimply girl behind the counter, cracking gum. Odd, the park so deserted on such a fine day — dead, in fact, except for an old couple strolling the beach, some boys scaling the slippery black rocks by the water. "NO CHILDREN," reads the warning, in large white letters painted on stone.

With no one in the way, it was an ideal time to run, despite the heat. Locking the car, already I could feel the sweat on my brow. As I knelt to fix a shoelace, I heard a voice call, "Hello." Bright, cheerful; a voice full of promise and fun. Happy. It took a minute to register, but when I looked up, my God, there she was! Gloria, in black cycling shorts and a white top baring her midriff. You could see her ribs, her stomach muscles ridged like a washboard.

"Hey there," she called, coming closer, and I could see she'd just wound up a run. There were dots of sweat beneath her tight little breasts, and between her shoulder blades, along the V of her crotch.

"You're the doctor, right? A girlfriend — this friend of mine, she works with—"

"Right, right," I mumbled, for the first time in my life fumbling for what to say. I couldn't even think of the other gal's name, for Chrissake.

"We've met—?" I finally managed, unlocking the driver's side. Reaching across to the glovebox, producing the glasses. When I handed them over, she flashed that huge smile of hers, upper and lower teeth, clear back to the molars. And then she told me her name.

"So." She clapped her hands together, backing away. "We'll be running into each other again, no doubt, now we're acquainted." She spoke with such certainty, turning and sprinting to her car, a blue, late-model Honda. I watched her get in and buff the nape of her neck with a towel, waving as she tooted once and drove off.

The sun was almost straight overhead by the time I started my run, so I chose a shady route past the gazebo, a narrow stony path leading uphill towards the centre of the park. Not a leaf stirred, it was so hot; not so much as a sparrow or squirrel. The path trailed off in a stand of pine, the ground covered with needles so dry you could imagine the glare through a shard of glass igniting them.

I leaned against a tree for a quick stretch, breathing in the smell like dried gin. The sap left a sticky smudge on my T-shirt, grey now with sweat. As I pushed out my calves, tensing then releasing my Achilles', a memory came to me: the stickiness of spruce gum, the sun's warmth on bare skin, dead needles and twigs pocking kneecaps. The girl's soft breath, her annoying giggle. My determination to say nothing and ignore it because we were alone, there was no one to hear us. On the island, one hazy afternoon. My first time. And afterwards, Mom complaining about the tree gum on my Tee Kays, how no amount of washing would remove it. The girl — what a little schmuck I was; I couldn't've told you her name even if I'd wanted to.

Anyway. I finished stretching and left the woods for the wide gravel path past the Martello tower, an old, rusty-stoned fortification stolid as a toadstool through the trees. Glimpsed a young couple kissing, having their picture snapped beside the dungeon door. Everything about them said "honeymoon". How else, I thought trotting by, could they dawdle so in the heat?

Looping back towards the parking lot, I made myself do one more kilometre, past the HMCS *Bonaventure* anchor honouring dead servicemen, and started cooling down, slowing to a brisk walk. Near the canteen I found a park bench and stretched out my hamstrings, my calves — bent-kneed, one foot then the other hoisted to the seat, to maximize the effort.

Generally, by this stage I feel exhilarated — exhausted, yes, but relaxed, refreshed. Satisfied by the sweat, the tautness of my muscles. But now, as I walked towards the car, my pulse levelling nicely, I felt a sudden sluggishness, a churlish discomfort — not physical exactly, but a twinge much like post-operative despair, something I'd thought was behind me. A restlessness — I don't know what else to call it, nor could I begin to explain why. Aside from the fact that when I got back, Barbara would be waiting, both garage doors raised and a path cleared to the lawn-mower.

Turning the key in the ignition, I remembered Gloria — that incredible smile, her turtle's-back tummy — and I have to admit, during the short drive home at least, it made me feel better.

Better and better, it turned out, as we started bumping into each other on a regular basis, usually in the parking lot, either warming up or cooling down. I got into the habit of driving to the park, jogging on sidewalks can cause shin splints, and for once I heeded Barbara's caution "Better safe than sorry." And another adage, one so obvious I've never been able to bring myself to use it, even on patients who'd most take it to heart: "An ounce of prevention's worth a pound of cure."

Some mornings it was still dark when I got to the parking lot — I could've used the time I saved driving to read the paper or wolf down an extra slice of toast — dry, of course, no butter. But old habits die hard, as they say. And Gloria was nothing if not regular. I admired that. So after a while I'd kill time in the car with the radio on, till the sky brightened and her blue Honda tore in, Gloria pulling a big, wide U-ie when she saw the Celica. We had the parking lot to ourselves; at that hour there was seldom anyone in sight, apart from a few other joggers and people walking dogs. At that hour there is nobody to tell you to slow down or stop.

After a couple of weeks we began jogging together. Perhaps I timed it that way, my leaving the house precisely at six, no earlier, no later. Or perhaps it simply happened that she would be getting out of her car as I arrived, or vice versa. The first time I was a little nervous that she would outdistance me, or that I'd be forced to overdo it — panting, tense with fear — to keep up. I needn't have worried; being an instructor, Gloria was full of patience. She could match my pace with no trouble at all; if she ever slowed on my account, she had the extreme grace not to show it.

I had vowed, when I recovered, to be kinder to myself. To seek some sort of balance between playing God all the time and being a regular guy. A husband, a father. Devastating, to be just shy of one's peak and forced to resign oneself to letting go — even slightly. I speak of my career. Perhaps it's a little like being an alcoholic and struggling to say no to every beer. Or a bulimic, always weighing the line between healthy nourishment and guilt over food. This is how I try explaining it to Barbara, the best analogy I can summon for describing my sense of professionalism to my wife. Except in my case the tendency to overdo things isn't out of self-contempt but self-regard, the urge to do a job well. To excel.

Since that episode two years ago, I have had to cut back a bit on my work, the stress involved. Running definitely helps. And my colleagues have been good in picking up the slack. So it was a little unusual — dare I say fortuitous — to get a call one night at three. Lismore was off in Hawaii, the residents run off their feet. The hospital could've found somebody else, I suppose, but they chose to call me. Some things may have changed since the heart attack, but not my Hippocratic duty.

The patient was in his sixties or seventies. They had cut off his shirt, his upper torso exposed, waiting. His arms and chest were covered with muddy tattoos, the smudged blue lines blending with the horrid pigment of his skin. I figured perhaps he was an old navy man — until he opened his mouth and I glimpsed the rotten black stumps of his teeth. A bum. Breath like a tavern floor. He was cursing everyone in sight — myself, the nurses, even the orderly going about his business, moving a stretcher from the cubicle.

The fellow was pissed out of his mind; a nurse whispered that the ambulance attendants had found him on the floor of a washroom, some dive up in the north end.

"Next of kin?" I asked — most of his chart was blank; he was too incoherent to give any details. Address unknown, no known family. Lovely. Rushing in, I'd noticed a scrawny-looking woman seated outside, half-cut as well. She might've been his age, maybe younger — with people like that it's difficult to tell. She was very frightened; when the nurse tried to pry something out of her, she just shrugged her skinny shoulders. She was wearing a dirty red cardigan with something disgusting spilled down the front — that much I had time to notice.

As I went to work on the fellow, I could hear her out in the hall, saying she didn't know "nothing", she'd just met the guy, they were having some drinks. "Vincent", she thought the man's name was. "Yeah, that was it: Vincent somebody."

"Someone find that woman a cab," I hissed, as the guy started to go into arrest. For a second, the stink of beer and urine and unwashed flesh was so overwhelming I almost hesitated — yes, hesitated — before pounding on his chest, driving all the strength I could muster into my arms. I paused — a split second, no longer — then pounded again, so hard I could feel the sickening snap of his ribs giving way.

And do you know, twenty seconds later I managed to get the heart going again, the line on the screen pulsing into a feeble zigzag. We saved the guy. For the time being, anyhow.

Maybe it was the hour, and I was groggy, part of me still home in bed with my wife. Barbara's soft snore, her warm, maternal smell, God, of celery sticks and flannelette and Sesame Street shampoo. But it scared me, that second's hesitation. The others' eyes, grave above their masks, wondering what the hell I was waiting for. It was that close.

After we got him stabilized, I returned once to check

his condition. Sedated, unconscious, he didn't look as bad. You couldn't see his bloodshot, terrified eyes, motionless and slightly sunken now beneath the lids. I couldn't help wondering what he'd glimpsed while he was cursing us, before he lost consciousness. While we were struggling to save his life. Some small indelible stain, perhaps, or a light? Some we pull back from the brink of death report seeing a glow — a bright, warming presence beckoning them.

I wouldn't want to speculate. Not in this fellow's case.

There was bile in my throat while I washed up and changed. "Going home to catch up on your sleep?" one of the nurses asked, in a chipper, presumptuous tone. "Right," I said, bushed. The clock said ten to five.

I thought of driving home and crawling back in beside my sleeping wife. But instead I drove to the park and sat watching the sun rise over the oil refinery, the auto port. Watched a container ship come in, tall as a high-rise, the toy-size pilot boat and tugs plying the blue-black harbour. I sat in the car like that till the clock on the dash said 5:45 and, sure as shit, resolute as Revenue Canada, in turned Gloria's little Honda.

I waited till she got out, then went over. She started warming up against the car, smiling up at me, still a bit sleepy. There was a little speck of toothpaste on her chin, and she didn't appear to be wearing any makeup. Of course, in that light I couldn't be certain. Her face looked pale and tired, the lines around her mouth a little more pronounced. But lovely, all the same.

"You're not running?" She was taking in my clothes, wrinkled chinos, scuffed deck shoes — the things nearest the bed when I received the call. Peering up at my face, she gasped, "Oh God — Michael, what's *wrong?*"

I tried to smile, gazing away from her at the lighthouse stranded on a spit in the harbour, its oscillating flash so quick yet feeble you wondered how they'd catch it at sea.

"Almost lost a guy." I coughed, clearing my throat. Thrusting my hands in my pockets, I glanced at my toes. Some of the stitching had come away; I made a mental note for Barbara to have it repaired. "Very close." I coughed again.

Gloria, meanwhile, was unzipping her track suit, loosening the trousers and stepping out of them. "Well, it happens. I guess. Doesn't it? I mean, nobody's Ben Casey. And the guy's alive, right? Jeez, he must be thankful."

Underneath, she had on cropped black tights, a plain blue T-shirt. But as she lunged into a runner's stretch, I caught a glimpse of the narrow strip of jungle-print between her buttocks. Festive. Tropical. Her eyes on me, she straightened and, leaning upright against the car, did some pushups. When she glanced down to check her toe position, I stole a look at her flanks, curved and tight as a horse's, divided neatly as an apple. In spite of my weariness, I felt a pleasant tightening in the groin. Sensing it, perhaps, Gloria turned and smiled.

"Kind of chilly this morning. Probably wise to wait till it warms up a bit. Wouldn't want to get a cramp — I mean, this time of day, in the middle of the woods. A gal can never be too careful, can she?"

The next I knew, I was in my car following hers. Oh, I knew where she lived. It's not that big a city; after fifteen years I could probably drive it blindfolded. But I crept along behind her, a car's length between us. Cruising through the flashing ambers, we proceeded slowly — out of respect, perhaps, for the time, that hushed, suspended hour before the world awakes. Gloria had a habit, I noticed, of riding the brake — or maybe she was giving me time to change my mind. An out.

We'll just see, I told myself, tailing her into the underground garage. Her apartment was near the top of the Park Gardens, a decent enough high-rise not far from the hospital. A lot of nurses live there, the single ones. As we got off the elevator — Gloria looking radiant in the tastefully lit corridor — we could hear the faint sounds of people stirring: the buzz of clock radios, voices coming alive, coffee grinders. The soft hum of others showering, shaving....

"I suppose you don't drink coffee," she said, showing me into her small white living-room. The furnishings were inexpensive Scandinavian — a boxy white sofa and loveseat with a low, glass-topped table between. Modern, tasteful — pristine. A room marvellously unsullied by children's fingerprints or feet. On one wall were some chrome-framed prints of ballerinas, sepia-toned studies of ankles and feet, toes bent at an impossible angle. The only splash of colour a florist's arrangement of fresh-cut flowers in the centre of the room, reflected in the sparkling tabletop.

Peeling off her track suit again, Gloria disappeared into the kitchen and returned with two small bottles of grapefruit juice. Removing the lids, she set each on a coaster — souvenirs from the Boston Marathon. Turning her back to me, she pulled the blue T-shirt over her head, wandering towards what I supposed was the bedroom.

"Just gimme a sec, okay?" Her voice was muffled by the stretchy fabric. Her butt round and firm and beautiful as life, the thong between the cheeks. Her waist tiny and tight, the ribcage lifting above it.

I took a sip of juice, so sour it tasted bitter at first, bitter as the contents of a stomach. It made me think of that patient again — Vincent — the blackness of his mouth beneath the bright, greenish lights.

"Michael?" she called from the other room. Enticing. Inviting. Through the wall, I could hear the Weather

Channel come on in the next apartment, from somewhere else the time — 6:52.

"Michael?"

Without answering, I set down the juice, screwing on the lid as quietly as possible. Then, for some reason I still can't put my finger on, I rose and let myself out.

I don't know why. Hurrying for the stairs, I was already wondering what harm it would've done. Not much; maybe not any. Barbara need never have known. Getting into the car, I envisioned Gloria sitting Buddhist-style on the bed, the straps of her exerciser pulled down; rolling her head this way and that. Her large brown eyes daring me.

You know, I almost went back. But there was something about the street outside, my eyes adjusting from the underground parking — the brightness of the sky, perhaps? Traffic noises starting up, people already rushing to work. And I thought, move it. Move it. Before the kids wake up. If I get home now, my wife will still be in bed. Waiting.

SWIMMING POOLS, MOVIE STARS

I didn't always smoke — Lord, no. In fact, I didn't start till Barbara was in school. Now I'm glad, I am, just to have something in my hand, something to occupy me. I thank God for my cigarettes, especially now. If not for the Cameos I'd go stark raving mad. They'd be booking me into Dartmouth faster than it takes poor Art to get dressed these days, they would, the very ones always at me to quit — Barbara and that husband of hers, the doctor.

They're coming up for the day, the whole family. On the phone I said to bring their bathing suits. The kids', I meant — my grandson and granddaughter — though I suppose if they want to swim they can bring their own darned suits; they're not exactly babies. Besides, they're coming to see Arthur. Since the diagnosis not a weekend goes by Barbara doesn't drive up, mostly by herself, sometimes with the kids and Michael.

"Bring your suit, and we'll barbecue, too." I tried sounding as chipper as I could on the phone, as if there was nothing in the world wrong, not a thing different.

"Take each day as it comes" is what the volunteer

from the Cancer Society told Arthur.

"Life goes on," he says, being philosophical. Doesn't fool me though, not for a minute. I've heard him down the hall — crying, sometimes. More than once I've heard him praying: "Please God, I'll do this if only if only you'll, you'll—" Striking bargains, the way you do when you're a little kid. "Please, pleeease, God. I promise I'll never bite my nails again if you, if you, if you...."

Arthur, poor, poor Arthur.

It might even be funny, if he weren't my husband. If he weren't so sick.

I hear him now, scuffling around the bedroom, getting up. He knows Barb and them are on their way. He wants to be washed and dressed by the time they arrive, so they won't find him in bed. Doesn't like his girl to see him in bed, though for Pete's sake I couldn't begin to tell you how many times I've said: "You're gonna wear yourself out, hon. You've gotta do like the doctors say and pace yourself."

It must be a hundred degrees in this house. I've got all the shades drawn, even here in the kitchen. Arthur minds the heat something fierce, always did — but especially now, after his treatments.

"Lord," he tells me after those mornings at the hospital. "I must be burning up, Kaye. Roasting like something on a goddamn spit. If this isn't hell, I don't...." And I'll rush around pouring him a cool bath, shallow so the doctor's targets don't wash off, and turning on fans, every drape and blind and balloon shade in the house drawn so he won't get the least bit of sunlight.

Says he can't bear the sun or any light at all — which is why on this lovely July day I'm racooned inside, creeping around like an animal only comes out at night. Guess by now you could say I've adjusted — to the light, I mean. The heat, though, that's another story. Had a fellow in last week about an air conditioner, but Arthur got up out of bed to tell him we weren't interested. Couldn't justify the cost, he told the man, the sake of two weeks a year.

"Arthur," I said, ready to give up at that point, plain ready to give up. "It's worth it if it makes you more comfortable."

But he just hobbled into the bedroom, half shut the door in my face. I could hear him in there squirming back under the sheet, his breath wheezy and jagged as a saw.

I showed the fellow the door, then stood outside the bedroom. "Art? Art, honey, how 'bout a little drink of juice? I'll bring you a little drink of orange juice, how's that?" I coaxed and coaxed, the exact same way I used to Barbara, dragging her away from the TV.

After a long time he said, "All right then, that'd be fine," as if I'd offered turpentine — the orange juice, that is. Only thing he can enjoy and keep down any more — funny, though, since that's the one fruit they tell you to avoid, on account of it being hard on the stomach. Arthur says it's the only thing still tastes as it should, and not like something out of a small brown bottle.

"All these treatments," I finally asked his doctor this past week. "Do you think they're doing any good?" I was at rock bottom that day, as if the darkness in the house had got through my clothes and skin and settled inside.

"We won't know unless we try" was the answer.

Doctors, like God's puppets mouthing these things. Remind me of the man on *Ed Sullivan* Barbara used to get a kick out of, between Topo Gigio and the Beatles. What was his name? Charlie something. The puppet's mouth opened and closed like the trap door to a cave.

"Open sesame," Arthur used to say, watching that mouth, and Barbara would laugh.

Open sesame — how I miss hearing things like that.

Just this morning, I said it to make him open wide enough to let the toothbrush in. I was laughing, blinking back tears. Wanted him to laugh too, but then his hand came up to my wrist — his hand, grey as old wax paper, so thin you can see all the veins full of God knows what — and he tugged at me to stop. It's not funny, his eyes said, nothing's funny. His breath smelled cold and metallic as blood in a kidney pan — a queer, bitter, chemical smell not like a body's any more, but something taken over by pills. When he spat there was blood in the toothpaste, not a lot, but a swirl dark as the chocolate in ripple ice cream.

"Barb's coming up today," I reminded him, watching the spit twirl away under the tap. I took the facecloth and wiped his mouth.

"I'd rather be dead than this," he said in this tight, fussy voice, fed up. Petulant as a child sick of school or a game of tag gone awry — as if it were somebody's fault.

"I'd rather be dead, I said. Do you know that, Kaye?"

And I started to cry — not so much because of the unfairness or the fact of what he said. But because it got me thinking again: where does that leave me?

He looked at me with those eyes that have no shine any more, eyes that know things I don't, but seem to be waiting. Waiting and watching for me to slip up somehow.

"You want to look good for Barbie, now don't you. Barbie and the kids," I said.

Thinking he'd be glad about seeing her, I waited for a flicker, something, in his eyes. Steady as a reptile's, they were. Gave me the creeps to meet them, like staring down a turtle or snake, something cold-blooded, dead. What I wanted was to say "Arthur. Arthur, *why* are you blaming me?"

"Give me a hand with the shaver now, would you, Kaye?" he said, watching me in the mirror. For a minute our eyes played cat-and-mouse, his daring mine to hold still long enough till this awful, ugly truth could jump out and take root in me. Breathing in slow, I tried facing him without letting my eyes reflect what we've both been told. *Well, yes, Arthur. The doctors say....*

"There you go, dear," I said, running the razor over his cheek. It buzzed up into my fingers. Under the stubble his skin felt like rubber left in the sun too long, limp but dry, so dry — better, perhaps, since they stopped the chemo — but dry and dead as the peelings from a sunburn.

"We want to try and shrink the tumour," they told me, "To make him more comfortable."

Her last visit, he told Barbara it felt like he was being barbecued. When he said that, she about had a fit.

"Come on now." I patted on shaving lotion, Old Spice, his favourite. Fought the urge to slap it on like a barber, going gently, gently as if powdering an infant's bottom.

In the bedroom I laid out his clothes — the blue golf shirt, some cream-coloured slacks, socks, his blue-checked boxers. I had to turn away as he got out of his pyjamas, old and slow as Noah, I thought, without the beard.

"Need any help there?" I said in this cheerful voice, fussing with the bedskirt, fluffing the pillows. "Barb should be here any time."

"I'm just gonna sit here now and wait to die."

That's what he said when he found out. We'd just gotten home from the hospital; he'd been in having tests. "Inoperable", "three months to a year" — the words were still flying around the top of my brain like comets.

Goodness only knows what they told him when I wasn't there — the nurses, I mean, once visiting hours ended and he was lying there quiet. The room was semiprivate, the other patient usually off padding around in his johnny shirt. At the time I figured that was good; better than having some terminal case in the next bed.

But now I think it might've done Arthur good if there'd been someone sicker — just their breathing, their snoring, between my visits, once the lights were out. God only knows what poor Arthur was thinking the hours he put in, them figuring out what was wrong.

Started with his breathing; he said he was having trouble catching his breath. Next it spread to his stomach — heartburn, I figured, like when I was pregnant with Barbara. But then he started having trouble keeping things down.

What exactly the doctors told him, I can't say. I wasn't there when he got the news; they only told me afterwards. It was a resident took me aside, a sweet-faced young woman with a long, fat braid down her back, her feet in Nikes. I didn't know she was a doctor at first — she couldn't've even been Barbara's age.

"We can't give you a prognosis, Mrs. Mossman. With treatment, who knows? Without — well, the most we can hope for is three, maybe four months. At the most."

I wanted to reach back and yank the braid, pull it till it stretched her eyes. Like Barbara screeching *Mum, Mum, it's too tight!* when I was fixing her hair.

He was diagnosed in February. I'll never forget that day, driving Arthur home from the hospital. There was freezing rain, ice sticking to the windshield fast as the wipers could swish it off. Arthur sat beside me in the front seat, his blue shaving kit on his lap, hands folded so tight you swore the knuckles would split.

"Arthur," I said, the news finally starting to settle like the blob of mercury in an old-fashioned thermometer. The kind I put under Barbara's arm when she had chickenpox, not the kind they've got now, hooked to computers.

I wanted to reach over and put my hand on his

clutching the zipper on the blue nylon bag, clutching, clutching then letting go. I wanted to, but it was all I could do to keep the car going straight and not veer over the line. Everything inside me seemed to quake like a tall dish of Jell-O, from the thin, hard skin on top down to the jiggly bottom.

When I let him in the front door, he went straight to his chair in the living-room, the stiff blue wing-chair he chooses when there's company. Sat there staring out the picture window at the road, the junipers at the end of the driveway, glazed with ice.

I should've gone and put my arms around him. I wanted to. I could've held him and wept, and rocked him the way I used to Barbara. I would've, if there hadn't been such hate in his eyes. Hate, despair — I don't know what you'd call it, him sitting there stiff as if nailed to a plank, staring, this haughty, betrayed look on his face. I remember looking at him, thinking, oh, if only he were of paper — a ball crumpling in a bonfire, or newsprint, a big sheet left outside, wet, grey and limp. It would've been easier; then I could've comforted him.

"You're just bringing me home to die, aren't you?"

The way he said it enough to slice me in two. As if the whole universe had cooked this thing up and turned against him. And I, more than anybody, were the one that set the pot to boil.

"Let me get you a cup of tea, dear," I finally said, when I couldn't take it any more — the hard, stubborn silence of two people married forty-two years, not like the prickly chill in the air after a fight, but worse, a million times worse. I swear the only sounds were those from the road, the slushy noise of cars passing, and the whirr of the furnace starting up, a sound that normally made me feel çosy. But then I felt a coldness glide down my back — like the dumb-waiter in some big old house, dropping with a full load of dishes. I got up and went to plug in the kettle.

After a few minutes Arthur came into the kitchen. He stood with his hands in his pockets, looking out at the deck, the gas barbecue Barbara and the kids gave him the year before for Father's Day, crusted with ice. Still in his sock feet — I hadn't had a chance to unpack his slippers — he rocked back on his heels, staring out at the grey, frozen yard as if it were summer and he deciding whether to cut the grass.

It was the pool he had his eyes on, the white-fenced enclosure, the bright blue cover sagging under some slush, and beyond it, the bare trees bent like wires at the end of the yard.

"If I'd of known then, I wouldn't've bothered having it put in," he said, looking right at me taking tea-bags from the goose-patterned canister. "Blue Geese" it says on the bottom; "Microwave-safe". He tried to laugh, his eyes glistening as if there were ice on them, too.

"Oh no," I told him. "No, Arthur — don't be silly, you mustn't talk that way." My hand was shaking and all of a sudden I felt my stomach buckle, a bad-tasting lump at the back of my tongue. But that's what I said, in a voice sure as a Sunday School teacher's. Not a pinch of doubt. The same voice I used when Barbara was a child fretting over homework.

"I'll never get this project done," she'd complain, like it was the end of the world. "Oh yes you will." I'd leave no room for her to do otherwise.

"You're going to be all right," I said to him, holding the canister lid, its blue china knob smooth as a worry stone in my hand, a pet rock. The hard coolness a comfort somehow, definite as a marble under a blanket. But it was all I could do not to drop the thing, let it roll and shatter on the blue cushion floor.

"Yes," he said after a while, watching me with this

huffy, suspicious look.

"You'll get your swims, don't worry." The Sunday School voice again — if I spoke loud enough, maybe, just maybe my good sense would rub off.

"The treatments start next week...," he said in an off-hand way.

I turned to pour the kettle, steam breezing back and scalding my hand.

"...I don't want you going and telling Barbara, now."

I don't suppose he noticed me stop to lick my finger, squeezing it tight to still the pain.

"She's got enough on her plate, Kaye, without this too."

Barbara has this big job now, you see, doing some sort of research at the Bedford Institute. Now her kids are in school, she acts as if she's making up for lost time. *Lost?* I'd like to say to her. *Lost?*

She's told me what she does: some kind of science, there's a name for it, I can never remember. Something to do with parasites, tiny crawly things in the ocean that get into sea urchins — or maybe it's mussels. When she talks about her work, all I picture is a clip from the news a few years ago, something to do with toxic mussels, a woman in a lab coat swirling yellow slime in a blender. I had to look away — Arthur too — each time they showed it, over and over: the shot of this woman looking happy and natural, as if home blending banana shakes for her kids.

Well. Barbara's job is more important than that person's — it has to do with opening up new kinds of fisheries. I don't tell her, of course, but it calms me somehow, thinking of her as that lady with the blender. Still, you have to give her credit for going back to work and applying herself after being home with Amy and Tyler.

Especially with her husband so busy, the two of them busy and in the money — two ships passing in the night, that would sum up their marriage. But Arthur, poor Arthur, is awful proud of his little girl and I have to say I am too. Even if there are times I wish the two of us could just sit down and share a recipe, or some cute craft for the kids — those kits they sell in *Canadian Living*, for instance, that make you go, "Why didn't I think of that?" Though Amy and Tyler are past that now; they're older. We all are, which is why I appreciate Barbara's visits, especially now with her father so bad. And so when she comes I try to forget she's a scientist, and think of her — just like her mother — fixing meals, concocting desserts. Never mind that the male half of the equation is usually missing: Michael, either at work or winding down from it. "Taking time for himself," she always explains, which is what they told him to do after his trouble.

Doctors! Just ask Arthur what he thinks of them. And he'll tell you, just as I would now, they're only out for one thing.

"Ha!" Arthur said by the pool last summer, right after we had it put in. "Looks like a doctor lives here now!"

It was a big debate, see, whether to get one in-ground or out. We finally opted for the pricier kind — safer for the grandchildren, Arthur decided, having a shallow end. I started reminding him, of course, how they have their red-blue-green-maroon or whatever badges, how they're not that little any more. But then I stopped myself.

"Yes, dear. I think we'd get more enjoyment out of the better model. Plus it would look so much nicer."

And so we had the thing installed — took a backhoe two whole days just to dig the hole! After the decking was laid, the pump primed, Arthur stood at the deep end with his arms spread out like a little boy, whistling through his teeth.

"Whoooo-eeee!" he yelled, laughing as if he'd just beat the world at chess or croquinole. "Looks like a doctor lives here now!"

"Yes," I said, setting up the new 'chaise-lounge' from Sears. "That or some kind of celebrity!" Silly, but I couldn't help thinking of *The Beverly Hillbillies*, Granny in her rocker on top of the truck.

Arthur cupped his hand to his ear.

"What was that?"

"You know," I yelled back, my laughter rippling like waves the length of the pool. "'Swimmin' pools, movie staaarrrrs'!"

He stopped, looked at me funny, then leaned over to push off his sandals, puffing a little from the effort. This smug, content smile spreading ear to ear.

"But honey. Those people never get to retire!"

I'll always remember that. Even now, waiting for Barbara, it makes me want to smile. Even though since February it's not too funny any more.

Retirement — seems this is what Arthur should've looked forward to his whole life, ever since I've known him anyway. Whether he'd admit it or not; heaven knows when he turned sixty-five, do you think I could get him to quit? Some would've called him a workaholic. "You're wishing your life away, Arthur Mossman" — that's what I used to say when he complained about his job, the hours, the driving. The mess of papers in the basement, later, when he finally retired from the office but kept on working at home — small claims, sporadic jobs, just to keep a finger in the pie. Because, you see, deep down I knew he liked his work. Can't imagine what he'd have done all those years without it, actually. Oh, I know the awful things used to get to him sometimes — Lord, I used to tell him, you'd have to be made of granite not to be affected. But Arthur loved working — well, not so much that, as he loved excitement, being in the thick of things. I used to kid that if someone gave him the choice between a day home with me — just me, no one around to disturb us — or on the road, at a disaster scene, well...we both knew which would win hands down.

Arthur always was the type enjoyed being on the move, the hum of tires. Never could sit too long at home, even quiet times like Christmas, though in the accident business there were precious few of these. But me, now, I could sit warming his pie in the oven — for ever if need be. To me it just didn't seem necessary being overly busy, like a gerbil running a wheel, faster, faster, till after a while you wear yourself out and fall off. Not complaining, of course. But exhausted, once you realize the running's like a cat chasing its tail. Pointless.

Sure, there were a few times I'd have liked to be in the thick of something too. But of the two of us — of all the people it could've happened to — queer it had to be Arthur who got sick. Never smoked or drank in his life, well, not once we were married. Barb would say I've smoked enough for both of us.

Some days after lunch, in the bedroom watching *Coronation Street* (Arthur always watches TV before drifting off for a nap, just like a baby sleeping afternoons), I'll steal a glance at him — the greyish tinge to his face, the stubbly patches I've missed with the razor; the way his skin almost seems too big — and I'll wonder if it's always been there inside him, the cancer, this terrible growth. If he was born with it already rooted, whatever "it" is that triggers sickness. If it was in there lurking, hidden deep and dark where no one could see, the day we met, the day he took me to lunch. The day Barbara was born, or the baby.

The baby — my memory of him's a dull itch. Maybe Arthur's sickness is like he was inside me, a secret that turns you upside-down once let out. Arthur saw him, you see, not me. Nobody else, besides the doctors and nurses. They wouldn't let me see him. Only Arthur was allowed to hold him a minute or two before they took the body. The perfect little body, Arthur told me later, after I nagged and nagged; except the face resembled a little old man's, wrinkled and shrunken, dehydrated. The skin was grey; no colour sprang when you touched it, he said, when you stroked the cheeks with your finger. Failure to thrive in the womb, something to do with the cord.

Arthur saw. He said by looking you couldn't see anything awfully wrong, just the way the face appeared wilted — "wilted as a daisy" was how he put it. But otherwise perfect, a perfect little baby. I've never gotten over that, or the nurses whispering: "Try keeping busy, Mrs. Mossman, doing for others. It'll help take your mind off...."

At the time I thought there could be nothing worse; now I know that's not true. But I can't help thinking whatever it was made the baby die has gotten into Arthur now. The last person you'd expect, always the type put a brave face on things, kept you believing there's a reason, somewhere, to smile. Though don't get me wrong, we've had our ups and downs — what marriage hasn't?

Sounds foolish — foolish as Simple Simon fishing for whales in a bucket — but till last winter the baby was alive somewhere, somehow, in the hopefulness in Arthur's eyes, the fun, the impatience even. Even when he used to come in late, keep me waiting with his supper all evening, then ask why I didn't just go to bed. Even when I thought he liked his work better than me, I could look at him and feel, at least, the baby wasn't my imagination, a kernel of something I'd dreamed and lost; an excuse.

Funny, its dad being the only one who ever saw it, after me feeling its weight there, under my ribs, all those

months. For a long time afterwards, I'd lie beside Arthur
in bed, shivering as if I were out on the doorstep naked.
Oh, my.

"I just want you to be happy," he'd sigh.

Now, pray tell, what on earth does a person say to
that?

The night after Arthur's diagnosis I had an awful dream,
one hell of a dream. Woke up cold and wet with perspiration, the only warmth in my lips from dreaming about
kissing him.

We were somewhere in the States; it was flat, with
miles of low brick buildings: schools or warehouses, or
clinics, maybe. There were acres and acres of these buildings, looped with freeways — just like where my sister
Ardith lives in Florida, the time Arthur and I drove down
to visit and kept getting lost, palm trees and boulevards
all the same after a while.

But in the dream I was alone, and I was looking for
my husband. Getting panicky, I went into this building,
could've been a clinic, could've been an office, yes, the
big, sprawling office of an insurance company. But inside was a funeral home, with little black-and-white signs
for each viewing room. And someone at a desk got up
and told me they had him, but it wasn't too late.

The person led me to a stretcher where Arthur lay,
already grey. He had a tube up his nose, and another snaking down to a bag hanging over the wheels. And he looked
at me, at least I *felt* he could see me, his eyes just slits, the
dullest glint between the lids. And he said in this weak,
dry croak, "Kaye? Kaye Rushton? Will you come out to
eat? Will you meet me round the corner at twelve? Twelve
sharp, for lunch?"

I squeezed his hand, could already feel it going cold,
his fingertips blue. There wasn't time to answer. I bent

down and kissed his forehead. And he whispered in this soft, parting voice:

"Hug me, Kaye. Hug me."

But before I could do it he was gone.

And do you know, when I woke I could still feel the warmth of his forehead on my lips — Arthur snoring beside me, his mouth open on the pillow, chest lifting and falling, just like always.

But then I knew.

Come on, Barbara, if you don't get here soon your father'll be asleep. The afternoon'll be gone. If I take chicken out now, it'll be thawed in time for supper. How many pieces? One for you, one each for the kids, one for Michael if he comes, a few bites off one for Arthur....

I'll sit down and have a cigarette while I'm waiting, that's what I'll do.

Oh God, did you hear that? I'm talking to myself again.

Reaching on top of the fridge for the package, I notice the coat of dust. It doesn't feel greasy, though, the way it would if I were doing more cooking. Laying the green and white pack on the table, I go off to get a dust rag, a ragged piece of tea towel. Dampening it, I push aside the shade for a glimpse of the pool, the water sparkling flat and bright in the sun. I imagine how a dip would feel, the coolness like pinpricks, sharp at first as splintered crystal.

That's what the sparkle puts me in mind of — good lead crystal with candlelight flickering through. Don't know why exactly, since Arthur and I never were ones for candlelit dinners. Too busy; his crazy, unpredictable hours. I figured once he retired maybe things would change, we'd have more time for things like candles, flowers, the odd glass now and then of rosé. Still haven't gotten around to it, though. But for some reason, looking out at the pool reminds me of beautiful stemmed glasses — the clarity that lets you see clean to the bottom.

This is what I like about pools, the fact that you know exactly what's down there, unlike the ocean. No squiggly, slimy surprises. Though it's something Arthur, with his love of salt water, can't quite appreciate.

He used to laugh at me, you know; once we were picnicking near Peggy's Cove and he kept badgering me to come in. Well. It wasn't too bad when the tide was low and the seaweed stayed put and you could see what was what and where not to step. I had my monthly visitor so I wasn't going in past my knees anyway. Barbara was just a little thing — two, maybe three years old. Arthur kept pestering, "Come on in, hon! It's not so bad once you get used to it!"

It wasn't the coldness I minded. "I don't like to leave the baby," I yelled back, shivering, the water just over my shins.

"For Pete's sake" — he was laughing, shaking his head — "we're right *here*."

As I went to answer, something grabbed my toe — latched on, it did, nearly sent me out of my skin! I screamed and splashed out of that water so fast I got soaked. Barbara looked up from her little red pail and her face wrinkled in a howl, as if something had swum in and tried to gobble up her mum.

Arthur stumbled out laughing, his belly shivering from the cold. There was a tiny green crab cupped in his hands. Dripping all over the towels, he crouched down and dropped it in the pail. He took Barbara's little fist and touched it to the shell, giving her a squeeze as she looked up and started to giggle. For a while they watched it scamper around the bottom trying to claw its way up the sides, before he waded out and let it go.

"See?" he called. "Nothing to be scared of."

But that was enough for me. After that I stayed on the blanket.

Now I wonder — as I do waking, eating, going to sleep — has the cancer been inside him all along, like that creature hiding in the sand? "Nothing to be scared of," he told me. But it wasn't till he knew it was there that he said so.

The chemo was hellish — like watching a dog being poisoned alive. You hear about all the poisons out there in the ocean, the soil; in those half-baked things Barbara puts under her microscope.

All these poisons, and more, dripped through the needle into his vein.

"Don't move," they told him. "Any leakage will kill the flesh around the site. So, please, Mr. Mossman, please don't move your arm. Try to stay as still as you can."

"Picture the good cells" — a breath later they sounded cheery as Englishmen singing "God Save the Queen" — "the good cells fighting the bad like knights on horseback."

Arthur liked that; you could tell by his grim little smile the idea suited him. But at the time I found it skewed, wrong-headed. No, I preferred to think of big fish eating smaller ones: dark-finned sharks swimming against the current, swallowing fry tiny and quick as the striped electric fish in Barbara's family-room aquarium. It happens so fast, nobody sees the little ones dart by like flecks of dust through a sieve; "neon tetras", I believe that's the name the kids have for them.

I felt so helpless, holding his hand, later the basin, rubbing his back while he brought up. Helpless, yet comforted too, in the queerest, smallest way, knowing I was doing all I could — the cold comfort that follows years of fretting and hazy dread, once the axe falls and lands not far from your own neck. It was like watching dove-grey thread roll, unwinding, over a hard waxed floor, the white, empty spool come to rest under your chair; I could finally look at things and say, "So, yes. This is what was meant to be, all along. This is it."

I get up on a chair to wipe off the fridge. Down the hall I hear Arthur stir.

"Barbie'll be here soon!" I call out, raising my voice. No answer. Half the time I don't think he hears. God. It strikes me how I'm always tiptoeing around, scared to upset anything, disturb the peace, the awful peace, while I'm doing the usual and Arthur's in there sleeping. At least I think he's sleeping — could be the effort getting dressed flattened him out, the way the wind does the grass behind the pool. Lord knows the past few weeks he's had the strength for little else, precious little else.

Oh, the long, heavy silence, as if he's in there thinking up paces to put me through, getting me in shape for something — me! scared to put the radio on in case it bothers him. Arthur, who so loved his music: Charley Pride, Johnny Mathis.... Oh boy, when we first met I used to get after him, he'd play the car radio so loud. Used to make him turn it down so we could talk.

"Talk? Why this need all the time to talk?" he'd say, then a good song would come on and he'd be in seventh heaven, some crazy kind of glory I think now, tapping his hands on the wheel and singing, well, mumbling the words under his breath. His off-key monotone — my Dinah! what I'd give now to hear a bar or two of "Easy Lovin'" in that flat old voice.

"Hon?" I creep down the hall, tap on the door. "You okay, Art?" I whisper, as if even the sound of my voice must pain him. Every sound — like the waves of heat, the flakes of sunshine breaking round the shades — driving it home.

"I'm fine," he sighs after a long, long time. "Why don't you go fix yourself some lunch and I'll stay put till she gets here."

"Suit yourself, then," I whisper through the crack in the door, already backing away. "Can I bring you anything? A cup of tea? A sandwich? How 'bout that, or some juice — there's some mixed up...."

"No, nothing is fine." There's this slow creaking sound as he turns over on top of the spread. "I'll just rest until she comes."

In the kitchen it's hot enough now to cook the devil. My land, I've never seen such heat. I straighten the shade above the sink's grey glint. The cigarettes are still waiting on the table. Maybe I'll fix some iced tea for Barbara's visit — yes, she'll like that.

When I snap the lid from the tin, the sound seems to bounce off the walls. The wooden spoon thuds the sides of the pitcher. There's a tight, queasy feeling in my belly as I carry a glassful to the breakfast nook and pull out a chair. I sit there in my apron, sipping the iced tea. It tastes like the tin, the lemon flavour harsh as furniture polish. Barb should be here any second and I still haven't had my cigarette. My tongue pressed to my teeth, I shut my eyes for a moment and breathe in, imagining the menthol's coolness filling my chest, soothing as VapoRub. When at last I light one — just one, quick, before Barb gets here — my hand's shaking so hard I can hardly flick the lighter.

If only there were something I could do. Of course I think of the living-room, how it could use dusting; the pool vacuuming, the chemicals checked. Before Barbara and the kids arrive, I should go out and skim off the bugs. Fishing, I call it, with the long-handled scoop Arthur got at Canadian Tire.

Terrible problem last year with horse-flies; you should've seen Arthur one afternoon, treading water with the darned things buzzing around his head, this disgusted look on his face like a child with a burst balloon. Next thing, the two of us were laughing, the sun flashing in his face, his nose and forehead burned red as the back of his neck. Farmer tan — that's my husband, even the time we went to Florida: his neck and arms, the top of his head where the hair doesn't quite stretch across, all beet-red, the rest of him chalk-white.

But that day with the horse-flies — when he got over being mad and saw how silly he looked — for a moment you would've sworn he wasn't a day over fifty, certainly not sixty-nine going on seventy. Heck, he looked the picture of health; if you squinted you'd've almost thought he was young — not a fellow who'd worked forty-nine years, just starting to enjoy life. You know those "Freedom Fifty-five" ads? Well, Arthur could've been one of those trim, smiling men. God forbid they had ads like that when he was still selling. The *women* — can you credit those women, fifty-five and not a grey hair or dimple of cellulite! I wouldn't've been able to keep up.

Not that I have anything against those TV couples, I don't. As a matter of fact, you could say getting the pool was our "Freedom Fifty-five" — fifteen years late. Crazy, some said; hardly a sound investment. But after that one time in Florida we decided we weren't too crazy about it; Arthur would be lost without the change of seasons — heck, nothing to do all day, all year, but lie on a deck chair sipping fancy drinks. Not for me, Arthur said. A couple of months a year, maybe; any more and you'd start feeling like a deadbeat, it seems to me — aimless, the way I used to feel when Barbara started school and I filled up my time grocery-shopping. Some days I turned on the TV — but I never watched those dismal soap operas, oh no, not me. That was one temptation I never gave in to, afternoon television. But the idea of wide-open spaces, days with no plans, still makes me jumpy as a flea on a dead cat. Arthur too, until now.

Oops — I hear the Cherokee pull in out front! Quick, quicker than you can say "algicide", I jump up and run the half-smoked butt under the tap, poke it in the garbage. Same with the ashtray, which I shove under the sink, behind the Mr. Clean.

The door opens downstairs and Barbara comes bustling in, the whoosh of traffic, the drone of a lawnmower rushing in with her. Silence fills the hall again as she comes upstairs, her footsteps buried in the brown shag.

"Mum?" she calls. My heart sinks as I realize she's alone.

"Where're the kids?" I meet her at the top of the stairs; don't bother to hide my disappointment.

"Oh, you know," she says, distracted as if busy sniffing something out. I put my hand over my mouth as she leans forward to kiss me, waiting for her to pounce at the smell of smoke.

"Where's Dad?" she asks in a half-alarmed, half-irritated voice — as if she'd driven all this way and found nobody home.

"Resting. He's looking forward to seeing you, though." I don't mention the kids. Basketball practice? Swimming lessons, or is it gymnastics on Sundays? The thought of their strong, young bodies fills me with a sudden weariness, makes me yearn for another fag, a whole one this time.

"He would've liked — your father would've liked seeing—"

"It's Michael's turn, you know, to take them swimming. Talk about the week from hell, Mum — he hasn't seen them in days."

"They could've swum here. I told you to bring their suits—"

She lets out a long sigh, as if I've asked her for the moon, for goodness' sake.

"Maybe next weekend, Mum."

I follow her into the kitchen, this tall, wide-hipped woman. She's wearing shorts, those crisp knee-length things with all the pockets that she orders from that pricey place in Maine. She looks older to me somehow, still trim, but tired, middle-aged. Probably working too hard.

"New haircut, dear?" I barely look at her, arranging the placemats on the table, crescent-shaped ones like sections of fruit. Dories, we used to call oranges cut like that — Barbara and I, when she was little. "Rory's in the dory," I would sing to her, sprinkling on sugar.

"Hmmm?" She tucks her hair behind her ears, the edges curving underneath like a seashell. The hairdo reminds me of a small, shiny helmet. There are grey strands in her part. She could buy a rinse to cover them, I don't know why she doesn't; that's what I did, till they took over. Though goodness knows I never told anybody — I'd hide the box in the garbage afterwards, wait and see if Arthur noticed.

Barbara opens the fridge and takes out the iced tea. She holds it up, inspecting the ice cubes floating on top, then gets a spoon to give it a stir. Raising the shade a few inches, she pours herself some and leans over the sink, looking out at the pool. White-gold ripples flash over the wall, the ivy-patterned paper. Her hips stuck out, she bends there, drinking. She has her suit on; the elastic cuts in under the shorts. She should probably start watching her weight — I open my mouth to say so, but stop myself. It's at her age the weight creeps up, though I've always done my best to keep it down. But Barbara's build isn't like mine; I suppose somewhere down the line she takes after the Mossmans, if not her father. When she was small, she looked a bit like my sister.

She puts down her glass and starts talking — loud, too loud, I think — about the kids' lessons, their swimming instructor.

"Shhhh, shhhh. Your father's—"

"I'd rather they remember him being *well*," she blurts out, and there are tears in her eyes, a hard glitter like the chrome round the faucet. She rubs the end of her nose as if it's winter and she's got a bug. "God, what a week. Michael in surgery, the kids—" Then she looks at me with this mix of guilt and pity, as if she were four and had had an accident.

"I'm sorry, Mum. How've you been coping?"

Coping, that's a favourite expression nowadays, like "developmentally challenged", "palliative medicine" — making the best of bad situations, looking for silver linings. For me "coping" is a type of saw.

Under my blouse, the perspiration sends chills down my back; with the perm coming out, my hair sticks to my neck. Down the hall I hear Arthur getting up, creeping like a snail from the bedroom. Barbara assembles a smile, feature by feature, the way you'd put together a puzzle or a dress.

"Daddy!" She swivels towards him, her strong hips brushing mine. Holding onto the back of a chair, he stands stooped over, smiling with his mouth. The sides of his jaw look shiny, his teeth somehow sunken; for the tiniest second his eyes liven, just a flicker, then sink back into themselves, hollow. In the dimness you can't see the yellowness of his skin: he's the same shade as the light. For one quick instant he seems to blend into the gloom, disappearing like a shadow when a cloud passes, tinging everything a flat, shifty grey. In his eyes I've already glimpsed this happening, the same subtle fading from blue to no colour at all.

Barbara puts her arms around him, kisses his cheek. Her big, healthy body makes his look frail as straw. Hugging her, his lips pulled back in a tight, hopeless smile, he stares over her shoulder. His eyes are hard and dark above her light-coloured T-shirt. Pinching my lips together, I feel my cheeks tighten.

"That beige is nice on you," I say, reaching up to smooth her sleeve.

"It's unbleached cotton," she explains, as if it matters, trying to smile. "I bought one for Amy too, but she won't wear it — says they look like dishcloths." It's meant as a joke, but her father only grimaces, moving from her to sit down.

His golf shirt, pressed for the visit, hangs stiff as a section from the newspaper, as if there's nothing underneath but bones. Until a couple of months ago you wouldn't have guessed — my God, you wouldn't've guessed at all.

"Michael and the kids couldn't make it," I whisper.

"That's all right." But there's a queer loftiness to his voice, same as when clients filed false claims — not surprise exactly, but disappointment. Arthur starts to cough.

"Well, next time, perhaps," Barbara says. Loud, distant, she seems almost bossy. Since when, I'm not sure — her birthday, starting her job? Perhaps it's only been since her father got sick.

"Well, dear," I sigh, patting Arthur's back. Under the blue jersey, his shoulder blades jut small and sharp as chicken bones. "How 'bout a swim while your father goes back for his nap?"

Out by the pool the sun's bright as knives. As Barbara pulls off her T-shirt I catch a whiff of Arthur's Old Spice. That, and the water's Javex smell, and something else too: a dank, sour odour like rotting leaves or mildew. The smell seems to be spreading through the house, a little more each day, likely from the basement — dampness mixed with dryer lint, the scent of boxed detergent.

"My land, those tiles are hot!" Sliding off my flip-flops, I watch my daughter step out of her shorts. Hopping from foot to foot, I stand there in my SeaQueen suit, the green one I bought two winters ago for Florida. Paid way too much for it — call it vanity, a woman my age. But at the time I was anxious to make the most of my "good points", as they say in the magazines. "Choose what best suits your body type." So somehow I roped myself into this one, with its high V-neck and ruffled skirt meant to hide wobbly thighs. Truth is, in my own back yard I don't mind a little sun on my cleavage — and swimming's supposed to trim down one's "problems". This darn thing feels like a dress, wet.

Stripped down to her black Speedo, Barbara smiles approvingly — indulgently? I should've, yes, I *should've* gone with the hot pink suit Arthur liked. Sat outside the dressing-room at Margolian's, he did; wanted to see me in something skimpy, low-necked.

"Oh, go on," I said at the time, but you know, I was flattered. Forty years of marriage and he still wondered how I looked in a bathing suit. Well.

"Where's the vacuum thingy?" Barbara pads around the side in her bare feet, doesn't seem to mind the heat of the concrete. It's so hot I have to put on my flip-flops again to reach the ladder.

She goes into the pump-house and comes out with the thermometer; squats by the edge and dips it in, really careful. I half expect her to hold it up to the sun and check for bugs, those teeny-weeny things she studies at work, "invisible to the naked eye" as they say on *Jacques Cousteau* or *The Nature of Things*. Her legs are brown and strong, a little heavy at the top when she crouches. She straightens up from the knees, pointing her hands as if she's praying, and in she goes, a strong black arc against the sparkling turquoise. The water breaks and splashes, spilling over the sides.

"It's gorgeous," she says coming up, her head like a seal's. Her voice is rueful, though, distant, as if she'd be happier alone.

Slowly, slowly, clinging to the little metal ladder, I lower myself in, the blueness lapping at my thighs, my tummy. The cold makes my muscles jump, my bosom shrink in the stiff, padded cups. The water seems to darken somehow, my feet wavering yellowy-green on the bottom. The cold's always a shock, all the more so because of the colour. It's deceiving — makes me think of palm trees and those long, flat boulevards where Ardith lives; of other people my age with nice tans and white shoes. Not the ocean, or icebergs.

"Aren't you coming in?" Barbara calls, treading water at the deep end.

The cold hollows me out, makes me feel like an empty bottle. I bend over, rubbing water up and down my arms, till the top of my suit is dark. The foolish little skirt puffs and flounces around my middle like water wings.

"You'll love it once you're in," she coaxes.

Sucking in my breath, I splay my fingers. Water glints across my knuckles, my wedding ring. Slowly I spread my arms, lifting my feet from the soft, slippery bottom, letting go. I hate getting my face wet, so I hold it like a puppet's strung to the sky. Ahead of me Barbara's dark shape looms and scoots away, water shooting up as I stroke towards her, my eyes squeezed shut.

Then something queer gets into me, compelling me; something inside, small but weighty as a new penny glinting on the bottom. Fast, fast, before I can chicken out, I dunk my face — mouth, nose, eyes, everything — till my hair fans like the stingers on a jellyfish.

I open my eyes. The chlorine darts and burns, blinding as the light spiking down, glittering like dust motes — plankton, Barbara would say. For one split second there's nothing but brilliance, the hard, sharp brilliance of slivered glass.

Far above on the surface a dark speck flutters and hums — a stranded fly. I blow out a string of tiny glass beads; the water lifting my hair, the foolish ruffle. I feel it encirling me, soft as the edges of a bubble.

There's a burst, a splash, and something else buoys me — Barbara, her hard, cold bosom; her strong arms pulling around me. I come up gasping, stunned as a hooked mackerel, water singing in my sinuses. The two of us hooked together in this queer, stumbling embrace as she heaves me up, choking, onto the side.

"Mum! What happened? What're you *doing?*"

I can barely hear her through the burbling in my ears. *"Mum!"*

The sun is stabbing down. Her eyes are so green, her scalp white through her dark, ribbed hair; wet, you can't see the grey.

Her voice — when it finally breaks in   is puzzled, angry: the voice of someone betrayed, disgusted; and like a child's, frightened.

I'm dizzy, light-headed, the way you get leaning too long over a sinkful of something soaking in bleach. The chlorine smell rises like steam to the top of my skull. I cough up a little water, but I'm all right. Slouched over, I let my chin sag to my chest as I get my breath. Through the green Lycra, the concrete warms my bottom, my spreading thighs, the spidery blue veins beneath the skin.

Looking straight at my daughter, I think: "And what about me, what am *I* gonna do?" But instead my voice tells her, "I'm sorry."

FEMMES FATALES

W hen I came in they were putting away groceries. My stunned brother was sitting at the table playing Game Boy, the volume cranked. Even through his headphones you could hear each beep, that fake, jumpy music like ants on crack. Made me want to rip the thing out of his hands — I hadn't had much shuteye, see. It was Saturday, past noon, and I was just getting home from a sleepover at Natalie's. I was barely inside before *she* started in.

"That's a *different* blouse, Amy. Nice, I mean."

Barbie gave Daddy one of those moist, smarmy looks she's so good at. Ty kept punching buttons, talking to himself: *"Yesss!* I beat this level!"

"Just don't light a match near it, the blouse I mean." Daddy snickered, unwrapping brown bundles of food — you could see they'd spent all morning at the market. Barbie shot him a dirty look as she jammed something in the fridge.

"No, really. I used to have one just like it in grade 10."

"Oh God." Daddy, trying to be funny.

"Just 'cause your taste's in your feet, Mike—" I blurted out. "*Dad*." You have to be so bloody careful not to call parents by their real names; Mom — Barbie — really hates it when I do that.

Then *she* chimed in.

"Oh, give her a break, Michael. So how was Natalie's, hon?"

I picked the crust off a bagel. "What's it to you?"

She glared the way she does sometimes when I come out of the shower, Daddy moaning about hot water and who do I think I am, Madonna?

Barbie dug him in the ribs, the muscles around her mouth twitching.

"You did stay at Natalie's, didn't you?"

"What do *you* think?"

Barbie looked away, same stunned, excuse-me-for-living gaze as the clerks in those shops she drags me around sometimes, "just the two of us". Crafty places with a fruity smell, that sell dried flowers, those hats people hang on doors. The country-kitchen look.

"So. You like it, Mom?" (Better to lighten up a touch.) "I got it on Argyle Street, that coo-ol used-clothes place with the pink vinyl miniskirt in the window. Only five bucks. Nat and I—"

She sniffed, watching Daddy's back, his elbow going like a saw as he sliced bagels.

"It's real nice, Amy." She sighed, reaching up on her Nike tiptoes to get plates. "I just told you that."

Daddy said, "Get out the cheese, would you, Amy?" Rolling his eyes at Barbie. Meaning: at least it's not ripped. At least it covers her belly button and doesn't show her tits. God. Do they have to be so damn transparent?

Wolfing down the rest of the bagel, I went to my room, grabbing Daddy's cell phone on the way up. Slamming the door, I smiled at myself in the mirror, and stuck out my chest. The shirt looked excellent — "spiffin'" as Nat says. (I could just hear her giggling, "The slinkiness brings out your two best points!") The faces printed on the slippery yellow fabric winked back at me: pretty, long-necked women with swoopy eyes and puckered lips, like flappers from the twenties.

Femmes fatales, the girl in the store said when she took my money. She looked seventeen or eighteen — just a few years older than me and Nat. But with no Daddy or Barbie to nag her, you could tell. The whole time she waited on me, taking my five dollars plus ninety-five tax and sticking the blouse in a bag, we stared at her. Couldn't help it. One eyebrow had a gold sleeper through it, her nose and bottom lip too. And one side of her hair was shaved, the other dyed blue. *Soooo* cool. She had on a red velour minidress, like the seats in Nat's parents' van.

All the way to Scotia Square we went on about her. How Barbie and Daddy would cringe. What a piss-off it was never to be allowed to do what you want.

"It's your body," Nat said, once we'd found the wash-room. I was in a cubicle changing into the new blouse, stuffing my old black T-shirt into the bag. She was by the sinks putting on eyeliner.

"Yeah right. Tell them that."

I came out and modelled it for her. The cuffs had three buttons each, the collar big and droopy as beagle ears. There was a tiny rip under one of the arms and the bottom button was missing. But the colour picked up the glow of my lemon kiss lipgloss; the silkiness made my eyes shine. The sides were tapered, the clingy material showing off my long skinny waist. Sucking in my stom-ach, I let the shirt-tails flap over the top of my jeans.

"Awesome!" Nat giggled. "I know *somebody's* gonna love it. Just wait till he gets his fingers on *that.*"

"Oh buzz off Nat!" But I was giggling too. She could

see I was pleased.

"Skin dog!" Her voice dipped low and dirty as the floor.

"Pervert!" I gave her a nudge and she missed her eye, dark blue liner blotting her cheek. Suddenly she got all serious.

"What if your mom phones before you come in? What do I say?"

"Tell her I'm in the bathroom."

"What if she calls back?"

"Tell her I'm asleep."

A cleaning lady bustled in then, some fat old bag in a dirty blue uniform, pushing a mop.

"No loitering," she said, swabbing it past our Reeboks.

"Piss off," we mouthed at each other, swinging out into the mall, still giggling.

Paul O'Brien was waiting by the Orange Julius, just as he promised. He was wearing a brown suede jacket — well, a jacket that looked like suede, except the fringes, which curled a bit at the ends. He'd just washed his hair, dark and glossy, cut in a thick mushroom. With him were two guys in ballcaps and floppy jeans, boys I recognized from grade ten. Nat got all red and flustered when she saw who they were, kept flicking a piece of hair behind her ear and staring at her running shoes. I took a deep breath, waiting for her to say something stupid. Start elbowing me, and take up where we'd left off in the washroom.

But before we even had a chance to run back through my plan to sleep at her place, Nat took off up the escalator. She looked back once and yelled, "I'll leave the window open." Paul was too busy lighting a smoke to ask what she meant.

His friends moved off too, their pants dragging over the tops of their Docs. Paul stepped closer. He was an inch or two shorter than me, so close now I could see green specks in his eyes. He smelled like cigarettes and Juicy Fruit gum.

"Nice shirt," he said, his eyes swooping down the front of it. I couldn't quite tell if he was making fun or not. Paul has a weird sense of humour. One of the reasons I thought he was cute.

He ran his index finger over my sleeve as if to pick off a boogie.

"No. Really. It looks good on ya." His jacket zipper grazed my chin as he reached up and slung his arm around my shoulder. Joined like that we walked down the mall, hips bumping, his hand dangling over my front, till we reached the lineup outside the Cineplex. Then he let go and dug in his pockets for money.

"Two for—" He flipped a twenty out of his billfold, slid it towards the cashier.

"Under fourteen, adult accompaniment." She squinted, sizing me up, and I felt my face go hot. Not speaking, she ripped out two tickets and pushed them across the counter.

I followed Paul to the refreshments, stood back as he got a large Coke and a small buttered.

Not much bigger than our living-room, the cinema was almost full. We found two seats near the back and slid in, Paul swearing under his breath when some of the popcorn spilled. I stuck the bag with my T-shirt under the seat. The curtain went up and some ads came on, Paul gazing straight ahead, chewing. I could just make out his jaw moving in the shifty glow off the screen, the paper cup propped between his legs.

I wiggled closer — the air conditioning was enough to make your teeth chatter. The blouse's slinkiness didn't help. Laying my head on his shoulder I could feel my boobs against the scratchy new bra Barbie had gotten me.

As he slouched back in the hard, springy seat, Paul's shoulder sagged as he slurped away at his drink.

The film opened with a woman being stalked by a man in white shoes. Glassy and round as the globs in tapioca, Paul's eyes never left the screen as he passed the popcorn box. I fished through the kernels for some fluffy bits.

Onscreen, the woman was being stabbed and stuffed in a closet. Paul licked his fingers and sucked up the dregs of his pop. Same slurpy sound as when Barbie washes pots, lets the sink drain without picking out the mushy food scraps first.

"You want some money for a pop or anything?" he whispered. Sliding his arm around me, he let his empty cup roll under the seat ahead. In the movie a puddle of blood spread like jam from under the closet door.

Paul's fingers started playing with my collar, working their way underneath, stroking my neck. He smelled like butter, his chin shiny in the dim light, the fuzziest hint of a moustache above his lip. I shut my eyes, held my breath and smiled as he leaned over to kiss me, poking his tongue at my teeth. His breath tasted like burnt toast.

"What time you gotta be home?" he said, turning back to the screen. His hand was still under my collar, his elbow cocked at a crazy angle as he worked down my strap. God knows what the people behind us thought, if they even noticed.

Squirming, I watched his face. Goosebumps pricked up and down my arm, stiff now as the body on the screen.

Like a drunk spider his fingers crawled from my armpit down the side of my bra. I pinched in my arm, tried pinning his hand with it. Losing track of the killer, I rounded my shoulders to hide my chest, tilting like the leaning tower of Pisa, away from him and his groping.

It didn't do any good. His fingers kept searching,

reaching and probing like somebody learning Braille, till they hit the target. My boob, flat as an egg fried sunny-side up, if you have to know; the nipple tender as yolk in the middle. Then he squeezed — hard — his thumb kneading and rubbing, rubbing fast enough to raise a blister. Like men buying fruit in Sobeys, grabbing oranges and feeling for bruised spots. Except that, underneath, boobs are like bunches of grapes —that's if you believe the picture in that pink book Barbie made me read once, *What Girls Should Know.* Looking at that, you had to wonder why anyone would want to feel one.

Staring straight ahead, I bit my lip in pain as he pinched and rolled my nipple between his fingers. Same way he held a cigarette, smoking it down to the butt. He leaned his head back and let out a groan. I pressed my shoulder blades to the sticky upholstery.

"Are you all right?" I whispered after a minute or two.

The camera panned to the killer's shoes padding over a carpet, lurking in a doorway. A gasp came from the audience. You could almost hear them holding their breath.

"I got a pain," Paul hissed, his tongue flicking my ear. "Right *here.*"

Before I could pull it back, he grabbed my hand and shoved it in his pocket. I felt something move, thick as a rolled-up sock, and jerked my hand away.

The camera swept from the killer's feet to his neck, the muzzle of a gun stuck there. The credits started rolling and I jumped up. Thank God for credits. Though what a stupid thing to say, something Barbie would say, as if God had anything to do with it.

The lights flooded on. In my rush to get out I forgot the bag under my seat. It wasn't till later, walking up Duke Street to the bus, that I remembered. "We could go back," Paul said in a flat voice.

"Nah." I made it sound as though it didn't matter

about my old shirt. Really, I was thinking about Nat, how her parents liked lights out by midnight.

On the bus he sat beside me, slumped over with his legs apart. Hands folded together in his lap, he started playing with his fingers. "This is the church, this is the steeple...open 'er up and look...at...the—" Watching my face, he began to laugh. A mean, snarky laugh that made me feel I'd done something wrong, something awful, far worse than lying to my parents.

We got off at Quinpool, and he walked me the two blocks to Nat's house. The van was in the driveway. All the lights were out except hers in the basement. I stopped and waited for a minute on the sidewalk, my hands up inside my cuffs. Paul wouldn't look at me. Kicking something on the ground, he gazed up the street as if watching for somebody else. Sniffing at the air like a puppy chasing a scent.

"Thanks for the show," I said. Nat's light flashed off, then on again. I pictured her waiting in her purple baby-dolls, magazines spread out over the bed.

He didn't say a word, just started walking away. I thought of Nat's notepad, the lists we were going to make of things we wanted: haircuts, clothes and things to match. The lime-green sling-backs at that place on Argyle that Nat was saving up for.

"Well. See ya later," I called hopefully, more a question than a goodbye.

"Yeah."

He was already halfway up the block but I could see him shrug. The back of his jacket hiked over his pants, his shirt sticking out.

"Nice coat!" I wanted to sneer. But Nat's window scraped open, her whisper rasping across the lawn.

"Get in here! Quick!" She held the curtain back as I slid in feet first. "Tell me everything!" I stood there blinking.

"But what did he *say?*" she wanted to know. "Did you guys kiss?"

Curled up on her bed, I stared at the little green hearts on the wallpaper. After a while they made you feel sick.

"Amy? C'mon! Tell me. You gonna see him again, or what? I mean, what's *wrong?*"

"Nothing." I reached up and snapped off her lamp. Turning on my back, I lay studying the shadowy, stippled ceiling, stroking the cool, silky smoothness of my sleeve.

After a while Nat put out her hand and ran a finger over it, like a TV glove test for dust.

"Think Barb'll like it?" she whispered slyly, snorting into her pillow. I think it was then she made that remark about my "two best points". Must've been the hour, but something about her voice shook me out of my mood, set off a round of giggling. Giddy, I told her what I'd seen of the movie. Then she made a joke about Paul's fringe, which put us on the floor laughing. I guess we got pretty silly; twice Nat's parents thumped on their bedroom floor.

Alone in my room I start to undress, watching in the mirror as I unbutton the blouse. It makes me shiver, the feel of it slithering off my shoulders to the carpet. Downstairs, I can hear Daddy yelling at Ty to turn off the Nintendo.

The sun through the window makes me look sleepy and pale, my skin bluish-beige against the bright new bra. Nat and I hardly got an hour's sleep, laughing and talking till dawn. My eyes feel scratchy and raw, but I'm happy. She and I had a good time.

I put on clean clothes, then grab my blouse off the floor. As I go to hang it up, though, I notice the greasy spots on the collar, a couple more by the pocket. Out in

the hall Barbie comes creeping upstairs to use the bathroom. I hear her hovering for a second outside my door.

"Really, Amy. I like your new shirt, I do." Her voice
all sugary-sweet, coming through the crack like a draft. I
listen for her hand on the knob. And quick, before she
has a chance to barge in and start snooping around, I ball
up the blouse and stuff it in the back of the closet. With
all the other stuff that no longer fits.

THE CHAMPAYNE DAM

The street changed when the Whites moved in — some would've said it went straight to the dogs. In Jeremy's view, initially, the new blood improved it, lent an air of excitement to the hilly, potholed neighbourhood. Never mind that it was bad blood, dogpatch blood, that the air carried with it a stink of exhaust, danger. Jeremy willingly overlooked all this — a good thing, since he lived next door, his yard split from theirs by a shy strip of gravel.

In his forty-six years at 17 Hatcher Road, Jeremy had never seen the likes of the goings-on at number fifteen. The previous tenant, now in a nursing home, had scarcely spoken to him or his mother, Pearl. Despite their proximity, both sides had liked it that way. It was that kind of neighbourhood; people kept to themselves.

Now he could hardly credit the activity next door. The bevy of vehicles dead and alive, cars and visitors at all hours. Often he heard them pulling into the yard in the middle of the night. Since his mother's death a few months earlier, he'd become a bit of a night-hawk — nothing for him to be awake at three, sometimes four in the morning, flicking through the channels on TV.

He'd invested the proceeds of his mother's estate in a satellite dish. A sound idea at the time, it seemed; anything to consume the silence that so suddenly engulfed him. Four thousand dollars, access to eighteen different satellites, a hundred channels: the salesman's pitch was irresistible. Yet, had he foreseen the Whites moving in two weeks later, the hours of free viewing pleasure they provided, he mightn't have parted so quickly with his money.

But at the time, Jeremy cheerfully cleared a path through the cluttered front room to let the technician install the receiver, hook up his small, dusty set. He crouched patiently before the screen as the man demonstrated the remote while cracking jokes about getting stuck on the Playboy channel.

The seven-foot black mesh dish filled his tiny front yard, like a wide-open flesh-eating flower, stamens poised. Perched beside a rock, its presence at first made Jeremy blush. But once he got used to it, he believed it evinced a certain power. It made him feel important.

The day the Whites moved in, Jeremy dredged a tire from the woods behind his house, slashing it to make it fit around the base of the dish. When the large rented truck rattled up, he was in the crawl space under the kitchen, digging out whitewash and a brush.

A small crowd milled next door when he emerged, men in black T-shirts and tight, greyish jeans, a few women hanging off the bumpers, talking. Dressed more or less alike, the men looked, to Jeremy, like a small ragtag army parachuted in from somewhere. The sight made him itchy beneath his dark threadbare clothes, but he forced himself to breathe deeply, to let their jagged laughter drift to the top of his skull.

Swinging the bucket of paint, he slouched towards

the front of his place, humming the theme from *The Simpsons*. Concentrating on each note, the ticklish buzz the low ones left on the back of his tongue, he kept his head down and managed to pass the adjacent yard as if it were occupied only by rocks. Home free, he squatted beneath the dish. Rolling to his knees, he started painting the tire, slow, steady slaps, stealing glances every now and then at the bunch next door, the parade of mattresses, sofas and appliances spilling slowly from the truck to the yard and up into the house. Already the clink of beer bottles had begun to punctuate the blur of voices and barking laughter.

The house next door resembled Jeremy's — the same style and state of disrepair — except it was built on a tall, block foundation with a spindly porch, a steep flight of stairs tacked on the front. A couple of times he splotched paint watching two weedy-looking fellows negotiate the steps with a large plush sofa, a big-screened TV. He marvelled that the stairs could bear the weight; surveying the jumble of furniture heaped outside, he wondered where on earth the strangers expected it to fit. Once, he almost considered laying down his brush to wander over for a better look — until some cursing erupted, an emaciated-looking man with longish grey hair shouting at a woman in pressed jeans and white sneakers to go easy with the stereo. "For Chrissake, Dar, ding that and I'm tellin' ya, hon, you're dead meat!" Skulking inside, Jeremy went to the kitchen and took his time rooting for a rag to clean up the spills.

When he came back outside, the truck was gone. Only three people remained: the long-haired fellow, the stout, flat-reared woman with the sneakers, and a plump, pretty girl who looked to be about sixteen. Cleaning up the spots where the paint had slopped onto the dish's base, Jeremy couldn't help watching them. Dressed in high-tops, tight stonewashed jeans and a limp black T-shirt with orange wings on the front — colours that made Jeremy think of turkey — the man mimicked a teenager. But even at a distance his face looked ashen, and it dawned on Jeremy that he was older, his own age perhaps, or very ill. Curious, suddenly enthralled, he found himself gawking, watching the man's stringy arms, muscles flexing as he hoisted and ferried boxes up the shaky stairs, a cigarette dangling from his lip.

In the yard, meanwhile, the woman and girl sorted through cartons and crates without talking, listless and balky as if unsure what to do next. Jeremy got a good look at the girl. She had on a bright yellow tank-top and tight denim shorts that winked a white slice of buttock whenever she bent over — a view that made Jeremy bump the tire with his wrist. "Brandy", he heard the woman shout to her as she leaned over a lamp. He couldn't help staring, taking in the girl's flushed, wide-eyed face, her honey-coloured bangs swept up like a breaker. Brandy, he rolled the name over his tongue, thinking how it suited her hair, thick and stiff and sweet-looking as dried syrup or tree sap. He was trying to decide which, still staring, when the man emerged from the house and lolled over the railing with a beer. "Break-time, eh hon?" the woman yelled up. "Bring me one too, wouldja Russy? It's so friggin' hot, I got some thirst! Of all the bloody days to move!"

"Aw, quit your complainin'!" the fellow hollered down, taking a swig. As he did so, his eyes lit suddenly, squarely, on Jeremy. Smiling or sneering, Jeremy wasn't sure which, he raised his bottle. "You wanna take a pit-chure or what? Naw, I'm just jivin' ya, man. You wanna come over and give us a hand? Got lotsa beer, if you're in'erested. Name's White, Russy White. This here's my wife Darlene, my little girl Brandy."

"That's nice," Jeremy managed to croak, shaken,

twisting the rag till his palms stuck to it. "Pleased to meet you," he whispered, but not before the man shook his head and disappeared inside.

Ignoring Jeremy, the girl and her mother started carting things upstairs. Wiping his hands, he watched them tramp up and down, up and down. When he squinted, they resembled ants, the sturdy black carpenter ants that travelled the sills of his cramped, low basement. There was something mesmerizing about their movement. Something steady and reassuring, it seemed as he watched the pair, Brandy and her mom, the slowly shrinking pile of goods. He jammed the rag into his pocket, and felt himself relax.

But hammering the lid on the paint can, he happened to gaze a little too directly at Darlene stooping to catch her breath. Glancing up, she gave him a blank look; the girl, trailing behind, her arms laden, stopped and stared. Feeling as exposed as if the sun had just melted off his pants, the cool black shadow of the dish no help to him at all, he raised one pale hand and forced a smile. After what felt like a string of commercials near the end of a cliff-hanger, the girl finally set down her load and waved back.

He blinked and scurried inside to take a nap while the paint dried.

Once the dish was installed, Jeremy had trouble catching up on his sleep. Night after night he spent in front of the TV, late late nights, too. After a matter of weeks, the slow but subtle shift in his hours of shuteye took a toll on his inner clock. When he needed it most, sleep eluded him, leaving him high and dry as a dinghy at low tide, stranded by daylight; crusty-eyed, shaky. Not that it mattered when he napped, Jeremy being master of his day's routine.

Occasionally, deprived of sleep, his pride in his new

acquisition would slip. Agitated, bleary, he'd peek through the tattered curtains at the dish, descended like a relic from *Lost in Space*. And, depending on how tired he was, he'd worry. Worry that someone from Welfare would see it and mistake him for an imposter, a rich imposter, and reclaim his benefits.

In the greenish light of day, the mouldering silence of his bedroom, it was easy to fret. But in the velvety dark of his tiny, cosy front room, slumped before the glowing screen, he forgot about the social worker, the concerned young woman who had come to visit when his mother died; forgot about the cash from the monthly cheques she arranged for him, fives and tens bound together with a rubber band and stashed in a kitchen drawer. Tuned to smiling TV faces, their timed, toothy laughter, Jeremy could lose himself in spacious sitcom living-rooms, in endless joyful ads for hair dye and cleaning agents. Could almost forget his big, ungainly body, his crumbling surroundings.

Before the lively blue flicker, at three in the morning he could feel a little like God, his hand on the slender new remote. An eye on the universe, linked to all those satellites — satellites, whatever they were. He'd seen a newsclip once, some crazy-looking gizmo like a barrel-chested dragonfly all eyes and antennae hovering over the earth, the black veil of space behind. But it didn't matter how or why satellites worked; in the wee hours just before dawn, this seemed the sum of his existence: the black swirling cosmos instantly static, intact; Jeremy by turns dozing and alert on its cool, calm periphery. His hand on the right buttons, his television universe.

But everything changed after the Whites arrived, as if someplace out there a signal went awry, the reception knocked off kilter. "Do not adjust your set," was the advice announcers gave if and when one's screen went snowy — advice that began to percolate the instant Jeremy lay down that day to nap.

Paint fumes blending with the mildewed odour of the walls, his sour-smelling clothes melding with the ruined pinkish bedspread, he squeezed his eyes shut and tried to sleep. But the sound of voices kept wafting from next door; the scud of furniture over floors, the whiney roar of a vacuum, badgering and cajoling above it all like the lines from a jingle: "Brandy-this, Brandy-that.... Russy, come on Russy, put down that beer and gimme a hand, wouldja...? For shitsake, Dar, where's the fire? Can'tcha just fuck off and relax for two seconds?"

He did mental dot-to-dots lying there in his cramped little room, attaching names to voices. But the exercise made him anxious, so he rolled onto his stomach, tried picturing the tire drying in the sun. Which brought to mind the dish, of course, and a nagging urge to get up and see what was on such-and-such a channel, and then the worry...the worry....

Finally tuning out the noise from the window, he decided the key was to make the most of things, to enjoy the dish while he had it. To maximize his usage, as the salesman said. Whatever that entailed. No matter. In his mind he was already on the next step, a plan to make the dish look more at home, more natural. Rooted. He would plant flowers, yellow flowers the shade of the girl's tank top, yes, a ring of them inside the tire. Yellow, to match the peeling shingles on his house. Eventually Jeremy drifted off, counting blossoms.

The next day, just after noon, he walked to the mall where the supermarket garden centre was selling off the dregs of that year's stock. Wizened, leafless plants, leggy marigolds, brown-stemmed petunias. There were plenty of the first kind the very colour he'd dreamed of, their strong, mustardy scent on his fingers as he handed over the money, biting back a yawn. Clutching their crinkly pots, he stopped into the drugstore for a *TV Guide*. The cashier, new on the job, wearing large pink glasses that looked upside down, seemed vaguely familiar; with a little jolt he realized it was the woman from next door, the new one. "Hel-lo," he drawled, holding out his hand for his change, watching her face for some flicker of recognition. But she didn't so much as blink, her face bland, impervious; her magnified eyes ringed black as a racoon's, impassive. Heat flooding his cheeks, he quickly averted his gaze to his feet, the dirty speckled floor, and hurried off with his purchases.

From the foot of Hatcher Road, he noticed the change at number fifteen. Where the day before the yard had been piled with furniture, now it was full of vehicles. There was a yellow dirt-bike leaning against the cement-block foundation, a battered late-model sedan parked out front.

Near the edge of his gravel was a shiny silver pick-up truck — Jeremy thought it must be new because of the smell, like singed metal and carpet glue. Next to it, a small white car sat propped on blocks, its rusty exposed axles like something from the swamp out back. Heavy distorted rock music blared from the house — Jeremy knew it vaguely as something from the seventies, the type of tune that would've prompted his mother to turn off the radio. The door at the top of the steps gaped wide, as a blank screen without so much as a test pattern. But apart from the music, there were no signs of life.

To transform the tire into a flowerbed took more doing than he had expected. First, there was the problem of soil. Thankful for the patchy shade, he took a Sobeys bag into the woods and, using his hands, scraped up enough dead leaves and dirt to fill it. Finally, filling an apple-juice can with water, he set about planting.

He had just enough earth to half fill the tire. The marigolds lifted easily from their pots, his paint-speckled fingers clumsily tamping down their withered roots until, after a while, he succeeded in ringing the base of the dish with sparse, nodding blooms. He'd just finished watering them, was stepping back to admire his work, when a voice shot across the yard, spraying like gravel over the car tops.

"Hey, buddy! Nature boy!"

Nearly jumping out of his skin, Jeremy turned to see Russy leaning against the hood of the pick-up, half-naked and streaked with grease.

"How ya doin'?" Russy yelled, and Jeremy swivelled around to make sure he wasn't addressing someone else. "C'mon over and check out my new wheels. C'mon, the ol' lady's workin', see, me and a few buddies are havin' a drink, you know, just kinda mellowing out." He gave the hood a slap, the sharp metallic sound ringing like a gunshot through the trees. "Got some good deal, eh. I'se just checking her out underneath. C'mon and take a look — don't be scared, bud, I won't bite or nothing."

The blood draining from his face, Jeremy took a couple of sluggish steps forward.

"Th-th-the name's Jeremy," he muttered, feeling light-headed. "Jeremy M-M-Mossman." An instinct — God, it was like his mother's voice, the same put-upon nagging — warned him to turn and bolt back towards the shadow of the dish, the safety of his tire. But something about Russy's coaxing lassoed him.

"Two hundred-and-fifty horse, damn good deal. What's the matter, nature boy, you don't like trucks? I guess a guy like you is better plantin' flowers, that it? Man, I seen everything now." Russy shook his head, stroking the roof of the cab as one would a pet.

"Some nice, though, ain't she." Jeremy had to stop

for a minute and figure out whom he was referring to; craning up towards the open door, he expected to see the girl, his daughter.

"C'mon over. You live alone, I guess? Must be nice, eh. Party central, no old lady bitchin' at ya all hours. 'Get up, do this, do that.' Don't get me wrong, bud — Jeremy — Darlene's a good head, but lookit, when the cat's away, a guy's got to play. You know what I'm sayin'? So c'mon over and get to know your neighbours, eh, c'mon and have a drink wit' the boys."

As if something inside him had silently, subtly come unstuck, with a queer resolve Jeremy stalked to the truck. He was aware of the dirt on his hands, its dry gritty feel, and on the knees of his limp, shabby trousers. But as he approached, none of this appeared to register in Russy's eyes. Instead, they had a vacant, spiralling look like a dart board, the rings inside a tree, or on a small, muddy pool. Up close, Russy looked a lot older, sicker — his face creased and etched as blasted rock, patched with sparse stubble. A embarrassed kind of pity washed through Jeremy, limbering him. It caused him to flush, a timid smile to tighten his mouth.

He was close enough to read a decal on the truck's rear windshield: "Bad Ass Toys for Bad Ass Boys", and for a split second Jeremy heard that voice again, warning him.

"So — whaddyou drive?"

At such close range, Russy seemed to shrink, his chest sunken, bony. A pipsqueak, Jeremy marvelled, realizing with something approaching shame that in size he overtook the fellow like a bear.

"Oh, me," he stammered, "I-I prefer to walk. I-I never drove in my life, ac-tual-ly, never had no need to."

"G'wan, buddy — everybody got to drive."

Jeremy waited for him to laugh, or at least snort, but instead Russy eyed him as if awaiting an explanation.

"You lose yer licence or something? You get caught drunken-drivin' or what, bud?"

"Nope," Jeremy heard himself say, his voice pious, resolute, "never had one...just lost me nerve, maybe, before I got around to going to drivin' school...."

"Drivin' school!" Russy let out a good-natured guffaw. "Man, you don't go to school for to learn nothing! I could take ya down to the mall myself and learn ya! Drivin' school, my arse."

Jeremy hunched his shoulders, waiting for the mockery to begin. It usually started this way, faint like drizzle, a drop or two at first, then, next thing he knew, streaming cats and dogs.

But Russy seemed distracted, even a bit confused. "Whadja say your name was, again?"

"Jeremy, that's Jeremy with a J."

"Glad to meetcha, Jeremy." He stuck out his hand and Jeremy hesitated, noting the blurred inky heart on his wrist; the indistinguishable initials inside. "Big guy. Nature boy," Russy mused, as if struggling to commit him to memory. Then, twitching, he jerked his head towards the satellite dish.

"Some rig ya got there — bet you get some pile of channels on that. Keeps ya out of trouble, I guess, eh? Me, now, I could use somethin' like that, sure could. A nice big dish, eh, that'd be the cat's arse, like Dar says. 'Specially in my line of work...."

"And wha' would that be?" Jeremy blurted out, before he could catch himself.

"Oh, jeez...you gotta learn to keep your nose clean, fella. But since you asked — let's just say I'm in the home-amusement biz—"

Jeremy perked up, pushing from his mind the tattooed heart, the "Bad Ass" logo. "Like videos and that, right?"

"Sure, stuff like that, yeah, right." Russy shrugged. "So, you gonna come have a drink now, or wha'?" he coaxed again.

His feet glued to the gravel, Jeremy mulled it over.

"C'mon an' meet my buddies, Jer, before Dar gets home and gives us all the boot. Good head most of the time, 'cept when she's on the rag, then look out."

It was Russy's chumminess that finally enticed him; besides, he was curious to see where the Whites had put all the furniture. Slowly he followed Russy up the rickety stairs, pounding bass and electric guitar enveloping him at the top.

Nothing prepared him for the scene past the threshold. In the tiny, smoky living-room, two men slumped in chairs, one balding, thin like Russy, the other short, stocky, with shoulders like a penguin's. Both were wearing sunglasses, though the drapes were drawn, blotting up the fiercer strains of light that made it through the boxy picture window. Jeremy could smell what they were smoking, what they were drinking, too — something strong and sanitizing, he suspected, like Mr. Clean, only the colour of corn syrup, big tumblersful. That was about all he noticed — their drinks — the few short seconds before he bolted, taking the steps two at a time. Pebbled glasses full of whisky, the girl, too, darting past the room with a towel around her head. And the music, that awful, driving racket, its jackhammer rhythm inside his brain.

Rushing home, Jeremy locked both doors, shut all the windows and switched on the TV. He poured himself a glass of milk and, as he sipped it, realized his teeth were chattering. It was hot in the room, hot and stuffy, but he wrapped himself in the blanket from the couch and tried to concentrate on a cooking show, another on gardening. This prompted him to peek once at the marigolds, which seemed to be doing fine in the tire, a bit more wilted maybe, but otherwise unchanged.

For the rest of the afternoon and into the evening, he channel-surfed. But finding nothing too engaging, no *X-Files*, no dramas or decent sitcoms, heck, not even a good game show, only sports, finally he resigned himself to a single channel, one rerunning *Golden Girls* and ancient *Star Trek* episodes.

Captain Kirk had just uttered "Beam me up" for the umpteenth time when the fun began next door. The crunch of tires on gravel, doors slamming, boisterous, stroppy voices. Jeremy zapped to the info channel, the one with no pictures, just words, to check the time, 12:05. Flicking back the curtain, he watched as a cab pulled up, and the girl got out. The taxi waited in the yard, its lights on — Jeremy could see the driver inside checking his meter — and after a few minutes a man came out of the house and jumped in. But not before two more cars drove up, and two or three other people sauntered inside.

A housewarming party, Jeremy decided, with a restless, queasy envy. What nice folks, how lucky the Whites must be to have so many friends; what a "good head", Russy, to have such non-stop company.

Just how non-stop he realized an hour or two later when, after drifting in and out of a snooze, the TV jarred him awake like a fuzzy bolt of lightning. Peeking out again, he spied a police car parked at the foot of the hill, almost out of sight but unmistakable, even in the darkness, that time of night.

A numbness went through him as he hit the OFF button and slumped against the sagging cushions, pressing himself to the springs, the smelly, itchy blanket drawn over his head. He thought of the dish out there, big as life, a fly-trap. A dragnet. He wished there were some means of hiding it. Of having it vaporize the way things

did on *Star Trek* — temporarily — leaving only the
flowerbed, its circular moonlit glow. He prayed, finally,
that it might just disappear, if only for a while, its black
shape absorbed in the dark; beamed, dispatched
someplace else, to some other body heavenly or otherwise, aeons from his yard. Anywhere, he thought, not
here.

He lost track of how long he lay waiting for the swing
of headlights through his window, a knock at the door.
But when he summoned the nerve for another look, he
figured God had been listening, in His roundabout way.
The cruiser was gone, the dish unmoved. The traffic next
door in full jag, unswayed.

By the time he dragged himself to bed, scratchy-eyed,
nauseous, still in the pants he'd worn gardening, it was
nearly four in the morning.

He was awakened next day by a rapping at the back door,
gentle at first, then louder. Bewildered, zombie-like,
Jeremy threw on a shirt, fumbling with the buttons as he
stumbled through the kitchen. Sunlight streamed through
the greasy window, outlining stains on the curtains.

It was the girl — he nearly slipped on some garbage
when he saw her honey-coloured hair. "Oh my Dinah,
oh my Dinah," he muttered, panicking, pitching clutter
from the counter into the sink: dirty dishes, clean dishes,
whatever lay about. The girl knocked again, her smooth,
inquisitive face peering in, filling the door's tear-drop
panes. When something broke, his mother's favourite
mug, he turned and gaped. Her eyes were wide and
painted, and she had brows like the Golden Arches, shaved
or plucked, which gave her a frightened look. It was this
look that convinced him to let her in.

"Hiya, we met, right? I'm Brandy, with a 'y' not an 'i',
that's so tacky," she said pertly, almost insolently, gazing

at his skewed buttons, the pale flesh gaping between them. "I...um...was lookin' for something to do, see, and I...well, like, you got that dish, and I was just wondering if, like, sometime, it'd be okay if I came and watched some TV."

Fumbling with his shirt, his pants, hitching them higher and higher, Jeremy could only stare, jarred, stunned by her boldness. Her neighbourliness.

"You know, like, I don't mean to barge in. It's just that it's so boring. Like, my folks are too cheap to get a dish, so all we have is cable, what a drag.... Hey, do you get *NYPD Blue*?"

"I-I guess," he managed to reply, studying her. She had on the same tight shorts, but a different top, small and pink like something a baby would wear. "I,-listen," he mumbled, "would you know the time?"

Her lip curled and she rolled her eyes.

"I mean now, please, what time of day—?"

She shrugged, giggling as if he had two heads, or his fly was down. "I dunno, morning, noon, whatever." Then, backing away as coyly as she'd entered, she slipped outside, yelling, "Nice meeting yuz, anyway."

Jeremy tried going back to bed, but the noise next door started up again, a radio this time, loud and hectoring. He went and switched on the TV, flicking past some cartoons and a wrestling match to a show about groundhogs. Settling on a *Mod Squad* rerun, he tried to let the pictures lull him to sleep. But outside the racket mounted. A woman, probably Darlene, kept shouting above the deejay, the chain-saw whine of a motorbike behind her. His brow throbbing as if there were a drill bit poised above one eye, Jeremy decided the only thing to do was escape. Grabbing a grocery bag but forgetting to brush his teeth, he double-knotted his shoes, resolved to take a walk.

When he slipped from the house, Darlene was out on the porch beating a mop, screaming down at Russy who was shirtless, his head under the hood of the car on blocks. Ducking past, Jeremy stuffed the bag in his pocket, his eyes on the gravel till he reached the end of Hatcher Road that met the highway. There he trained them on the pavement ahead, without so much as glancing at the gutters or the houses and stores along his usual route.

Spurning the mall, the lake, he followed the broken sidewalk at a shambling clip, uncertain of his destination. His stomach growled, and he recalled with disinterest that he hadn't eaten. Despite the clouds the sun beat down, heat rippling off the asphalt. He wished he'd taken the time to fill something with water, the empty pop bottle by his bed. As traffic whizzed by, he thought how he could have rigged it, the bottle in the bag, its plastic handles looped to his belt, leaving both hands free, unencumbered.

He walked till muffler shops and laundromats gave way to subdivisions, brick and siding houses on large unlandscaped lots; till baby barns and pick-up trucks petered out entirely, yielding to scrub spruce, the road scooped from rock. Here it narrowed, winding towards a valley. At the top of a hill, beyond some barrens, the ocean came in sight, a hard level blue dotted with freighters and sailboats scudding the surface like bright, clean flies.

He hadn't planned to veer off the shoulder, to try and reach the water. But that sharp, unshifting view lured him to stumble over lichen-scalped rocks, through prickly, stunted drifts of huckleberry. Egged on, forgetting his hunger, he made it to a cliff and perched on a boulder that rocked like a loose molar. The sun paled, its heat bent by swooping wind; a fogbank loomed like a snowplow on the horizon. Shutting his eyes, he drew up his knees and listened to the sea's grating rumble through cracks and crevasses below; the same thunderous clatter, he mused, as the sound of the subway in New York City, the one

and only time he'd watched that cop show Brandy wanted
so badly to see.

The fog rolled in and he felt the first spatters of rain.
Skidding from his perch, he headed towards a ravine for
cover. At the base of the wide, rocky cleft was a stand of
spruce, stunted trees that sprung like fur from the barren.
High above, on the headland beyond, towered a crumbling bunker — a fortification from some war or another,
he speculated, as he made for the woods. Reaching the
trees, he pushed his way through the gnarled, scabby
branches.

But in the middle of the thicket he stopped short,
stumbling upon something more intriguing, more en-
trancing than the ocean. Like an oasis, hemmed by spruce
and hewn from the peat, lay a bowl-shaped pit. The dried-
up remains of a pond, its dark, muddy bed strewn with
rocks and sticks bleached like bones. At one end was a
steep cement wall, a foul-smelling spring seeping beneath
it, staining the rocks yellow where they plunged to the
sea.

Drawing closer, Jeremy glimpsed some workmanlike
letters carved in the lip of the concrete wall, traced them
with his fingers. *Champayne Dam, April 14, 1941.* Words
that meant nothing, nothing at all, but tickled him somehow, as if with a feather. They left him tingling oddly,
feeling somehow singled out. Like finding a golf ball on
the moon, he thought, recalling a space show he'd seen.
The same eerie thrill of crossing into lost or abandoned
territory.

With a peculiar delight he pondered the words, ignoring the shards of brown glass, the shiny bottle caps
scattered over the moss, the mud. The litter reminded
him of Russy, but he put this out of his mind, savouring
instead the sober, secret feeling of discovery. It was a bit
like food, he decided, something heavy and sweet; like

wolfing down a couple of doughnuts, the fullness afterwards, spreading through one's belly.

The fog thickened and it started to pour. Reluctantly,
Jeremy ducked back into the trees. Yanking the bag from
his pocket, he got out of his clothes, including his stained,
shapeless shorts, and shoved everything inside it. Stretching out beneath the branches, he shivered at the cool,
pleasant prickle of needles and moss on his skin. The bag
for a pillow, he folded his arms and lay still, the rain-
drops weighty and slow now as if falling from someplace
beyond the sky. He glanced past the bulge around his
navel to the nest of hair below; his thoughts flew to
Brandy — her round, pretty face, those eyebrows stark as
parentheses — then skipped like an ad through the fili-
gree of twigs. Beyond the burls and knotted bark, the fog
had broken like a plate, a furry warmth penetrating cracks
of blue. Hunkering down, he felt his bones yield, his flesh
meld with the moss. A lumpy mattress, a soft bier.

The Whites, he mused, his eyelids leaden, spruce balm
a potion as heady and rich as rain, as beer, as the peat-
coloured muck on the pond bottom. Beer. Champagne.
A drink with fizz, that much he knew from race-car shows,
like gingerale, or spit; a spring bubbling out of the ground
— a clear white fizz, not the black bubbling crude in the
Hillbillies' backyard....

He had no way of knowing how long he slept, blissful,
oblivious as Rip Van Winkle in the woods. When he woke
the sky was blue but pale, with rags of gilt-edged cloud.
Brushing twigs from his backside, he slid out from under
the skimpy boughs, shook his clothes from the bag and
put them on. They were dry, deliciously dry, warmed by
the oily heat of his scalp. His stomach yowled for food; it
was late, well past supper, the time *The Simpsons* aired.

Crashing through the bushes, his pulse like a compass, he found the road. He paused at the ditch to sort through some refuse — a rum bottle, clumps of Kleenex, faded wrappers. He poked the bottle into his bag and began the long, slow roller-coaster trek back to Hatcher Road. Plodding along, he walked until he thought his feet would give out, his knees refuse to bend. As cars sped by and dusk fell, he contemplated sticking out his thumb. But only bums begged rides from strangers, his mother had said once. And he knew, with a longing that swelled to briefly match his hunger, that he'd have only panicked and bolted for the bushes, had anyone stopped.

Fresh Prince of BelAir was just ending when he finally reached home. The soles of his feet felt burnt; a blister on his heel had bled and scabbed over, leaving a rusty stain through his sock. But the uproar next door had simmered down — thank the Lord for small mercies, he thought. Grabbing a loaf of stale bread, some tinned beans, he ate supper from the can, eyes on the screen, folding the last slice of bread in half to wipe out the juice. He was licking the last of it off his wrist when Brandy knocked.

Limping to the kitchen, he flicked on the light, blinking, then quickly let her in. He dodged her inquisitive eyes which dropped from his face to his toes, the thick yellow nails curving over their tips. "I just thought— Wow, like, are you okay?" Wearing jeans so tight her legs looked like freshly poured, encased cement, she had on that tight pink baby top. Its silky warmth brushed his arm as she squeezed past, making for the TV. "I mean, I figured you might like some company, right? But if you're sick or something, I can always—"

Following her into the front room, he saw that she'd been crying, her eyelids pouched like puffed wheat.

"I hate her," she shrugged, "my mother, she's such a bitch. You'd swear she was a communiss the way she tries to rule me. Not like the old man, like, with him anything goes. He's cool, but her? 'Don't you go nowheres lookin' like that, girl — someone'll think you're a hooker an' try to roll ya!' Can you believe it? Sayin' something like that to your own kid? But the old man, all he does is laugh, like it's some big frigging joke."

She sank into the couch, snorting back tears. Horrified, Jeremy changed channels.

"Hey" — she snuffled — "I was watching that."

Hobbling quickly to the kitchen, Jeremy pondered what to do. He went to the cupboard, rummaged until he put his hand on an aged Vachon Flakie he'd saved and forgotten. Pouring a glass of Tang, he shuffled back to the front room with an offering in each hand, eyeing the screen as he held them out.

"No thanks." She scowled, querulous. She'd grabbed the remote control, was switching stations so rapidly the screen jumped like an eye with a tic. "But listen, I was thinking — could you lend me five bucks?"

Sure he hadn't heard right, stumped, Jeremy folded his hands, listened to his supper settling inside. The jarring, crashing airwaves were making him dizzy.

"Like, I only need five bucks, I'll pay ya back — I'm not tryin' to rip you off, if that's what you're scared of. But I'm s'posed to go out tonight, and...God, I need some money."

Abruptly she hopped up, eyeing him, the TV stuck on some nether-channel, ghostly outlines of faces waving across the screen.

"So? You gonna lend me it, or what?"

Backing away, he fled to the kitchen, jerked open the drawer. His fingers sticky from supper, he peeled a five-dollar bill from the wad of cash. In his haste the rubber band snapped with a sound like someone being smacked. When he turned, she was in the doorway, watching, her palm held out.

"You're some sweet," she said, "I'll pay you back. Promise."

And as she slammed outside, the sagging storm door clapping the house, he thought with a shock how old she looked, for such a young girl, how old and in a way naked, bald, her face so smooth and raw with those eyebrows; bald as the rock he'd perched on before the rain, before finding the pond-bed, the dam, his Champayne dam.

Five dollars, he chided himself, what's that? Not much. Besides, she'll pay me back, sure she will. And if she doesn't, I won't miss it, no, I won't. What's five dollars anyway, if it makes somebody happy, whatever kids her age do. Five dollars to send her packing. Pretty little thing, but brazen. Rude. Five dollars well spent. A sound investment, he spoke aloud, mimicking the satellite-dish salesman. Good money after bad. Good riddance. *Hooker, roll you,* the girl's voice echoed back. Whatever that meant. Hook line sinker, his mind crept back to the woods, his dried-up pond; and then his mother's voice piped up, a spark out of nowhere arcing through his spine. Hooker: wasn't that the same as slut?

He filled a bucket with hot water, dumped in some salt, just as *she* would have advised, and sat before the TV soaking his feet. He tried to watch a movie about a tornado destroying a town. But the twister itself reminded him too much of a whirling, frantic housewife in a floor-polish ad, and the plot was hard to follow. He soon lost interest, switching to another show, one from the seventies called *Being There*. But the hero's childish grin put him off, made him unaccountably nervous. When he rose to empty the bucket, there was a cruiser outside, this time in front of his house.

A day or two later, the girl appeared once more. He was

in the middle of watering his marigolds, which weren't doing as well as he'd hoped. All day long the sun baked down and, despite the shade from the dish, the soil kept drying out, his plants showing the effects. He was at the sink filling his juice tin when Brandy slipped inside, not bothering to knock.

"There's nothing to do," she complained, and when he looked up she had both hands wedged in her pockets, those shorts cutting ridges in her thighs. He turned off the tap and timidly held out his hand, expecting his money. But she brushed past him into the front room.

Peering in at her, there was something about Brandy's manner that made him cringe — something brittle and sharp, he thought, like jagged threads of cooked sugar when he was small, very small, and his mother made candy. Yet he found something slovenly and soft about her, too, slouching there, her chubby legs crossed, pointing the remote the way Captain Kirk aimed a ray gun. He had no inkling at all of what to do.

Disappearing outside with his apple-juice can, Jeremy gave the flowers a long, slow dousing. When he crept back in to refill it, the TV was still burbling, but she was gone — as scarce as hen's teeth as his mother would've said. An exercise show was in progress, he saw, glancing around the small dishevelled room.

Haltingly, he coughed and called out, "Brandy?" But only the TV woman answered, her body like a crossword puzzle, shiny, flat, with all those muscle groups: *One more, two more, three more, that's it. Lookin' good, reeeal good....*

It took several days for Jeremy to realize the money was missing, almost a week. But one afternoon when he went to get a ten from the drawer, enough for milk, bread and fish sticks, he found it cleaned of everything but five cents' worth of Canadian Tire money. His lungs froze, his hand went limp pawing the bottom of the drawer. His cash was gone all right, vamoose, nothing left but the coupon, crumbs and a dried-up pen.

The cops, he figured crazily, thoughts flying out like an uncaged budgie. The dish, his mind hit upon it like a wall, showering suspicions. The government, the Welfare—

What if she was right? — that sweet-faced social worker who talked to him when his mother was so sick, again after she died. Her gentle, prying suggestions — maybe he shouldn't be on his own, managing money, his money, their money.... And maybe he was so inept, so susceptible, they'd decided to take it back. The government, the Indian-givers. Had sneaked in like thieves and snatched it, the moment his back was turned. While he was on an errand, or worse, so much worse, watching TV. Right under his nose.

In this frayed, irrational state, muddled as a bag of wires, Jeremy's mind fixed itself upon the dish. Everything pointed to it, a magnet attracting weird and rotten luck.

Worst of all, he thought, the ugly turn of events served him right, for being not just greedy, but prideful too.

Panic-stricken, unable to think clearly, it never occurred to him to suspect the neighbours, not even Brandy. For what it boiled down to, he believed, was a problem with satellites, stray ones; they were the culprits, if he had to place blame.

This time he was careful to bring along water and food, some peanut-butter sandwiches which he hurriedly slapped together, an orange and a can of luncheon meat. At the last minute he grabbed the blanket from the couch, and a spare pair of undershorts. The only option was to hide, he decided, knowing fully where if not for how long.

As he slipped past, the Whites' place seemed deserted despite the cars cramming the yard.

The hike seemed to take longer than before, time suspended with every curve and dip in the road. As he neared the barrens, his view of the rocks and the sharp blue horizon broadening, deepening, Jeremy felt his limbs relax and succumb to a soothing weariness. By the time he approached the Champayne Dam, his muscles ached and the sky had deepened to the shade of cream soda. The matter of his missing cash seemed as remote and trivial as the ring of marigolds in his yard, the giant black bloom they'd been meant to disguise.

The voices were faint at first, a thrumming in the trees that matched the spilling surf. It took him a while to hear them, longer to recognize and attach a name to one. But something about its pitch, its shiftless, smart-ass drone, sounded awfully familiar.

Freezing in his tracks, Jeremy glimpsed his neighbour through the sparse, prickly boughs. In the gloom Russy faced him, his back to the dam, feet braced against a rock. He was rolling a cigarette, licking it. Darkness had fallen and it was difficult to see, but what Jeremy guessed was a sugar-filled baggy lay on the concrete above Russy's head. There was a man with him, scrawny and squat like one of the fellows in Russy's living-room that day. But Jeremy didn't recognize him. He had his back to the trees, face obscured, his body like a stick against the deep black bowl in the ground.

Spellbound, open-mouthed, Jeremy craned closer. A twig snapped. The two spoke in low, growling voices; he realized they were arguing, conducting some sort of deal, bargaining as he had with God the times he couldn't sleep.

He couldn't help himself. Pushing aside a branch for a better view, Jeremy glimpsed the pale flash of bills rippling like a deck of cards in Russy's hand. Felt his stomach drop when he saw the rubber band, wide and dark like the one he'd saved from a bunch of broccoli. His broccoli. His money.

He might have had time to run, to heave himself back up the hill, through the bushes to the road. But something — a gasp, his sharp intake of breath, the soft smoosh of a toadstool underfoot — roused Russy's attention, yanked it from the man's demands, his own capitulations. His peaked face suddenly alert, almost fearful, Russy's eyes narrowed, piercing the fragrant black screen of needles to rest on Jeremy cowering there.

Russy's lips moved, his bottom one sagging then lifting in a sneer, his dim face melting.

"Well if it ain't nature boy...come on out, arsehole, I seen ya, don't think you can take off like that. I *said*, I seen ya, a'right?"

Jeremy felt his heart kick, every muscle leap, poised. He let the bag of food fall to his feet.

The fellow with Russy went dead still, his stick-arms limp at his sides. In another situation, another life, his stance would have reminded Jeremy of *Gunsmoke*; "Stick 'em up" he might have crowed, "Reach for the sky", had they been on TV.

Steeling himself, moaning slightly, Jeremy crept forward, branches bending, yielding soundlessly.

"You got my money," he muttered, in a voice that echoed across the small black crater, bouncing off the darkened trees.

"Wha'?" Russy's jaw dropped, aghast.

Springing to life, his friend moved towards Russy, made a lunge for the baggy. Adrenalin darting through his limbs, Jeremy stood transfixed, his eyes on the blackened moss.

"I said you got m-my money, Russy. You gotta gimme my money."

"Fuckin' idjit don't know what he's talking about—"

But the friend was already scrambling up the rocky bank, his backside knobbed like a burl as he scurried away.

"You got my money, Russy."

Inside his pockets Jeremy's fingers curled. Sweat stung his eyes. Through the smarting, he watched a moth buzz and light near Russy's cheek.

"I'm not leaving till you gimme it." His voice was a whisper, faint as the hiss of spray.

"So I got your money, who you gonna run to, huh? Your momma? The cops? Eh, Tarzan? Nature boy." Russy stood so close now Jeremy could smell his breath, a mix of liquor and something dead. "Listen, I know about you," he leered, "I know your kind, you after putting the make on my little girl. Eh? I know all about that, see, she tol' me about you, she did. So let's just say this is money you owed her. Eh, buddy? That's what she said. Think a guy like you can get it without paying?"

Stumbling backwards, Jeremy swung out, his fist flattening air.

"Get out," Russy jeered, mocking him. But something in his voice sounded cagey, tired.

Jeremy shut his eyes, felt his blood sing, his arm a dead weight, lank, useless.

He heard the flap of paper, a soft thud, scuttling stones; felt the wind stirring, a salty chill. When he opened his eyes, bills fluttered over the ground like dingy butterflies. He dropped to his knees, scooping up the money. Stuffing it like manna into his pockets, he turned for one last, bold look at his neighbour.

But Russy had vanished, darkness swallowing his jerky escape, leaving nothing but a clatter of pebbles down the steep cliff-face, the tiny splashes they made hitting the sea.

Tilting his head back, Jeremy gazed up, scrutinizing

the velvet sky. The wind in his ears, he watched a star appear, perhaps it was a plane — a strange steady light that, when he tracked it, seemed too bright to be either.

FAMILY HISTORY

Meantime a glorious revelry began
Before the Water-Monarch. Nectar ran
In courteous fountains to all cups outreach'd;
And plunder'd vines teeming exhaustless pleach'd
New growth about each shell and pendent lyre;
The which, in disentangling for their fire,
Pull'd down fresh foliage and coverture
For dainty toying. Cupid, empire-sure,
Flutter'd and laugh'd, and oft-times through the throng
Made a delighted way. Then dance, and song,
And garlanding grew wild; and pleasure reign'd.
In harmless tendril they each other chain'd,
And strove who should be smother'd deepest in
Fresh crush of leaves.

John Keats' Endymion, *Book III*

I t takes them the better part of the morning to find
the footpath, a narrow track behind a pub and some
grimy brick cottages. Laura is the one insisted they

keep looking, Kaye just as happy to go back to the room and repack her suitcase. But Laura feels determined to locate this place, a drab corner of town no tourist would visit. Not that Westbury, Wilts., is much of a holiday spot; an old milltown, its gins and looms long silent, it's more a place people pass through on their way to Stonehenge or Bath. For Laura this is the attraction; what she wants is a taste of the ordinary, of quiet village life. Never mind that the trail itself leads inauspiciously from the pub's parking lot, where last night's trash spills from a dumpster. At eighty years of age, Miss Laura Campbell has come in search of her family's history.

She has travelled from Canada with her cousin Kaye, in her late sixties, recently widowed. A keen travelling companion, Laura concedes, despite her sometimes over-weening sense of propriety. Still, Kaye has more than enough pep for both of them, it would seem, until this morning when Laura requires her to be spry.

"It *must* be this way," Laura says, marching past the garbage, a child's tricycle tipped over in the ditch. The only sign is one marked "No Trespassing". Kaye skulks behind in her slightly creased yellow dress as they pass some parked cars, then an unruly strip of garden, cabbages and pole beans sprouting amidst the weeds.

Just ahead, the footpath looms like the mouth of a tunnel, ringed with ivy entwining the trunks and branches overhead, the packed black earth bare and worn down by so many feet, centuries of feet. Now they've finally found it, Laura can see the place gives Kaye the creeps: so much growth blocking out the daylight, riotous, heavy, and from the swamp beyond the brambles, the stagnant slur of water. God knows who might be in here, lurking behind the vines. At home Laura would reluctantly avoid such a place, but not here.

She stoops to inspect a tightly closed bud, bending

the stem carefully in her papery hands while Kaye fusses
with the little camera around her neck. Laura knows her
cousin would like a picture of her — Kaye keeps saying
she ought to be taking more snaps to show her grandchildren — but even before they enter the path, they both
see it will be too dark, the air too still, vegetation too
dense to admit the slightest breeze. Where they come
from, the flora consists of spruce and alder; yes, Laura
can see how this place bothers her cousin, so much ivy
twisting everywhere, running rampant. She knows Kaye
is wishing they'd gone instead to the Victorian garden in
the town centre, with its neat beds of roses, its goldfish
pond. *An old millpond,* Kaye marvelled, reading from a
brochure; "the things that can be accomplished with
money and a little civic-mindedness!"

"Wait up!" Kaye calls to her now, still fussing with
the camera. Touching a sprig of ivy dangling in her path,
Laura doesn't seem to hear. She reaches into her handbag
for a nail file and takes a cutting, which she wraps in a
Kleenex and tucks carefully away. It doesn't faze her that
the cutting may dry out, or that Customs may not allow
it through.

"Smile!" Kaye says, and for a second Laura smiles wist-
fully, then waves her hand before the lens. Kaye shrugs
— it's too dark anyway, Laura's face shadowy, her pink
flowered dress subdued. "Maybe back there, maybe if I
still had the sun behind me," she says. But Laura turns
and keeps going, not interested in humouring anybody.

"Listen!" She stops abruptly, holding a gnarled finger
to her lips. All Kaye hears is the twitter of birds, the leafy
stillness.

"What is it, for goodness' sake?" Kaye bursts out. Laura
could hear earthworms tunnelling, she thinks, fixing the
collar of her blouse. Eight days together have started to
take their toll. All Kaye wanted this morning was a little

exercise, some fresh air after breakfast, a little time before they begin their real business here: a trip to the library, to search county records. This is what Laura wants to do. Tomorrow they leave for Bath, then London, the airport. A whirlwind trip — it seems they've been on the go non-stop since arriving in England just over a week ago.

"Now pace yourself," her cousin keeps telling her, though until today Laura has felt like suggesting, more than once, that Kaye heed her own advice. But pride makes Laura hold her tongue, though she herself is no slouch. At her age, it's hard to tell where she gets her energy — saved from a lifetime with only herself to look after, Kaye would say, though never to Laura's face. "Of course she's eighty years *young*, she never had kids!" Kaye is always telling people back home. Why, just this morning, while Laura was upstairs brushing her teeth, Kaye had to stop herself. "My, she's remarkable," said the woman at the bed-and-breakfast, who clucked her tongue when she heard Laura's age. Kaye immediately regretted divulging it, though she knew Laura wouldn't be too concerned. Being a spinster, it seemed, Laura wasn't jealous for her privacy — not the way a married woman might be, even a widowed one.

"So what are you ladies up to this morning?" the woman had enquired, whisking away the cloth seconds after they rose from the table. That was the trouble with these places, Laura had stolen a glance at Kaye, you had no idea what you were getting till you'd unpacked your bags.

"Perhaps we'll take a walk," Laura had replied off-handedly. After Kaye's remarks about how the bathroom was kept, Laura knew she wouldn't be too interested in the proprietress's suggestions.

"If you like the country, there's a lovely footpath at the foot of Leigh Road — it's right by the pub there, you can't miss it! So long as you don't mind getting your feet a little muddy — you'll be wanting your walking shoes, mind," the woman had blathered on, brushing away their crumbs, finally clattering off to the kitchen with a trayful of dishes.

The bed-and-breakfast was a tall, red-brick Victorian house that would've looked more at home in Toronto, Laura thought. It stood out on the narrow street, among the tiny, crowded front gardens sullied by passing trucks and buses. The rest of the houses, rows of brick cottages, had a forlorn look about them — Kaye had breathed a loud sigh of relief when the cabbie who took them from the station pulled up in front of "Belle Vista". Laura's spirits flagged when she saw their room, high-ceilinged, with peeling green wallpaper, a mottled carpet and a pair of cheap-looking twin beds. But no ashtrays, thankfully; no smoking in the rooms, to Laura's delight, and her cousin's dismay.

She had trudged to the bed nearest the window and lain down, shoes still on her feet, not bothering to spread a newspaper beneath them as she usually did. Mercifully, Kaye kept quiet until she'd managed a few moments with her eyes closed.

"Well, I don't care for the high ceilings, do you, they make me feel *lonesome* somehow," Laura had said, refreshed, sitting up from her nap. "But don't worry, dear, we'll get along. We'll get along fine, won't we."

Now, as she lingers under the canopy of leaves, there is a quality about Laura that's been present from the time the two of them were girls — though being thirteen years older, she seemed more an adult than another child to Kaye, while Kaye remained, to Laura, a baby. Their mothers were close, which made it no easier for Kaye, during occasional get-togethers, to accept Laura's gentle ministrations. Even then it was obvious that Laura, now counting the pale white petals of a flower, could never have been a mother. No, she was far too gentle and whimsical, too trusting, bound to see the best in people; motherhood would have smothered that. Yet no amount of exposure to the way-wardness of others' children has been able to destroy Laura's faith — which is how she managed as a princi-pal's assistant, the same school, all her working life.

And despite their differences, she and Kaye have re-mained close, at least in her cousin's eyes — more like sisters, as Kaye enjoys telling people, than cousins. And despite what Kaye would consider a squeamishness over certain things, Laura is full of spunk, the kind of dogged-ness that has landed them here on this path, as if there is some purpose to this walk.

"How far are you planning to go?" Kaye asks in a raspy whisper, needing secrecy though it's clear they are the only ones about. "It's one thing to be a tourist, you know, quite another to trespass...."

Laura knows they stand out, a bit like two rare, gaudy flowers in their bright travelling clothes, but pretends not to hear, so intent is she upon the plants, the lush, damp weight of honeysuckle and hawthorn. Her sensible white shoes are as soft and sure on the packed earth as the bare feet of those who have passed before. Their kin, Laura is convinced, as if their blood is in this soil. Clutching her camera, Kaye appears less comfortable. For one thing, she isn't dressed for such a trek, should have worn slacks in-stead of a skirt. Laura, on the other hand, could as easily be in her nightgown, wearing the same thing as yester-day and the day before, for that matter. Marching ahead, she pauses to sniff a wildflower the same shade as her dress. Glancing back, she sees that they've come farther than she realized, the beginning of the path now a tiny circle of light.

"Laura!" Kaye yells, one hand to her chest. In the shadows her face looks grey. Laura can tell she's unnerved, being in such a secluded place, just the two of them — let's face it — two elderly ladies. Kaye is right, you never know who could be around the next bend, though so far the trail does not seem to meander much.

"I'll bet they took this path to go to market!" Laura exclaims as Kaye catches up. There's a lightness in Laura's cheeks, visible in the dimness; a brightness to her eyes that disappears when Kaye opens her mouth to speak.

"*Shhhhhh!*" She scowls and Kaye stops in mid-sentence.

"Listen!" Laura hisses, her voice again soft as the whisper of leaves, of some small, unseen animal scurrying through the grass. From the slow, reedy stream hidden now by willows comes the faint buzz of dragonflies, the laziest trickle of water.

"Can't you hear them?" she asks gently, her imagination spinning, her grey eyes intent.

"Can't you just see them walking through here on their way to market!" Her voice rises — firmer, demanding: wake up! she seems to prod — then trails off, suddenly resigned. Kaye nods patiently, embarrassed; glad for the first time all morning that they are alone, that there is no one around to witness this display, Laura's imagination working overtime.

It's as if she can see generations: mothers and their swaddled babies; sturdy, work-worn fathers; their homespun clothes, aprons, breeches, bonnets; their broken shoes. It's as if she can hear them speaking in their quaint, quirky dialect, hear them singing as they go about their chores, whistling and singing ballads, *singing*, because of course they are happy. Oh, perhaps Laura can hear them crying too, the screams and curses of women delivering, the men's bragging and brawling, but it's not Laura's business to dwell on such things. No. Instead, closing her eyes, breathing deeply, she tries to intuit the love that's been between them, the bond as close and entangling as the pleached boughs above her head.

Kaye senses faintly what Laura is feeling, but as for seeing and hearing it herself — well, what she sees are the vines, the twigs of hazel and hawthorn entwined beside the path. Just that: the leaves of what few plants she can name after eight days' listening to Laura, Laura the walking encyclopaedia of wildflowers and weeds.

"Well" — Kaye tugs at her sleeve — "have you had enough?" In the distance, from somewhere farther up the path, they hear voices, real, living voices; a dog barking. There's somebody coming, a flash of colour in the greenery ahead. An elderly couple out walking their dog, she in a kilt and chunky brown shoes, the man in grey tweed, a woollen cap, the mongrel waddling along on its lead. It barks at the sight of Kaye and Laura, the owners cajoling it in brisk, convivial voices. The man raises his walking stick, tips his cap in greeting. Relieved, Kaye's face tightens to a smile as Laura reaches out instinctively to take her arm, the two of them stock-still as if caught at something.

"Lovely day!" the couple call as they approach. "Don't mind the dog, she won't bite!"

"Oh, so it *is* a public path, we weren't quite sure—" Kaye falters. The two give her a queer look, fixing smiles upon Laura.

"Oh yes, you're almost to the end — if you stay on the path it'll take you to the middle of town, you see, to the millpond, the garden there below the square," the man prattles. "Stick with it and it's a lovely shortcut, you know."

"Yes," says the woman, still smiling, "you can almost lose yourself in here, can't you? You could be miles from anything here, you'd hardly know the town exists...."

The man gives a nod, pulling on the dog to make it heel, and the couple carry on, disappearing towards the pub.

"Well," says Kaye, suddenly chipper. "Shall we keep going? We might as well see where it comes out."

But Laura feels sated, if not tired. Her pink chiffon scarf (a slight match to her dress) is a little askew; her feet drag as if, for now, she's had her fill of exploring. "I suppose," she replies vaguely, "though I think that's enough for this morning, don't you?" She doesn't mention that landing in the town centre, the sudden intrusion of people and noise, would leave her unsettled. And before Kaye can answer, Laura lets go of her arm and turns back in the direction they have come.

Though it's lunchtime, Laura still feels full from breakfast. She's not used to so much heavy food first thing in the day, enough to keep her going until suppertime, even after their walk. Content to sit while Kaye goes off in search of snacks, she waits on a bench in the churchyard, her ankles crossed delicately, hands clasped over her purse. Her eyes are closed, as if she has fallen asleep gazing up into the boughs of a nearby yew. Its ancient trunk is wrinkled and furrowed as skin, the ground beneath littered with cigarette ends.

Through the branches the sky is a perfect blue; a light breeze tugs at her scarf. Laura looks so at ease as to belong here, though they've only been visiting a day. Perhaps it's her age that enables her to blend in so easily; or the dress, the shoes. More precisely, there's something about her manner, a kind of gentle presupposition, that makes her so at home here, outside the Church of All Saints. The cathedral has been here since 1342; "Please respect this place where there has been Christian worship for 1,000 years," reads the sign at the gate. Laura believes her ancestors were baptized and married here.

She watches Kaye browsing outside some shops across the square. Even from a distance her cousin's brisk, sure movements make Laura long to drift off, to look up into the branches waving softly overhead and somehow lose herself there. That is all: to become lost in this place so charged with the past, a past she fears others barely sense.

Being here makes Laura feel as old herself as the tree, the lichen-crusted stone of the church, so ancient it appears part of the ground. She feels as though she too has always been here, old but restful, at peace somehow, as if this is *it*, where her life has led, from mute beginnings to knowing. Knowing what, she isn't quite sure, except that she finds satisfaction believing that the bones of her ancestors may lie underfoot in the churchyard. May or may not, because from what she has been told — snippets of stories, yarns passed on long ago by her mother, her grandmother — these people were too poor for tombstones.

It may be that none of them are buried here at all, but lie in unmarked graves all over the county. Lost, except for those who emigrated and are buried in Canada, inscriptions on their headstones. *Back home*, thinks Laura with a brief pang for the ocean; the small, shabby village sloping up from the river; her tidy white house. But what is this place if not home? It's as if everything that has ever happened to her, known and unknown, has brought her here.

Laura starts as her cousin approaches, calling out in a shrill, cheery voice, as if embarrassed to find this old lady dozing in public.

"Laura!" she says sharply, paper rustling as she pulls something from her net shopping bag. "Honestly, dear, there was nothing in the tea shop you'd like, so I went to the greengrocer's and got these." Laura hates it when Kaye

calls her "dear", as if she is of another generation, one
that needs protecting. As if she is in her cousin's care.
"See what I've got!" Kaye waves apples before Laura's nose,
unwraps a wedge of hard white cheese. "No, nothing in
the tea shop you'd eat," she repeats, causing Laura to sniff.
She would have enjoyed a chocolate bar; what Kaye means
is that nothing suited *her*. Kaye, slim and striking as a
woman half her age, hardly a speck of grey in her reddish
hair, full and cut in a style Laura's wouldn't have held
when she was twenty. The only giveaway to Kaye's age
the ruddy, wizened looks of a smoker.

"That's all right, dear," Laura sighs, to be nice. Kaye
was good enough, after all, to accompany her on this trip
— to make the arrangements, book the bed-and-breakfast, even set up the meeting with the town archivist.
They are to see him at one, in the library opposite the
yew tree and Laura's park bench.

"I'd have brought you a coffee but there just doesn't
seem to be a place," Kaye rattles on, smoothing the stray
hair in her part. "Except for the tea shop, and I know you
like your caffeine. They only had instant — imagine."

In retirement, Laura has taken to drinking coffee,
having read somewhere of its health benefits in thinning
the blood. "Tea would've been fine," she says quietly, not
wishing to linger over it. She accepts one of Kaye's apples, rubs it carefully on her skirt, takes a bite. The flesh is
hard and yellow, more tart than the kind she gets at home,
a cooking apple. She nibbles a narrow band of peel around
the core, then wraps the fruit in a Kleenex, waiting for
her cousin to finish hers. Kaye takes a couple of bites and
makes a face.

"Ooops," she says, apologetic, solicitous. "Let me get
you something else."

"I'm fine."

Kaye breaks off a piece of cheese as Laura moves to

the edge of the bench. The iron hands on the church clock spring forward, five minutes to one. She stands up, anxious now to make their appointment. Sighing, Kaye shoves the cheese back into her bag and gets up, still chewing. "Laura," she says, "we don't have to go this *second*."

Laura cannot wait. It was for this she wished to come to England, though yes, it was Kaye who wrote the letters, did the necessary legwork. It was Kaye who managed, Laura isn't quite sure how, to have a transcript sent, a copy of their grandmother Emma's marriage certificate, dated 1893. She herself expressed little interest, merely passing it on to Laura with some other papers. Letters mainly, between their mothers, that Kaye found one day cleaning house before the trip. These Laura found disappointing, full of references to weather and housework, but the transcript she cherishes. She carries it with her now, inside the folder with her passport, her traveller's cheques.

In the library the archivist sits behind a cluttered wooden desk beside the returns counter. He is stout, round-faced and balding, and wears glasses. *T. Holden, BA*, announces the plastic name-plate on his desk. Right away Laura notices his bad teeth, war teeth, she thinks. *If this were Canada*, she knows Kaye is thinking, poised behind her, anxious to make their presence known. When at last the archivist glances up, Laura's breath catches.

"How may I help you?" he says drily, and she's aware of Kaye glancing away to avoid viewing his teeth.

"We've come—" Laura starts to explain as Kaye cuts in, louder.

"It's Mrs. Mossman, I wrote you a couple of months ago," she says, "and this is my cousin Miss Campbell." Behind them the drone of a photocopier, the whisper of pages, the librarians' hushed voices. "Miss Campbell is interested in" — Kaye hesitates, searching for the quickest way of putting it — "whatever you might have...about our family history." The way she says "family" makes Laura want to laugh, Kaye's voice remote and cool as if requesting a simple call number. The archivist pushes back his thinning hair and clears his throat, then quietly, non-committally, as though they've taken him from lunch or some other, more important task, rises and leads them to a shelf of worn red volumes, census listings from the year 1841 onwards.

"You might try your luck with these," he says, waving them towards a broad green table where others sit before similar books, charts and photocopies. "I shall be here till three should you need further assistance," he says, retreating to his desk. Kaye pulls down an armload of books and drops them with a thud on the table.

"There," she says, dragging out a chair for Laura. "Now I'm just going to find the Ladies'. You go ahead though, dear — don't wait for me."

Likely dying for a cigarette, Laura thinks, sighing.

If only, *if only* she knew where to start. She lets one of the books fall open to the centre, the 'M's; flips backwards through the thin, smudged pages till she finds the 'G's, then runs her fingernail over the pale, mimeographed list. Goddard, Godley, Godling, Godsoe, Gold, Golding, Good, *Gooding*.... Her grandmother's maiden name, but no Emmas, not for that year, 1881, when she would have been a child of five or six. Laura wonders if she's simply missed it; half the names are indecipherable, the mauve typescript faded and illegible in spots. She wishes she had younger eyes — her cousin's eyes. But Kaye has vanished, not that she would have the patience for such a chore.

("I'd sooner be looking for *live* relations, if you asked me," she heard Kaye telling the woman before breakfast. "But my cousin, now she likes digging up old things.")

A paper chase, a dusty, dog-eared trail of unrelated

names and dates. Laura flips ahead to the next census, 1891, one every decade. Two years before her grandmother's marriage — but there's no mention of her at all. Still hopeful, Laura opens the volume for 1871; could there have been some family confusion over Emma's year of birth? Back then, she tells herself, people were somewhat less vigilant keeping track of such things. Her heart flutters as she scours the pages, lifts as her eyes suddenly light upon the name, *Emma Gooding*. It dives just as quickly when she spies, farther down, three identical entries. Four altogether, without so much as a middle initial.

In the margin are their ages, though some families show two, three, sometimes four children with the same birthdate. A few are distinguished by a characteristic affliction, "blind", "cripple", "deaf mute"; others by occupation, mostly "labourer" for men, "servant" for women. *Emma Gooding, servant. Emma Gooding, scholar. Emma Gooding, nursemaid. Emma Gooding, seamstress.* And then there are the siblings — a dozen different Josephs and Sarahs, names that tweak Laura's memory of half-forgotten stories, bits and pieces of unconnected detail about So-and-so, uncles and aunts, the namesakes of her mother's siblings. Frederick, Kenneth, Margaret, Beatrice, Penelope, Eleanor — Kaye's mother. Just a bunch of names now, as Kaye herself said so bleakly over breakfast, in the same dismissive tone she applied to the food. ("Sausages? Oh no, I don't care much for sausages — not this early in the day. Do you?")

Laura stares at the page, willing herself to recall any scraps of these stories from childhood, the hours listening to her mother telling her father, her sisters, Alma and Elizabeth — all of them dead now — about growing up in England. Before her mother emigrated, before her parents met. The scraps are like memories of a particularly savoury but undersized meal, fleeting as the taste of some unusual food, yet distinct enough to convince her it was, at one time, real.

Childhood-forged images of people Laura never knew appear and fade — an uncle, blind, playing the pipe organ in a cathedral; a brother, born without a right hand, a millworker. Lost, all of them, the real ones as much as the imagined. Lost like the photograph of Laura's grandmother in her garden, a tiny crowded English garden, hands tucked into her starched white apron, eyes stern, staring away from the camera. And the one of her own mother, Ruth, a round-cheeked, ringleted child in a pinafore, chubby legs showing above tiny buttoned boots. Laura wonders what's become of these pictures, and thinks perhaps Kaye has them. Somewhere, lying around the house. She takes a pencil from her purse, jotting notes on the back of an envelope. Names, dates. She tries to do some arithmetic, but runs out of space.

The print becomes even harder to read. *Golding, Goode, Gooding, Goodman, Goodship....* She knows the trail is fading. The air in the library is suddenly dry, almost parching. So much dust and paper. Laura puts her hand to her throat and coughs quietly, as unobtrusively as possible. A man glances up from his book. Laura would die for a drink of water; she tries to recall whether there's a drinking fountain near the door where they entered.

The archivist, meanwhile, is helping someone find something in a drawer; Laura wonders if it will be as hard to read as the census listings. She returns to 1881 — there must be something — and, inspecting the volume more closely, realizes much of that year's records are missing. The trail goes dead, entries for *Gooding* abruptly tailing off.

When at last Kaye returns from the washroom — it's been a good while since she left, given her lengthy stopover at the magazines — she finds Laura dozing again, or, as Laura says, resting her eyes.

"How's it going?" Kaye says, a touch too brightly.

"I'm afraid if you want to chat, you must do so outside." The archivist's voice is a hoarse growl above the scrape of drawers being opened and closed.

"I...I wonder if you can tell me where I would find...," Laura looks up at him, feels herself blushing.

"Some listings for 1881 are on microfilm," he says, pointing to a filing cabinet. Kaye marches over and removes some small, red-labelled boxes as cautiously as if they contained something caustic, dangerous. Gripping them delicately between her glossy red nails, she stalks to the machine. Kaye has lovely hands, Laura can't help thinking, hands inherited from her mother, of which Kaye has always been proud.

"I don't know how to work it," Laura whispers as her cousin pulls the metal reels from their boxes. Laura hates feeling so helpless; it makes her impatient with herself, fills her with a kind of despair, her lifelong incompetence with things mechanical. Still smiling — her lips freshly painted to match her fingernails — Kaye loops the plastic film through the machine, flicks on the light and sets the reels spinning. She curses under her breath when the film flies off, making a tattering sound, the empty spool whirring. Around the room, people look up from their reading. Spotting the little half-moons of perspiration on Kaye's blouse, Laura longs for the simplicity of the bulky red books, their pale mauve type.

Kaye threads the film again, diligently twisting the knobs to roll it through. The illuminated print flies past too quickly for Laura to read, let alone ponder. Kaye fiddles with another knob; words leap into focus. More names and dates, street names and numbers, a few of which Laura recognizes from something she read at the bed-and-breakfast. Some of this information has been transcribed into neat typescript, the rest is in a jagged, nineteenth-century hand. Kaye shakes her head.

"Wait now." Laura pulls in her wooden chair, squinting up at the screen.

"What exactly is it you're looking for?" Kaye's voice grates with boredom, a quiet agitation, as if she's being forced to study a phone book.

"Let me have a look." Laura presses closer. She would just as soon have Kaye leave her to the machine.

"How can you stand it?" Kaye mutters, exasperated. "This sort of thing drives me *batty*."

Her mouth set in a tight little line, Laura's old, tired eyes scan the lists, up and down, left to right, the hum of the machine drowning out Kaye's sighs. She makes little headway, except to discover the death in 1891 of a Samuel Gooding, father of one of the Emmas.

Kaye is staring out the window into the churchyard when the archivist announces that it is three p.m., that they will have to adjourn their search until Monday. The records room is closed for the weekend, he sniffs, and Kaye can't help smiling at his British emphasis on "end". Laura doesn't tell him they're leaving Saturday. Instead, she gives him a look of quiet indignation.

"How might I find where someone's buried?" she asks, trying to sound polite.

"For that you'd have to search the baptismal and burial records, the parish registers...."

Laura rises slowly and pushes in her chair. The room is so stuffy even she is anxious now to get outside for a breath of fresh air. She feels in need of sleep, a lengthy nap this time, not merely a rest.

"If there's anything you'd care to leave with us," the archivist says without interest. Laura can't think what to ask, there are so many things....

Outside, it has misted over. Threatening rain, clouds

have thickened along the escarpment overlooking the town; they blot out the white chalk figure of a horse, reputedly cut there in the cliff during King Alfred's reign.

"A cup of tea would be nice," Laura ventures, plodding ahead though she is exhausted now, her eyes raw. There's a throbbing in her forehead, a heaviness in her chest, as if she has come very close to holding something and lost her grasp of it. She has no better sense of *them* now than before, little more than what she brought to her task, a few names and birthdays. Laura struggles in her imagination to give the lost ones hearts, lungs, stomachs, *breath*. Legions of faces and histories, brief, mundane, unaccountable histories, lives. Walking along the broken sidewalk with Kaye, Laura is filled with sadness, as much for them as for herself, a feeling of having lost them not once but twice, the flash of a fish on a hook, then nothing, only the froth and pull of the current.

"What's the matter, dear?" Kaye asks as they pause to enter the tea shop. She's alarmed by Laura's sudden moodiness, her silence. (Laura is known for her equanimity, if anything.) Looking over the slim assortment of tea cakes on a trolley — it is mid-afternoon, after all, the place is nearly empty — Kaye suddenly puts her hand over her mouth, stifles a giggle.

"Oh. Did you find out something...you know, *bad*, about somebody?"

Coming from Kaye it sounds so childish, child*like*, that Laura is taken aback. Choosing a small cake with Devon cream, she sits down at one of the little tables. Kaye slips in across from her, waiting. She rummages for cigarettes, then slips the package back inside her purse.

"Well?" she prods, after the shopgirl brings their tea. But Laura isn't listening; she is savouring the sweet, thick cream, feeling it settle inside her. It has begun to rain outside, drops pelting the window, and people hurry past, ducking into shops for shelter. It occurs to Laura how alike they seem, mostly older people like her, smallish and stocky, but strong, plain-faced; the women dressed in similar fashion, shapeless dresses. But it's something more than looks, she thinks, stirring sugar into her tea — two lumps, as she used to take it, always two lumps. There's a gentleness, a *kindliness* about these strange, fleeting faces that strikes Laura as somehow familiar.

"So," says Kaye, daintily nibbling her pastry as Laura brushes crumbs from her lap. "Tell me what ne'er-do-wells we're descended from."

Passing the window, a woman catches Laura's eye as she hurries by. There is nothing particularly remarkable about her; she appears past middle age, as ordinary as the others, grey-haired and dressed in a shapeless raincoat.

"*What?*" Kaye urges, amused.

"Oh." Laura seems startled. "There was nothing like that," she says. The worst her afternoon has uncovered is a man, a great-great uncle perhaps, who died in the workhouse.

She watches the woman cross the street and disappear into a butcher shop. Her cousin sighs, putting down her teacup.

"Well," Kaye finally says. "I hope you've found what you were looking for. Now we can concentrate on the sights — there's still Bath, the abbey, the canal.... The shopping there is supposed to be grand, I read somewhere."

Laura nods and finishes her tea, waiting for another glimpse of the woman. She watches for her while Kaye pays the bill, carefully counting out pennies. After a moment or two the woman reappears, stopping outside the butcher's to tie on a plastic rainbonnet. Gripping her parcels, she continues down the street, Laura following with her eyes until the woman vanishes into the churchyard.

"Everything all right, dear?" Kaye reaches out to pat her wrist. Laura summons a smile and gives her cousin's hand a tired squeeze.

"Fine." She breathes in and sighs. "Just fine," she repeats, trailing slightly behind as Kaye holds the door and they step into the wet, empty street.